B.J. Daniels is a *New York Times* and *USA TODAY* bestselling author. She wrote her first book after a career as an award-winning newspaper journalist and author of thirty-seven published short stories. She lives in Montana with her husband, Parker, and three springer spaniels. When not writing, she quilts, boats and plays tennis. Contact her at bjdaniels.com, on Facebook or on Twitter, @bjdanielsauthor

Debra Webb is the award-winning *USA TODAY* bestselling author of more than one hundred novels, including those in reader-favourite series Faces of Evil, the Colby Agency and the Shades of Death. With more than four million books sold in numerous languages and countries, Debra has a love of storytelling that goes back to childhood on a farm in Alabama. Visit Debra at www.debrawebb.com

Also by B.J. Daniels

Also by Debra Webb

Discover more at millsandboon.co.uk

IRON WILL

B.J. DANIELS

THE STRANGER NEXT DOOR

DEBRA WEBB

This book is produced from independently certified FSC™
paper to ensure responsible forest management.

For more information visit: www.harpercollins.co.uk/green

Printed and bound in Spain
by CPI, Barcelona

MILLS & BOON

All rights reserved including the right of reproduction in whole or in part in any form. This edition is published by arrangement with Harlequin Books S.A.

This is a work of fiction. Names, characters, places, locations and incidents are purely fictional and bear no relationship to any real life individuals, living or dead, or to any actual places, business establishments, locations, events or incidents. Any resemblance is entirely coincidental.

This book is sold subject to the condition that it shall not, by way of trade or otherwise, be lent, resold, hired out or otherwise circulated without the prior consent of the publisher in any form of binding or cover other than that in which it is published and without a similar condition including this condition being imposed on the subsequent purchaser.

® and ™ are trademarks owned and used by the trademark owner and/or its licensee. Trademarks marked with ® are registered with the United Kingdom Patent Office and/or the Office for Harmonisation in the Internal Market and in other countries.

First Published in Great Britain 2019
by Mills & Boon, an imprint of HarperCollins*Publishers*
1 London Bridge Street, London, SE1 9GF

Iron Will © 2019 Barbara Heinlein
The Stranger Next Door © 2019 Debra Webb

ISBN: 978-0-263-27430-1

0819

MIX
Paper from
responsible sources
FSC™ C007454
www.fsc.org

CITY AND COUNTY OF SWANSEA LIBRARIES	
6000350137	
Askews & Holts	04-Jul-2019
	£5.99
SWHQ	

IRON WILL

B.J. DANIELS

This one is for Paula Morrison, who believes like I do that if one schlep bag is a great idea, then let's make a dozen. Thanks for making Quilting by the Border quilt club so fun.

Chapter One

Hank Savage squinted into the sun glaring off the dirty windshield of his pickup as his family ranch came into view. He slowed the truck to a stop, resting one sun-browned arm over the top of the steering wheel as he took in the Cardwell Ranch.

The ranch with all its log-and-stone structures didn't appear to have changed in the least. Nor had the two-story house where he'd grown up. Memories flooded him of hours spent on the back of a horse, of building forts in the woods around the creek, of the family sitting around the large table in the kitchen in the mornings, the sun pouring in, the sound of laughter. He saw and felt everything he'd given up, everything he'd run from, everything he'd lost.

"Been a while?" asked the sultry, dark-haired woman in the passenger seat.

He nodded despite the lump in his throat, shoved back his Stetson and wondered what the hell he was doing back here. This was a bad idea, probably his worst ever.

"Having second thoughts?" He'd warned her about his big family, but she'd said she could handle it. He wasn't all that sure even he could handle it. He prided himself on being fearless about most things. Give him a bull that hadn't been ridden and he wouldn't hesitate to climb right on. Same with his job as a lineman. He'd faced gale winds hanging from a pole to get the power back on, braved getting fried more times than he liked to remember.

But coming back here, facing the past? He'd never been more afraid. He knew it was just a matter of time before he saw Naomi—just as he had in his dreams, in his nightmares. She was here, right where he'd left her, waiting for him as she had been for three long years. Waiting for him to come back and make things right.

He looked over at Frankie. "You sure about this?"

She sat up straighter to gaze at the ranch and him, took a breath and let it out. "I am if you are. After all, this was your idea."

Like she had to remind him. "Then I suggest you slide over here." He patted the seat between them and she moved over, cuddling against him as he put his free arm around her. She felt small and fragile, certainly not ready for what he suspected they would be facing. For a moment, he almost changed his mind. It wasn't too late. He didn't have the right to involve her.

"It's going to be okay," she said and nuzzled his neck where his dark hair curled at his collar. "Trust me."

He pulled her closer and let his foot up off the brake. The pickup began to roll toward the ranch. It wasn't that he didn't trust Frankie. He just knew that it was only a matter of time before Naomi came to him pleading with him to do what he should have done three years ago. He felt a shiver even though the summer day was unseasonably warm.

I'm here.

Chapter Two

"Looking out that window isn't going to make him show up any sooner," Marshal Hud Savage said to his wife.

"I can't help being excited. It's been three years." Dana Cardwell Savage knew she didn't need to tell him how long it had been. Hud had missed his oldest son as much or more than she had. But finally Hank was coming home—and bringing someone with him. "Do you think it's because he's met someone that he's coming back?"

Hud put a large hand on her shoulder. "Let's not jump to any conclusions, okay? We won't know anything until he gets here. I just don't want to see you get your hopes up."

Her hopes were already up, so there was no mitigating that. Family had always been the most important thing to her. Having her sons all fly the nest had been heartbreak, especially Hank, especially under the circumstances.

She told herself not to think about that. Nothing was going to spoil this day. Her oldest son was coming home after all this time. That had to be good news. And he was bringing someone. She hoped that meant Hank was moving on from Naomi.

"Is that his pickup?" she cried as a black truck came into view. She felt goose bumps pop up on her arms. "I think that's him."

"Try not to cry and make a fuss," her husband said even as tears blurred her eyes. "Let them at least get into the yard," he said as she rushed to the front door and threw it open. "Why do I bother?" he mumbled behind her.

FRANKIE KNEW THE sixty-two-year-old woman who rushed out on the porch had to be Dana Cardwell Savage. Hank had told her about his family. She thought about the softness that came into his voice when he talked about his mother. She'd heard about Dana's strength and determination, but she could also see it in the way she stood hugging herself in her excitement and her curiosity.

Hank had warned her that him bringing home a woman would cause a stir. Frankie could see his mother peering inside the pickup, trying to imagine what woman had stolen her son's heart. She felt a small stab of guilt but quickly pushed it away as a man appeared behind Dana.

Marshal Hud Savage. She'd also heard a lot about him. When Hank had mentioned his dad, she'd seen the change not just in his tone, but his entire body. The trouble between the two ran deep. While Dana was excited, holding nothing back, Frankie could see that Hud was reserved. He had to worry that this wouldn't be a happy homecoming considering the way he'd left things with his oldest son.

Hank's arm tensed around her as he parked and cut the engine. She had the feeling that he didn't want to let her go. He finally eased his hold on her, then gave her a gentle squeeze. "We can do this, right? Ready?"

"As I will ever be," she said, and he opened his door. The moment he did, Dana rushed down the steps to throw her arms around her son. Tears streamed down her face unchecked. She hugged him, closing her eyes, breathing him in as if she'd thought she might never see him again.

Frankie felt her love for Hank at heart level. She slowly slid under the steering wheel and stepped down. Hud, she noticed, had descended the stairs, but stopped at the bottom, waiting, unsure of the reception he was going to get. Feeling for him, she walked around mother and son to address him.

"Hi, I'm Frankie. Francesca, but everyone calls me Frankie." She held out her hand, and the marshal accepted it in his large one as his gaze took her measure. She took his as well. Hud Savage was scared that this visit wasn't an olive branch. Scared that his son was still too angry with him. Probably more scared that he was going to let down his wife by spoiling this reunion.

"It's nice to meet you," the marshal said, his voice rough with what she suspected was emotion. A lot was riding on what would happen during this visit, she thought, and Hud didn't know the half of it.

"Frankie," Hank said behind her. His voice broke. "I want you to meet my mom, Dana."

She turned and came face-to-face with the ranch

woman. Dana had been a beauty in her day; anyone could see that. But even in her sixties, she was still very attractive with her salt-and-pepper dark hair and soft, gentle features. She was also a force to be reckoned with. Dana eyed her like a mama bear, one who was sizing her up for the position of daughter-in-law.

Whatever Dana saw and thought of her, the next thing Frankie knew, she was being crushed in the woman's arms. "It is so wonderful to meet you," Dana was saying tearfully.

Behind her, Frankie heard Hud say hello to his son.

"Dad," Hank said with little enthusiasm, and then Dana was ushering them all into the house, telling her son that she'd baked his favorite cookies and made his favorite meal.

Frankie felt herself swept up in all of it as she told herself this would work out—even against her better judgment.

"HANK SEEMS GOOD, doesn't he," Dana said later that night when the two of them were in bed. She'd told herself that things had gone well and that once Hank was home for a while, they would get even better. She hadn't been able to ignore the tension between her son and husband. It made her heart ache because she had no idea how to fix the problem.

"He seems fine." Hud didn't look up from the crime novel he was reading.

"Frankie is pretty, isn't she."

"Uh-huh."

"She's not what I expected. Not really Hank's type, don't you think?"

Hud glanced over at her. "It's been three years since we've seen him. We have no idea what his type is. He probably doesn't know either. He's still young. I thought Naomi wasn't his type." He went back to his book.

"He's thirty-three, not all that young if he wants to have a family," she said. "It's just that Frankie isn't anything like Naomi."

"Maybe that's the attraction."

She heard what he didn't say in his tone. *Maybe that's a blessing.* Hud had never thought Naomi was right for Hank. "I suppose it might be why he's attracted to her. I just never thought he'd get over Naomi."

Hud reached over and, putting down his book, turned out his bedside light. "Good night," he said pointedly.

She took the hint and switched off her own lamp as her husband rolled over, turning his back to her. Within minutes he would be sound asleep, snoring lightly, while she lay awake worrying. The worst part was that she couldn't put her finger on what made her anxious about Hank coming home now and bringing a young woman.

"He wants to move on, put Naomi and all that ugliness behind him, don't you think?" She glanced over at Hud's broad back, but knew he wasn't going to answer because he didn't have the answer any more than she did.

She was just glad that Hank was home for however long he planned to stay and that he wasn't alone anymore. "As long as he's happy…" Hud began to snore softly. She sighed and closed her eyes, silently mouthing her usual nightly prayers that her family all be safe and happy, and thanking God for bringing Hank home.

"IT'S BEAUTIFUL HERE," Frankie said as she stood on the guest cabin deck overlooking the rest of the ranch in the starlight. The cabin was stuck back high against the mountain looking down on the ranch and the Gallatin River as it wound past. "I feel like I can see forever. Are those lights the town?" she asked as Hank joined her.

"Big Sky, Montana," he said with little enthusiasm.

She turned to him. "How do you think it went?"

He shook his head. "I'm just thankful that my mother listened to me and didn't have the whole family over tonight. But maybe it would have been less uncomfortable if they'd all been there. Tomorrow you'll meet my sister, Mary, and her fiancé, Chase."

"There's your uncle Jordan and aunt Stacy."

"And a bunch of my mother's cousins and their families," he said with a sigh.

She couldn't imagine having all that family. Her father had left when she was three. Her mother had married several times, but the marriages didn't last. Her mother had died in a car accident right after she'd graduated from high school, but they'd never been close. The only real family she'd ever felt she had was an uncle who'd become her mentor after college, but he was gone now too.

"You could just tell them the truth," she said quietly after a moment. She envied Hank his family, and felt lying to them was a mistake.

He shook his head. "This is difficult enough." He turned to go back inside. "You can have the first bedroom. I'll take the other one." With that, he went inside and closed the door.

Frankie stood on the deck, the summer night a fra-

grant blend of pine and water. There was just enough
starlight that she caught glimpses of it shining off the
surface of the river snaking through the canyon. Steep,
rocky cliffs reflected the lights of the town, while the
mountains rose up into the midnight-blue star-filled
canopy.

She felt in awe of this ranch and his family. How
could Hank have ever left it behind? But the answer
seemed to be on the breeze as if everything about
this place was inhabited by one woman. Naomi. She
was what had brought Hank home. She was also why
Frankie was here.

Chapter Three

Hank rose before the sun and made his way down the mountainside to the corral. He'd missed the smell of saddle leather and horseflesh. He was breathing it in when he heard someone approaching from behind him.

He'd always been keenly aware of his environment. Growing up in Montana on a ranch, he'd learned at a young age to watch out for things that could hurt you—let alone kill you—in the wild. That instinct had only intensified in the years he'd been gone as if he felt a darkness trailing him, one that he could no longer ignore.

"You're up early," he said to his father without turning around as Hud came up behind him.

"I could say the same about you. I thought you and I should talk."

"Isn't that what we did at dinner last night?" Hank asked sarcastically. His father hadn't said ten words. Instead his mother had filled in the awkward silences.

"I'm glad you came back," Hud said.

He turned finally to look at his father. The sun glowed behind the mountain peaks to the east, rimming them with a bright orange glow. He studied his father in the dim light. They were now both about the same height, both with broad shoulders and slim hips. Both stubborn to a fault. Both never backing down from a fight. He stared at the marshal, still angry with him after all these years.

"I'm not staying long."

Hud nodded. "That's too bad. Your mother will be disappointed. So am I. Son—"

"There really isn't anything to talk about, is there? We said everything we had to say three years ago. What would be the point of rehashing it?"

"I stand by what I did."

Hank laughed. "I'd be shocked if you didn't." He shook his head. "It must be wonderful to know that you're always right."

"I'm not always right. I just do the best I can with the information and evidence I have."

"Well, you're wrong this time," he said and turned back to the horses. One of the mares had come up to have her muzzle rubbed. Behind him, he heard his father head back toward the house and felt some of the tension in his chest release even as he cursed under his breath.

DANA HAD INSISTED on making them breakfast. After a stack of silver-dollar-sized pancakes swimming in butter and huckleberry syrup, a slab of ham, two eggs over easy and a tall glass of orange juice, Frankie sat back smiling. She couldn't remember the last time she'd eaten so much or liked it more.

No matter what happened on this visit to the ranch, she planned to enjoy herself as much as was possible.

"I thought dinner was amazing," she told Dana. Hank's favorite meal turned out to be roast beef, mashed potatoes, carrots and peas and homemade rolls. "But this breakfast... It was so delicious. I never eat like this."

"I can tell by your figure," her host said, beaming. Clearly Dana equated food with love as she looked to her son to see if he'd enjoyed it. He'd cleaned his plate, which seemed to make her even happier. "So, what do you two have planned today?"

"I thought I'd show Frankie around Big Sky," Hank said.

"Well, it's certainly changed since you were here," his mother said. "I think you'll be surprised. Will you two be back for lunch? Your father still comes home every day at twelve."

"I think we'll get something in town, but thanks, Mom. Thanks for everything."

Tears filled her eyes and her voice broke when she spoke. "I'm just glad to have you home. Now, plan on being here for supper. Your dad's doing steaks on the grill and some of the family is stopping by. Not everyone. We don't want to overwhelm Frankie."

"I appreciate that," he said.

Frankie offered to help with the dishes, but Dana shooed them out, telling them to have a fun day.

Fun was the last thing on the agenda, she thought as she left with Hank.

HANK HAD BEEN restless all morning, but he'd known that he couldn't get away from the house without having one of his mother's breakfasts. The last thing he wanted to do was hurt her feelings. It would be bad enough when she learned the truth.

Pushing that thought away, he concentrated on his driving as he headed downriver. He'd grown up with the Gallatin River in his backyard. He hadn't thought much about it until Frankie was doing her research and asked him, "Did you know that the Gallatin River begins in the northwest corner of Yellowstone National Park to travel one hundred and twenty miles through the Gallatin Canyon past Big Sky to join the Jefferson and Madison Rivers to form the Missouri River?"

That she found this so fascinating had surprised him. "I did know that," he told her and found himself studying her with renewed interest. The river had been part of his playground, although he'd been taught to have a healthy respect for it because of the current, the deep holes and the slippery rocks.

Now as he drove along the edge of the Gallatin as it cut through the rocky cliffs of the canyon, he caught glimpses of the clear green water rushing over granite boulders on its way to the Gulf of Mexico and felt a shiver because he'd learned just how deadly it could be.

A few miles up the road, he slowed to turn onto a dirt road that wound through the tall pines. Dust rose behind the pickup. He put down his window and breathed in the familiar scents. They made his heart ache.

Ahead, he could see the cliffs over the top of the pines. He parked in the shade of the trees and sat for a moment, bracing himself.

"This is the place?" Frankie whispered, her gaze on the cliff that could be seen over the top of the pines.

He didn't answer as he climbed out. He heard her

exit the pickup but she didn't follow him as he walked down through the thick pines toward the river, knowing he needed a few minutes alone.

An eerie silence filled the air. When he'd first gotten out of the truck, he'd heard a squirrel chatting in a nearby tree, a meadowlark calling from the tall grass, hoppers buzzing as they rose with each step.

But now that he was almost to the spot, there was no sound except the gentle lap of the water on the rocks. As he came out of the pines, he felt her—just as he always had. Naomi. It was as if her soul had been stranded here in this very spot where she'd died.

His knees went weak and he had to sit down on one of the large boulders along the shore. He put his head in his hands, unaware of time passing. Unaware of anything but his pain.

Like coming out of a daze, he lifted his head and looked across the river to the deep pool beneath the cliff. Sunlight glittered off the clear emerald surface. His heart in his throat, he lifted his gaze to the rock ledge high above the water. Lover's Leap. That was what it was called.

His gaze shifted to the trail from the bridge downriver. It was barely visible through the tall summer grass and the pines, but he knew that kids still traveled along it to the ledge over the water. The trick, though, was to jump out far enough. Otherwise...

A shaft of sun cut through the pine boughs that hung out over the water, nearly blinding him. He closed his eyes again as he felt Naomi pleading with him to find out the truth. He could feel her arguing that he knew her. He knew she was terrified of heights. She would never have gone up there. Especially alone. Especially at night. Why would she traverse the treacherous trail to get to the rock ledge to begin with—let alone jump?

It had made no sense.

Not unless she hadn't jumped to her death. Not unless she'd been pushed.

Hank opened his eyes and looked up through the shaft of sunlight to see a figure moving along the narrow trail toward the rock ledge high on the cliff. His throat went dry as shock ricocheted through him. He started to call to her even as he knew it was his mind playing tricks on him. It wasn't Naomi.

He opened his mouth, but no sound came out and he stared frozen in fear as he recognized the slim figure. Frankie. She'd walked downriver to the bridge and, after climbing up the trail, was now headed for the ledge.

HUD HEAVED HIMSELF into his office chair, angry at himself on more levels than he wanted to contemplate. He swore as he unlocked the bottom drawer of his desk and pulled out the file. That he'd kept it for three years in the locked drawer where he could look at it periodically was bad enough. That he was getting it out now and going over it as he'd done so many times over those years made it even worse.

He knew there was nothing new in the file. He could practically recite the report by heart. Nothing had changed. So why was he pulling it out now? What good would it do to go over it again? None.

But he kept thinking about Hank and his stubborn insistence that Naomi hadn't committed suicide. He didn't need a psychiatrist to tell him that suicide was the most perverse of deaths. Those left behind had to deal with the guilt and live with the questions that haunted them. Why hadn't they known? Why hadn't they helped? Why had she killed herself? Was it because of them? It was the why that he knew his son couldn't accept.

Why would a beautiful young woman like Naomi Hill kill herself? It made no sense.

Hud opened the file. Was it possible there was something he'd missed? He knew that wasn't the case and yet he began to go over it, remembering the call he'd gotten that morning from the fisherman who'd found her body in the rocks beneath Lover's Leap.

There had been little doubt about what had happened. Her blouse had caught on a rock on the ledge, leaving a scrap of it fluttering in the wind. The conclusion that she'd either accidentally fallen or jumped was later changed to suicide after more information had come in about Naomi's state of mind in the days before her death.

Add to that the coroner's report. Cause of death: skull crushed when victim struck the rocks below the cliff after either falling or jumping headfirst.

But his son Hank had never accepted it and had never forgiven his father for not investigating her death longer, more thoroughly. Hank had believed that Naomi hadn't fallen or jumped. He was determined that she'd been murdered.

Unfortunately, the evidence said otherwise, and Hud was a lawman who believed in facts—not conjecture or emotion. He still did and that was the problem, wasn't it?

Chapter Four

Hank felt dizzy and sick to his stomach as he watched Frankie make her way out to the edge of the cliff along the narrow ledge. She had her cell phone in her hand. He realized she was taking photos of the trail, the distance to the rocks and water below as well as the jagged rocky ledge's edge.

As she stepped closer to the edge, he heard a chunk of rock break off. It plummeted to the boulders below, and his heart fell with it. The rock shattered into pieces before dropping into the water pooling around the boulders, making ripples that lapped at the shore.

He felt his stomach roil. "Get down from there," he called up to her, his voice breaking. "Please." He couldn't watch. Sitting down again, he hung his head to keep from retching. It took a few minutes before his stomach settled and the need to vomit passed. When he looked up, Frankie was no longer balanced on the ledge.

His gaze shot to the rocks below, his pulse leaping with the horrible fear that filled him. There was no body on the rocks. No sign of Frankie. He put his head back down and took deep breaths. He didn't know how long he stayed like that before he heard the crunch of pine needles behind him.

"I'm sorry," Frankie said. "I should have known that would upset you."

He swore and started to get to his feet unsteadily. She held out a hand and he took it, letting her help him up. "I'm usually not like this."

She smiled. "You think I don't know that?"

"You should have told me you were going up there," he said.

"You would have tried to stop me," she said and pulled out her phone. "I needed to see it." She looked up from her screen. "Have you been up there?"

"Not since Naomi died, no."

She frowned, cocking her head. "You've jumped from there."

"When I was young and stupid."

Nodding, Frankie said, "You have to push off the cliff wall, throw your body out to miss the rocks and to land in the pool. Daring thing to do."

"Helps if you're young, stupid and with other dumb kids who dare you," he said. "And before you ask, yes, Naomi knew I'd jumped off the ledge. She was terrified of heights. She couldn't get three feet off the ground without having vertigo. It's why I know she didn't climb up there on her own. Someone made her."

"Sometimes people do things to try to overcome fears," Frankie said and shrugged.

"Naomi didn't. She was terrified of so many things. Like horses. I tried to teach her to ride." He shook his head. "I'm telling you, she wouldn't have climbed up there unless there was a gun to her head. Even if she'd wanted to kill herself, she wouldn't have chosen that ledge as her swan song."

With that, he turned and started toward the truck, wishing he'd never come back here. He'd known it would be hard, but he hadn't expected it to nearly incapacitate him. Had he thought Naomi would be gone? Her soul released? Not as long as her death was still a mystery.

Frankie didn't speak again until they were headed back toward Big Sky. "At some point you're going to have to tell me why your father doesn't believe it was murder."

"I'll do one better. I'll get a copy of the case file. In the meantime, I'll show you Big Sky. I'm not ready for my parents to know the truth yet."

She nodded and leaned back as if to enjoy the trip. "I timed how long it took me to walk up the trail from the bridge to the ledge. Eleven minutes. How long do you think it would have taken Naomi?"

"Is this relevant?"

"It might be." She turned to look at him then. "You said the coroner established a time of death because of Naomi's broken wristwatch that was believed to have smashed on the rocks. We need to examine the time sequence. She left you at the ranch, right? The drive to the cliff took us ten minutes. She could have beat that because at that time of the evening in early fall and off season, there wouldn't have been as much traffic, right?"

He nodded.

"So if she left the ranch and went straight to the bridge—"

"She didn't. She met her killer at some point along

the way. Maybe she stopped for gas or… I don't know. Picked up a hitchhiker."

Frankie shot him a surprised look. "From what you've told me about Naomi, she wouldn't have stopped for a hitchhiker."

"It would have had to be someone she knew. Can we stop talking about this for just a little while?" He hated the pleading in his voice. "Let me show you around Big Sky, maybe drive up to Mountain Village."

She nodded and looked toward the town as he slowed for the turn. "So Big Sky was started by Montana native and NBC news co-anchorman Chet Huntley. I read it is the second-largest ski resort in the country by acreage." She gazed at Lone Mountain. "That peak alone stands at over eleven thousand feet."

He glanced over at her and chuckled. "You're like a walking encyclopedia. Do you always learn all these facts when you're…working?"

"Sure," she said, smiling. "I find it interesting. Like this canyon. There is so much history here. I've been trying to imagine this road when it was dirt and Yellowstone Park only accessible from here by horses and wagons or stagecoaches."

"I never took you for a history buff," he said.

She shrugged. "There's a lot you don't know about me."

He didn't doubt that, he thought as he studied her out of the corner of his eye. She continued to surprise him. She was so fearless. So different from Naomi. Just the thought of her up on that ledge— He shoved that thought away as he drove into the lower part of Big Sky known as Meadow Village. His mother was right. Big Sky had changed so much he hardly recognized the small resort town with all its restaurants and fancy shops along with miles of condos. He turned up the road to Mountain Village, where the ski resort was located, enjoying showing Frankie around. It kept his mind off Naomi.

"So you met the woman Hank brought home?"

Dana looked up at her sister, Stacy. They were in the ranch house kitchen, where Dana was taking cookies out of the oven. "I thought you might have run into them this morning before they took off for some sightseeing."

Her sister shook her head. Older than Dana, Stacy had been the wild one, putting several marriages under her belt at a young age. But she'd settled down after she'd had her daughter, Ella, and had moved back to the ranch to live in one of the new cabins up on the mountainside.

"I stopped over at their cabin this morning to see if they needed anything," Stacy said now, avoiding her gaze.

Dana put her hands on her hips. She knew her sister so well. *"What?"*

Stacy looked up in surprise. "Nothing to get in a tizzy over, just something strange."

"Such as?"

"I don't want to be talking out of turn, but I noticed that they slept in separate bedrooms last night." Her sister snapped her lips shut as if the words had just sneaked out.

Dana frowned as she put another pan of cookie dough into the oven and, closing the door, set the timer.

Hadn't she felt something between Hank and Frankie? Something not quite right? "They must have had a disagreement. I'm sure it is difficult for both of them being here after what happened with Naomi. That's bound to cause some tension between them."

"Probably. So, you like her?"

"I do. She's nothing like Naomi."

"What does that mean?" Stacy asked.

"There's nothing timid about her. She's more self-assured, seems more…independent. I was only around her for a little while. It's just an impression I got. You remember how Naomi was."

Her sister's right brow shot up. "You mean scared of everything?"

Dana had been so surprised the first time Hank had brought Naomi home and the young woman had no interest in learning to ride a horse.

I would be terrified to get on one, she'd said.

Naomi isn't…outdoorsy, was the way Hank had described her. That had been putting it mildly. Dana couldn't imagine the woman living here. As it turned out, living at Cardwell Ranch was the last thing Naomi had in mind.

"Frankie looks as if she can handle herself. I saw Hank gazing at her during dinner. He seems intrigued by her."

"I can't wait to meet her," Stacy said now.

"Why don't you come to dinner? Mary's going to be here, and Chase. Jordan and Liza are coming as well. I thought that was enough for one night." Her daughter and fiancé would keep things light. Her brother and his wife would be a good start as far as introducing Frankie to the family.

"Great. I'll come down early and help with the preparations," her sister said. "I'm sorry I mentioned anything about their sleeping arrangements. I'm sure it's nothing."

FRANKIE LOOKED OUT at the mountain ranges as she finished the lunch Hank had bought them up at the mountain resort. This was more like a vacation, something she hadn't had in years. She would have felt guilty except for the fact that technically she *was* working. She looked at the cowboy across the table from her, remembering the day he'd walked into her office in Lost Creek outside of Moscow, Idaho.

"Why now?" Frankie had asked him after he'd wanted to hire her to find out what had really happened to his girlfriend. "It's been three years, right? That makes it a cold case. I can't imagine there is anything to find." She'd seen that her words had upset him and had quickly lifted both hands in surrender. "I'm not saying it's impossible to solve a case that old…" She tried not to say the words *next to impossible*.

She'd talked him into sitting down, calming down and telling her about the crime. Turned out that the marshal—Hank's father—had sided with the coroner that the woman's death had been a suicide. She'd doubted this could get worse because it was clear to her that Hank Savage had been madly in love with the victim. Talk about wearing blinders. Of course he didn't want to believe the woman he loved had taken a nosedive off a cliff.

"I thought I could accept it, get over it," Hank had said. "I can't. I won't. I have to know the truth. I know this is going to sound crazy, but I can feel Naomi pleading with me to find her murderer."

It didn't sound crazy as much as it sounded like wishful thinking. If this woman had killed herself, then he blamed himself.

Her phone had rung. She'd checked to see who was calling and declined the call. But Hank could tell that the call had upset her.

"Look, if you need to take that…" he'd said.

"No." The last thing she wanted to do was take the call. What had her upset was that if she didn't answer one of the calls from the man soon, he would be breaking down her door. "So, what is it you want me to do?"

Hank had spelled it out for her.

She'd stared at him in disbelief. "You want me to go to Big Sky with you."

"I know it's a lot to ask and this might not be a good time for you."

He had no idea how good a time it was for her to leave town. "I can tell this is important for you. I can't make you any promises, but I'll come out and look into the incident." She'd pulled out her standard contract and slid it across the table with a pen.

Hank hadn't even bothered to read it. He'd withdrawn his wallet. "Here's five hundred dollars. I'll pay all your expenses and a five-thousand-dollar bonus if you solve this case—along with your regular fee," he'd said, pushing the signed contract back across the table to her. As the same caller had rung her again, Hank had asked, "When can you leave?"

"Now's good," she'd said.

Chapter Five

Frankie had tried to relax during dinner later that night at the main ranch house, but it was difficult. She now understood at least the problem between Hank and his father. From what she could gather, the marshal was also angry with his son. Hank had refused to accept his father's conclusion about Naomi's death. The same conclusion the coroner had come up with as well.

Hank thought his father had taken the easy way out. But Frankie had been around Hud Savage only a matter of hours and she knew at gut level that he wasn't a man who took the easy way out. He believed clear to his soul that Naomi Hill had killed herself.

During dinner, Hank had said little. Dana's sister, Stacy, had joined them, along with Dana's daughter, Mary, and her fiancé, Chase, and Dana's brother, Jordan, and wife, Liza. Hank had been polite enough to his family, but she could tell he was struggling after going to the spot where Naomi had died.

She'd put a hand on his thigh to try to get him to relax and he'd flinched. The reaction hadn't gone unnoticed by his mother and aunt Stacy. Frankie had smiled and snuggled against him. If he hoped to keep their secret longer, he needed to be more attentive. After all, it was his idea that they pretend to be involved in a relationship. That way Frankie could look into Naomi's death without Hank going head-to-head with his father.

When she'd snuggled against him, he'd felt the nudge and responded, putting an arm around her and pulling her close. She'd whispered in his ear, "Easy, sweetie."

Nodding, he'd laughed, and she'd leaned toward him to kiss him on the lips. It had been a quick kiss meant to alleviate any doubt as to what was going on. The kiss had taken him by surprise. He'd stared into her eyes for a long moment, then smiled.

When Frankie had looked up, she'd seen there was relief on his mother's face. His mother had bought it. The aunt, not so much. But that was all right. The longer they could keep their ruse going, the better. Otherwise it would be war between father and son. They both wanted to avoid that since it hadn't done any good three years ago. Frankie doubted it would now.

"Cake?" Dana asked now, getting to her feet.

"I would love a piece," Frankie said. "Let me help you." She picked up her plate and Hank's to take them into the kitchen against his mother's protests. "You outdid yourself with dinner," she said as she put the dishes where the woman suggested.

Taking advantage of the two of them being alone with the door closed, Dana turned to her—just as Frankie had known she would. "I'm not being nosy, honestly. Is everything all right between you and Hank?"

She smiled as she leaned into the kitchen counter. She loved this kitchen with the warm yellow color, the photographs of family on the walls, the clichéd saying carved in the wood plaque hanging over the door. There was a feeling of permanency in this kitchen, in this house, this ranch. As if no matter what happened beyond that door, this place would weather the storm because it had survived other storms.

"It's hard on him being back here because of Naomi," Frankie said.

"Of course it is," Dana said on a relieved breath. "But he has you to help him through it."

She smiled and nodded. "I'm here for him and he knows it. Though it has put him on edge. But not to worry. I'll stand by him."

Tears filled the older woman's eyes as she quickly stepped to Frankie and threw her arms around her. "I can't tell you how happy I am that Hank has you."

She hadn't thought her generic words would cause such a response but she hugged Dana back, enjoying for a moment the warm hug from this genuine, open woman.

Dana stepped back, wiping her tears as Stacy and Jordan's wife, Liza, came in with the rest of the dirty dishes and leftover food. "We best get that cake out there or we'll have a riot on our hands," Dana said. "If you take the cake, I'll take the forks and dessert plates."

"I'M SORRY," HANK SAID when they reached their cabin and were finally alone again. Dinner had been unbearable, but he knew he should have played along better than he had. "You were great."

"Thanks. Your mother was worried we were having trouble. I assured her that coming back here is hard on you because of Naomi. Your family is nice," she said. "They obviously love you."

He groaned. He hated lying to his mother most of all. "That's what makes this so hard. I wanted to burst out with the truth at dinner tonight." He could feel her gaze on him.

"Why didn't you?"

Hank shook his head. He thought about Frankie's kiss, her nuzzling against him. He'd known it would be necessary if they hoped to pass themselves off as a couple, but he hadn't been ready for it. The kiss had taken him by surprise. And an even bigger surprise had been his body's reaction to it, to her.

He turned away, glad it was late so they could go to bed soon. "I think I'm going to take a walk. Will you be all right here by yourself?"

She laughed. "I should think so since I'm trained in self-defense and I have a license to carry a firearm. You've never asked, but I'm an excellent shot."

"You have a gun?" He knew he shouldn't have been surprised and yet he was. She seemed too much like the girl next door to do the job she did. Slim, athletic, obviously in great shape, she just kept surprising him as to how good she was at this.

If anyone could find out the truth about Naomi, he thought it might be her.

AFTER HANK LEFT, Frankie pulled out her phone and looked again at the photographs she'd taken earlier from the ledge along the cliff. Standing up there being buffeted by the wind, her feet on the rocky ledge, she'd tried to imagine what Naomi had been thinking. If she'd had time to think.

Hank was so sure that she'd been murdered. It was such a strange way to murder someone. Also, she suspected there were other reasons his father believed it was suicide. The killer would have had to drag her up that trail from the bridge and then force her across the ledge. Dangerous, since if the woman was that terrified of heights, she would have grabbed on to her killer for dear life.

How had the killer kept her from pulling him down with her? It had been a male killer, hadn't it? That was what Frankie had imagined. Unless the couple hadn't gone up to the ledge with murder in mind.

Frankie rubbed her temples. People often did the thing you least expected them to do. Which brought her back to suicide. What if Hank was wrong? What if suicide was the only conclusion to be reached after this charade with his family? Would he finally be able to accept it?

The door opened and he came in on a warm summer night gust of mountain air. For a moment he was silhouetted, his broad shoulders filling the doorway. Then he stepped into the light, his handsome face twisted in grief. Her heart ached for him. She couldn't imagine the kind of undying love he'd felt for Naomi. Even after three years, he was still grieving. She wondered at the size of Hank's heart.

"I'd like to talk to Naomi's mother in the morning," she said, turning away from such raw pain. "Lillian Brandt, right?"

"Right." His voice sounded hoarse.

"It would help if you told me about the things that were going on with Naomi before her death, the things that made the coroner and your father believe it was a suicide." When he didn't answer, she turned. He was still standing just inside the door, his Stetson in the fingers of his left hand, his head down. She was startled for a moment and almost stepped to him to put her arms around him.

"There's something I haven't told you." He cleared his throat and looked up at her. "Naomi and I had a fight that night before she left the ranch." He swallowed.

She could see that this was going to take a while and motioned to the chairs as she turned and went into the small kitchen. Opening the refrigerator, she called over her shoulder, "Beer?" She pulled out two bottles even though she hadn't heard his answer and returned to the small living area.

He'd taken a seat, balancing on the edge, nervously turning the brim of his hat in his fingers. When she held out a beer, he took it and tossed his hat aside. Twisting off the cap, Frankie sat in the chair opposite him. She took a sip of the beer. It was icy cold and tasted wonderful. It seemed to soothe her and chase away her earlier thoughts when she'd seen Hank standing in the doorway.

She put her feet up on the well-used wooden coffee table, knowing her boots wouldn't be the first ones that had rested there. She wanted to provide an air of companionship to make it easier for him to tell her the truth. She'd learned this from her former cop uncle who'd been her mentor when she'd first started out.

"What did you fight about?" she asked as Hank

picked at the label on his beer bottle with his thumb without taking a drink.

"It was stupid." He let out a bitter laugh as he lifted his head to meet her gaze. "I wasn't ready to get married and Naomi was." His voice broke again as he said, "She told me I was killing her."

Frankie took a drink of her beer before asking, "How long had you been going out?" It gave Hank a moment to collect himself.

He took a sip of his beer. "Since after college. We met on a blind date. She'd been working as an elementary school teacher, but said she'd rather be a mother and homemaker." He looked away. "I think that's what she wanted more than anything. Even more than me."

She heard something in his voice, in his words. "You didn't question that she loved you, did you?"

"No." He said it too quickly and then shook his head. "I did that night. I questioned a lot of things. She seemed so…so wrong for me. I mean, there was nothing about the ranch that she liked. Not the horses, the dust, the work. I'd majored in ranch management. I'd planned to come home after college and help my folks with the place."

"And that's what you were doing."

He nodded. "But Naomi didn't want to stay here. She didn't like the canyon or living on my folks' place. She wanted a home in a subdivision down in Bozeman. In what she called 'civilization with sidewalks.'" He shook his head. "I had no idea sidewalks meant that much to her before that night. She wanted everything I didn't."

"What did she expect you to do for a living in Bozeman?"

"Her stepfather had offered me a job. He was a Re-altar and he said he'd teach me the business." Hank took a long pull on his beer. "But I was a rancher. This is where I'd grown up. This is what I knew how to do and what I…"

"What you loved."

His blue eyes shone as they locked with hers. She saw that his pain was much deeper than even she'd thought. If Naomi had committed suicide, then he blamed himself because of the fight. He'd denied her what she wanted most, a different version of him.

"So she left hurt and angry," Frankie said. "Did she indicate where she was going? I'm assuming the two of you were living together here at the ranch."

"She said she was going to spend the night at her best friend Carrie White's apartment in Meadow Village here at Big Sky and that she needed time to think about all of this." He swallowed again. "I let her go without trying to fix it."

"It sounds like it wasn't an easy fix," Frankie commented and finished her beer. Getting up, she tilted the bottle in offer. Hank seemed to realize he still had a half-full bottle and quickly downed the rest. She took both empties to the kitchen and came back with two more.

Handing him one, she asked, "You tried to call her that night or the next morning?" As she asked the question, she knew where his parents would have stood on the marriage and Naomi issue. They wouldn't want to tarnish their son's relationship because of their opinions about their choice for a partner, but they also wouldn't want him marrying a woman who was clearly not a good match for him. One who took him off the ranch and the things he loved.

"That night, I was in no mood to discuss it further, so I waited and called her the next morning." He opened his beer and took a long pull. "Maybe if I'd called not long after she left—"

"What had you planned to say?" she asked, simply curious. It was a moot point now. Nor had his plans had anything to do with what happened to Naomi. By then, she was dead.

"I was going to tell her that I'd do whatever she wanted." He let out a long sigh and tipped the beer bottle to his lips. "But when she didn't answer, I changed my mind. I realized it wasn't going to work." His voice broke again. "I loved her, but she wanted to make me over, and I couldn't be the man she wanted me to be." His eyes narrowed. "You can dress me up, but underneath I'm still just a cowboy."

"Did you leave her a message on her phone?"

He nodded and looked away, his blue eyes glittering with tears. "I told her goodbye, but by then it would have been too late." His handsome face twisted in pain.

Frankie sat for a moment, considering everything he'd told her. "Was her cell phone found on her body or in her car?"

He shook his head. "Who knows what she did with it. The phone could have gone into the river. My father had his deputies search for it, but it was never found." His voice broke. "Maybe I did drive her to suicide," he said and took a drink as if to steady himself.

"I'm going to give you my professional opinion, for what it's worth," she said, knowing he wasn't going to like it. "I don't believe she killed herself. She knew that you loved her. She was just blowing off some steam when she headed for her friend's house. Did her friend see her at all?"

He shook his head.

"So she didn't go there. That would explain the discrepancy in the time she left you and when her watch was broken. Is there somewhere else she might have gone? Another friend's place? A male friend's?"

His eyes widened in surprise. "A male friend's? Why would you even ask about—"

"Because I know people. She was counting on you to change and do what she wanted, but after four years? She would have realized it was a losing battle and had someone else waiting in the wings."

He slammed down his beer bottle and shoved to his feet. "You make her sound like she was—"

"A woman determined to get married, have kids, stay home and raise them while her husband had a good job that allowed all her dreams to come true?"

"She wasn't—she—" He seemed at a loss for words.

"Hey, Hank. Naomi was a beautiful woman who had her own dreams." He had showed her a photograph of Naomi. Blonde, green-eyed, a natural beauty.

Ignoring a strange feeling of jealousy, Frankie got to her feet and finished her beer before she spoke. She realized that she'd probably been too honest with him. But someone needed to be, she told herself. It wasn't just the beer talking. Or that sudden stab of jealousy when she'd thought of Naomi.

In truth, she was annoyed at him because she knew that if he'd reached Naomi on the phone that night, he would have buckled under. He would have done whatever she wanted, including marrying her. On some level, he would have been miserable and resented her the rest of his life, but being the man he was, he would have made the best of it. Naomi dying had saved him and he didn't even realize it.

"We need to find the other man," Frankie said as she took her bottle to the recycling bin before turning toward the bedroom.

Hank let out a curse. "You're wrong. You're dead wrong. I don't know why I—"

She cut off the rest of his words as she closed the bedroom door. She knew he was angry and probably ready to fire her. All she could hope was that he would cool down by the morning and would trust that she knew what she was talking about. Oh, she'd known women like Naomi all her life—including her very own mother, who chewed up men and spit them out one after another as they disappointed her. That was the problem with trying to make over a man.

HANK COULDN'T SLEEP. He lay in the second bedroom, staring up at the ceiling, cursing the fact that he'd brought Frankie here. What had he been thinking? This had to be the stupidest idea he'd ever come up with. Clearly, she didn't get it. She hadn't known Naomi.

Another man?

He thought about storming into her bedroom, telling her to pack her stuff and taking her back to Idaho tonight. Instead, he tossed and turned, getting more angry by the hour. He would fire her. First thing in the morning, he'd do just that.

Who did she think she was, judging Naomi like that? Naomi was sweet, gentle, maybe a little too timid… He rolled over and glared at the bedroom door. Another man in the wings! The thought made him so angry he could snap off nails with his teeth.

As his blood pressure finally began to drop somewhere around midnight, he found himself wondering if Naomi's friend Carrie knew more than she'd originally told him. If there had been another man—

He gave that thought a hard shove away. Naomi had loved him. Only him. She'd wanted the best for him. He rolled over again. She thought she knew what was best for him. He kicked at the blanket tangled around his legs. Maybe if she had lived she would have realized that what was best for him, for them, was staying on the ranch, letting him do what he knew and loved. Sidewalks were overrated.

Staring up at the ceiling, he felt the weight of her death press against his chest so hard that for a moment he couldn't breathe.

You don't want to let yourself believe that she committed suicide because you feel guilty about the argument you had with her before she left the ranch, his father had said. *Son, believe me, it took more than some silly argument for her to do what she did. We often don't know those closest to us or what drives them to do what they do. This wasn't your fault.*

Hank groaned, remembering his father's words three years ago. Could he be wrong about a lot of things? He heard the bedroom door open. He could see Frankie silhouetted in the doorway.

"If there is another man, then it would prove that

she didn't commit suicide," the PI said. The bedroom
door closed.

He glared at it for a long moment. Even if Frankie
had gone back to her bedroom and locked the door,
he knew he could kick it down if he wanted to. But as
Frankie's words registered, he pulled the blanket up
over him and closed his eyes, exhausted from all of
this. If there had been another man, then he would be
right about her being murdered.

Was that supposed to give him comfort?

Chapter Six

"I told my mother that we were having breakfast in town," Hank said when Frankie came out of the bedroom fully dressed and showered the next morning. He had his jacket on and smelled of the outdoors, which she figured meant he'd walked down to the main house to talk to his mother.

"I'm going to take a shower," he said now. "If you want to talk to Naomi's mother, we need to catch her before she goes to work." With that, he turned and went back into his bedroom.

Frankie smiled after him. He was still angry but he hadn't fired her. Yet.

She went into the kitchen and made herself toast. Hank didn't take long in the shower. He appeared minutes later, dressed in jeans and a Western shirt, his dark, unruly hair still damp at his collar as he stuffed on his Stetson and headed for the door. She followed, smiling to herself. It could be a long day, but she was glad she was still employed for numerous reasons, number one among them, she wanted to know now more than ever what had happened to Naomi Hill.

Lillian Brandt lived in a large condo complex set

back against a mountainside overlooking Meadow Village. She'd married a real-estate agent after being a single mother for years, from what Hank had told her. Big Sky was booming and had been for years, so Lillian had apparently risen in economic stature after her marriage compared to the way she'd lived before Naomi died.

From her research, Frankie knew that Big Sky, Montana, once a ranching area, had been nothing more than a sagebrush-filled meadow below Lone Mountain. Then Chet Huntley and some developers had started the resort. Since then, the sagebrush had been plowed up to make a town as the ski resort on the mountain had grown.

But every resort needed workers, and while milliondollar houses had been built, there were few places for moderate-income workers to live that they could afford. The majority commuted from Gallatin Gateway, Four Corners, Belgrade and Bozeman—all towns forty miles or more to the north.

Lillian was younger than Frankie had expected. Naomi had been four years younger than Hank. Frankie estimated that Lillian must have had her daughter while in her late teens.

"Hank?" The woman's pale green eyes widened in surprise. "Are you back?"

"For a while," he said and introduced Frankie. "Do you have a minute? We won't take much of your time."

Lillian looked from him to Frankie and back before she stepped aside to let them enter the condo. It was bright and spacious with no clutter. It could have been one of the models that real-estate agents showed prospective clients. "I was just about to leave to go to the office." She worked for her husband as a secretary.

"I just need to ask you a few questions," he said as she motioned for them to take a seat.

"Questions?" she asked as she moved some of the pillows on the couch to make room for them.

"About Naomi's death."

The woman stopped what she was doing to stare at him. "Hank, it's been three years. Why would you dig all of it back up again?"

"Because he doesn't believe she killed herself," Frankie said and supplied her business card. "I didn't know your daughter, but I've heard a lot about her. I'm sorry for your loss, ma'am." Then she asked if it would be okay if Mrs. Brandt would answer a few questions about her daughter. "She was twenty-six, right? Hank said she was ready to get married."

Lillian slumped into one of the chairs that she'd freed of designer pillows and motioned them onto the couch. "It's all she wanted. Marriage, a family."

"Where was she working at the time of her death?" Frankie asked.

"At the grocery store, but I can't see what that—"

She could feel Hank's gaze on her. "Is that where she met her friend Carrie?"

Lillian nodded. Her gaze went to Hank. "Why are you—"

"I'm curious," Frankie said, drawing the woman's attention back again. "Was there anyone else in her life?"

"You mean friends?"

"Yes, possibly a male friend," Frankie said.

The woman blinked before shooting a look at Hank. "She was in love with Hank."

"But she had to have other friends."

Lillian fiddled with the piping along the edge of the chair arm. "Of course she had other friends. She made friends easily."

"I'm sure she did. She was so beautiful," Frankie said.

The woman nodded, her eyes shiny. "She got asked out a lot all through school."

"Do you remember their names?"

Lillian looked at Hank. "She was faithful to you. If that's what this is about—"

"It's not," Hank assured her.

"We just thought they might be able to fill in some of the blanks so Hank can better understand what happened to Naomi. He's having a very hard time moving on," Frankie said.

The woman looked at Hank, sympathy in her gaze. "Of course. I just remember her mentioning one in particular. His name was—" she seemed to think for a moment "—River." She waved her hand wistfully. "Blame it on Montana, these odd names."

"You probably don't remember River's last name," Frankie said.

"No, but Carrie might. She knew him too." Lillian looked at her watch. "I really have to go. I'm sorry."

"No," Frankie said, getting to her feet. "You've been a great help."

"Yes," Hank agreed with much less enthusiasm. "Thank you for taking the time."

"It's good to see you," the woman said to him and patted his cheek. "I hope you can find some peace."

"Me too," he said as he shared a last hug with Mrs. Brandt before leaving.

HANK CLIMBED BEHIND the wheel, his heart hammering in his chest. "You aren't going to give up on your other man theory, are you?"

"No, and you shouldn't either," Frankie said from the passenger seat.

He finally turned his head to look at her. Gritting his teeth, he said, "You think she was cheating on me? Wouldn't that give me a motive for murder?"

"I don't think she was cheating. I said she had someone waiting in the wings. Big Sky is a small town. I suspect that if she'd been cheating on you, you would have heard."

"Thanks. You just keep making me feel better all the time."

"I didn't realize that my job was to make you feel better. I thought it was to find a killer."

He let out a bark of a laugh. "You are something, you know that?"

"It's been mentioned to me. I'm hungry. Are you going to feed me before or after we visit Naomi's best friend, Carrie?"

"I'm not sure I can do this on an empty stomach, so I guess it's going to be before," he said as he started the pickup's engine.

"Over breakfast, you can tell me about Carrie," she said as she buckled up.

"I don't know what you want me to tell you about

her," he grumbled, wishing he'd gone with his instincts last night and stormed into her bedroom and fired her. Even if he'd had to kick down the door.

"Start by telling me why you didn't like her."

He shot her a look as he pulled away from the condo complex. "What makes you think…?" He swore under his breath. "Don't you want to meet her and decide on your own?"

"Oh, I will. But I'm curious about your relationship with her."

Hank let out a curse as he drove toward a local café off the beaten path. The place served Mexican breakfasts, and he had a feeling Frankie liked things hot. She certainly got him hot under his collar.

It wasn't until they were seated and had ordered— he'd been right about her liking spicy food—that he sat back and studied the woman sitting across from him.

"What?" she asked, seeming to squirm a little under his intent gaze.

"Just that you know everything about me—"

"Not everything."

"—and I know nothing about you," he finished.

"That's because this isn't about me," she said and straightened her silverware. He'd never seen her nervous before. But then again, he'd never asked her anything personal about herself.

"You jumped at this case rather fast," he said, still studying her. She wasn't the only one who noticed things about people. "I suspect it was to avoid whoever that was who kept calling you." He saw that he'd hit a nerve. "Angry client? Old boyfriend?" He grinned. "Old boyfriend."

"You're barking up the wrong tree."

"Am I? I don't think so." He took her measure for the first time since he'd hired her. She was a very attractive woman. Right now her long, dark hair was pulled back into a low ponytail. Sans makeup, she'd also played down the violet eyes. And yet there was something sexy and, yes, even sultry about her. Naomi wouldn't leave the house without her makeup on.

That thought reminded him of all the times he'd stood around waiting for her to get ready to go out.

This morning Frankie was more serious, more professional, more hands-off. Definitely low-maintenance in a simple T-shirt and jeans. Nothing too tight. Nothing too revealing.

And yet last night at dinner when she'd snuggled against him, he'd felt her full curves. Nothing could hide her long legs. Right now, he could imagine her contours given that she was slim and her T-shirt did little to hide the curve of her backside.

"Why isn't a woman who looks like you married?" he asked, truly surprised.

"Who says I'm not?"

He glanced at her left hand. "No ring."

She smiled and looked away for a moment. "Isn't it possible I'm just not wearing mine right now?"

Hank considered that as the waitress brought their breakfasts. "*Are* you married?" he asked as the waitress left again.

"No. Now, are you going to tell me why you didn't like Naomi's best friend or are you going to keep stalling?"

Chapter Seven

Johnny Joe "J.J." Whitaker tried the number again. Frankie hadn't been picking up, but now all his calls were going to voice mail. Did she really think he would quit calling? The woman didn't know him very well if she did. That was what made him so angry. She *should* know him by now. He wasn't giving up.

He left another threatening message. "Frankie, you call me or you're going to be sorry. You know I make good on my threats, sweetheart. Call me or you'll wish you had."

He hung up and paced the floor until he couldn't take it anymore. She had to have gotten his messages. She had to know what would happen if she ignored him.

He slammed his fist down on the table, and the empty beer bottles from last night rattled. One toppled over, rolled across the table and would have fallen to the floor if he hadn't caught it.

"Frankie, you bitch!" he screamed, grabbing the neck of the bottle. He brought the bottle down on the edge of the table.

The bottom end of the bottle broke off, leaving a lethal jagged edge below the neck in his hand. He held it up in the light and imagined what the sharp glass could do to a person's flesh. Frankie thought he was dangerous?

He laughed. Maybe it was time to show her just how dangerous he could be.

CARRIE WHITE HAD gotten married not long after Naomi died, Hank told her on the way over to the woman's house. She had been about Naomi's age, and they'd met at the grocery store where Naomi had worked. Carrie had worked at one of the art shops in town. They became friends.

"Was she a bad influence?" Frankie asked.

Hank shrugged. "I don't know."

"How was Carrie with men?"

"She always had one or two she was stringing along, hoping one of them would pop the question."

Frankie laughed. "Is this why you didn't like her?"

"I never said I didn't like her. I just didn't think she was good for Naomi. You have to understand. Naomi was raised by her mother. Her father left when she was six. It devastated her. Lillian had to go to work and raise her alone without any more education than a high school diploma."

"So they didn't have much money?"

"Or anything else. Naomi wanted more and I don't blame her for that."

"Also Naomi didn't want to end up like her," Frankie supposed.

"She wanted a husband, a family, some stability. When her mother started dating the real-estate agent, she wanted that for us."

"Seems pretty stable at the ranch," Frankie said.

"I would have been working for my parents. Naomi couldn't see how I would ever get ahead since even if they left me the ranch, I still have a sister, Mary, and two younger brothers, Brick and Angus. I could see her point. She wanted her own place, her own life, that wasn't tied up with my family's."

Frankie held her tongue. The more she found out about Naomi, the more she could see how she would not have been in the right place emotionally to be involved in a serious relationship. But she was having these thoughts because the more she learned about Hank, the more she liked him.

"So Carrie encouraged her how?"

Hank seemed to give that some thought as he pulled up in front of a small house in a subdivision in Meadow Village. "Carrie encouraged her to dump me and find someone else, someone more…acceptable. Carrie married a local insurance salesman who wears a three-piece suit most days unless he's selling to out-of-staters, and then he busts out his Stetson and boots."

Frankie got the picture. She opened her door, anxious to meet Carrie White and see what she thought of her for herself. She heard Hank get out but could tell that he wasn't looking forward to this.

At the front door, Frankie rang the bell. She could hear the sound of small running feet, then a shriek of laughter followed by someone young bursting into tears.

"Knock it off!" yelled an adult female voice.

She could hear someone coming to the door. It sounded as if the person was dragging one of the crying children because now there appeared to be at least two in tears just on the other side of the door.

"Naomi's dream life?" she said under her breath to Hank.

The woman who opened the door with a toddler on one arm and another hanging off her pants leg looked harried and near tears herself. Carrie was short, dark-haired and still carrying some of her baby weight. She frowned at them and said, "Whatever you're offering, I'm not inter—" Her voice suddenly broke off at the sight of Hank. Her jaw literally dropped.

"Fortunately, we aren't selling anything," Frankie said.

"We'd just like a minute of your time," Hank said as the din died down. The squalling child hanging off Carrie's leg was now staring at them, just like the toddler on her hip. "Mind if we come in?"

The woman shot a look at Frankie, then shrugged and shoved open the screen door. "Let me just put them down for their morning naps. Have a seat," she said over her shoulder as she disappeared down a hallway.

The living room looked like a toy manufacturing company had exploded and most of the toys had landed here in pieces. Against one wall by the door was a row of hooks. Frankie noticed there were a half-dozen sizes of coats hanging there.

They waded through the toys, cleaning off a space on the couch to sit down. In the other room they could hear cajoling and more crying, but pretty soon, Carrie returned.

Frankie could see that she'd brushed her hair and put on a little makeup in a rush and changed her sweat-shirt for one that didn't have spit-up on it. The woman was making an effort to look as if everything was fine. Clearly the attempt was for Hank's benefit.

"It's so good to see you," Carrie said to him, still looking surprised that he'd somehow ended up on her couch.

Frankie guessed that things had not been good between Carrie and Hank after Naomi's death. It seemed Carrie regretted that.

"How have you been?" she asked as she cleared toys off a chair and sat down. She looked exhausted and the day was early.

"All right," he said. "We need to ask you some questions."

The woman stiffened a little. She must have thought this was a social call. "Questions about what?"

"I understand you didn't see or hear from Naomi the night she died," Frankie said. Carrie looked at her and then at Hank.

He said, "This is Frankie, a private investigator. She's helping me find out what happened that night."

The woman turned again to her, curiosity in her gaze, but she didn't ask about their relationship. "I've told you everything I know," she said to Hank before turning back to Frankie. "I didn't hear from her or see her. I told the marshal the same thing."

"Were you planning to?"

The question seemed to take Carrie off guard. "I can't…" She frowned.

"Hadn't your best friend told you that she was going to push marriage that night and if Hank didn't come around…"

The woman's eyes widened. "I wouldn't say she was pushing marriage exactly. It had been four years! How long does it take for a man to make up his mind?" She slid a look at Hank and flushed a little with embarrassment.

"How long did it take your husband?"

Carrie ran a hand through her short hair. "Six months."

Frankie eyed her, remembering the coats hanging on the hooks by the door. "Were you pregnant?"

The woman shot to her feet, her gaze ricocheting back to Hank. "I don't know what this is about, but—"

"She was your best friend. You knew her better than anyone," Frankie said, also getting to her feet. "She would have told you if there was someone else she was interested in. I'm guessing she planned to come back to your place that night if things didn't go well. Unless you weren't such good friends."

Carrie crossed her arms. "She was my *best* friend."

"Then she would have told you about River."

That caught the woman flat-footed. She blinked, looked at Hank again and back to Frankie. "It was Hank's own fault. He kept dragging his feet."

She nodded. "So Naomi must have called to tell you she was on her way."

Carrie shook her head. "I told you. I didn't see her. I didn't hear from her. When I didn't, I just assumed everything went well. Until I got the call the next morning from her mother."

Frankie thought the woman was telling the truth. But Naomi would have called someone she trusted. Someone she could pour her heart out to since she left the ranch upset. "Where can we find River?"

HANK SWORE AS he climbed into his pickup. "I don't want to go see River Dean," he said as Frankie slid into the passenger seat.

"After Naomi left you, she would have gone to one of two places. Carrie's to cry on her shoulder. Or someone else's shoulder. If the man waiting in the wings was River Dean, then that's where she probably went. Which means he might have been the last person to see her alive. If he turned her down as well, maybe she did lose all hope and make that fatal leap from the cliff. You ready to accept that and call it a day?"

Without looking at her, Hank jerked off his Stetson to rake a hand through his hair. "You scare me."

"She wanted to get married and have babies and a man who came home at five thirty every weekday night and took off his tie as she gave him a cocktail and a kiss and they laughed about the funny things the kids had done that day. It's a fantasy a lot of people have."

He stared at her. "But not you."

She shrugged.

"Because you know the fantasy doesn't exist," he said, wanting to reach over and brush back a lock of dark hair that had escaped from her ponytail and now curled across her cheek.

"I'm practical, but even I still believe in love and happy-ever-after."

Surprised, he did reach over and push back the lock of hair. His fingertips brushed her cheek. He felt a tingle run up his arm. Frankie caught his hand and held it for a moment before letting it go. He could see that he'd invaded her space and it had surprised her. It hadn't pleased her.

"You said you wanted the truth," she reminded him, as if his touching her had been an attempt to change the subject. "Have you changed your mind?"

RIVER DEAN OWNED a white-water rafting company that operated downriver closer to what was known as the Mad Mile and House Rock, an area known for thrills and spills.

Frankie could still feel where Hank's fingertips had brushed her cheek. She wanted to reach up and rub the spot. But she resisted just as she had the shudder she'd felt at his sudden touch.

Hank got out of the pickup and stopped in front of a makeshift-looking building with a sign that read WHITE-WATER RAFTING.

The door was open, and inside she could see racks of life jackets hanging from the wall. A motorcycle was parked to one side of the building. Someone was definitely here since there was also a huge stack of rafts in the pine trees, only some of them still chained to a tree. It was early in the day, so she figured business picked up later.

All she could think was that Naomi was foolish enough to trade ranch life for this? A seasonal business determined by the weather and tourists passing through? But maybe three years ago, River Dean had appeared to have better options. And if not, there was always Naomi's stepfather and the real-estate business.

Hank stood waiting for her, staring at the river through the pines. She felt the weight of her cell phone and her past. She'd turned off her phone earlier, but now she pulled it out and checked to see that she had a dozen calls from the same number. No big surprise. She didn't even consider checking voice mail since she knew what she'd find. He'd go by the office and her apartment—if he hadn't already. He would know that she'd left town. She told herself he wouldn't be able to find her even if he tried. Unfortunately, he would try, and if he got lucky somehow...

"You ready?" Hank said beside her.

She pocketed her phone. "Ready as *you* are."

He chuckled at that and started toward the open door of the white-water rafting business. She followed.

The moment she walked in she spotted River Dean. She'd known men like him in Idaho. Good-looking ski bums, mountain bikers, river rafters. Big Sky resembled any resort area with its young men who liked to play.

River Dean was tanned and athletically built with shaggy, sexy blond hair and a million-dollar smile. She saw quickly how a woman would have been attracted to him. It wasn't until she approached him that she could tell his age was closer to forty than thirty. There were lines around his eyes from hours on the water in sunshine.

Hank had stopped just inside the door and was staring at River as if he wanted to rip his throat out.

"You must be River," she said, stepping in front of Hank. River appeared to be alone. She got the feeling that he'd just sent some employees out with a couple of rafts full of adventure seekers.

"Wanting a trip down the river?" he asked, grinning at her and then Hank. His grin faded a little as if he recognized the cowboy rancher Naomi had been dating.

"More interested in your relationship with Naomi Hill," Frankie said.

"You a...cop?" he asked, eyeing her up and down.

"Something like that. Naomi came to see you that night, the night she died."

River shook his head. "I don't know who you are, but I'm not answering any more of your questions."

"Would you prefer to talk to the sheriff?" Frankie snapped.

"No, but..."

"We're just trying to find out what happened to her. I know she came to see you. She was upset. She needed someone to talk to. Someone sympathetic to her problem."

River rubbed the back of his neck for a moment as he looked toward the open door and the highway outside. She could tell he was wishing a customer would stop by right now.

"We know you knew her," Hank said, taking a threatening step forward.

River was shaking his head. "It wasn't like that. I was way too old for her. We were just friends. And I swear I know nothing about what happened to her."

"But she did stop by that night," Frankie repeated.

The river guide groaned. "She stopped by, but I was busy."

"Busy?" Hank said.

"With another woman." Frankie nodded since she'd already guessed that was what must have happened. "Did you two argue?"

"No." He held up his hands. "I told her we could talk

the next day. She realized what was going on and left. That was it," River said.

Hank swore. "But you didn't go to the sheriff with that information even though you might have been the last person to see her alive."

"I wasn't why she jumped," River snapped. "If you're looking for someone to blame, look in the mirror, man. You're the one who was making her so unhappy."

Frankie could see that Hank wanted to reach across the counter and thump the man. She stepped between them again. "Tell me what was said that night."

River shook his head. "It was three years ago. I don't remember word for word. She surprised me. She'd never come by before without calling."

Behind her, Frankie heard Hank groan. River heard it too and looked worried. Both men were strong and in good shape, but Hank was a big cowboy. In a fight, she had no doubt that the cowboy would win.

"It's like I just told you. She was upset before she saw what was going on. I told her she had to leave and that we'd talk the next day. She was crying, but she seemed okay when she left."

"This was at your place? Where was that?"

"I was staying in those old cabins near Soldiers' Chapel. Most of them have been torn down since then."

"Did you see her leave?" Frankie asked. "Could she have left with anyone?"

River shook his head and looked sheepish. "Like I said. I thought she was all right. I figured she was looking for a shoulder to cry on over her boyfriend and that she'd just find someone else to talk to that night."

"Was there someone you thought she might go to?" she asked.

River hesitated only a moment before he said, "Her friend Carrie maybe? I don't know."

Chapter Eight

"You should have let me hit him," Hank said as he slipped behind the wheel and slammed the door harder than he'd meant to.

"Violence is never the answer."

He shot her a look. "You read that in a fortune cookie?" He couldn't help himself. He couldn't remember the last time he was this angry.

He saw Frankie's expression and swore under his breath. "Yes, I'd prefer to blame River Dean rather than the dead woman I was in love with. You have a problem with that?"

She said nothing, as if waiting for his anger to pass. His father had warned him that digging into Naomi's death would only make him feel worse. He really hated it when his father was right—and Hud didn't even know that was what he was doing.

He drove back to the ranch, his temper cooled as he turned into the place.

"I had no idea about what was going on with Naomi," he said, stating the obvious. "You must think me a fool."

Frankie graced him with a patient smile as he drove down the road to the ranch house. "She loved you, but you both wanted different things. Love doesn't always overcome everything."

"Don't be nice to me," he said gruffly, making her laugh. Her cell phone rang. She checked it as if surprised that she'd left it on and quickly turned it off again.

"You're going to have to talk to him sometime," Hank said, studying her.

"Is there anyone else you want to go see?"

He shook his head, aware that she'd circumvented his comment as he parked at the foot of the trail that led to their cabin on the mountainside. "I need to be alone for a while, Frankie. Is that all right?"

"Don't worry about me."

He smiled at her. "You can take care of yourself, right? Never need any help."

"I wouldn't say that." She opened her door and got out.

He swore and, after throwing the pickup into Park, got out and went after her. "Frankie, wait."

She stopped and turned back to him.

"I don't know what your story is, but I do know this," he said. "You have closed yourself off for some reason. I recognize the signs because I've done it for the past three years. In your case, I suspect some man's to blame, the one who keeps calling. One question. Is he dangerous?"

She started to step away, but he reached for her arm and pulled her back around to face him again. "I'm fine. There is nothing to worry about."

He shook his head but let go of her arm. "You are one stubborn woman." He couldn't help but smile because there was a strength and independence in her that he admired. He'd never known a woman quite like her. She couldn't have been more different from Naomi, who he'd always felt needed taking care of. Just the thought of Naomi and what he'd learned about her before she died was like a bucket of ice water poured over him. He took a step away, needing space right now, just like he'd told her.

"I'll see you later." With that, he turned to his pickup and drove off, looking back only once to see Frankie standing in the ranch yard, a worried expression on her face.

"Nothing to worry about, huh?" he said under his breath.

As FRANKIE TURNED toward their cabin on the mountain, she saw movement in the main house and knew that their little scene had been witnessed. They didn't appear to be a loving couple. She didn't know how much longer they could continue this ruse before someone brought it up.

But this was the way Hank wanted it. At least for the time being. She felt guilty, especially about his mother. Dana wanted her son to move on from Naomi's death and find some happiness. Frankie wasn't sure that was ever going to happen.

She hated to admit it to herself, but the moment Hank had told her about the problems they'd been having, she'd nailed the kind of young woman Naomi had been.

The weight of her cell phone in her pocket seemed to mock her. She was good at figuring out *other* people, but not so good when it came to her own life.

"Frankie!" She turned at the sound of Dana's voice. The older woman was standing on the ranch house porch, waving at her. "Want a cup of coffee? I have cookies."

She couldn't help but laugh as she started for the main house. Dana wanted to talk and she was using cookies as a bribe. Frankie called her on it the moment she reached the porch.

"You've found me out," Dana said with a laugh. "I'll stoop to just about anything when it comes to my son."

"I understand completely," she said, climbing the steps to the porch. "Hank is a special young man."

"Yes, I think he is," the woman said as she shoved open the screen door. "I thought we could talk."

Frankie chuckled. "I had a feeling." She stepped inside, taking in again the Western-style living room with its stone fireplace, wood floors, and Native American rugs adjacent to the warm and cozy kitchen. She liked it here, actually felt at home, which was unusual for her. She often didn't feel at home at her own place.

"I never asked," Dana said as she filled two mugs with coffee, handed one to Frankie and put a plate of cookies on the table. "How did you two meet?" She motioned her into a chair.

Hank hired me to pretend to be his girlfriend. "At a bar." It was the simplest answer she could come up with. She wondered why she and Hank hadn't covered this part. They should have guessed at least his mother would ask.

"Really? That surprises me. I've never known Hank to be interested in the bar scene and he isn't much of a drinker, is he?" Dana let out an embarrassed laugh. "I have to keep reminding myself that he's been gone three years. Maybe I don't really know my son anymore."

Frankie chuckled and shook her head. "Hank only came into the bar to pick up some dinner. Apparently it had been a long day at work and he'd heard that we served the best burgers in Idaho. I just happened to be working that night, and since it was slow, we got to talking. A few days later, he tracked me down because I was only filling in at the bar. A friend of mine owns it. Anyway, Hank asked me out and the rest is history."

It was pure fiction, but it was what she saw Dana needed to hear. Hank was no bar hound. Still, she felt guilty even making up such a story. It would have been so much easier to tell the truth. But her client had been adamant about them keeping the secret as long as they could.

Dana took a sip of her coffee and then asked, "So when not helping a friend, what do you do?"

"I'm a glorified secretary for a boss who makes me work long hours." That at least felt like the truth a lot of days. "Seriously, I love my job and my boss is okay most of the time. But I spend a lot of time doing paperwork."

"Oh my, well, you must be good at it. I'm terrible at it. That's why it is such a blessing that our Mary stayed around and does all of the accounting for the ranch."

"These cookies are delicious," Frankie said, taking a bite of one. "I would love your recipe." The diversion worked as she'd hoped. Dana hopped up to get her recipe file and began to write down the ingredients and explain that the trick was not to overbake them.

"So you cook," Dana said, kicking the conversation off into their favorite recipes. Frankie had no trouble talking food since she did cook and she had wonderful recipes that her grandmother had left her.

FRUSTRATED AND ANGRY at himself and Naomi, Hank drove out of the ranch, not sure where he was going. All he knew was that he wanted to be alone for a while.

But as he turned onto the highway, he knew exactly where he was headed. Back to the river. Back to the cliff and the ledge where she'd jumped. Back to that deep, dark, cold pool and the rocks where her body had been found.

He knew there was nothing to find there and yet he couldn't stay away. It was one of the reasons he'd left after Naomi died. That and his grief, his unhappiness, his anger at his father.

After pulling off the road, he wound back into the pines and parked. For a moment he sat behind the wheel, looking out at the cliff through the trees. What did he hope to find here? Shaking his head, he climbed out and walked through the pines to the rocky shore of the river. Afternoon sunlight poured down through the boughs, making the surface of the river shimmer.

A cool breeze ruffled his hair as he sat down on a large rock. Shadows played on the cliff across from him. When he looked up at the ledge, just for a moment he thought he saw Naomi in her favorite pale yellow dress, the fabric fluttering in the wind as she fell.

He blinked and felt his eyes burn with tears. Frankie was right. He and Naomi had wanted different things. They hadn't been right for each other, but realizing that didn't seem to help. He couldn't shake this feeling he'd had for three years. It was as if she was trying to reach him from the grave, pleading with him that he find her killer.

Hank pulled off his Stetson and raked a hand through his hair. Was it just guilt for not marrying her, not taking the job with her stepfather, not giving up the ranch for her? Or was it true? Had she been murdered?

He reminded himself that this was why he was back here. Why he'd gone to Frankie to begin with and talked her into this charade. He realized, as he put his hat back on to shade his eyes from the summer sun, he trusted Frankie to find out the truth. Look how much she'd discovered so far. He told himself it was a matter of time. If they could just keep their…relationship secret…

At the sound of a twig breaking behind him, Hank swung around, startled since he'd thought he was alone. Through the pines he saw a flash of color as someone took off at a run.

He jumped to his feet, but had to work his way back through the rocks, so he couldn't move as fast. By the time he reached the pines, whoever it had been was gone. He told himself it was probably just a kid who was as startled as he was to see that there was someone at this spot.

But as he stood, trying to catch his breath, he knew it hadn't been a kid. The person had been wearing a light color. The same pale yellow as Naomi's favorite dress or just his imagination? He'd almost convinced himself that he'd seen a ghost until, in the distance, he heard the sound of a vehicle engine rev and then die away.

Chapter Nine

After her visit with Dana, Frankie realized that she and Hank had to move faster. His mother was no fool. Frankie could tell that she was worried.

"Is there a vehicle I could borrow?" Frankie asked after their coffee and cookies chat.

"Of course." Dana had moved to some hooks near the door and pulled down a set of keys. "These are to that blue pickup out there. You're welcome to use it anytime you like. Hank should have thought of that. Where did he go, anyway?"

"He had some errands to run and I didn't want to go along. I told him I would be fine exploring. I think I'll go into town and run a few errands of my own." She gave the woman what she hoped was a reassuring smile and took the keys and the pickup to head into town.

Frankie felt an urgency to finish this. It wasn't just because their pretense was going to be found out sooner rather than later. Nor was it because she'd left a lot of things unfinished back in Idaho, though true. It was being here, pretending to be in love with Hank, pretending that there was a chance that she could be part of this amazing family at some time in the future.

That, she knew, was the real problem. Hank was the kind of man who grew on a woman. But with his family, she'd felt instant love and acceptance. She didn't want to hurt these people any longer. That meant solving this case and getting out of here.

At the local grocery store, she found the manager in the back. She'd assumed that after three years, the managers would have changed from when Naomi had worked here. She was wrong.

Roy Danbrook was a tall, skinny man of about fifty with dark hair and eyes. He rose from his chair, looked around his incredibly small office as if surprised how small it really was and then invited her in. She took the plastic chair he offered her, feeling as if being in the cramped place was a little too intimate. But this wouldn't take long.

"I'm inquiring about a former worker of yours, Naomi Hill," she said, ready to lie about her credentials if necessary.

Roy frowned and she realized he probably didn't even remember Naomi after all this time. The turnover in resort towns had to be huge.

"Naomi," he said and nodded. "You mentioned something about an insurance claim?"

She nodded. She'd flashed him her PI credentials, but he'd barely looked at them. "I need to know what kind of employee she was."

He seemed to think for a moment. "Sweet, very polite with customers…" She felt a *but* coming. "But I had no choice but to let her go under the circumstances."

This came as a surprise. Did Hank know Naomi had

been fired? "The circumstances?" That could cover a lot of things.

The manager looked away for a moment, clearly uncomfortable with speaking of past employees, or of the dead? "The stealing." He shook his head.

"The stealing?" All she could think of was groceries.

"Unfortunately, she couldn't keep her hand out of the till. Then there was the drinking, coming in still drunk, coming in late or not coming in at all. I liked her mother, so I tried to help the girl." He shook his head. "Finally, I had to let her go, you understand."

Frankie blinked. He couldn't be talking about the same Naomi Hank had been involved with. "We're talking about Naomi Hill, the one who—"

"Jumped off the cliff and killed herself. Yes."

Stealing? Drinking? Partying? Blowing off work? She tried to figure out how that went with the image Hank had painted of Naomi, but the two didn't fit.

A thought struck her. "She wasn't doing all this alone, right? There had to be someone she hung out with that might be able to give me some insight into her character."

He nodded. "Tamara Baker."

"Is she still around?"

"She works at the Silver Spur Bar." She didn't have to ask him what he thought of Tamara. He glanced at the clock on the wall. "She should be coming to work about now. If she is able to." He shook his head. "I hope this has helped you. I find it most disturbing to revisit it."

"You have been a great help, thank you." She got to her feet, feeling unsteady from the shock of what she'd learned. Sweet, timid little Naomi. Frankie couldn't wait to talk to her friend Tamara.

WHEN HUD CAME home for lunch, as he always did, Dana had sandwiches made and a fresh pot of coffee ready. She hadn't planned to say anything until he'd finished eating.

"What is it?" her husband demanded. "You look as if you're about to pop. Spit it out."

She hurriedly sat down with him and took half of a sandwich onto her plate. Broaching this subject was difficult. They'd discussed Hank on occasion but it never ended well. Sometimes her husband could be so mule-headed stubborn.

"It's Hank."

"Of course it is," Hud said with a curse.

"Something's wrong."

Her husband shook his head as he took a bite of his lunch, clearly just wanting to eat and get out of there.

"This relationship with Frankie, it just doesn't feel... real."

"You have talked about nothing else but your hopes and prayers for Hank to move on, get over Naomi, make a life for himself. Now that he's doing it—"

"I don't believe he's doing it. Maybe coming back here was the worst thing he could do. I can tell it's putting a strain on him and Frankie. Earlier, I saw them... They aren't as loving toward each other as they should be."

Hud groaned as he finished his sandwich and reached for a cookie, which he dunked angrily into his coffee mug. "What would you like *me* to do about it?"

"Why is it we can't talk about Hank without you getting angry?" she demanded. They hardly ever argued, but when it came to the kids, she was like a mama bear, even with Hud. "I want to know more about Frankie." She said the words that had been rolling around in her mind since she'd first met the woman.

"You don't like her."

"No, I do. That's the problem. She seems so right for Hank."

Hud raked a hand through his hair before settling his gaze on her. "What am I missing here?"

"That's just it. I like her so much, I have to be sure this isn't— I mean, that she's not— Can't you just do some checking on her to relieve my mind so I can—"

"No." He stood up so abruptly that the dishes on the table rattled, startling her. "Absolutely not. Have you forgotten that the trouble began between my son and me when I did a background check on Naomi?"

"Because he was so in love with her. It was his first real crush. I asked you to make sure that she was all right for him because he seemed blind to her…"

"Blind to the fact that she didn't want what he wanted more than anything? That she would never have been happy with Hank if he settled here? She wanted marriage so badly that it was all she talked about. That she was pressuring our son and I could see that he felt backed against a wall?" Hud demanded. "Yes. Those were all good reasons. Along with the fact that I sensed a weakness in her. A fragility…"

"You questioned her mental stability, not to mention she'd been arrested for shoplifting."

He nodded, looking sick. "Something I never told our

son. As it turned out, maybe I should have. I was right about her, which gives me no satisfaction." He raised his head to meet her gaze. His eyes shone. "I lost my son. I'm not sure I will get him back because of everything that happened. I can't make that mistake again." He reached for his Stetson on the wall hook where he put it each time he entered the kitchen. "Thank you for lunch." With that, he left.

Dana looked after him, fighting tears. She couldn't help the knot of fear inside her. Something was wrong, but she had no idea what to do about it.

TAMARA BAKER WAS indeed behind the bar at the Silver Spur. The place was empty, a janitor was just finishing up in the restroom, and the smell of industrial-strength cleanser permeated the air.

"Tamara Baker?" Frankie asked as she took a barstool.

"Who wants to know?" asked the brunette behind the bar. She had a smoker's rough voice and a hard-lived face that belied her real age. Frankie estimated she was in her midthirties, definitely older than Naomi.

"You knew Naomi Hill."

Tamara's eyes narrowed to slits. "You a reporter?"

Frankie laughed. "Not hardly. I heard that you and Naomi used to party together."

"That's no secret." That was what she thought. "But if you aren't with the press, then—"

Frankie gave her the same story she had Roy, only Tamara wasn't quite as gullible. When Frankie flashed her credentials, the bartender grabbed them, taking them over into the light from the back bar to study them.

"You're a PI? No kidding?"

"No kidding. I was hoping you could tell me about Naomi. Other people I've spoken with have painted a completely different picture of her compared to the stories I've heard about the two of you." She was exaggerating, but the fib worked.

Tamara laughed. "Want something to drink?" she asked as she poured herself one.

"I'd take a cola."

"I knew a different side of Naomi," the woman said after taking a pull of her drink. "She let her freak flag fly when she was with me."

"How did you two meet?"

"At the grocery store. She helped me out sometimes when I didn't have enough money to feed my kids." Tamara shrugged. "I tried to pay her back by showing her a good time here at the bar."

Frankie understood perfectly. Naomi would steal out of the till at the grocery store for Tamara, and Tamara would ply her with free drinks here at the bar. "What about men?"

"*Men?* What about them?"

"Did this wild side of her also include men?"

Tamara finished her drink and washed out the glass. "Naomi wasn't interested. She had this rancher she said she was going to marry. She flirted a little, but she was saving herself for marriage. She had this idea that once she was married, everything would come up roses." The bartender laughed.

"You doubted it?"

"I've seen women come through here thinking that marriage was going to cure whatever ailed them," Tamara said. "I've been there. What about you?" she asked, glancing at Frankie's left hand. "You married?"

She shook her head. "You must have been surprised when you heard that Naomi dove off the cliff and killed herself."

The woman snorted. "I figured it was just a matter of time. She was living a double life. It was bound to catch up with her."

"You mean between the bar and the cowboy?"

Tamara looked away for a moment as if she thought someone might be listening. "Naomi had a lot more going on than anyone knew."

"Such as?"

The front door opened, sending a shaft of bright summer sun streaming across the floor like a laser in their direction. A man entered, the door closing behind him, pitching them back into cool darkness.

"Hey, Darrel," she called to the man as he limped to the bar. "What ya havin'?" The bartender got a beer for the man and hung around talking to him quietly for a few minutes.

Frankie saw the man glance in her direction. He was about her age with sandy-blond hair, not bad-looking, but there was something about him that made her look away. He seemed to be suddenly focusing on her a little too intensely. She wondered what Tamara had told him about her.

When the bartender came back down the bar, Frankie asked, "You didn't happen to see Naomi that night, the night she died, did you?"

"Me?" She shook her head. "I was working until closing. It's my usual shift. You can ask anyone."

Frankie noticed that the woman now seemed nervous and kept glancing down the bar at the man she'd called Darrel.

As she straightened the shirt she was wearing, Tamara asked, "Can I get you anything else?" She didn't sound all that enthusiastic about it.

"You said Naomi was into other things. Like what?"

"I was just shooting my mouth off. You can't pay any attention to me. If I can't get you anything else, I really need to do some stocking up." She tilted her head toward the man at the end of the bar. She lowered her voice. "You know, want to look good in front of the customers."

"Sure." She could tell that was all she was going to get out of Tamara. But she wondered what it was about the man at the end of the bar that made her nervous.

As she left, she found herself still trying to piece together what she'd learned about the woman known as Naomi Hill. The pieces didn't fit. She tried to imagine what Naomi could have been involved in that would get her murdered—if that had been the case.

More and more, though, Frankie believed that the woman had come unhinged when she'd seen her planned life with Hank crumbling, and it had driven her to do the one thing that terrified her more than her so-called double life.

HANK KNEW HE couldn't put it off any longer. He swung by his father's office, knowing the man was a creature of habit. Marshal Hudson Savage went home every day for lunch. And every day, his wife would have a meal ready. Hank used to find it sweet. Then his father went back to his office. If nothing was happening, he would do paperwork for an hour or so before he would go out on patrol.

He found his father sitting behind his desk. The marshal looked up in surprise to see Hank standing in the doorway. "Come on in," he said, as if he knew this wasn't a personal visit. "Close the door."

Hank did just that, but he didn't take the chair his father offered him. "I want a copy of Naomi's file." Hud started to shake his head. "Don't tell me I can't have it. She'd dead. The case is closed. Pretend I'm a reporter and give me a copy."

His father sighed as he leaned back in his chair, gazing at him with an intensity that used to scare him when he was a boy and in trouble. "Your mother and I had hoped—"

"I know what you'd hoped," he interrupted. "Don't read too much into my wanting a copy of the file."

"What am I supposed not to read into it? That you still haven't moved on?"

Hank said nothing.

"What's the deal with you and Frankie?" the marshal asked, no longer sounding like his father. "Are you in love with her?"

"Seriously? Mother put you up to this?"

"We're concerned."

Hank laughed. "Just like you were concerned when I was in love with Naomi."

"Are you in love with Frankie?"

"Who wouldn't be? She's a beautiful, smart, talented woman. Now, if we're through with the interrogation, I still want that file. Let's say I need it to get closure."

"Is that what it is?"

He gave his father an impatient look.

The marshal leaned forward, picked up a manila envelope from his desk and held it out to him.

Hank stared at it without taking the envelope from him for a moment. "What is this?"

"A copy of Naomi's file."

"How—"

"How did I know that you would be asking for it?" His father asked the question for him as he cocked his head. Hank noticed his father's hair more graying than he remembered. "Maybe I know you better than you think."

Hank took the envelope from him. "Is everything in here?"

"Everything, including my notes. Will there be anything else?"

He shook his head, feeling as if there was something more he should say. "Thank you."

His father gave him a nod. His desk phone rang.

Hank opened the door, looking back as his father picked up the phone and said, "Marshal Savage." He let the door close behind him and left.

Chapter Ten

J.J. went by Frankie's apartment and banged on the door until the neighbor opened a window and yelled out.

"I'm going to call the cops."

"Call the cops. Where's Frankie?"

"The woman who lives in that apartment? She packed up and left with some man a few days ago."

"What?" He described Frankie to the man since it was clear the fool didn't know what he was talking about.

"That's her," the man said. "I know my own neighbor. She left with a cowboy—that's all I can tell you. She's not home, so please let me get some sleep."

He thought he might lose his mind. Where could she have gone? He'd been by her office. It was locked up tight. He told himself she was on a case. But why wouldn't she answer her phone? Why wouldn't she call him back? She knew what a mistake that would be once he got his hands on her.

He'd called her number, left more messages, and still she hadn't gotten back to him. What if she'd left for good?

She wouldn't do that. She was just trying to teach

him a lesson, playing hard to get. Once he saw her again, he'd teach *her* a lesson she wouldn't soon forget. No one pulled this kind of crap on him. Especially some woman.

He knew there was only one thing to do. Track her down and make her pay.

After all, he had the resources. He just hadn't wanted to use them. He'd hoped that Frankie would have come to her senses and realized she couldn't get away from him. But she had.

And now he was going after her.

FRANKIE FOUND HANK poring over papers on the small table in their cabin.

Hank looked up, surprised as she came in the door, as if he'd forgotten all about her. "Where have *you* been?"

"I've been working. You all right?"

He nodded. "I stopped by the marshal's office and got a copy of Naomi's file."

"Your dad gave it to you?" She couldn't help being surprised.

"He'd already made a copy for me." He grunted. "He says he knows me better than I think he does. You're probably right about them seeing through us. Mom said you took one of the pickups into town. I'm sorry I didn't think to give you keys for a vehicle."

"It was fine," she said, pulling out a chair at the table and sitting down. "I had coffee and cookies with your mother before I left."

He raised a brow. "How did that go?"

"She quizzed me about us, about me. She wanted to know how we met. We should have come up with something beforehand. I had to wing it." She told him the story she'd given to his mother.

Hank nodded. "Sorry about that, but it sounds like you covered it."

"We had a nice visit. I don't like lying to her, though. She's going to be hurt."

"I know." He got to his feet. "You hungry? I haven't had lunch."

"Me either."

"I know a place up the canyon, the Corral. They used to make great burgers. Want to give it a try?"

She smiled as her stomach rumbled loudly.

It was one of those beautiful summer days. Frankie breathed it in as Hank drove them through the canyon. Sunlight glimmered off the pines and the clear green of the river as the road and river wound together through cliffs and meadows.

Frankie sat back and enjoyed the ride. She'd decided she would tell Hank later what she'd learned so as not to spoil his lunch. It could wait, and right now she was enjoying just the two of them on this amazing day. Even Hank seemed more relaxed than she'd seen him. He turned on the radio, and as a country song came on from a local station, they both burst into song. Frankie had grown up on the old country classics, so she knew all the words.

They laughed as the song ended and fell into a companionable silence as the news came on and Hank turned off the radio.

"You said you were working while I was gone—"

"We can talk about it later."

He shot her a look before going back to his driving, as if he knew it wasn't going to be good news. Not far up the road he turned into the Corral. The place had originally been built in 1947. It had changed from when Hank was a boy, but it still served great burgers and fries. Now you could also get buffalo as well as beef and sweet potato fries or regular. The booths had been replaced with log furniture and yet he still felt as at home here as he had as a boy when his grandfather used to play guitar in a band here.

After they ordered, Hank said, "I like your hair." He reached over and caught a long lock between his thumb and finger. "Do you ever wear it down?"

She eyed him suspiciously.

"What? I can't compliment you? You said we needed to act like lovers."

"Lovers?" She broke into a smile. "Something happen I don't know about?"

He let go of her hair and glanced toward the bar. "Before I went down to my father's office for a copy of Naomi's file, I stopped by the river again where she died. There was someone else there. I heard them behind me and when I turned around they ran. I caught only a glimpse of fabric through the trees and then I heard a car engine start up and the vehicle leave."

FRANKIE COULD SEE that the incident had spooked him. She wasn't sure why, though. Nothing about it sounded sinister. "Who do you think it was?"

He shook his head. "I thought I caught a glimpse of Naomi up on the ledge, wearing this pale yellow dress she loved."

"Was anyone up on the ledge?"

He shook his head. "But there was someone behind me. Someone wearing a light-colored garment running through the trees."

"You thought it was Naomi?"

"Naomi is dead. She can't step on a twig and break it directly behind me and startle me." He picked up his napkin and rearranged his silverware. "I'm not losing it."

"I know you're not. You saw someone. But that doesn't mean it had anything to do with Naomi. Unless you think you were followed."

He shook his head. "Why would someone follow me?"

She shrugged. Clearly neither of them knew. He realized that she was right. It was just someone who was looking for a spot on the river. He'd probably startled them more than they had him.

"But then again," Frankie said, "if you're right and Naomi was murdered, then her murderer is still out there."

"If you're trying to scare me—"

"What you have to figure out is why anyone would want to kill Naomi in the first place. I have some thoughts that I'll share on the way back to the ranch. But in the meantime—"

"Just a minute. You learned something?"

Fortunately, their burgers and fries came just then. They'd both gone for beef, regular fries and colas. Hank looked down at the food, then at her. She picked up a fry and dragged it through a squirt of ketchup she'd poured onto her plate before taking a bite.

"I can't remember the last time I had a burger and

fries," she said with enthusiasm. Picking up the burger, she took a juicy hot bite and made a *hmmm* sound that had him smiling.

He could see that she didn't want to talk about what she'd found out. Not now. He decided to let it go until after their lunch because it was a beautiful day and he was sitting here with a beautiful woman. "Did I just see you put mayo on your burger?"

"You have a problem with that?" she joked.

He reached for the side of mayo she'd ordered. "Not if you share. I guess it's just one more thing we have in common."

"We have something in common?"

Hank met her gaze. "Maybe more than you realize." He took a bite of his burger and they ate as if it might be their last meal.

HANK COULDN'T REMEMBER the last time he'd enjoyed a meal more—or his dining companion. Frankie was funnier than he'd expected her to be. The more time he spent around her, the more he liked her. She'd definitely been the right choice when he'd gone looking for a private investigator.

He'd asked around and was told he couldn't beat Frankie Brewster. At that point, he'd thought Frankie was male. It wasn't until he saw her that he knew how to come back to the ranch without drawing attention to his reason for returning. So far, it seemed to be working, even if his parents were suspicious of their relationship. Let them worry about that instead of his real reason for bringing her home.

"Okay, let's hear it," he said as they left the Corral

and headed the five miles back toward Big Sky and the ranch.

She started to say something when she glanced in her side mirror. "Do you know the driver of that truck behind us?"

He glanced in his rearview mirror and saw a large gold older-model truck behind them. As he watched, he saw that the truck was gaining speed on them. "No, why?"

"I saw it behind us earlier on the way to the Corral."

"You think whoever is driving it is following us?" The idea sounded ludicrous until he reminded himself of the person he'd seen by the river earlier—and the reason he was home. She was right. If Naomi had been murdered, then her killer was still out there.

Looking in the rearview again, he saw that the truck was coming up way too fast. The canyon road was winding with tight curves and few straightaways, and yet the driver of the truck acted as if he planned to pass—and soon—given the speed he was traveling.

"Hank, I have a bad feeling," Frankie said as the driver of the truck closed the distance.

He had the same bad feeling. Earlier there'd been more traffic, especially close to Big Sky, but other than a few semis passing by, they seemed to be the only two vehicles on this stretch of the highway right now.

Hank looked for a place to pull off and let the truck pass. Maybe it was a driver who didn't know this canyon and how dangerous it could be. Or maybe— The front of the truck filled his rearview mirror.

"He's going to ram us," he cried. "Brace yourself."

The driver of the truck slammed into the back of

them. Hank fought to keep the pickup on the road. This section of highway was bordered on one side by cliffs and the river on the other. Fortunately, there was a guardrail along the river, but up ahead there was a spot where the guardrail was broken apart from a previous accident and hadn't been replaced yet.

All thoughts of the driver of the truck behind them being new to the area dissolved. Whoever was at that wheel knew exactly what he was doing. Hank knew going faster wasn't going to help. He couldn't outrun the truck.

"He's going to try to knock us into the river at this next curve," he told Frankie as the bumper of the truck banged into them again and he had to fight the wheel to keep from wrecking. "There is nothing I can do, so I have a bad feeling we will be swimming soon."

As he came around the curve, the trucker did exactly what he'd anticipated he would do. Hank tried to stay on the highway, but the truck was too large, the driver going too fast. The large truck smashed into the side of his pickup, forcing them off the road. Fortunately, Hank saw that the riverbank wasn't steep. Rather than let the trucker roll the pickup off into the river, he turned the wheel sharply toward the water and yelled, "Hang on!" and hoped for the best as the pickup left the highway and plunged into the Gallatin River.

Chapter Eleven

"I was just at the grocery store," Dana said without preamble when her husband answered his phone at the marshal's office. "I overheard the manager talking to one of his employees about Naomi."

"Dana, I'm right in the middle of—"

"Roy said that a woman named Francesca Brewster with some insurance company had come in and was asking questions about Naomi and her death. Why would Frankie be asking about Naomi's death?"

"Maybe she's curious," her husband said after a moment. "After all, Naomi was Hank's former girlfriend. Frankie probably wants to know what happened to her and I doubt Hank is very forthcoming. Hell, he still thinks she was murdered."

"I'm worried. You know how I felt about Naomi and I'm afraid Hank did too. Now it's like he doesn't trust me. I have no idea how he feels about Frankie."

"He brought her home with him. That should tell you something."

"It would if they were getting along. Stacy said they aren't sleeping in the same bed and earlier I saw them having another argument. If she's asking people questions about Naomi—"

"I think you're making too much out of this."

"We don't know anything about her."

"Dana—"

"He's our son, Hud. I don't want to see him make a terrible—"

"There is nothing we can do about it. If either of us says anything…" He swore. "Honey, we have to let him make his own mistakes. We both tried to warn him about Naomi and look where that left us."

"It's just that I don't think he can take another woman breaking his heart." She hated how close to tears she sounded.

"He's a grown man. He can take care of himself. Give him a little credit. Maybe Frankie is exactly what he needs."

IT HAPPENED SO FAST, Frankie didn't have time to react. One minute they were on the highway, the next in the river. The pickup plunged into the water, the front smashing into the rocks. Water rushed around them and began to come in through the cracks, building up quickly at her side window.

"We have to get out of here," Hank yelled over the roar of the river and the sound of water as it began to fill the cab.

She saw him try to open his door and fail against the weight of water. Her door was facing upstream, so she knew there was no opening it. She unhooked her seat belt, only then aware of her deflated airbag in her lap. Water was rising quickly. Hank was right. They had to brave the river because if they stayed in the pickup much longer—

Next to her, Hank had unsnapped his seat belt and was trying to get his side window to slide down, but it didn't appear to be working. He moved over and leaned back against her. "Get ready," he said. "Once I kick out the window…" He didn't need to tell her what would happen. She could see the water rushing over the cab of the pickup and forming an eddy on his side of the truck.

Hank reared back and kicked. The glass turned into a white spiderweb. He kicked again and the window disappeared out into the river. Cold water rushed in. Hank grabbed her hand. "Hang on," he said as the cab filled faster.

She held on as if her life depended on it. It did. For a moment, the force of the water rushing in wouldn't let them escape. But Hank kicked off the side of the pickup, dragging her with him. For a few moments, which felt like an eternity, she saw and felt nothing but water all around her. Her chest ached from holding her breath. She needed air, would have done anything for one small intake of oxygen. Hank never let go of her hand, or her his, even as the river tried to pull them apart.

And then, gloriously, they surfaced, and she gasped for breath. Nothing had ever felt so good as she took air into her lungs. As Hank pulled her toward shore, she looked back, surprised by how far downriver they'd surfaced. The truck cab was completely submerged in the water. She coughed and gasped for air as she stumbled up onto the rocks.

Hank pulled her to him, rubbing her arms as if to take away the chill. She hadn't realized how hard she was trembling until his strong body wrapped around her. She leaned into him, taking comfort in his warmth as what had just happened finally hit her. Someone had tried to kill them—and she'd lost her purse as well as her gun.

On the highway, vehicles had stopped. People were calling to them. Someone said they'd phoned for help and that the marshal was on his way.

DRENCHED TO THE skin and still shivering from the cold water and the close call, Hank climbed into the back of his father's patrol SUV with Frankie. His father had given them blankets, which they'd wrapped up in. Still he put his arm around her, holding her close to share his body heat. He still couldn't believe what had happened and was just thankful they were both alive.

He'd gotten her into this. So of course he felt responsible for her. But he knew it was more than that as he pulled her closer. He wasn't sure when it had happened but they felt like friends. Almost dying did that to a person, he thought.

He became aware of how her wet clothes clung to her, revealing curves he'd always known were there but hadn't seen before. The fact that he could think about that now told him that he was definitely alive—and typically male.

"Why would someone want to force you off the road?" his father asked after he'd told him what had happened.

He heard the disbelief in his father's tone. He'd been here before. Hud hadn't believed that Naomi was murdered. He didn't believe that someone had just tried to kill them. "Believe whatever you like," he snapped. "But this was no accident. The truck crashed into us twice before it forced me off the road. It wasn't a case of road rage. Frankie had seen it behind us on the way to the Corral. The driver must have followed us and waited until we came out."

"Okay, son. I've called for a wrecker. I'll have your truck taken to the lab. Hopefully there will be some paint from the other truck on it that will help us track down the make and model, along with the description you've already given me of the driver. Even if the driver wasn't trying to kill the two of you, he left the scene of an accident. I've put a BOLO out. Later, after the two of you get a shower and warm clothes on, I'll take your statements."

Hank rested his head on the top of Frankie's as she leaned into his chest and tried not to let his father get to him. The man always had to be Marshal Hudson Savage, all business. The show-me-the-evidence lawman. Just for once, Hank would have liked him to believe his own son.

He drew Frankie closer and closed his eyes, just thankful to be alive. Thankful he hadn't gotten her killed. And more aware than ever of the woman in his arms.

FRANKIE FELT AS if she was in shock. After they were dropped off at their cabin, Hank led her into the bathroom and turned on the shower. *It's probably hypothermia*, she thought, since she'd felt fine in Hank's arms, but the moment he'd let her go, she'd begun to shake again.

The mirror in the bathroom quickly steamed over. "Get in with your clothes on." She looked at him as if he'd lost his mind. "Seriously," he said and, opening the glass shower door, pushed her toward the warm water streaming down from the showerhead. "Just toss your wet clothes on the floor of the shower. I'll take care of them later. I'll use the other shower. You need to get warm and dry as quickly as possible. Trust me."

Trust him? She looked into his handsome face and had to smile. Surprising herself, she did as he suggested and stepped into the walk-in shower, clothes and all. She did trust him. More than he knew. The warm water felt so good as it soaked her clothing and took away the cold. With trembling fingers, she began to peel off the wet garments to let the warm water get to her bare skin.

She felt something heavy in her jeans pocket. Her cell phone. She pulled it out and reached out to lay it next to the sink. At least she wouldn't have to worry about getting any more calls she didn't want to take since she could see that the screen was fogged over, the phone no doubt dead.

Worse, earlier, she'd put her gun into her purse. She could only hope that her purse had stayed in the pickup. Otherwise, it had washed downriver.

A shiver moved through her and she stepped back into the shower. But she knew that it would take more than warm water to stop her from shaking. Someone had tried to kill them. She thought about the truck that had forced them off the highway and into the river. She'd only glimpsed the driver. A man. A large angry man.

It wasn't him, she told herself. It couldn't have been.

Where would he have gotten a truck like that and how would he—

Unless he had somehow tracked her to Big Sky. She glanced at her phone and felt her heart drop. Tracking her phone would have been child's play for anyone who knew how. Especially for a cop.

She leaned against the shower wall, suddenly weak with fear. The last thing she wanted was her past catching up with her here. She told herself that she was only running scared. He hadn't found her. The man in the truck hadn't been him. All of this was about Naomi—not about her.

Refusing to give in to her fears that she might have been responsible for almost getting Hank killed, she concentrated on the feel of the warm water cascading down her body. As she turned her face up to the spray, she assured herself that she was fine. Hank was fine. Better than fine. She thought of how he'd held on to her until they were both safe on shore and then hugged her in his arms, sharing his warmth, protecting her, taking care of her even when he had to be as cold as she was.

She felt her nipples pucker to aching tips at the memory of his hard body against hers. It had been so long since she'd felt desire for a man. It spiked through her, turning her molten at her center at just the thought of Hank in the other shower, warm water running down his naked body.

Frankie shut off the water and, stepping over her wet clothes, reached for a towel. Hank was her employer. Nothing more. She was reacting to him like this only because they'd just shared a near-death experience.

But even as she thought it, Frankie knew it was much

more than that. She'd never met anyone like Hank. His capacity to love astounded her. Look how he'd mourned Naomi's death for three long years and still refused to give up on finding out the truth. Frankie couldn't imagine a man loving her like that.

She toweled herself dry and pulled on the robe she saw that Hank had left for her. After drawing it around her, she pulled up the collar and smelled the freshly washed scent. Hugging herself, she realized she was crying softly. She'd never been so happy to be alive.

Frankie quickly wiped her tears and busied herself wringing out her clothes and hanging them in the shower to dry. Then, bracing herself, she tied the robe tightly around her and stepped out of the bathroom.

HUD RETURNED TO his office. He quickly checked to make sure that a deputy and a highway patrol officer were taking care of traffic while the wrecker retrieved Hank's pickup from the river.

He realized he was still shaken. He didn't want to believe that the driver of the truck who'd run them off the road had been trying to kill them. But the driver had forced them off the road where the guardrail was missing—as if he knew exactly where to dump them into the river. That made the driver a local and that was what worried Hud.

Hank believed this had something to do with Naomi's death. But Hud had seen Frankie's face in the rearview mirror. She'd just been through a terrifying experience, no doubt about it. Yet he'd seen a fear in her eyes long after she'd been safe and warm in the back of his patrol SUV.

Swearing under his breath, he turned on his computer, his fingers hovering over the keys for a moment as he considered what he was about to do. He ticked off the reasons he had to do this. Hank's unexpected return. His son bringing a woman home after three years. Françesca "Frankie" Brewster, someone they'd never heard about before. The two were allegedly a couple, but their behavior was in question by Dana, who was good at these things. Add to that, Frankie had been asking around about Naomi's death. Throw in the "accident" that ended up with them in the river and what did it give you?

With a curse, he put his fingertips on the computer keys and typed Francesca "Frankie" Brewster, Lost Creek, Idaho.

What popped up on the screen made him release the breath he'd been holding. He sat back, staring at the screen. What the hell? Frankie Brewster Investigations?

It took him only another minute to find out that she was a licensed private investigator in the state of Idaho and had been in business for four years. Her name came up in articles in the local paper. She'd actually solved a few cases that had made the news.

He sat back again, berating himself for looking and, at the same time, wondering what he was going to do now with the information. Just because she was a PI didn't mean that she and Hank weren't really a couple. In fact, Hud thought that might be what attracted his son to her to begin with. So why make waves?

If he said anything to Hank, his son would be furious. He would know that his father did it again, checked up on Frankie—just as he had with Naomi. Only with

Frankie there was no sign that she'd ever been arrested or put under mental evaluation, at least.

"That's a plus," he said to himself and turned off the computer to rub the back of his neck and mentally kick himself. "Frankie's investigating Naomi's death," he said to himself, realizing that was what was going on. His son thought he could pull a fast one, bring Frankie home, pretend to be an item, and all the time the two were digging into Naomi's death.

He swore under his breath. Was it possible that someone was getting nervous? Was that why that truck had forced them off the road? To warn them to stop? But if that was the case…

Hud picked up the phone and called the lab. "I want information on the vehicle that forced that pickup off the road ASAP. Call me at home when you get it."

In all his years in law enforcement, he'd never felt this unsettled. What if Hank had been right all along and Naomi had been murdered? Enter Frankie, and the next thing he knew, his son and the PI were run off the highway and into the river. A little too coincidental to suit him.

With a sigh, he knew what he had to do. He had to stop them from investigating even if it meant making his son mad at him again. Hank had to let him look into it. Even as he thought it, Hud knew hell would freeze over before his son would trust him to do that. There would be no stopping Frankie and Hank if they were doing what he suspected they were.

He thought of all the mistakes he'd made with his oldest son. As he got to his feet, he just prayed that he wasn't about to make an even bigger one. But he had to stop the two of them before they ended up dead.

HANK CAME OUT of the bathroom only moments after Frankie. He'd stood under the warm spray for a long time. His emotions were all over the place. The trucker running them off the road proved what he'd been saying all along, didn't it?

So why didn't he feel more satisfaction? He'd been right. But as he stood letting the water cascade over his body, all he'd been able to think about was Frankie. He kept picturing her soaking wet, her clothes clinging to every curve. The memory had him aching.

He had turned the shower to cold and tried to get a handle on his feelings. Shivering again, he'd turned off the shower and had stood for a moment, still flooded with a desire like none he'd ever felt. He'd loved Naomi but she hadn't stirred this kind of passion in him. Was that another reason he hadn't wanted to rush into marriage?

Shaking his head, he'd stepped out of the shower and grabbed a towel to roughly dry himself off. He didn't want to be feeling these yearnings toward Frankie, not when he'd come home to set things right with Naomi. He told himself that he would keep her at a distance. But try as he might, he still felt an aching need at even the memory of her in his arms in the back of the patrol SUV.

He'd hung up his wet clothes and pulled on one of the guest robes that his mother supplied to the cabins. He promised himself that he would keep his mind on the investigation. If he was right, then they had rattled

Naomi's killer. They were getting close. Maybe too
close, he'd thought as he'd stepped out of the bedroom.

At the sight of Frankie standing there, his bare feet
faltered on the wood floor. Her long, dark hair was
down, hanging below her shoulders to the tips of her
breasts beneath the robe. Her face was flushed, as was
her neck and throat. Water droplets still clung to her
eyelashes, making her eyes appear even larger, the violet a darker purple.

She looked stunning. When their gazes met, he saw
a need in her that matched his own and felt all his re-
solve to keep her at arm's length evaporate before his
eyes. He closed the distance between them without a
word, without a thought. She didn't move, her gaze
locked with his, a vein in her slim neck throbbing as
he approached.

He took a lock of her long hair in his fingers. It felt
silken even wet. She still hadn't moved. Still hadn't
broken eye contact. His heart pounded as he brushed
her hair back on one side before leaning in to kiss that
spot on her neck where her blood pulsed. The throbbing
beat quickened beneath his lips and it was as if he could
feel his own heart drumming wildly to the same beat.

It had been so long since he'd felt like this. As his lips
traveled down her neck into the hollow at her shoulder,
she leaned back, giving him access. He heard her sharp
intake of breath as he stroked her tender flesh with the
tip of his tongue. From the hollow at her shoulder, it
would have been too easy to dip down to the opening
of her robe and swell of her breasts he could see rising
and falling with each of her breaths.

He lifted his head again to look into her eyes before

he cupped the back of her neck and drew her into a kiss, dragging her body against his. Desire raced along his veins to the riotous pounding of his heart. She looped her arms around his neck as he deepened the kiss and pulled her even closer until their bodies were molded together, almost as one. He could feel her breasts straining against the robe. He wanted desperately to lay open her robe and press his skin to hers. He wanted her naked body beneath his more than he wanted his next breath.

Reaching down, he pulled the sash of her robe. It fell away. He untied his own. As their robes opened, he pushed the fabric aside. He heard a gasp escape her lips as their warm, naked bodies came together. He felt her hard nipples press against his chest. Desire shot through him.

The knock at the door startled them both. "Hank? Frankie? I need to talk to you." Another knock and then the knob turned slowly.

They burst apart, both frantically retying their robes as the marshal stuck his head in the door. "Sorry. I…" He started to close the door.

"It's all right," Hank said. His voice sounded hoarse with emotion and need even to his ears. He shot a look at Frankie and saw that she was as shaken as he was. If only he had thought to lock the door. If only his father had picked any time but now to stop by.

And yet, now that he'd cooled down some, he knew it was for the best. He had enough problems without jumping into bed with Frankie—as much as he would have loved to do just that. But life was complicated enough as it was. A part of him was still in love with Naomi. He wasn't sure he'd ever get over her—and he had a feeling that Frankie knew that.

"Did you find out something about the truck that ran us off the road?" Frankie asked, her voice breaking.

They shared a look. Both of them struggling not to laugh at the irony of the situation. He wondered if she felt as disappointed as he did—and maybe just as relieved. Their relationship was complicated enough without this. And, he reminded himself, there was that man who kept calling her, the one Frankie didn't want to talk to. The one he suspected was her lover, past or present. Whoever the man was, Frankie hadn't dealt with him, he thought as his father stepped into the cabin, Stetson in hand and a sheepish, amused and yet curious look on his face.

HUD LOOKED FROM his son to Frankie. Both were flushed and not just from their showers. He hadn't known what he was going to say, but after walking in on what he'd just seen, he surprised himself.

"I've decided to reopen Naomi's case," he said as the two hurriedly moved away from each other like teenagers caught necking on the couch. Dana had thought they weren't lovers. If he hadn't come along when he did, they would have been. Maybe his wife was wrong about the two of them. Maybe he was too.

"Why would you reopen the case?" Hank asked as Frankie straightened her robe.

"I'm going to get dressed," she said. "If you'll excuse me." She hurried off toward the bedroom.

"I'm sorry," Hud said. "Clearly I interrupted something."

His son waved a hand through the air. "I thought you didn't believe that Naomi was murdered?"

"I'm still not sure I do. But after what happened today, I want to take another look."

Hank shook his head, mumbling under his breath as he turned toward the kitchen. "I'm going to get dressed and have a beer. You want one?"

He glanced at his watch. He was off the clock. Normally he would pass because he wasn't in the habit of drinking before dinner, but today he'd make an exception. "I would love one." That apparently had taken Hank by surprise, because he felt his son studying him as Hank returned in jeans and a Western shirt with two bottles of beer.

As Hank handed him one and twisted off the top on his own, he said, "Thank Mom for stocking our refrigerator."

"You know your mother. She wanted you and Frankie to be…comfortable up here." Earlier, he'd come up to the cabin, planning to bust them, exposing Frankie as a PI and their relationship as a fraud. But seeing them together, he'd changed his mind and was glad of it. He could eat a little crow with his son.

Anyway, what would it hurt to reopen the case unofficially? He still had misgivings about Hank's accident earlier today. Maybe all it had been was road rage. Either way, he was determined to track down the truck—and driver.

Frankie came out of the bedroom dressed in a baggy shirt and jeans, her feet still bare. Without asking her, Hank handed her his untouched beer and went into the kitchen to get another one.

Hud stood for a moment, he and Frankie somewhat uneasy in each other's presence. He was sure that his son had given the PI an earful about him. He'd lost Hank's respect because of Naomi's case. He'd thought he wouldn't get another chance to redeem himself. Maybe this would be it.

Hud took a chair while Frankie curled up on the couch, leaving the chair opposite him open. Hank, though, appeared too restless or stubborn to sit. He stood sipping his beer.

"Any word on the truck that put us in the river?" Frankie asked into the dead silence that followed.

"Not yet. I've asked that it be moved to priority one," he said. "I also have law enforcement in the canyon watching for the truck. It will turn up." He sounded more confident than he felt. He needed that truck and its driver. He needed to find out what had happened earlier and why—and not just to show his son that he knew what he was doing. If Hank was right and the driver of that truck was somehow connected to Naomi's death… well, then he needed to find Naomi's killer—before his son and Frankie did.

"If I was wrong, I'll make it right," he told his son, who nodded, though grudgingly. As he finished his beer, his cell phone rang. "That will be your mother. Don't tell her about this," he said, holding up his empty bottle. "We'll both be in trouble," he joked, then sobered. "Dinner isn't for a while. But I also would play down what happened earlier in the river during the meal. You know your mother."

Hank smiled. "I certainly do." Hud saw him glance at Frankie. A look passed between them, one he couldn't read, but he could feel the heat of it. He really wished his timing had been better earlier.

FRANKIE WAS STILL shaken from those moments with Hank before the marshal had arrived. She'd come so close to opening herself up to him, to baring not just her naked body, but her soul. She couldn't let that happen again. She reminded herself that their relationship was fake. He was her employer. He was still in love with the memory of Naomi.

That last part especially, she couldn't let herself forget. Not to mention the fact that she had her own baggage he knew nothing about. With luck, he never would. Once she was finished with this job, she would return to Idaho. Who knew what Hank would do.

Clearly, he loved the ranch and wanted to be part of the family's ranching operation. Would what they discovered free him from the past? Free him from Naomi enough that he could return?

"We have time for a horseback ride," Hank said out of the blue as the marshal left. "It's time you saw the ranch. You do ride, don't you?"

"I grew up in Montana before I moved to Idaho," she said. "It's been years since I've ridden, but I do know the front of the horse from the back."

"Good enough," Hank said. "Come on."

Frankie got the feeling that he didn't want to be alone with her in their cabin for fear of what would happen between them. She felt relieved but also a little disappointed, which made her angry with herself. Had she learned nothing when it came to men?

They walked down to the barn, where Hank saddled them a couple of horses. She stood in the sunlight that hung over Lone Mountain and watched him. She liked the way he used his hands and how gentle he was with the horses. There were many sides to this handsome cowboy, she thought as he patted her horse's neck and said, "Buttercup, you be nice to Frankie, now."

He handed her the reins. "Buttercup said she'll be nice. You need to do the same. No cursing her if she tries to brush you off under a pine tree." He turned to take the reins of the other horse.

"Wait," Frankie cried. "Will she do that?"

He shrugged as he swung up into the saddle and laughed. "Let's hope not." He looked good up there, so self-assured, so at home. He spurred his horse forward. "Also, Buttercup's got a crush on Romeo here, so she'll probably just follow him and behave. But you never know with a female." He trotted out of the barn, then reined in to wait for her.

She started to give Buttercup a nudge, but the mare was already moving after Romeo and Hank.

They rode up into the mountains through towering pines. The last of the summer air was warm on her back. She settled into the saddle, feeling more comfortable than she'd expected to be. Part of that was knowing that she was in good hands with both Buttercup and Hank.

Frankie stole a glance at him, seeing him really relax for the first time since she'd met him. He had his head tilted back, his gaze on the tops of the mountains as if soaking them into his memory for safekeeping. Was he sorry he'd left? It didn't really matter, she realized. He couldn't come back here—not with Naomi's ghost running rampant in his heart and mind. Until he knew what had happened to her, Frankie doubted he would ever find peace.

In that moment, she resolved to find out the truth no

matter what it was. She wanted to free this man from his obvious torment. But even as she thought it, she wondered if he would ever really be free of Naomi and his feelings for the dead woman.

"Wait until you see this," Hank said and rode on a little ahead to where the pines opened into a large meadow. She could see aspens, their leaves already starting to turn gold and rust and red even though summer wasn't technically over. This part of Montana didn't pay much attention to the calendar.

As she rode out into the meadow, she was hit with the smells of drying leaves and grasses. It made her feel a little melancholy. Seasons ended like everything else, but she hated to feel time passing. It wouldn't be long before they would be returning to Idaho and their lives there. That thought brought back the darkness that had been plaguing her for the past few months. She was going to have to deal with her past. She only wished she knew how.

Hank had ridden ahead across the meadow. She saw that he'd reined in his horse and was waiting for her at the edge. Buttercup broke into a trot across the meadow and then a gallop. Frankie surprised herself by feeling as if she wasn't going to fall off.

She reined in next to Hank. He was grinning at her and she realized she had a broad smile on her face. "I like Buttercup."

"I thought you might. She's a sweetheart. Except for when she tries to brush you off under a pine tree." His grin broadened.

"You really are an awful tease," she said as he came over to help her off her horse.

"You think so?" he said as he grabbed her by her waist and lifted her down to stand within inches of him. Their gazes met.

Frankie felt desire shoot like a rocket through her. She'd thought she'd put the fire out, but it had only been smoldering just below the surface. She wanted the kiss as much as her next breath.

He drew her closer. "What is it about you that is driving me crazy?" he asked in a hoarse whisper.

She shook her head, never breaking her gaze with his. "I could ask you the same thing."

He chuckled. "I want to kiss you."

She cocked her head at him. "So what's stopping you?"

"I've already had my heart broken once. I'm not sure I'm up to having it stomped on just yet," he said, but he didn't let her go. Nor did he break eye contact.

"You think I'm a heartbreaker?" she said, surprised how breathy she sounded. It was as if the high altitude of the mountaintop had stolen all her oxygen.

He grinned. "I know you are and yet…" He pulled her to him so quickly that she gasped before his mouth dropped to hers.

The kiss was a stunner, all heat. His tongue teased hers as he deepened it, holding her so tightly against him that she felt as if their bodies had fused in the heat.

He let her go just as quickly and stepped away, shaking his head. "We should get back, but first you should see the view. My mother is bound to ask you at dinner what you thought of it."

She was still looking at the handsome cowboy as she swayed under the onslaught of emotions she didn't believe she'd ever felt before. "The view?" she said on a ragged breath.

Hank laughed and took her hand. "It's this way." He led her to the edge of the mountaintop, still holding her hand in his large warm one. "What do you think?"

She thought that, for a while, they'd both forgotten Naomi. "I've never enjoyed a horseback ride more in my life," she said, her gaze on the amazing view of mountains that seemed to go on forever.

He gently squeezed her hand. "It is pretty amazing, isn't it?"

bellow, she murmured before "I'm sorry," she said on
a ragged breath. . . .

Chapter Twelve

Dinner was a blur of people and laughter and talk as more relatives and friends gathered around the large dining room table, including Dana's best friend, Hilde, and her family. Fortunately, most of it was going on around Frankie, and all she had to do was smile and laugh at the appropriate times. She avoided looking at Hank, but in the middle of the meal, she felt his thigh brush against hers. She felt his gaze on her. When he placed his hand on her thigh, she wasn't able to control the shiver of desire that rocketed through her. She moved her leg and tried to still her galloping pulse. Getting her body to unrespond to his touch wasn't as easy.

Once the meal was over, she and Hank walked back up to their cabin. For a long way, neither said a word. It was still plenty light out.

"Are you all right?" Hank asked over the evening sounds around them. She could hear the hum of the river as it flowed past, the chatter of a squirrel in the distance and the cry of a hawk as it caught a thermal and soared above them.

"Fine. You?"

He stopped walking. "Damn it, Frankie. You can't pretend that the kiss didn't happen. That things haven't changed."

She stopped walking as well and turned to face him. Was he serious? They were pretending to be in a relationship and had almost consummated it. Worse, it was all she could think about. And maybe even worse than that, she wanted it desperately. "It hasn't changed anything."

He made a disbelieving face. She wanted to touch the rough stubble on his jaw, remembering the feel of it earlier when he'd kissed her. Not to mention the memory of their naked bodies molded together for those few moments was so sharp that it cut her to the core. "Don't get me wrong. I wanted you more than my next breath. I still do. But—"

"But?" he demanded.

"But you're my employer and this is a job. For a moment we let ourselves forget that."

"So that's the way we're going to play it?" he asked, sounding upset and as disappointed as she felt.

"Let's not forget why we're here. You're still in love with the memory of Naomi after three years of mourning her death. Let's find out who killed her—if she really was murdered—and then…" She didn't know what came after.

"Do you doubt Naomi was murdered after what happened when we left the Corral?" he demanded.

She thought there could be another explanation, though not one she felt she could share with him until she knew for sure. She still wanted to believe that no one knew where she was, especially the man who'd left her dozens of threatening messages on her phone.

Choosing her words carefully, she said, "Based on that and what I've learned about Naomi, I think there is a very good chance that she was murdered."

He stared at her for a moment. "That's right. You haven't told me what you learned about her today." He started walking again as if bracing himself for the worst. "So let's hear it."

HANK LISTENED, GETTING angrier by the moment. They'd reached the cabin by the time she'd finished. "This woman, Tamara Baker, is lying. Naomi hated the taste of booze."

"Tamara insinuated that Naomi was into something more than booze. Not men. But something more dangerous."

"Like what? Money laundering? Drugs? Prostitution?" He swore. "Stop looking at me like that. Go ahead, roll your eyes. You think I didn't know my own girlfriend?"

"Why would Tamara lie?"

"I have no idea. But she's wrong and so is Roy at the grocery store. Naomi wouldn't steal. He's thinking of the wrong girl. Naomi sure as heck didn't get fired. She was one of his best workers. She showed me the bonus she got for…" His voice trailed off. "I can't remember what it was for, but I saw the money."

Frankie said nothing, which only made him even angrier. He shoved open the door to the cabin, let her go in first and stormed in behind her. "What if it's all a lie to cover up something else?" He knew he was reaching.

He couldn't imagine why these people would make up stories about Naomi.

She shrugged. "I only told you what I'd learned. Maybe she had another life when she wasn't with you."

He shook his head and began pacing, angry and frustrated. "You didn't know her. She was afraid of everything. She was…innocent."

"All right, maybe that's how she got involved in something she didn't know how to get out of."

He stopped pacing. "Like what?"

"She had a boyfriend before you, right?"

"Butch Clark. Randall 'Butch' Clark. But she hadn't seen him in years."

"I want to talk to him. Alone," she added before he could say he was going with her.

"Why? I just told you that she hadn't seen him in years."

She said nothing for a moment, making him swear again. "Just let me follow this lead. I'll go in the morning. Any idea where I can find him?"

"His father owns the hardware store. He'd probably know." He felt sick in the pit of his stomach as he recalled something. "He was at Naomi's funeral. I recognized him."

"So you knew him?"

He shook his head. "Naomi pointed him out once when we first started dating. He didn't seem like her type. I asked her about him, but she didn't want to talk about him, saying he was her past."

Frankie nodded knowingly and he caught a familiar glint in her eye.

"I don't even want to know what you're thinking right now," he said with a groan.

She shrugged. "Naomi had a past. That's all."

He cocked his head at her, waiting.

"That she didn't want to talk about," she added. "Happy?"

"You are so sure she had some deep dark secret. I might remind you that you have a past you don't want to talk about."

"True, but you and I aren't dating."

"We're supposed to be," he said, stepping toward her. "I don't see that as being so unbelievable given what almost happened earlier. How about I fire you, end this employer-employee relationship, and we quit pretending this isn't real?"

FRANKIE LOOKED INTO Hank's blue eyes and felt a shiver of desire ripple through her. It would have been so easy to take this to the next level—and quickly, given the sparks that arced between them. Common sense warned her not to let this happen. But the wild side of her had wanted him almost from the first time he'd walked into her office. The chemistry had been there as if undercover, sizzling just below the surface.

Any woman in her right mind would have wanted this handsome, strong, sexy cowboy. She doubted Hank even knew just how appealing he was. Naomi had held his sensuality at arm's length, using herself as a weapon to get him to the altar. Frankie could see that the wild side of Hank wanted out as badly as she wanted to unleash it.

He stopped directly in front of her, so close she could

smell the musky outdoor male scent of him. She felt her pulse leap, her heart pounding as she waited for him to take her in his arms.

Instead, he touched her cheek with the rough tips of his fingers, making her moan as she closed her eyes and leaned into the heavenly feel of his flesh against hers.

At a tap on the door, Hank groaned. "If that's my father—"

"Hello?" Dana called. "Are you guys decent?"

Hank swore softly under his breath and then, locking his gaze with Frankie's, grinned. "Come on in, Mom," he said as he grabbed Frankie, pulled her to him and kissed her hard on the mouth. Breaking off the kiss only after the door had opened, he said, "We are now, Mom."

Chapter Thirteen

It was late by the time Dana left. She'd seemed in a talkative mood, and it was clear that she wanted to spend more time with her son. Frankie excused herself to go to bed. She hadn't been able to sleep, though. Her body ached with a need that surprised her. She hadn't felt this kind of desire in a very long time and definitely not this strong.

Trying to concentrate on something, anything else, she considered what she'd learned about Naomi Hill. Sweet, quiet, timid, scared of everything, a nondrinker who was honest as the day was long with only one desire in life—to get married and settle down.

Frankie frowned. Was her reason for giving Hank an ultimatum that night only because of that desire? Or was she running from something?

The thought wouldn't go away. Hours later, she heard Dana leave. She lay on her back, staring up at the ceiling, hardly breathing, wondering if Hank would come to her bed.

He didn't. She heard the creak of the bed in the other bedroom as he threw himself onto it. She smiled to herself hearing how restless he was. Like her, he was having trouble sleeping.

Frankie didn't remember dozing off until she awakened to daylight and the sound of rain pinging off the panes in her window. By the time she'd showered and dressed, determined to do what she had been hired to do, the rain had stopped and the sun had come out. Droplets hung from the pines, shimmering in the sunlight.

When she came out of the bedroom, she found that Hank was also up and dressed.

"I'm going to go talk to Tamara and then maybe go by the grocery store and talk to Roy," he said, not sounding happy about either prospect.

She nodded. He'd shaved and she missed the stubble from last night, but he was still drop-dead handsome. "I'd call you when I get back from seeing Butch Clark, but my phone…"

"Mine too. Why don't we meet back here and have lunch together and share whatever information we come up with? Be careful. I'm sure you haven't forgotten yesterday."

Not hardly. "See you before lunch." She could feel his gaze on her and knew their conversation wasn't over yet.

"About last night—"

"Did you have a nice visit with your mother?"

He grinned, acknowledging that he'd caught her attempt to steer the subject away from the two of them. "I did, but I wasn't referring to yet another interruption just when things were getting interesting. I was going to say, I didn't come to your bed last night not because I didn't want to. Just in case you were wondering. You say you want to keep this strictly professional, but should you change your mind…all you have to do is give me a sign."

She tried to swallow the lump in her throat. He was throwing this into her court. If she wanted him, she'd have to make the next move. Her skin tingled at the thought. "That's good to know," she said and headed for the door.

"No breakfast?" he said behind her. There was humor in his tone, as if he knew she needed to get away from him right now or she might cross that line.

"I'll get something down the road," she said over her shoulder without looking at him because he was right. The thought of stepping into his arms, kissing those lips, letting him take her places she could only imagine, was just too powerful. She turned up the hood on her jacket against the rain and ignored the cold as she kept walking.

HANK SWORE AS he watched Frankie leave. He would have loved to have spent this day in bed—with her. He almost wished he had gone to her bed last night.

As much as he wanted Frankie, he hadn't forgotten why they'd come back to the ranch, back to Big Sky, back to where Naomi had died. He would always love Naomi, he told himself. But for the first time in years, he felt ready to move on. Maybe he could once they'd found out the truth.

He saw his cell phone sitting in the bowl where he'd put it this morning and went to look for Frankie's. He found it beside the sink. It was still wet. He tried to open it. Nothing. Well, at least now she couldn't get those calls that she'd been ignoring.

Who was so insistent? Someone she didn't want to talk to. He'd seen her reaction each time she'd recognized the caller. She'd tensed up as if…as if afraid of the person on the other end of the line? Definitely a man, he thought, and wondered if anyone had ever tried to kill her before yesterday.

He could almost hear her say it went with the job.

But he'd felt her trembling in the water next to him after their escape from his pickup. She'd been as scared as he had been, so he doubted nearly dying went with the job. Although he had a bad feeling that someone *had* tried to kill her. Maybe the person who kept calling.

"Well, now he can't find you, just in case he's been tracking your phone," he said to the empty room.

Hank couldn't put it off any longer. He needed to get to the truth about Naomi. Confronting Tamara and Roy were at least places to start. He wasn't looking forward to it. He doubted they would change their stories, which would mean that he hadn't known Naomi.

He sighed, wishing he was curled up in bed with Frankie, but since that wasn't an option, he grabbed his jacket and headed out into the cool, damp summer morning.

RANDALL "BUTCH" CLARK was easy to find—in the back of his father's hardware store, signing in the most recent order. As the delivery driver pulled away, Butch turned and stopped as if surprised to see that he had company. He was short, average-looking with curly sandy-blond hair and light brown eyes.

"Frankie," she said, holding out her hand as she closed the distance between them.

Butch hesitated. "If this is about a job, my dad does the hiring. I'm just—" He waved a hand as if he wasn't sure exactly what his title was.

"I'm not looking for a job. I'm here about Naomi."

"Naomi?" he repeated, both startled and suddenly nervous as he fiddled with the clipboard in his hands. "Is there something new with her that I don't know about?"

Frankie decided to cut to the chase. "I'm a private investigator looking into her death." If he asked for her credentials, she was screwed. Fortunately, he didn't.

His eyes widened in surprise. Or alarm? She couldn't be sure. "Why? It's been three years. I thought her death was ruled a suicide?" His voice broke.

She closed the distance between them, watching the man's eyes, seeing how badly he wanted to run. "You and I know it wasn't suicide, don't we, Butch?"

"I don't have any idea what you're talking about."

Frankie went on instinct based on Butch's reaction thus far. He was scared and he was hiding something. "You and Naomi were close." She saw him swallow as if he feared where she was headed. "So if anyone knew what was going on with her, it was you."

Butch didn't deny it. "Why are you asking about this now?"

"The marshal has reopened the case."

He took a step back, put down the clipboard on one of the boxes stacked along the delivery ramp and wiped his palms on the thighs of his dirty work pants. "Look, I don't want to get involved."

"You're already involved, Butch. But I might be able to help you. No one needs to know about your…part in all this if—" he started to object but she rushed on "—you tell me what you know. The marshal didn't question you the first time, right?" She saw the answer. Hud hadn't known about the old boyfriend. "So there is no reason for your name to come up now, right?"

His eyes widened in alarm. "I didn't do *anything*."

"But Naomi did."

He looked down at his scuffed sneakers.

"Could we sit down?" she asked and didn't wait for an answer. There were three chairs around a folding card table that appeared to be used as a break room. Probably for the smokers since there was a full ashtray in the middle of the table along with several empty soda cans.

"Just tell me what you know and let me help you," she said. "I'm your best bet."

He pulled out a chair, turned it around and straddled it, leaning his chin on his arms as he looked at her with moist brown eyes. "I don't even know who you are or who you work for."

"Probably better that you don't if you want me to keep your name out of it, but—" She reached for her shoulder bag.

He quickly waved it off. "You're right. I don't want to know. But if you work for them, I had nothing to do with this. I told her not to keep the money. It was like she'd never seen a movie and known that they always come after the money."

Frankie did her best not to let her surprise show as she quickly asked, "Where did she find it?"

"She told me on the highway." His tone said he didn't believe her.

"Did she tell you how much money was in it?"

He looked away. "I told her not to count it. Not to touch it. To put it back where she found it and keep her mouth shut. But she saw there was a small fortune in the bag. She'd never seen that much money."

"What did she plan to do with it?"

Butch let out a bark of a laugh. "Buy a big house, marry that rancher she was dating, move down here in the valley, raise kids, go to soccer practice. She had it all worked out except…" He shook his head.

"Except?"

He looked at her as if she hadn't been listening. "The rancher didn't want to marry her, she thought someone was following her and she ended up dead."

Frankie caught on two things he'd said. Butch knew that the night of Naomi's death, Hank said he wasn't ready to get married. Someone was following her that night. "Did she tell the rancher about the money?"

"No way. She said he was too straitlaced. He'd want to turn it in to his father. He'd be too scared to keep it."

But timid little Naomi apparently wasn't. "You said someone was following her?" He glanced down, obviously just realizing what he'd said. "The night she died. That's when you talked to her."

He looked up but she shook her head in warning for him not to lie. "She called the bar where I was having a drink with friends and told me that she thought she was being followed."

"What did you tell her to do?"

He rubbed a hand over his face. "I didn't know what

to tell her. She sounded hysterical. I said give it back. Stop your car, give it to them. She said she couldn't, that she'd put some of the money down on a house and couldn't get it back."

"So then what did you tell her to do?"

"I thought that maybe if she explained the situation…"

Frankie groaned inside. If the money Naomi had found was what she thought it was, negotiating was out of the question. "So she pulled over and tried to bargain?"

He shrugged, his voice breaking when he spoke. "I don't know. The line went dead. I tried to call her back but there was no answer."

"Did she know who she'd taken the money from?" Frankie asked.

"If she did, she never said anything to me. I swear it." He rose from the chair. "Please, I thought this was over. I thought your people… Whoever you're working for. I thought they got most of their money back. At least, what was left." He frowned. "I thought it was over," he repeated.

Frankie got up from her chair. "As far as I'm concerned, it is over."

Relief made him slump and have to steady himself on the back of the chair he'd abandoned. He let out a ragged breath and straightened. "So we're good?"

She nodded as a loud male voice called from inside the store.

"That's my father. I have to—" He was gone, running through the swinging doors and disappearing from sight.

Frankie went out the back way and walked around to the pickup Dana Savage had lent her. Climbing behind the wheel, she wished she had a cell phone so she could call Hank. Up the block she spotted the time on one of the banks. It was about forty minutes back to Big Sky. She'd tell Hank when she saw him. But at least now she knew the truth.

Naomi Hill had been murdered—just as he'd suspected. It didn't put them any closer, though, to knowing who'd killed her, but at least now they knew why.

HANK DROVE INTO Meadow Village after he left the ranch. Frankie had told him that Tamara worked at the Silver Spur Bar. But when he parked and went inside, he was told that it was her day off. He asked for her address and wrangled for a moment with the bartender before the man gave it over. Hank dropped a twenty-dollar bill on the bar as he left.

He knew the old cabins the bartender had told him about. But as he neared the row of four cabins, he spotted marshal office vehicles parked out front. Crime scene tape flapped in the wind.

Swearing, he pulled in and, getting out, started past the deputy stationed outside.

"Hold up," the deputy said. "No one goes inside. Marshal's orders."

"Tell him I need to see him," Hank said. He held up his hands. "Tell him his son is out here, Hank. Hank Savage. I'll stand right here until you get back and won't let anyone else get past. I promise."

The deputy disappeared inside and almost at once returned with Hud.

"What's going on?" Hank asked in a hushed voice as the two of them stepped over to the ranch pickup he'd driven into town.

"What are you doing here?"

"I came by to see Tamara Baker. Frankie had spoken to her about Naomi. I wanted to talk to her." Immediately he realized his mistake as he saw his father's eyes narrow. "Tamara said some things about Naomi that didn't seem right."

"Like what?"

He didn't really want to discuss this out here, let alone voice them at all, especially to his father. Also, the marshal hadn't answered his question. He pointed out both.

"Tamara's dead."

"Dead? Not—" He didn't have to say "murdered." He saw the answer in his father's expression.

"When I get through here, I think we'd better talk." With that, his father turned and went back inside as the coroner's van pulled up.

Chapter Fourteen

Back at the ranch, Frankie went straight to the cabin to wait for Hank. She felt anxious. What she'd learned was more than disturbing. Naomi had apparently found the answer to her prayers—or so she thought. Where had she picked up the bag of money? It seemed doubtful that it had been tossed out beside the road.

At the sound of the door opening, she spun around and saw Hank's face. "What's happened?" she asked, feeling her pulse jump and her stomach drop.

"I went over to talk to Tamara Baker. She wasn't at the bar. I got directions to her cabin. My father was there along with a crime team and the coroner." He met her gaze. "She'd been murdered."

The news floored her. Stumbling back, she sat down hard on the sofa. The ramifications rocketed through her. She'd talked to Tamara and now she was dead. Swallowing down the lump in her throat, she said, "There's more. I'm pretty sure I know why Naomi was murdered."

Hank moved to a chair and sat down as if suddenly too weak to stand. "You talked to Butch."

"He said she found a bag of money."

"What?" he asked in disbelief.

"Drug money, I would imagine. Enough money that she put some of it down on a house in Bozeman for when the two of you got married."

He dropped his head into his hands. "This can't be true," he mumbled through his fingers.

"She called Butch that night at the bar where he was meeting his friends—"

"So this bastard knew about this the whole time?" Hank demanded as his head came up, his blue eyes flaring.

"She told him she was being followed. She was afraid it was them, whoever the money belonged to. She debated stopping and giving back what she had left with a promise to pay back the rest."

He groaned. "She was going to make a deal with a bunch of drug dealers?"

"Her phone went dead. He tried to call her back but there was no answer."

Hank shook his head. "She told him all of this? So he knew she was in trouble and he didn't do anything?"

Frankie knew that the tough part for Hank was that Naomi hadn't trusted him with her secret. It wasn't just that she'd been living a lie, the bonus at work, not telling him about getting fired, the drinking with Tamara, the close connection with her old boyfriend when she felt she was in trouble, and River Dean, the backup if things didn't work out with Hank.

It was a lot for the cowboy to take. She wondered how Naomi had planned to explain all this money she'd come into, including the house she was in the process of buying. Maybe an inheritance? Maybe Hank would have bought the explanation, except that he hadn't wanted to get married and move to Bozeman.

Naomi had been so naive that she'd thought the drug dealers wouldn't find out who'd taken their money? Especially if it had been a lot. A small fortune to Naomi might not have been that much to some people in the wealthy part of Big Sky. But the drug dealers would have wanted it back.

"I suspect, given what you just told me," Frankie said, "that Naomi also confided in Tamara."

Hank pushed to his feet, a hand raking through his hair as he walked to the window, his back to her. "I didn't know her at all." He sounded shocked. "I loved her so much and I had no idea who she really was."

"You loved the idea of her. You fell in love with what she wanted you to see. Eventually, you would have seen behind the facade. Hopefully, before it was too late to walk away unscathed."

HANK HEARD SOMETHING in her voice. Regret. He turned to study Frankie. "Is that what happened with this man who keeps calling you?" He didn't expect an answer. He thought of Naomi. "I'm not sure it was love—at least on her part. With love comes trust. She didn't trust me enough to tell me about the money."

"Your father is the marshal."

He let out a snort. "She really thought I'd go to my father with this?"

"Wouldn't you have?"

Hank laughed and shook his head. "I would have made her turn the money over to my father." He nodded. "It would have been the only smart thing to do and she would have hated me for it."

Frankie gave him a that's-why-she-didn't-tell-you shrug.

"Well, he has to know about all of this now. He probably has people he suspects are dealing drugs in the area. What are the chances that they killed Naomi and now Tamara?" His gaze came up to meet hers and his quickly softened. "You can't blame yourself."

"I talked to her and now she's dead. Who should I blame?"

"The man you said was sitting down the bar. He was the only witness when the two of you were talking, right?"

She nodded. "But she could have told someone after that."

He shook his head as all the ramifications began to pile up. "I knew she'd been murdered. I damn well knew it. But I would never have guessed..." He sighed. "When I saw my father at Tamara's cabin, I told him that you'd talked to Tamara about Naomi. I'm sorry. I slipped up."

"Don't you think it's time we tell your parents the truth? It's pretty obvious that we're investigating Naomi's death."

"Come on. Let's go." He headed for the door.

"Just like that?"

He shook his head. "My father could be here any moment. Let's go get some lunch. I don't want to be interrogated on an empty stomach."

They left the ranch with him driving the ranch pickup he'd borrowed that morning. "I know this out-of-the-way place." He turned onto the highway and headed south toward Yellowstone Park.

Lost in thought, he said little on the drive. He could see that Frankie was battling her own ghosts. He wondered again about the man in her life who kept calling. All his instincts told him that the man was dangerous.

As he neared the spot they would have lunch, he dragged himself out of his negative thoughts, determined to enjoy lunch with Frankie and put everything behind them for a while.

"My father and grandfather used to tell stories about driving down here in the dead of winter to get a piece of banana cream pie," he said as they turned into a place called the Cinnamon Lodge. "It used to be called Almart. Alma and Art owned it and she would save pieces of banana cream pie for them."

"That's a wonderful story," Frankie said, as if seeing that he wanted to talk about anything but Naomi. "Something smells good," she said as they got out and approached the log structure.

Hank figured she wasn't any more hungry than he was. But he'd needed to get out of the cabin, away from all of it, just for a little while. It wasn't until after they'd had lunch and were in the pickup again that he told her what he'd been thinking from the moment he saw the crime scene tape around Tamara's cabin.

"It's time for you to go back to Idaho. You can take one of the pickups and—"

"I'm not leaving," she said as he started the pickup's engine, backed out and pulled onto the highway.

"You don't understand. You're fired. I have no more use for your services."

FRANKIE LAUGHED AND dug her heels in. "You think you can get rid of me that easily?"

"I'll pay you the bonus I promised you as well as your per diem and—"

"Stop! You think I don't know what you're doing?"

He glanced over at her, worry knitting his brows. "It's too dangerous. I should have realized that after what happened yesterday with that truck. But now that we know what we're dealing with—"

"Exactly. What *we're* dealing with. I want to see this through. With you." Her last words broke with emotion.

Hank sighed and reached for her, pulling her over against him on the bench seat of the older-model pickup. She cuddled against him, finding herself close to tears. She couldn't quit this now. She couldn't quit Hank. "Frankie—"

She touched a finger to his lip. "I'm not leaving."

"Yesterday was a warning," he said. "I see that now. If we don't quit looking into Naomi's death—"

"Her *murder*," she said, drawing back enough to look at him. "Are you telling me that you can walk away now that you know the truth?" She could see that he hadn't thought about what he would do.

"We have no idea who they are. Unless my father can track down that truck and find the driver…"

"So you think that makes us safe? You think they won't be worried about what we know, what we found out?"

"I don't want to think about it right now." He pulled her close again, resting his head against the top of hers for a moment as he drove.

She could hear the steady, strong thump of his heart

as she rested her head against his chest. This man made her feel things she'd never felt before. Together there was a strength to them that made her feel safe and strong...and brazen.

"Then let's go back to the cabin and not think at all," she said, taking that unabashed step into the unknown as if she was invincible in his arms.

HANK MEET HER gaze and grinned as he slowed for the turnoff to the ranch. "Are you making a move on me, Miss Brewster?"

She sat up and started to answer when she looked out the windshield at the road ahead and suddenly froze. Following her gaze, he could see a large dark sedan parked on the edge of the road into the ranch. He looked over at Frankie as she moved out from under his arm to her side of the pickup. All the color had drained from her face.

"Frankie?" he asked as he made the turn into the ranch and drove slowly by the car. He could see a man sitting behind the wheel. Frankie, he noticed, hadn't looked. Because, he realized, she knew who it was.

"Frankie?" Her gaze was still locked straight ahead, her body coiled like a rattler about to strike.

"Stop," she said and reached for her door handle.

He kept going. "No way am I letting you face whatever that is back there alone."

She shot him a desperate look that scared him. "Damn it, Hank, this has nothing to do with you. Stop the pickup and let me out. *Now!*"

Frankie was right. He'd opened up his life to her, but

hers had been off-limits to him from the get-go. Nothing had changed.

He gritted his teeth as he brought the pickup to a stop. Her door opened at once and she jumped out, slamming the door behind her as she started to walk back to where the car and driver waited.

Watching in the side mirror, he cursed under his breath as he remembered her frightened expression every time her cell phone had rung with a call from whoever the man had been. Hank would put his money on that same man now sitting in that car, waiting for her.

All his instincts told him that whoever this man was, he was trouble. Frankie could pretend he wasn't, but Hank knew better. Except that she'd made it abundantly clear she wanted to handle this herself.

With a curse, he shifted into gear and headed the pickup down the road toward the ranch. She didn't need his help. Didn't want it. The PI thought she could handle this herself. She probably could.

After only a few yards up the road, he slammed on the brakes. Like hell he was going to let her handle this on her own, whether she liked it or not.

Throwing the pickup in Reverse, he sped back up the road, coming to a dust-boiling stop in front of the car.

Frankie had almost reached the vehicle. He saw that the driver had leaned over to throw the passenger-side door open for her to get in. The jackass wasn't even going to get out.

He could hear the man yelling at her to get in. Grabbing the tire iron from under the seat, Hank jumped out.

"She's not getting into that car with you," he said as he walked toward the driver's-side window. He could feel Frankie's angry gaze on him and heard her yell something at him, but it didn't stop him. "You have a problem with Frankie? I want to hear about it," he said, lifting the tire iron.

Chapter Fifteen

The man behind the wheel of the car threw open his door and climbed out. He was as tall as Hank and just as broad across the shoulders. The man had bully written all over him from his belligerent attitude to the bulging muscles of his arms from hours spent at the gym. Hank heard Frankie cry, "J.J., don't!"

"Who the hell are you and what are you doing with my fiancée?" the man she'd called J.J. demanded.

Hank shot a look at Frankie across the hood of the man's car.

"She didn't mention that she's engaged to me?" J.J. said with obvious delight. "I see she's not wearing her ring either. But you haven't answered me. Who the hell are—" His words were drowned out by the sudden *whop* of a police siren as the marshal pulled in on the other side of Hank's pickup.

J.J. swore. "You bitch," he yelled, turning to glare at her. Frankie had stopped on the other side of his car. She looked small and vulnerable, but even from where he stood, Hank could see that she would still fight like a wild woman if it came to that. "You called the law on me?"

The man swung his big head in Hank's direction. "Or did you call the cops, you son of a…" He started to take a step toward Hank, who slapped the iron into his palm, almost daring him to attack.

J.J.'s gaze swung past him. Out of the corner of his eye, he saw his father standing in front of his patrol SUV. J.J. saw the marshal uniform as well, swore and hurriedly leaped back into his car. The engine revved and Hank had to step back as J.J. took off, tires throwing gravel before he hit the highway and sped away.

"What was that about?" Hud asked after he reached in to turn off the siren before walking over to his son.

Hank looked at Frankie, who was hugging herself and shaking her head. "It was nothing," he said. "Just some tourist passing through who wanted to give us a hard time."

His father grunted, clearly not believing a word of it. "I need to talk to the two of you. Your cabin. Now."

Hank nodded, his gaze still on Frankie. "We'll be right there."

J.J. DROVE AWAY, fuming. *She called the cops on me? Had she lost her mind? And that cowboy…* Hank Savage had no idea what he'd stepped into, but he was about to find out.

"The cowboy's name is Hank Savage. His father's the marshal of the resort town of Big Sky, Montana," his friend at the station told him after he'd managed to get the license plate number off one of the business surveillance cameras near Frankie's office. The camera had picked up not just the man's truck but a pretty good image of the cowboy himself going into Frankie's office and coming out again—with her. She'd gone down the block, gotten into her SUV and then followed the pickup.

"You recognize the cowboy?" his friend had asked.

"No. It must be a job." But she'd left her rig in her garage.

"Well, if it is a job, she went with him, from what you told me her neighbor said."

That was the part that floored him. Why would she take off with a man she didn't know? Unless she did know him. He thought of how the man had defended her. Hell, had she been seeing this cowboy behind his back?

He drove down the highway, checking his rearview mirror. The marshal hadn't come after him. That was something, anyway. But how dare his cowboy son threaten him with a tire iron. That cowboy was lucky his father came along when he did. He swore, wanting a piece of that man—and Frankie. He'd teach them both not to screw around with him.

He pulled into the movie theater parking lot and called his friend back in Lost Creek. After quickly filling him in, he said, "I'm going to kill her."

"Maybe you should come on back and let this cool down until—"

"No way. I don't know what's going on, but she's my fiancée."

Silence. Then, "J.J., she broke off the engagement. You can't force her to marry you."

"The hell I can't. Look, she's mad at me. I screwed up, got a little rough with her, but once we sit down and hash this out, she'll put the ring back on. I just can't have some cowboy get in the middle of this."

"Where'd she meet this guy?"

"That's just it. I have no idea. Why would she just leave with him unless she knew him before? The neighbor said she packed a small bag and left. If she'd been seeing this cowboy behind my back, I would have heard, wouldn't I?"

"It's probably just what you originally thought. A job."

He shook his head. "She was sitting all snuggled up next to him in the pickup. It's not a job. The bitch is—"

"Come back and let yourself cool down. If you don't, you might do something you're going to regret. You already have a couple strikes against you at work. You get in trouble down there—"

"Not yet. Don't worry. I'll be fine." He disconnected. Fine once he got his hands on Frankie. He sat for a moment until he came up with a plan. He'd stake out the ranch. The next time she left it, he'd follow her. But first he had to get rid of this car. He needed a nondescript rental, something she or the cowboy wouldn't suspect.

"I DIDN'T WANT you involved," Frankie said with rancor the moment they were in his pickup, headed back to the ranch. The marshal had waited and now followed them into the ranch property.

"You made that clear. None of my business, right?" He looked over at her, his eyes hard as ice chips. "It isn't like you and I mean anything to each other. Still just employer and employee. Why mention a fiancé?"

"I told you, I broke it off."

He continued as if he hadn't heard her. "It isn't like we were just heading up to our cabin to… What was it we were going to do, Frankie?"

She sighed and looked away. "J.J. and I were engaged. I called it off two months ago. He didn't take it well."

"So I gathered. Now he's still harassing you. Why haven't you gone to the authorities?"

"It's complicated. I don't have the best relationship with the local cops in Lost Creek."

"Because you're a private investigator?"

"Because J.J. is one of them. He's a cop."

"A cop?" Hank shook his head. He was driving so slowly, he knew it was probably making his father crazy. It was his own fault for insisting he follow them into the ranch. As if he thought they might make a run for it?

"How long did you date him?"

"Six months. He seemed like a nice guy. The engagement was too quick but he asked me at this awards banquet in front of all his friends and fellow officers. I… I foolishly said yes even though I wasn't ready. Even though I had reservations."

"He doesn't seem like the kind of guy who takes no for an answer." When she said nothing, he added, "So he put a ring on your finger and then he wasn't a nice guy anymore. Nor does he seem like a guy who gives up easily." Hank met her gaze.

She dragged hers away. "It's his male pride. All his buddies down at the force have been giving him a hard time about the broken engagement. It isn't as if his being unable to accept it has anything to do with love, trust me. He just refuses to let this go. I gave him back his ring and he broke into my house and left it on my dining room table. But this isn't your problem, okay? I'll handle it."

He shook his head. "He comes back, *I'll* handle it," he said. "I can see how terrified you are of him and for good reason. I asked you if he was dangerous. I know now that he is. That man's hurt you and next time he just might kill you. I'm not going to let that happen as long as you're—" their gazes met "—in my employ," he finished.

After parking next to his father's patrol SUV, he sat for a moment as if trying to calm down. He'd been afraid for her. She understood he'd been worried that she would have stupidly gotten into that car.

Through the windshield, she could see the marshal was standing next to his patrol SUV, arms crossed, a scowl on his face as he waited.

Beside her in the pickup cab, she could feel Hank's anger. "Right now I don't even know what to say to you. Would you have been foolish enough to climb into that car with that man?" He glanced over at her. "You make me want to shake some sense into you until your teeth rattle. Worse, you stubbornly thought you could handle a man like J.J. and didn't need or want my help."

She wanted to tell him that she'd been on her own for a long time. She wasn't used to asking for help, but he didn't give her a chance.

"I thought you trusted me," he said, his voice breaking with emotion as he parked in front of the house and climbed out.

FOR A MOMENT, Frankie leaned back against the seat, fighting tears. Hank had shot her a parting look before getting out and slamming the door behind him. It was filled with disappointment that wrenched at her heart. He'd thought she was smart. Smart wasn't getting involved with J.J. Whitaker. Worse was thinking she could handle this situation on her own. Hank was right. J.J. was dangerous. If he got her alone again, he would do more than hurt her, as angry as he was.

Wiping her eyes, she opened her door and followed the two men up the mountain to the cabin. She ached with a need to be in Hank's arms. J.J. had found her at the worst possible time. Had he been delayed a few hours, she would have been curled up in bed with Hank. Instead, Hank was furious at her, and with good reason.

She should have told him the truth way before this. J.J. was a loose cannon. What would have happened if the marshal hadn't come along when he did? She just hadn't thought the crazed cop would find her. Why hadn't she realized he would use any and every resource he had at his disposal to get to her? Especially if her nosy neighbor had told him that she'd left with some cowboy.

J.J. would have been jealous even if her relationship with Hank were strictly business because he thought every man wanted what he had. With Hank acting the way he did…well, J.J. would be convinced she and Hank were lovers. They would have been, she thought as a sob bubbled up in her chest and made her ache.

Not that it would have solved anything. In fact, it would have complicated an already difficult situation. But now she was drowning in regret.

Chapter Sixteen

The marshal and Hank were both waiting for her when she topped the hill at the cabin. Hank held the door open for her and his father. She walked past him, feeling his anger and his fear. She'd told him to let her handle it and yet he'd come back to save her. She loved him and wanted to smack him for it.

"Anyone else want a beer besides me?" Hank asked as he went straight to the kitchen. His father declined as he took a seat in the living area. Frankie could have used something stronger, but she declined a beer as well. She felt as if she needed to keep her wits about her as she sat down on the couch.

"You want to tell me what that was about on the highway?" Hud said quietly to Frankie since he'd already heard Hank's version.

"An old boyfriend who won't take no for an answer," she said. "He's a cop in Lost Creek, where I live. He tracked me here."

The marshal nodded. "He going to be a problem?"

She swallowed. "I hope not."

Hank came back into the room carrying a bottle of beer, half of it already gone. "If he comes back here—"

"You call me," Hud interrupted. "You call me and let me handle it. I mean it."

Hank said nothing, his face a mask of stubborn determination mixed with anger. She couldn't tell how much of it was anger at her for not telling him or wanting to handle it herself or being frustrated by the J.J. situation as well as the two of them and where they'd been headed earlier.

The marshal cleared his voice. "We found the truck that ran you off the road. It's an old one that's been parked up at an abandoned cabin. Lab techs are checking for prints, but they're not hopeful. Anyone who knew about the truck could have used it. I'm surprised the thing still runs. Anyway, the paint matched as well as the damage to the right side."

"So it was someone local," Hank said. He looked at Frankie and saw her relief that it hadn't had anything to do with her and J.J. The woman had so many secrets. He thought of Naomi and cursed under his breath. Except Naomi had been needy. Frankie was determined to handle everything herself. He shook his head at her and turned back to his father.

"That makes sense given what we've learned about Naomi's death," he said and looked to Frankie again to see if she wanted to be the one to tell him. She gave him a slight nod to continue.

She was on the couch, her legs curled under her with one of Hank's grandmother's quilts wrapped around her. He could tell that her run-in with her former fiancé had rattled her more than she'd wanted him to see.

He was still angry and had a bad feeling that J.J. might come to the ranch next time looking for her. He'd obviously tracked her as far as the main entrance. How crazy was the cop? Wasn't it enough that they had drug dealers wanting to kill them?

"Naomi found a bag of money," Hank began and told his father what Frankie had found out about Naomi's final phone call to an old boyfriend saying she was being followed and asking him what she should do. Give what money she had left back? "And then apparently her phone went dead or she turned it off."

Hud swore under his breath. "Drug money?"

"That's the assumption."

"Did this old boyfriend, whose name I'm going to need, did he say where she'd found it?" He looked to Frankie. She shook her head. "And you knew nothing about this?" he said, turning back to Hank.

"Nothing." He chewed at his cheek for a moment, trying to hold back his hurt and anger, realizing that he was more angry at Naomi than Frankie, though both had kept things from him. He was aware of the distinction between the two. Naomi was his girlfriend, the woman he'd planned to marry. Frankie… He looked over at her. She was a hell of a lot more than his employee—that much he knew. "Apparently Naomi didn't trust me. Must be something about me that women don't trust."

Frankie groaned and shook her head. "Let's leave you and me out of this."

He saw his father following the conversation between them with interest for a moment before getting back to Naomi and the drug money.

"If she had told you, I hope you would have been smart enough to come to me. Wouldn't you?"

Hank nodded. "I certainly wouldn't have let her keep the money, which I'm sure is why she didn't tell me."

"So the two of you have been digging around in Naomi's death," Hud said after a moment. Hank glanced over at Frankie and considered telling his father about his arrangement with the PI. But he had a feeling his father already knew. Anyway, their arrangement was beside the point.

"Tamara must have at least suspected who the drug dealers were," Hank said.

"And contacted them to let them know that we were asking questions," the marshal said.

"Would explain how we ended up in the river."

"I'm pretty sure she was involved." They both looked over at Frankie, surprised that she'd spoken.

"You talked to Tamara," Hud said. "Did you get the feeling she knew more than she was telling you?"

"She hinted that Naomi was wilder than anyone knew, that she had secrets and lived a double life. But from what Hank had told me about her," Frankie continued, "I had the feeling Tamara was talking about herself."

"Well, whatever she knew, she is no longer talking," the marshal said. "And the two of you…" He took a breath and let it out. "I wish you'd been honest with me about what you were doing."

"You didn't believe that Naomi had been murdered," Hank pointed out, feeling his hackles rise a little.

"I know, and I'm sorry about that. You were right. I was wrong. But now you have to let me handle this. I need you both to promise that you're done investigating."

"I promise," Hank said, looking at Frankie.

"Fine," she said. "If that's what you want," she said to him, rather than the marshal.

"Do you have some suspects?" Hank asked.

"I hear things," his father said. "The problem is getting evidence to convict them. Are there drugs being distributed in Big Sky? Maybe even more than in other places in Montana just because of the amount of money here." He rose to leave. "I'm expecting you both to keep your promise. Otherwise, I'm going to lock you up. I'm tempted to anyway, just to keep you both safe. As much as I hate to say this, it might be a good idea for the two of you to go back home to Idaho. At least for a while."

Hank looked at Frankie. "We'll leave in the morning."

"After breakfast. Your mother will be upset enough, but at least have one more meal with her before you take off," Hud said and met Hank's gaze. "You might want to tell your mother the truth. I don't want her planning a wedding just yet."

Hank walked his father out. "Dad, that car earlier? It was Frankie's former fiancé. She broke up with him two months ago but he's continued to stalk her. He's a cop from Lost Creek."

"I'll keep an eye out for him."

"Thanks." He felt his father's gaze on him and seemed about to say something but must have changed his mind.

"See you at breakfast," Hud said, turned and left.

FRANKIE FELT AS if her heart would break. She felt ashamed. She should have known better with J.J. She'd ignored all the red flags. It made her more ashamed when she remembered how she'd given Hank grief for ignoring the obvious signs with Naomi. She prided herself on reading people, on seeing behind their masks, on using those skills to do her job.

But when it came to her own personal life? She'd failed miserably. It didn't matter that J.J. had hidden his real self from her. She still should have seen behind the facade. Now she couldn't get away from him. He must have tracked her phone. How else could he have found her? At least he hadn't tried to kill them in that old truck that forced them into the river. She could be thankful for that.

Throwing off the quilt, she headed for the shower, feeling dirty and sick to her stomach. She'd never wanted Hank to know about J.J., let alone have the two meet. After turning on the shower, she stepped under the warm spray and reached for the body gel to scrub away her shame and embarrassment.

Tomorrow she and Hank would go back to Idaho. She hated leaving anything unfinished. She'd at least found out why Naomi Hill had died. But she had no idea who might be behind the murder. As she tilted her face up to the water, she remembered the man sitting at the end of the bar the day she went to talk to Tamara. He'd been acting like he wasn't paying them any attention, but he'd probably been listening to their conversation. Also, Tamara had gone down the bar and the two had been whispering. What if he was—

The shower door opened, making her spin around in surprise, all thoughts suddenly gone as she looked into Hank's baby-blue eyes. "Mind if I join you?"

She stepped back and watched as he climbed in still

dressed in everything but his boots. "You don't want to take off your clothes?"

"Not yet," he said as he closed the shower door behind them and turned to take her in. "Damn, woman, you are so beautiful."

"I'm so sorry that you had to find out about J.J.," she said, close to tears. "He's the big mistake of my life and I'm so ashamed for getting involved with such a loser."

He touched his finger to her lips and shook his head. "We all make mistakes. Look at me and Naomi. But you don't have to worry. I'm not going to let J.J. hurt you ever again. I promise."

"I don't want you—"

"Involved? Once I take off my clothes and get naked with you? We'll be in this together, you understand?"

She swallowed the lump in her throat, but could only nod.

He slowly began to unsnap his Western shirt.

"I think you'd better let me help you with that," she said, grabbing each side of the shirt and pulling. As the shirt fabric parted, revealing his muscled, tanned chest, she ached to touch him. As he drew her to him, she pushed her palms against the warmth of his flesh and leaned back for his kiss.

"Last chance," Hank said as he ended the kiss and reached for the buttons of his jeans. "There won't be any going back once these babies come off."

She laughed and pushed his hands away to unbutton his jeans and let them drop to the floor of the shower along with his underwear and his socks. She looked at his amazing body—and his obvious desire—and returned her gaze to his handsome face. "No going back," she said as she stepped into his arms again and molded her warm, wet body to his.

HANK KISSED HER passionately as he backed her up against the tiled wall of the shower, before his mouth dropped to her round, full breasts. Her nipples were dark and hard, the spray dripping off the tips temptingly. He bent his head to lick off a droplet before taking the erect nipple into his mouth and sucking it.

Frankie leaned her head back, arching her body against his mouth, a groan of pleasure escaping her lips. He took the other nipple in his mouth as his hand dropped down her belly and between her legs. He felt her go weak as his fingers found the spot that made her tremble. She clung to him as he made slow circles until she cried out and fell into his arms again.

He reached around to turn off the water and opened the shower door. After grabbing several large white bath towels from the hooks, he tied one around his waist and wrapped Frankie in the other. Sweeping her into his arms, he carried her toward his bedroom. His heart pounded. He meant what he'd told her. They were now in this together. No more secrets.

She looped her arms around his neck and leaned her face into the hollow of his shoulder as he kicked open the door to the bedroom, stalked in and, still holding her, kissed her, teasing her lips open with his tongue. The tip of her tongue met his and he moaned as he laid her on the bed.

She grabbed him and pulled him down with her. "I want you, Hank Savage," she said, the words like a blaze she'd just lit in his veins. "Oh, how I want you."

MUCH LATER THEY lay in each other's arms, Frankie feeling as if she was floating on a cloud. She couldn't remember ever feeling this happy, this content. But there was another emotion floating on the surface with her. She had trouble recognizing it for a moment because it was so new to her. Joy.

It made her feel as if everything was going to be all right. She usually wasn't so optimistic. She was too rational for that. But in Hank's arms, she believed in all the fairy tales. She even believed in true love, although she knew it was too early to be thinking this way. Look at the mistake she'd made with J.J. Six months hadn't been long enough to date him before getting engaged.

She looked over at Hank. And here she was curled up in bed with a man she'd only known for days.

"Are you all right?" he asked as she sat up to sit on the edge of the bed.

The reality of it had hit her hard. "I was just thinking this might be too fast."

He caressed her bare back. "I can understand why you're scared, but is that what your heart tells you?"

Gripping the sheet to her chest, she turned to look at him. She knew only too well what her heart was telling her. She just wasn't sure she could trust it right now.

Finding safer ground, she said, "I remembered something when I was in the shower—before you joined me. The man sitting at the bar. He was more than a regular. He and Tamara…they had a connection. I'm sure of it and it wasn't romantic. He had to overhear our conversation, which could mean…that if he was involved in the drug distribution and Tamara knew about it or was involved, he could have ordered the driver of that truck to either scare us or kill us."

"You're purposely avoiding the question."

Frankie gave him an impatient look. "Sandy blond, about your height, a little chunkier." That made him raise a brow. "You know what I mean."

Hank stopped her. "I know who you're talking about. I know exactly who you're talking about. I went to school with him. Darrel Sanders. He has a snow removal business in the winter. I have no idea what he does in the summer." He reached for his phone and realized the late hour. "I'd better wait and tell Dad at breakfast."

He drew her back onto the bed, turning her to spoon against her. "We can take all the time you want," he whispered into her ear, sending a shiver through her. "I'll wait."

She pressed her body against his in answer and felt his desire stir again. Chuckling, she turned in his arms to kiss him. He deepened the kiss and rolled her over until she was on top of him.

Frankie looked into his blue eyes and felt so much emotion that it hurt. Too fast or not, she was falling hard for this cowboy.

Chapter Seventeen

Dana noticed right away that there was something different about her son and Frankie. She shot a look at Hud. He shrugged, but as he took his seat at the breakfast table, she saw him hide a knowing grin. She knew that grin.

"So, how are you two this morning?" she asked, looking first at her son, then Frankie.

"Great," they both said in unison and laughed.

She noticed that they were sitting closer together, and if she wasn't wrong, her son's hand was on Frankie's thigh. Whatever problems they'd been having, she was relieved to see that they'd moved on from them. At least for the time being. She feared that the ghost of Naomi was still hanging around.

"I made a special breakfast," she said. "Waffles, eggs, ham and bacon, orange juice and fresh fruit."

"Mom, you shouldn't have gone to all this trouble," Hank said, "but we appreciate it. I'm starved." He picked up the plate of waffles, pulled three onto his plate and passed the plate to Frankie.

"I can't remember the last time I had waffles," Frankie said and helped herself.

"Try the huckleberry syrup," he suggested. "It's my grandmother's recipe. Or there is chokecherry syrup, also my grandmother Mary's recipe." Dana had named her daughter after her.

She loved seeing her son and Frankie in such a good mood. She watched with a light heart as they helped themselves to everything she'd prepared. They both did have healthy appetites. She smiled over at Hud, remembering how he'd appreciated hers, back when she was that young.

She looked at the two lovebirds and wondered, though, if she'd really ever been that young. Nothing could spoil this moment, she thought, right before the phone rang.

Hud excused himself to answer it since it was probably marshal business.

Hank got up too, to follow his father into the other room.

Dana pushed the butter over to Frankie. "You look beautiful this morning. I love that shirt." It wasn't one of those baggy ones like she wore most of the time.

"Thank you." Frankie looked down at the shirt as if just realizing that she'd put it on that morning. When she looked up, her eyes clouded over.

"I'm sorry—was it something I said?"

"No, it's just that I love being here and—"

Hank came back into the room, followed by his father. Dana saw their expressions and said, "What's happened?"

Hud put a hand on his wife's shoulder. "It's just work, but Hank and Frankie are going back to Idaho today. They're leaving right after breakfast."

Dana shook her head as she felt her eyes burn with tears. "So soon?" she asked her son. "It feels like you just got here."

"It's for the best right now," Hank said. "We both have jobs to get back to, but don't worry. I'll be home again before you know it."

Her gaze went to Frankie as she recalled how close the young woman had been to tears just moments ago. Because she knew they were leaving? Or because she wouldn't be coming back?

"She'll be coming back too," Hank said quickly as if reading her expression. Her son sat back down at the table to finish his breakfast and gave Frankie a look that was so filled with love, Dana felt choked up.

"I certainly hope you'll both be back," she said, fighting tears.

"I have to go," her husband said as he leaned down to give her a kiss on the cheek. She reached back to grab his hand and squeeze it. She wished he would retire. There were days he left the house when she wasn't sure he would make it home alive again. It was a thought that filled her with fear. She couldn't wait for the days when the two of them would be here together on the ranch with their grandchildren and the phone wouldn't ring with marshal business.

"You told your dad about the man I saw at the bar?" Frankie asked as they left the ranch house.

"Darrel Sanders." He nodded as they walked up to the cabin to get their things.

She could tell that leaving here was hard on Hank.

Probably because it was so hard on his mother. "Your mom is so sweet."

"Yeah, she is. Frankie, I know all this is new between us, but I have to be honest with you. Being here, it makes me wish I'd never left. I miss it."

She nodded. "I can see that."

"Not because of Naomi. Maybe in spite of her. I miss my family. I miss ranch work."

"There's no reason you shouldn't come back. This is your family legacy." Frankie could feel his gaze on her.

"You have to know that if, down the road, once you've had enough time to accept that we belong together..."

"What are you saying?" she asked, stopping on the trail to face him.

"That if my coming back here was a deal breaker with us, I would stay in Idaho and I would be fine at my job."

She shook her head. "I would never keep you from what you love or your family. But we still need to slow down. This is way too fast."

"Not for me, but I can see it is for you. Plus we still have to deal with your ex-fiancé. I get it. Like I told you, I'll wait." He leaned toward her, took her face in his big hands and kissed her. "Umm, you taste like huckleberries."

She saw the look in his eye and laughed. Why not? It wasn't as if they were in a hurry to get back to Idaho.

As HANK DROVE out of the ranch, he couldn't help looking back. Frankie noticed and reached over to put her hand on his thigh.

"You'll be back."

He nodded. "*We'll* be back."

She smiled and looked out her window. He realized she was looking in her side mirror.

His gaze went quickly to his rearview mirror. No sign of J.J. "Let's hope he gave up and went back to Idaho."

"I doubt it. But since that's where we're headed…"

"What are we going to do about him when we get back?"

"I've hesitated to get a restraining order because, one, I know it won't do any good, and, two, it will only infuriate him and make things worse."

He stole a look at her as he drove. He still couldn't believe this. He was crazy about her. She was all he'd thought about. But the J.J. situation scared him. They weren't out of the woods yet. Until J.J. was no longer a problem, he and Frankie couldn't move forward. "What other option is there?"

"Short of shooting him?" She brushed her hair back. This morning she'd tied back her long mane. Tendrils had escaped and hung in a frame around her face. She couldn't have looked more beautiful.

"I understand why he doesn't want to lose you. I feel the same way. But his methods are so desperate, so…"

"Insane?" She nodded. "Also his reasons. He wants me back to save face. If he loved me he wouldn't—" Her voice broke.

"I'm guessing he's been violent with you," he said as he drove away from Big Sky headed north.

She nodded without looking at him. "Please, I don't

want to talk about him. It's a beautiful day and I don't want to spoil it."

It was. A crisp blue cloudless sky hung over the tall pines and rocky cliffs of the canyon. Beside them, the river flowed, a sun-kissed clear green. He felt her gaze on him.

"Are you all right with leaving? I mean, we came here to—"

"Because I was convinced Naomi was murdered. We have good reason now to believe it's true. It's up to my father now to find out the truth."

She nodded. "It feels unfinished."

He glanced over at her. "Once we knew what Naomi had gotten involved with, it was too dangerous to stay because I know you. You wouldn't stop looking. I couldn't let you do that. It was getting too dangerous. Not to mention my father would have locked us up if we continued to investigate it."

FRANKIE STARED AT him in surprise. "But you wouldn't have stayed and kept looking if I wasn't with you."

"I just told you. My father would have probably thrown me in jail is what would have happened."

"Hank—"

"There is no way I'm putting you in that kind of danger."

"That isn't your choice. This is what I do for a living."

"I've been meaning to ask you how you came to be a private eye."

She could see that he was changing the subject, but she answered anyway. "I had an uncle who was a private investigator. I started out working for him in his office. He took me on a few cases. I was pretty good at it. When he moved to Arizona and closed his office, I opened mine." She shrugged. "I kind of fell into it. Would I do it over? I don't know." She looked at him. "That day we went on the horseback ride up into the mountains?" He nodded. "I felt the kind of freedom I've always felt with my job. It was…exhilarating. If I could find a job that let me ride a horse every day…"

"As a rancher's wife, you could ride every day."

She'd been joking, wanting to change the subject. But now she stared at him and saw that he was completely serious. They hadn't even said that they loved each other and he was suggesting she become his wife.

But as she looked at him, she knew it in her heart. She did love him. She'd fallen for him, for his lifestyle, for his family. She'd fallen for the whole ball of wax and now he was offering it to her?

Frankie looked away. As she did, she saw the man stagger out into the highway. "Hank, look out!"

HANK HIT THE BRAKES. The pickup fishtailed wildly, but he got it stopped before he hit the man who'd dropped to his hands and knees in the middle of the highway.

He threw open his door, jumped out and rushed to the man gasping for breath, whose face was smeared with blood.

"Help me," the man said. "My car went off the road back in the mountains."

Hank reached down to help him up. Traffic had been light. What few drivers passed slowed down to look, but didn't stop.

"Here, let me help you to my pickup," he said as he half lifted the man to his feet. As they approached the passenger side, Frankie moved over to give him room to climb in with Hank's help.

After closing the door, Hank hurried around to slide behind the wheel. "I can take you to the hospital in Bozeman."

"That won't be necessary," the man said, no longer wheezing.

Hank shot a look at the man and felt his eyes widen as he saw the gun now pressed to Frankie's temple.

"Drive up the road," the man ordered. "I don't want to kill her, but I will."

Chapter Eighteen

J.J. had parked down the road from the ranch turnoff. He'd been able to see anyone coming or going. Stakeouts were something he was good at because he required so little sleep. He was usually wired. Catching bad guys was his drug of choice.

Catching Frankie and straightening her up was enough motivation to keep him awake for days. His dedication paid off in spades this morning when he saw the pickup coming out of the ranch with both the cowboy and Frankie.

The pickup turned north and J.J. followed in the SUV he'd rented. It cost him a pretty penny to rent, but he would spare no expense to get Frankie back. As he drove, he admitted to himself that he'd made mistakes when it came to her. He'd put off the actual wedding, stringing her along for a while because while he liked the idea of having her all to himself, he wasn't ready to tie himself down.

He'd been happy knowing that no other man could have her as long as she was wearing his ring. So when she'd wanted to break up, he'd been caught flat-footed. He'd thought it was because he hadn't mentioned setting a date for the wedding. But in that case, he would have expected her to start talking about making wedding plans or leaving bride magazines around or dropping hints and crying and giving him ultimatums.

Instead, she'd said she didn't want to marry him, that the engagement had been a mistake and that she wanted out. She'd handed him his ring. Hadn't even flung it at him in anger.

That was when he'd gotten scared that she was serious. No recriminations, no tears, just a simple "I don't want to marry you. I'm sorry."

It had hit him harder than he'd expected. He'd been relieved, and yet the thought of her just tossing him back like a fish that didn't quite meet her standards really pissed him off. He'd thought, *Like hell you're going to walk away from me.*

He'd gotten physical. But what guy wouldn't have under those conditions? That was when she stopped answering his calls, refused to see him, basically cut him off entirely. At first, he thought it was just a ploy to get him to the altar. Of course she wanted to marry him. He was a good-looking guy with a cool job. Didn't all women go for a man in uniform?

Since then he'd been trying to get her back every way he could think of. But it became clear quickly that she was serious. She wanted nothing more to do with him. That was when he got mad.

Now, as he followed the pickup north out of town, he considered what to do next. He had no idea where they were headed. But wherever they were going, they didn't seem to be in a hurry.

It was early enough that traffic was light, so he stayed

back, figuring he couldn't miss them if they stopped anywhere in the canyon. Once out of it, he'd have to stay closer. After his all-night stakeout, he wasn't about to lose them now.

They were almost out of the canyon when he saw the pickup's brake lights come on. He quickly pulled over to see what was going on. There was no place for them to turn off, so what the—

That was when he saw the cowboy jump out and rush up the road. A few moments later, the cowboy returned and helped a man into the passenger side of the truck. The man appeared to be injured.

As the pickup pulled back onto the highway, so did J.J. This put a new wrinkle in things, he thought. When not far out of the canyon, the cowboy turned off before the town of Gallatin Gateway. Maybe they were taking the man to his house on what appeared to be the old road along the river. Still, it seemed strange.

J.J. followed at a distance, telling himself this might work out perfectly for him. When they dropped the man off, maybe that was when he'd make his move.

"What is this about?" Hank asked, afraid he knew only too well.

"You'll find out soon enough," the man said. "Right up here around the next corner, take the road to the left toward the mountains."

Hank couldn't believe he'd fallen for this. But in Montana, you stopped to help people on the road. He hadn't given it a second thought, though he regretted that kindness now.

He shot a look at Frankie. She appeared calm, not in

the least bit worried, while his heart was racing. The man had a gun to her head! He couldn't imagine anything worse, and then realized he could. At least Frankie wasn't standing on a ledge over the river, looking down at the rocks, knowing she was about to die.

He saw the turn ahead and slowed to take it, glancing into his rearview mirror. There was a vehicle way back on the road. No way to signal that they needed help.

They were on their own. He knew they would have to play it by ear. He would do whatever it took to keep Frankie safe—even if it meant taking a bullet himself.

He turned onto the road. As it wound back into the mountains, he told himself that it made no sense for the drug dealers to kidnap them, let alone kill them. They'd gotten away with murder for three years. If he and Frankie had uncovered evidence against them, they would have been behind bars by now.

So why take them? That was the part that made no sense. Running them off the road had been a warning to back off, but this…this terrified him. Maybe they were cleaning up loose ends, like with Tamara, since she obviously had known more than she'd told Frankie.

THE FIRST THING the marshal did when he left the ranch after breakfast was drive over to Darrel Sanders's house. He'd hoped to catch him before he got up. He remembered the boy Darrel had been as a classmate of Hank's. A nice-looking kid with a definite chip on his shoulder.

Darrel had moved into his mother's house after she died. It was a small house in a subdivision of other small houses away from Meadow Village.

But when he pulled up, he saw that Darrel's vehicle,

an old panel van, was gone. He tried his number, let it ring until voice mail picked up before hanging up.

It made him nervous that Darrel wasn't around. The man worked in the winter but, as far as Hud could tell, did nothing in the summer to earn a living. The supposition was that he made so much with his snow removal business that he had summers off.

Hud sat for a moment, letting his patrol SUV idle in front of the house before he shut off the engine, got out and crossed the yard. He'd always gone by the book. But there was no way he could get a warrant based on what he had, which was simply suspicion.

At the house, he knocked and then tried the door. Locked. Going around the small house, he tried to look in the windows, but the curtains were pulled.

At the back, he stepped up onto the small porch. A row of firewood was stacked head high all along the back side of the house and down the fence, cutting off any view of most of the neighbors.

Hud tried the back door and, finding it locked, he put his shoulder into it. He wasn't as young as when he used to do this. The door held and his shoulder hurt like hell, but he tried again.

The lock gave and he opened the door and quickly stepped in, telling himself that he smelled smoke and thought he'd better check to make sure nothing was on fire inside. A lie, but one he would stand behind. The inside of the house wasn't as messy as he'd expected it to be. He'd wondered if Darrel had gone on the lam after Tamara's death, but if he'd packed up and taken off, there was no sign of it.

A pizza box sat in the middle of the table. He opened

it and saw that several pieces were still inside. There were dishes in the sink and beer in the refrigerator. He had the feeling that Darrel hadn't gone far.

He thought about waiting for him, but after looking around and finding nothing of interest, he left by the way he'd come in, feeling guilty and at the same time vindicated.

He'd insisted before Hank left that he get a new cell phone before he left town. He tried his number now.

FRANKIE STARTED AS Hank's cell phone rang. She hadn't replaced her own, saying she'd take care of it once she got home. She wanted a new number, one that J.J. probably wouldn't have any trouble getting, though. That thought had come out of nowhere. A foolish thought to be worrying about J.J. when a stranger had a gun to her head.

Hank's cell rang again.

"Don't touch it," the man ordered, pressing the barrel of the gun harder against her temple and making her wince.

"It's probably my father, and if I don't answer it, he'll be worried and put a BOLO out on us."

The man swore. "Give me your phone." Hank dug it out and handed it over. The man stared down at it for a moment and said, "Answer it. Tell him you're fine but can't talk because of the traffic and will call him later. Say anything more and the last thing your father will hear is this woman's brains being splattered all over you. Got it?"

"Got it." He took the phone back and did just as the

man had told him before being ordered to hand the phone back.

Frankie watched the man pocket the phone. She hadn't been able to hear the other side of the conversation. But it appeared the marshal had accepted that Hank couldn't talk right now.

She took even breaths, letting herself be lulled by the rocking of the pickup as Hank drove deeper into the foothills. She knew better than to try to take the gun away from the man in these close quarters. She would wait and bide her time. She hoped Hank was on the same page. He appeared to be since he hadn't tried to get a message to his father.

They came over a rise and she saw a small cabin set back against rocks and pines. Several rigs were parked in front of it, including a panel van that she'd seen before. It took her a moment to remember where. In front of the Silver Spur Bar in Big Sky. Darrel Sanders's rig. So this was just as they suspected, about the drug money and Naomi's death.

"Park over there and then we're going to get out very carefully," the man said. "This gun has a hair trigger. If you try anything—"

"I get the picture," Hank said impatiently. "But now this. If you shoot her, you'd better shoot me as quickly as possible because if you don't—"

"I get the picture," the man interrupted, and she saw him smile out of the corner of her eye.

Even knowing what this was about, she couldn't understand why they were being brought here. She didn't think it was to kill them, but she knew she could be wrong about that. The thought made her breath catch and her mouth go dry. She and Hank had just found each other. She had hardly let herself believe in this relationship. She didn't want it to be over so soon— and so tragically.

She'd said she needed time, but even after her bad experience with J.J., she knew in her heart that Hank was nothing like the cop. He was the kind of man who made a woman feel loved and protected. The kind of man who loved horses and wanted to make babies and raise a family.

Frankie felt tears burn her eyes as she let herself admit that she wanted that as well. Wanted to come back here to the ranch and raise their kids here. She wanted Hank.

The man opened his door and grabbed her with his free hand to pull her out of the pickup, the gun still pointed at her head. Hank had gotten out on the other side of the pickup and stood waiting, his gaze on the man as if hoping for an opportunity to get the gun away from him.

She willed Hank to look at her, and when he shifted his gaze, she smiled, hoping to reassure him that they were going to get through this. They had to. She'd seen their future and she wasn't ready to give that up. If it meant a fight…well, she was ready.

"WHAT A CHUMP," J.J. said as he looked after Hank and Frankie. He couldn't believe how accommodating the fool was. First he picked up a complete stranger from the middle of the road and then what? Offered to drive him home? And his home ended up being way down a dirt road, back in the foothills?

J.J. had gone on past the turnoff when he'd seen the pickup begin working its way back into the foothills. After turning around, he'd found a place to park, pulled his gun out of the glove box, checked to make sure it was fully loaded, then stuck it in the waistband of his jeans as he got out of the rental car.

It might be a hike back in to wherever the cowboy had taken the man, but J.J. thought the area couldn't be more perfect for what he had in mind. Even if they dropped the man off and were headed back this way before he reached the man's house on foot, he could work with it.

Feeling as if Lady Luck had smiled on him, he couldn't imagine a more perfect place to end this. Once he explained things to the cowboy, he hoped that was the end of any problem from him.

Frankie was his. Period. End of discussion. True, right now she was giving him some trouble, but he would try humbling himself, sweet-talking her, spoiling her, and if that didn't work then he'd have to get physical. It wasn't something he wanted to do, but she had to understand how things were going to be. She couldn't embarrass him in front of his friends and his coworkers. She had to behave. No one respected a man who couldn't keep his woman under control.

Once they established the rules, hell, maybe he'd suggest they pick a wedding date. Marrying her might be the only way to keep her in line. If that was what he had to do, then he'd bite the bullet and get it over with. It wasn't like he had someone else he wanted to marry. There were some he wanted to get into bed, but he could do that easily enough after he was married to

Frankie. She had to understand that he had his needs. Real men did.

J.J. was feeling good as he headed up the road. He'd gone a quarter mile when he realized that he couldn't hear the sound of a vehicle engine anymore. He came over a rise and saw why.

In the distance was a small cabin with four rigs parked in front of it, including the cowboy's pickup. What he didn't see was any sign of Frankie or the cowboy, though. Maybe the man they'd rescued had invited them in for something. A drink to pay them back for saving him?

Fine with J.J. He was in no hurry. He kept to the trees along the edge of the foothills until he was close enough to the cabin that he would see them when they came out.

Maybe he'd just hitch a ride with them when they left, he thought, feeling the weight of the gun pressing against his stomach. He pulled it out and sat down on a rock to wait, thinking about the future he and Frankie would have. Everything was going to be fine now. Like his boss had warned him, he just needed to get his life under control or he could be in trouble at work.

The memory made him grit his teeth. This was all Frankie's fault. But he would get the bitch in line—one way or the other.

THE MAN LED them into the cabin at gunpoint. Hank stepped through the door, Frankie and the man behind him, the gun still to Frankie's head. The cabin appeared larger on the inside than it had from outside. At a glance he took it all in as his mind raced for a way out of this that didn't get them both killed.

He saw a small kitchen against one wall, a bed and a half-dozen mismatched chairs around a table. Darrel was sitting in one of the chairs. A large man he didn't recognize was standing against the wall, looking tough. Hank didn't miss the holstered gun visible under the man's jacket.

He went on the defensive, determined not to let him see how worried he actually was. "What the hell, Darrel?"

His former classmate smiled. "Sit down, Hank. There's no reason to get all worked up. Les," he said to the man they'd picked up in the middle of the highway, "why don't you and Frankie sit over there." He pointed to the bed. "That way we can all see each other."

Hank hadn't moved. Darrel kicked out one of the chairs across the table from him. "Take a load off and let's talk."

"I can't imagine what we might have to talk about."

"Hank, we've known each other for too long to lie to each other. So let's cut the bull. You know perfectly well why you're here. Sit."

Hank took the chair, turning it around to straddle the seat and rest his arms on the back. He'd be able to move faster this way—if he got the chance.

Darrel smiled, seeing what Hank was up to, but said, "Your father was by my house this morning looking for me and snooping around, I heard. I suspect it's your doing. Yours and your—" his gaze shifted to Frankie "—your lady friend's." He eyed Frankie with interest for a moment before turning back to Hank. "Picked yourself up a private eye, did you? Why would you do that?"

He considered several answers before he said, "I never believed that Naomi killed herself."

Darrel nodded with a grimace. "No, you never did."

"So I hired Ms. Brewster to help prove I was right."

"And did you?" He could feel the man's intense gaze on him.

"No. Suspecting is one thing. Proving is another. It's why Frankie... Ms. Brewster and I were leaving town." He didn't want Darrel thinking there was anything more between him and Frankie than employer and employee. He knew the man well enough to know he would use it against them.

Darrel raised a brow in obvious surprise. "Leaving? Giving up that easy? Just doesn't sound like you, Hank. Remember how you were when it came to competitive sports? You couldn't stand to let me win. So why give up now?" His former classmate seemed to consider it for a moment before his gaze swung to Frankie. "Things get a little too complicated for you?"

He saw no reason to lie. "They did. So we decided to put all of this behind us and go back to our lives in Idaho."

Darrel shifted his weight to lean across the table toward him. "I'm happy for you. Personally, I thought you were never going to get over Naomi, but apparently you've now found a woman who's made you forget her. Under normal circumstances, I'd wish you well. But here is the problem. I still want my money that your former girlfriend stole. I thought it was lost forever, but then you came back to the canyon and I figured, 'Hank's come back to pick up the money. He was in on it the whole time.' I actually admire you for waiting three years. I kept track of you and knew you hadn't spent it. For a while, I thought maybe Naomi hadn't even told you about it. So where is it? In your pickup? Trent, go take a look."

"Wait a minute," Frankie said, making them all turn to look at her. "Naomi didn't have the money on her that night, the night you killed her?"

Chapter Nineteen

As J.J. had approached the cabin, he considered climbing in the back of the cowboy's pickup. From the hill where he sat, he could see that there appeared to be some old tarps in the back. He could hide, and when the time was right, he could pop up. *Surprise!*

The idea had its appeal. He just wasn't sure he could reach the pickup before they came out, and given the number of vehicles parked outside the cabin, he couldn't be sure how many people were inside.

The rock where he sat was far enough away that he could see the cowboy and Frankie when they came out, but they probably wouldn't notice him. It wouldn't take much for him to trot down to the road and stop them once they were out of sight of the cabin.

They seemed to have been in there for a while now, he thought, frowning. Maybe the man was more injured than he'd thought. What if they'd sent for an ambulance? Worse, the cops?

But as time passed with no sign of either, he was beginning to wonder what could be going on inside that cabin. Maybe he should get a little closer. The rock he was sitting on wasn't that comfortable anyway, he thought as he began to work his way down the hillside through the pines.

The front door of the cabin opened. He jumped back behind a pine, thinking it was about time they came out. But the man who emerged wasn't the cowboy. He was a big, tough-looking dude. Sunlight caught on the gun in the man's holster.

What the hell?

J.J. watched as the man went straight to the cowboy's pickup. It didn't take long to understand what was going on. The man was searching the truck. He obviously didn't find what he was looking for—even after going through their bags behind the seat. When he slammed the pickup door, he glanced at the tarps in the back and quickly climbed in to search there as well.

"Glad I wasn't under one of those tarps," J.J. said to himself as he watched the man finish his search and go back inside the cabin.

Something was definitely wrong and Frankie was in there. He considered what to do. No way was he busting in there, gun blazing. The way he saw it, all he could do was wait. Maybe if he heard screams from Frankie, he might have to change his mind.

Since the man had searched the pickup, it made sense that he wouldn't be looking in the back again. He continued down the hill, keeping his gun ready and his eyes focused on the cabin door.

Staying low, he made his way through the vehicles to the cowboy's pickup and leaped into the back, covering himself with the tarps to wait.

TRENT RETURNED MINUTES later from searching the truck. "Not there."

Frankie watched Darrel's jaw muscle bunch as the tension in the room became thick as smoke. But beside her, Les had released her arm and now merely sat with the gun pressed into the side of her head.

"I thought we were going to be straight with each other," Darrel said, clearly trying to contain his anger.

Frankie could see that Hank was getting angrier by the moment. "That was you the day at the river," Hank said. "That was you I saw running through the trees."

"I followed you thinking you were going for the money. Instead, you were doing what you always did, sitting and staring at that cliff. Three years, I've waited. When you came back after all this time, I thought it was finally to get the money."

Hank shook his head. "You had us forced off the road and into the river. You could have killed us."

"I doubted you would die, but at that point, you hadn't gone for the money and I was losing patience."

"When are you going to get it through your head?" Hank demanded. "We don't have your money. Now let us go."

"I don't think you realize your circumstances," Darrel shot back as he got to his feet and limped over to where Les had his gun to Frankie's head. He grabbed a handful of Frankie's dark hair in his fist as a switchblade suddenly appeared in his other hand. Frankie cried out in pain as he jerked hard on her hair, exposing her throat to the knife.

"I could cut her throat right now, and I will if you don't stop lying to me."

Hank leaped to his feet and took a step toward him. Behind him, Trent moved too quickly. She felt Darrel release her hair and turn.

"Don't!" Darrel yelled at Trent, but his command wasn't quick enough. The man had pulled his gun and now brought the barrel down hard on Hank's head.

Frankie screamed and jumped to her feet, only to be pulled back down by Les.

Darrel swore as Hank toppled to the floor. From where Les held her, she could see that his head was bleeding.

"Help him!" she cried.

Darrel, still swearing, limped over to him and checked for a pulse. "He's not dead." Hank moaned and struggled to sit up. "Get a towel for his head," he ordered. "Now!" Trent disappeared into the bathroom. "Everyone just calm down. I don't like things to get violent but I'm tired of being lied to. I want my money." He said the last through gritted teeth.

"Hank doesn't know where your money is," Frankie said, her voice breaking. She could see that he was dazed and bleeding, but alive. At least for now.

"Tie him up," Darrel ordered when Trent returned with the towel. He tossed the towel to Hank, who put it against the side of his head and flinched.

"Is that necessary?" Frankie demanded. "He's injured. He needs to go to the hospital, not be tied up." She got a warning side look from Darrel.

"You both brought this on yourselves," he said. "Maybe you didn't know about the money, but obviously you do now. So stop lying. Since Hank and Naomi were going to get married and she had put money down on a house, don't tell me he doesn't know where she hid the rest of it."

Trent pulled out duct tape and, after helping Hank into a chair, bound him to it.

"I told you, I don't know," Hank mumbled and seemed to be fighting unconsciousness.

"I know who has your money," she said.

Hank's head came up. He shot her a pleading look. "Frankie—"

She turned her gaze on Darrel, who slowly swiveled around to look at her. "If you're lying, something much worse is going to happen to you. Do you understand?"

"Perfectly. But there's something I need to know first."

"You don't seem to be in a position to be making ultimatums," Darrel said, sounding almost amused.

"You're wrong. I'm the only person in this room who can get you your money." Darrel glanced at Hank. "He doesn't know," she said. "So if you didn't find the money on Naomi that night, then you're right—she hid it somewhere. But what I don't get is why you killed her before she told you where."

He seemed to consider whether to answer or not, and then swore. "One of my associates was handling it and made an error in judgment."

"That's what you call killing her?" Hank said through clenched teeth. She could see he was in pain from the head wound. "An error in judgment?"

"Tamara didn't kill her," Darrel said. "She took her up on the ledge to scare her since she knew Naomi was afraid of heights. All Naomi had to do was tell her where the money was. It wasn't in her vehicle. Nor her apartment, which had already been searched. We suspected it was hidden on the ranch, but we needed the location. Naomi refused to give it to her. Tamara argued with her. Naomi tried to push past her on the ledge to leave, making it clear that she was never going to tell. She took a misstep and fell to her death. Killing her was the last thing we wanted to do."

"Until you got the money," Frankie said. She could see that Hank was struggling to stay conscious, struggling with the news about Naomi.

"You both misjudge me," Darrel said. "Dead bodies complicate things. I prefer not to shed blood unless I have to. Unfortunately, some of my other associates are less reasonable." He rose unsteadily from his chair, and Frankie was reminded of his limp when he'd come into the bar.

Stepping back, he lifted his pant leg to expose a mass of red and purple scar tissue. When he spoke, there was fury in his voice. "You have no idea how much your former girlfriend has cost me, and not just in money and pain. I came close to getting my throat cut—and that would have been the faster and least painful in the long run, I realize now. My associates had much worse plans for me. I've been busting my ass for three years to pay them back. I've been waiting for you to return to town to collect the money after that foolish, stubborn woman took it and refused to tell us where she'd hidden it. Now," he said as he covered his injured leg again and slowly lowered himself into his chair.

He turned his attention to Frankie. "You say you know who has my money?"

She nodded. "One more question first, though," she said, making him groan. She knew she was trying his patience, but she also knew that she had leverage and she planned to use it. She had to use whatever she could to get them out of this. "How was Naomi able to steal the bag of money that she referred to as a small fortune? I would have thought you'd be watching it closer than that. Unless she was one of your associates."

Darrel laughed at that. "Hardly. She and Tamara had become friends. Naomi gave Tamara free groceries and even money out of the till sometimes when she came in and no one else was around." He swung his gaze back to Hank. "Your girlfriend was a shoplifter. Did you know that? She got her kicks by stealing. Tamara failed to mention that until later when my money went missing."

"So you didn't know who took it at first," Frankie said.

"No," Darrel admitted. "I waited to see who started spending."

Frankie thought of the house that Naomi had put a down payment on, hoping Hank would marry her. "How much money are we talking?" she asked.

Darrel shook his head.

"So you knew that Naomi had a larcenous streak and yet you left it lying around?"

Darrel gave her a warning look and then said, "I didn't leave it lying around. I'd brought the money to the bar that afternoon to meet someone. The person was running late and some men came into the bar. I didn't like their looks. I sensed trouble, so I hightailed it into the office. Unfortunately, I didn't have time to put the money into the safe. So I stuck it behind some liquor boxes. Two men jumped me as I walked out of the office. They didn't get far in their plan, but in the confusion of throwing them out of the place with some help from a couple of friends…the money disappeared."

"How did you know Naomi took it?"

He sighed. "It took a little while to figure it out. I had to go through a few possibilities first. In the end, Tamara and I both remembered Naomi being in the bar and disappearing when the trouble started. Tamara thought Naomi might have gone to the restroom before the fight broke out. My office is right across from the women's bathroom. When I heard she'd put money down on a house in Bozeman… Now, no more questions. Who has my money?"

Frankie thought of Randall "Butch" Clark. It hadn't taken much to get the truth out of him and that had worried her at the time. He'd seemed scared enough, but he had wanted her to believe that Naomi had the money on her that night. That she was thinking about stopping and giving the drug dealers what she had left.

But it seemed he'd lied about that. Still, she didn't want to get him killed. "I'm going to take you at your word that you're not into bloodshed," Frankie said, getting to her feet. Les leaped up as well as he tried to keep the gun on her and get a better grip on her. She didn't think he would shoot and knew she was taking a chance, but she'd bluffed her way this far. "Tell him to get that gun out of my face."

Darrel looked from her to Les. "Sit down, Les. I have a gun under the table. I can kill them both if necessary.

You can put your piece away." He turned his gaze on her. "You have a lot of guts. He could have killed you just then before I could stop him."

She had a feeling that Les wasn't that quick-thinking, but kept it to herself. "Let me get this straight. Naomi didn't have the money on her that night, right?"

"I believe we already covered that."

"Tamara was following her that night, right? So what if she had the money and Tamara lied? She killed Naomi and kept the—"

"Tamara didn't have the money," Darrel said, talking over her. "Trust me, some of my more bloodthirsty associates talked to her about this at length before she…expired. She stuck to her story. Tamara took her up on the ledge to force her to tell what she did with it, but Naomi refused. Then the stupid woman slipped and fell."

HANK FELT AS if he was in a nightmare, one of his own devising. If he hadn't come back here, if he hadn't brought Frankie, if he'd just let Naomi go. His head ached and his vision blurred.

Frankie was scaring him, but he didn't know how to stop her—especially injured and bound to a chair.

"But if Naomi was being followed, how could she have dumped the money before she stopped or was pulled over?" Frankie asked.

Darrel shrugged. "You tell me."

"She'd already hidden the money," Frankie said, nodding as if to herself. "She called someone to tell the person where the money was in case something happened to her."

Frankie was right. Naomi had hidden the money

and called the person she trusted—her old boyfriend, Butch. It was the only thing that made any sense. Naomi thought the money was safe. She didn't think the drug dealers would really kill her until they had it. If she hadn't slipped—

He felt Darrel's gaze on him. "That's exactly how I saw it. She hid the money and made a call to tell her lover where he could find it. How about it, Hank? Isn't that the way you see it?"

"Naomi didn't call Hank," Frankie said.

But Hank knew who Naomi had called—and so did Frankie. He looked at her and felt his heart drop. He could see what she was thinking, but wasn't sure how to head her off.

"Why wouldn't Naomi tell on that cliff?" Hank demanded, stalling for time, afraid that Frankie was only about to get herself in deeper. "That makes no sense." And yet he knew. He didn't even have to look at Frankie and see that she knew too. He felt his stomach drop.

"She wasn't giving up the money," Frankie said, sounding sad for the woman she'd been investigating and sad for him. "It meant that much to her."

He shook his head, unable to accept that he'd never really known Naomi. He knew that she'd always felt deprived and wanted desperately to have the life she dreamed of having. Still, he didn't want to believe that she would put money before her own life.

"That's crazy. She's standing on the edge of the ledge over the river and she'd rather die than give up the money?" he said.

No one said anything, but he saw that Darrel was staring at Frankie.

Hank felt as if he was on a runaway train with no way to stop it. No way to jump off either.

"I can get you your money," Frankie said to Darrel. "But you're going to have to let me leave."

"Frankie, no," Hank said, feeling dizzy. "You can't trust him." He let out a curse, feeling helpless and scared. "You can't expect him to stick by any deal, Frankie. He used to cheat at every sport I ever played with him."

Darrel shook his head at Hank but he was smiling. "I had to cheat. You were too good for me. But right now, I think I have the upper hand."

"Frankie—"

"Put some tape over his mouth," Darrel ordered, and Trent sprang to it.

Hank tried to put up a fight but it was useless. He felt weak even though he hadn't lost that much blood. He wondered if he had a concussion. Right now his only concern, though, was Frankie. He'd foolishly gotten to his feet, knowing that Trent was behind him. He hadn't expected the man to hit him. Neither had Darrel. Now he found himself duct-taped to a chair and gagged. And Frankie was about to make a deal that could get her killed.

SHE'D KNOWN HANK wasn't going to like this and would have tried to stop her if he could have. "Let me go get your money," she said again to Darrel.

"Do I look stupid? If I let you go, you'll hightail it straight to the authorities, and the next thing I know, there'll be a SWAT team outside my door."

"You have another option?" Frankie asked. "We can't

tell you where the money is because we don't know. We didn't even know about it until recently. If you kill us, you'll never get the money and Hank's father will never stop looking for you. Stupid would be making your situation worse. Can't you see we're trying to help you figure this out?"

Darrel shook his head. "You make it sound like if you hand over the money, we all just walk away as if nothing ever happened. I just kidnapped the two of you."

"You are merely detaining us," Frankie said. "Until you get your money. Then you'll let us go. No harm, so to speak," she said, looking pointedly at Trent, "no foul. That's the deal."

"Trent goes with you."

She shook her head. "Not a chance. I go alone. It's the only way I have a chance of getting the person who took your money to admit the truth."

"How do I know you'll come back?"

"I'll come back. You have Hank."

"Good point," Darrel said. "I just wasn't sure you were that invested in him. If you don't come back, he dies. You call in the cops—"

"Save your breath. I'm not going to the authorities, but I need your word that he'll be safe until I get back," she said. "No more tough-guy stuff. The thing is, I don't know how long it will take me."

"You'd better not be playing me."

Frankie met Darrel's gaze. "You want your money. Hank and I want to get on with our lives." Her gaze went to Hank. He gave a small shake of his head and looked pointedly at Trent leaning against the wall again. Frankie knew this was dangerous, but she could see only one way out. Hank was already injured. She could imagine all of this going south quickly if she didn't do something. But what she was suggesting was a gamble, one she had no choice but to take.

"I'll give you until sundown."

Frankie shook her head. "I might need longer. Like I said, this could take a while."

Darrel shook his head. "Sundown or he's dead."

She wanted to argue but she could see she'd pushed the man as much as he was going to take. "Sundown, but promise me that I won't be followed. You need to trust me to handle this."

Darrel wagged his head. "You're asking a lot, sweetheart."

"It's Frankie. And I have a lot to lose," she said and looked at Hank. "There's one more thing that I need," she said to Darrel. "A gun."

Chapter Twenty

All of her bravado gone, Frankie's hands were shaking as she climbed into the pickup. She laid the unloaded gun on the seat next to her. Darrel said he wasn't about to hand her a loaded gun.

"I'm taking one hell of a chance on you as it is," he'd said. "I give you a loaded gun..." He'd smiled as he'd shaken his head. "I'm betting a whole lot on you as it is, lady."

It was mutual, she thought now. She'd just gambled Hank's life on her suspicion of what had happened to the stolen drug money. What if she was wrong? Even if she was right, the money could be gone. Or Butch might refuse to give it to her. For all she knew, he could have gone on the lam after she'd talked to him at his father's hardware store.

Hank was depending on her. She drove toward Bozeman, checking behind her for a tail, trying not to speed for fear of being pulled over. She considered calling the marshal, but couldn't risk it. Not yet, anyway.

After parking behind the hardware store, she tucked the gun into her jeans and covered it with the shirt and jacket she'd put on earlier that morning. Taking a breath, she climbed out and entered the hardware store at the back through the delivery entrance. In the dim light of the empty area, she did her best to pull it together. Butch wouldn't be excited to see her to begin with. If he sensed how desperate she was, she feared he would run.

He wasn't in the office at the back. She started through the store, keeping an eye out for him. She was almost to the front when an employee asked if she needed help.

"I'm looking for Butch," she said, surprised that her voice sounded almost normal.

"He's on vacation and not expected back for a couple of weeks," the young man said.

Vacation? "It's urgent that I contact him. When did he leave?"

"I believe he planned to leave today."

"Could you give me his address? Maybe I can catch him if he hasn't left yet."

The young employee hesitated.

"Please. It's urgent."

"Well, I suppose it will be all right." He rattled off the address, and Frankie raced back the way she'd come.

Butch lived in a small house on the north side of town that, like most of Bozeman, had been completely remodeled. She wondered when and how much money it had cost. She prayed that he hadn't left yet and that he had been too scared to dip into the money.

As she parked on the street and got out, she noticed that the house looked deserted. The garage door was closed and there was a newspaper lying on the front step, unread. Her heart dropped to her feet as she walked toward the house, wondering what to do next.

That was when she heard a noise inside the house. As she approached the garage, she glanced into one of the small windows high on the door. Butch Clark was hurriedly packing for what looked like more than a two-week vacation.

HANK WATCHED DARREL, seeing him become more anxious and irritated with each passing hour. It hadn't been a surprise when the man had broken his word immediately, sending Trent after Frankie.

"Stay back. Don't let her spot you tailing her," Darrel had ordered. "She takes you to the money, you know what to do."

He'd felt his heart drop, afraid he knew exactly what Trent would do. All he could hope was that Frankie was as good at her job as he knew her to be and would spot the tail or be able to deal with Trent if she had to.

Darrel began pacing again. His pacing the cabin floor had turned out to be a godsend. He'd paid little attention to Hank as if he'd forgotten about him. Les had lain down on the bed and quickly gone to sleep.

Meanwhile, Hank had been working on the duct tape Trent had used to bind his wrists behind him to the chair. He'd found a rough spot on the wood where a screw was sticking out. He could feel the tape weakening as he sawed through layer after layer. It was tedious, but he had time, he kept telling himself. He had to be free when Frankie returned.

His head ached, but if he had a concussion it wasn't a bad one. The dizziness had passed and he was feeling stronger by the moment.

When Darrel's cell phone rang, the man practically

jumped out of his thin skin. Hank stopped what he was doing for a moment. He could hear the entire conversation at both ends since Trent was talking so loudly.

"What do you mean you lost her?" Darrel demanded.

"She was headed toward the north end of town but then suddenly veered off on a street. I stayed back like you said but then she was headed toward Main Street and she was gone."

Darrel swore. "You say she was headed toward the north side of town?"

"Yeah. I don't know why she suddenly—"

"She spotted a tail," he snapped. "Go back to the north side of town, where she was originally headed. Drive the streets until you find her. *Find her.*"

"Okay, I'll try, but—"

"Either you find her or you'd better keep going and hope I never find *you*. That clear enough for you?"

"I'll find her. I won't give up until I do."

J.J. WAS GETTING sick of lying in the back of the moving pickup under the tarps. He wasn't sure how much more of this he could take. But he had to know what Frankie was up to.

When she'd stopped the pickup the first time, she'd gotten out. He'd waited for a few moments and then taken a peek. He'd watched her go into the back of a hardware store before quickly covering up again. What was this about? None of it made any sense. She'd left the cowboy and gone shopping? Was it possible Hank Savage had known the man he'd picked up in the road? If so, then…

She'd come back sooner than he'd anticipated, the

pickup door opening, closing, the engine starting and the truck moving again. Maybe she'd had to pick up something. An ax? A shovel? He'd shuddered at the thought.

The truck didn't go far before he felt something change. Frankie had been driving at a normal pace when suddenly she took off, turning this way and that. He had to hang on now or be tossed around the back of the pickup like a rag doll. What was going on?

When she finally slowed down and quit turning, she seemed to be backtracking. He'd been listening to the sounds around him. They'd been in traffic but now it had grown quieter. She brought the pickup to a stop. He heard her exit the truck. He listened, afraid to take a peek yet. He definitely had the feeling that they were in a residential part of town. He could hear the sound of someone using a leaf blower some distance away.

When he couldn't take the suspense any longer, he carefully rose and pushed back the edge of the tarp aside to peer out. What he saw shocked him. Frankie had pulled a gun and was now about to open someone's garage door. But before she could, the door suddenly began to rise with the sound of the mechanical engine pulling it up.

He heard an engine start up in the garage and saw Frankie step in front of the idling car, the gun raised to windshield level. "Stop, Butch!"

The car engine revved. Whoever was behind the wheel had backed the vehicle into the garage. For a fast getaway? The fool either had a death wish or was playing his luck. Either way, J.J. could see that Frankie was in trouble. The driver didn't seem afraid of the gun she was holding.

He threw back the tarp and jumped down to run at her, shoving her out of the way as the car came screaming out of the garage. He had drawn his own gun, but when he saw that the fool behind the wheel wasn't going to stop, he threw himself onto the hood and crashed into the windshield.

The driver hit his brakes hard. J.J. groped for something to hang on to but, failing, slid to the concrete, coming down hard. As he started to get up, he heard the engine rev again. He saw Frankie had the passenger-side door open and was screaming for the man behind the wheel to get out of the car.

He rolled to the side, but not quick enough. The door had caught him in the back of the head and the lights went out.

Chapter Twenty-One

Butch rattled the handcuffs holding him restrained to the passenger-side door of his car. "How do I know you aren't going to kill me?" His voice squeaked—just as it had when she'd jumped into the car as he was trying to get away. She'd shoved the barrel of the gun into the side of his head and told him she was going to kill him if he didn't stop. He'd stopped.

"You don't." She'd grabbed the keys and forced him at gunpoint into the passenger seat to handcuff him to the door.

"Who was that back there?" Butch asked now as they drove away from his house.

"A cop." She glanced in the rearview mirror over the top of all Butch's belongings he'd loaded. So far no tail. Also no J.J. She'd checked for a pulse. He had still been breathing but wasn't conscious. She'd taken his cop gun. At least now she had real bullets and a vehicle that whoever Darrel had sent to follow her wouldn't know. Her tail would find the pickup at the house—if he found the house at all.

"*A cop?* You said you wouldn't go to the cops."

Frankie shook her head, keeping her attention on her

driving. "I wanted to keep you out of it, Butch. Unfortunately, I had no idea just how deep you really were in all this. You lied to me, but for your sake and mine, you'd better not be lying to me now."

"I'm not." He sounded whiny. She could see why Naomi had dumped him. But he must have been the closest thing she had to a friend she could confide in.

"Why didn't you tell Naomi to give the money back right away?" she asked.

"I did. She wouldn't listen. She really thought she could get away with it."

Frankie shot him a look. "Kind of like you."

"Hey, what could I have done? They didn't know about me. I didn't know them. Naomi was dead. I knew where the money was hidden. So I waited to see what happened. Nothing happened. Until you showed up."

"You could have gone to the cops," she snapped. And then none of this would be happening. Hank wouldn't be in serious trouble back at the cabin and she wouldn't be racing out of town with two guns, one actually loaded, with a man handcuffed to the car and only a hope and a prayer that he wasn't lying to her.

She glanced over at Butch. He looked scared. That, she decided, was good. "I have to ask. Why did you wait to get the money?"

He turned to look out his side window. They'd passed Gallatin Gateway and were almost to Big Sky and Cardwell Ranch, where he swore Naomi had buried the money. "I had this crazy idea that they were watching the place where she buried it, you know, just waiting for me to show up so they could kill me like they did her."

Frankie thought about telling him what Darrel had

said about Naomi's death. That was if he was telling the truth. Either way, Butch might have been able to save her—if he'd gone to the cops right away.

Nor did she point out that there was little chance Darrel would be watching the ranch 24/7 even if he knew where the money was buried.

She turned onto the dirt road into the ranch, her mind racing. What would she do when she found the money? Hank had been right. She couldn't trust Darrel to keep his word. He said she wouldn't be followed. A lie. Once she handed over the money...

As she drove into the ranch yard, Butch pointed in the direction of a stand of trees. The land dropped to a small creek. Frankie groaned inwardly. She just hoped that Naomi was smart enough to bury the money where the rising water didn't send it into the Gallatin River. It could be in the Gulf of Mexico by now otherwise.

"Tell me exactly where it is," she said as she brought the car to a stop at the edge of the incline to the creek.

"There's a statue or something, she said, near the water."

Frankie frowned. "A statue?" she asked as she looked down the hill and saw pine trees and a babbling brook but no statue.

"Maybe not a statue, but—"

"A birdbath," she said, spotting it in a stand of trees. She quickly put the keys in her pocket, opened the door and, grabbing the shovel she'd taken from his garage, got out. As she did, she glanced toward the house and saw no one. Maybe she would get lucky. She needed some luck right now.

It was a short walk down to a stand of trees on a

rise above the creek. Someone had put a birdbath down here. Near it were two benches as if someone in the family came down here to watch the birds beside the river. Dana? She couldn't see the marshal sitting here patiently.

The birdbath, apparently made of solid concrete, proved to be heavier than it looked. She could have used Butch, but she didn't trust the man. She tried dislodging it and inching it over out of the way, wasting valuable minutes.

Finally, she just knocked it over, which took all her strength as it was. Then she began to dig. She wondered how Naomi had managed moving the birdbath and realized it had probably been her idea, the benches and the birdbath—after she'd buried the rest of the money.

The bag wasn't buried deep. Frankie pulled it out, sweating with the effort and the constant fear of what might be happening back at the cabin. The bag looked like one used by banks. It was large and heavy. She opened it just enough to see that it was stuffed with money, lots of money in large bills, and quickly closed it.

Leaving the shovel, she climbed back up the incline. As she topped it, she saw Dana standing by the side of the car.

WHEN J.J. CAME TO, he was lying on the grass with a monstrous headache. His gun was gone. So was Frankie and the car and its driver. All she'd left behind was the cowboy's pickup.

J.J. limped into the house through the open garage door. The house felt deserted. He was moving painfully through the living room when he thought he heard a car door slam. Was it possible Frankie had come back? He couldn't believe she'd left him passed out on the concrete and hadn't even called an ambulance. But she'd managed to take his gun.

He pressed himself against a wall out of sight of the hallway as he heard footfalls in the garage. One person moving slowly, no doubt looking for him. Why had Frankie come back now? It didn't matter. He was ready for her.

He smiled to himself as he waited to pounce. She wouldn't know what hit her.

As a figure came around the corner, he lunged. He didn't realize his mistake until it was too late. The figure spun as if sensing him coming and caught him square in the face with his fist. As he took the blow, he realized that the figure was way too large to be Frankie, way too powerful and way too male.

"Who the hell are you?" he heard the man say as he crashed on the floor at the man's feet. Before he could answer, he heard the man pump a bullet into his gun. He rolled over, struggling to pull out his badge, when he heard the first shot echo through the room. The burn of the bullet searing through his flesh came an instant later.

He tried to get up, tried to get his badge out. The second shot hit him in the chest and knocked him back to the floor. As the big man moved closer, J.J. saw that it was the tough guy who'd searched the pickup earlier at the cabin.

"You've really screwed up now," J.J. managed to say as he felt his life's blood seeping from him. "You just killed a cop."

"I'D LIKE TO tell you that this isn't what it looks like," Frankie said as she approached Dana. She saw that the woman had her cell phone clutched in her hand and knew at once that she'd already called the marshal.

"I thought you and Hank had gone back to Idaho," Dana said. Her voice trembled as her gaze took in the weapon Frankie had stuck in the waist of her jeans. Her shirt and jacket had come up during her battle with the birdbath.

"How long before Hud gets here?" Frankie asked.

"Where's Hank?" the older woman asked. She sounded as scared as Frankie felt.

"He's in trouble. I need to get back to him, Dana. I'm a private investigator. It's too long a story to get into right now. I need to leave before Hud gets here."

Dana shook her head, tears in her eyes. "I knew something was wrong. But I hoped…" Inside the car, Butch began to yell for Dana to help him. "That man is handcuffed and you have a…gun."

Frankie knew she couldn't stand here arguing. She started past Dana when she heard the sound of a siren. Moments later she saw the flashing lights as the SUV topped a rise and came blaring into the ranch yard.

She let out a shaky breath and felt tears burn her eyes. There was still time before sundown. But that would mean talking her way out of this, and right now, covered in mud, holding a bag of even dirtier drug money, she wasn't sure she had the words. All she knew was that she had to convince the marshal before sundown.

HUD SHUT OFF the siren. As he climbed out, he took in the scene. The man handcuffed in the car tried to slide down out of sight. Dana stepped to Hud, and he put his arm around her before he turned his attention to the young woman his son had fallen in love with. "Frankie?"

She held out the bag. "It's the drug money. They have Hank. If I don't give the money to them by sundown…" Her voice broke.

He nodded and stepped to her to take the money. "And that?" he asked, tilting his head toward the man in the car.

"It's Butch Clark, Naomi's old boyfriend. He's known where the money was buried all these years."

Hud nodded and glanced at his watch. "We have a little time. Whatever's happened, we will deal with it. You say they have Hank." She nodded. "Tell me everything," he said as he walked her toward the house.

"What about him?" Dana asked behind them.

"He's fine where he is for the time being," Hud said without a backward glance. Inside the house, Frankie quickly cleaned up at the kitchen sink as she told him about the man stumbling out onto the highway, being taken to the cabin, the demand for the money and Hank being injured.

Dana gasped at that point, her eyes filling with tears, but she held it together. Hud had to hand it to her—she was a strong woman and always had been. Her son was injured and being held by drug dealers. It scared the hell out of him, but Dana fortunately wasn't one to panic in a crisis. He appreciated that right now.

"Okay," he said when Frankie finished. "You say Darrel gave you an unloaded gun." He picked up the Glock he'd taken from her. "This one is loaded."

She nodded. "J.J. must have followed us. He was hiding in the back of the pickup. He tried to stop Butch when Butch was attempting to flee. He was hit by the car, but he was alive the last time I saw him."

Hud studied the woman, amazed by her resilience as well as her bravery. "You don't think Darrel will let the two of you go when you take him the money, right?"

She shook her head. "He doesn't want to kill us, but…"

"What will you do?" Dana asked her husband.

"The first thing is read Butch Clark his rights and get him locked up in my jail so he's not a problem." Hud pulled out his phone and called a deputy to come handle it. As he hung up, he looked at Frankie. "I need to take you back to Hank's pickup. There's time before sundown. Then you drive back to the cabin with the bag of money."

"Where will you be?" Dana asked.

"In the back of the pickup. I'll need to grab a few things and have Bozeman backup standing by." He got to his feet. "Let's go get Hank."

HANK WATCHED DARREL pace the cabin floor and worked surreptitiously at the thick tape binding his wrists behind him to the chair. He'd made a point of acting like he was still dizzy and weak from the blow, mumbling to himself incoherently until Darrel had removed the duct tape.

"Water," Hank had mouthed. "Please."

Darrel had gotten him some, holding it to his lips so he could take a few gulps. "She'll be back," Hank said when he took the water away. "With the money." And that was the part that terrified him the most, because he had no doubt that his former classmate would go back on his word. No way were he and Frankie walking out of here alive. "She does what she says she's going to do."

Darrel had started pacing again. Hank saw him looking out the window where the sun was dropping toward the horizon at a pace that had them both worried. Now the man turned to look at him and laughed. "You sure about that? If I were her, I'd take the money and go as far away from here as I possibly could."

"That's you. Frankie isn't like that." But right now, he wished she was. At least she would be safe. He'd gotten her into this. He deserved what he got. But Frankie… He couldn't bear to think of her being hurt, let alone—

"You'd better be right." Darrel sounded sad, as if he would be sorry for killing him. "I hate the way this whole thing spiraled out of control, and all because of that girlfriend of yours."

Hank couldn't argue with that. "I fell in love with a woman I didn't know. She hid so much from me, including stealing your money."

"And you think you know this one?" Darrel scoffed at that. "All women are alike. You really haven't learned anything since high school, have you. They will double-cross you every time. I knew this one—" He stopped talking to turn and look out the window again. He'd heard what Hank had.

The sound of his pickup's engine could be heard as the truck approached the cabin. Frankie had come back with the money. And before sundown.

"I've got to hand it to you, Hank. This woman really is something. If she's got the money, then I'd say this one is a keeper."

"Keep your promise. Let us go. We want nothing to do with any of this and you know it."

"Yeah, I hear you," Darrel said, actually sounding as if he regretted what was going to happen next. "We're going to have to talk about that." He stepped over to the bed and kicked the end of it. Les stirred from a deep sleep. "Wake up. We've got company. Go out and make sure she's alone."

"Me? Why do I have to—"

Darrel cuffed the man on the head. "Go!"

Les stumbled from the bed, clearly still half-asleep, and headed for the door. Darrel stood at the window, his back to him. Hank worked feverishly at the tape. Just a little more. He felt it give.

FRANKIE DID AS Hud had told her and parked next to the panel van, out of sight of the cabin. She stayed in the pickup, sitting behind the wheel, after she'd turned off the engine, waiting.

She desperately wanted to see Hank. She had to know that he was all right. But the marshal had assured her—Hank was safer if they did things his way.

She wasn't going to argue. She was thankful that she wasn't facing this completely alone. Because she had a bad feeling that once she got out of the pickup with the money, both she and Hank were as good as dead.

Les frowned as he saw where she was parking. He walked around the front of the vehicles to stop in front of the pickup. "Get out!" he ordered, still frowning. He looked as if he'd just woken up, which made her heart race. What had Darrel done with Hank after she'd left that he'd let Les sleep?

When she didn't get out, he stepped up to try the door and, finding it locked, glanced back at the cabin before he began to fumble for his gun. That was when Hud rose and coldcocked him with the butt end of a shotgun. The man dropped between the pickup and panel van without a sound.

As the marshal hopped down out of sight of the cabin windows, Frankie opened her door.

"Leave the bag with the money here," Hud said as he cuffed and gagged Les before rolling his body under the pickup. "Go into the cabin to check on Hank. When Darrel asks, tell him that Les took it from you. I need to know how many men are in there."

She nodded and whispered, "Trent was following me. I don't see his vehicle, so I don't think he's back yet. It should just be Darrel."

"Let's hope," Hud said and motioned for her to go before Darrel got suspicious.

Frankie headed for the cabin, praying with each step that Hank was all right. As she pushed open the door, the first thing she saw was Darrel. He had a gun in his hand, pointed at her heart. Her gaze leaped past him to Hank. She saw pleasure flash in his blue eyes at seeing her, then concern. He was still in the chair, but he seemed to feel better than the last time she'd seen him.

"Where's my money?" Darrel demanded, already sounding furious as if he'd worked himself up in the time she'd been gone. The door was open behind her, but he was blocking her from going to Hank.

"Les has it. He took it from me." She could see that

he didn't believe her. She described the bag. "I didn't touch the money, but the bag is heavy, and when I looked inside… I think all but the five grand she used for a down payment on the house is in there. Or at least enough to get you out of hot water. Now let us go."

Darrel shook his head, still blocking her from going to Hank, and yelled, "Les!" Not hearing an answer, he yelled again. "Bring the money in here."

She looked past him and saw Hank slowly pull his wrists free from behind him. He shook them out as if he'd lost all feeling in his arms after all this time of being taped to the chair. She gave a small shake of her head for him not to move.

"Les is probably out there counting the money," Frankie said, hoping the man would step outside, where the marshal was waiting. "Or has already taken off with the bag."

"On foot?" Darrel demanded and grabbed her as they both heard the scrape of chair legs on the floor.

HANK MOVED QUICKLY. Darrel was right about one thing. He'd always been better at sports than his classmate. Fortunately, that athletic prowess benefited him now when he needed it the most.

As Darrel turned, there was a moment of surprise, a hesitation that cost him. He was about to put the barrel of the gun to Frankie's head when Hank hit him in the side of his head with his fist and grabbed the gun. Darrel staggered from the blow but didn't go down. His grip on Frankie seemed to be the only thing holding him up.

Hank twisted the gun from the man's hand. The two grappled with it for a moment before Darrel let out a cry of pain. Frankie shoved him off her and pulled the Glock from behind her to point it at the drug dealer as he went down. She looked over at Hank, who stood beside her, the gun in his hand pointed at Darrel's heart as well.

Behind them Frankie heard the marshal say, "Well, look at the two of you. It appears you didn't even need my help." There was a smile in his voice as well as relief as he reached for his phone to let the cops know that he'd take that backup now. "I have two perps who need to be taken to jail. Also going to need a medic as well," he said, looking at the dried blood on his son's temple. "And I'm going to need a ride back to Big Sky."

"We could have given you a ride," Hank said after his father cuffed Darrel and read him his rights. Frankie could hear sirens in the distance. She leaned against Hank, his arm around her. She told herself that all she needed was a hot shower and she'd stop shaking.

"I thought you two might like some time together. But I guess you know this means you can't leave for Idaho for a while," the marshal said.

Hank glanced at her. "I think we're good with that."

FRANKIE HELPED HERSELF to another stack of silver-dollar-sized pancakes, slathered on butter and then drowned them in chokecherry syrup. She couldn't remember ever being this hungry.

So much had happened and in such a short time. She would have worried about that before Hank. She was no longer worried about it happening too fast. Instead, she was ready for the future in a way she'd never been before. She felt free, everything looking brighter, even before she'd heard the news about J.J.

Trent had been arrested and confessed everything, including killing the cop. He'd said it was self-defense, that J.J. had been reaching for his gun. But the Glock hadn't been found on the cop—or at the scene—because Frankie had taken it.

After hearing what all the cops had against him, including assaulting Hank and dealing drugs, along with killing an unarmed cop, Trent decided to make a deal for a lesser sentence for what he knew about the drug ring and Darrel's part in it.

Frankie could feel Dana watching her eat and smiling. "So you're a private investigator," she said. "Sounds dangerous. I was thinking that if you were to get married and have babies…"

Swallowing the bite in her mouth, Frankie grinned at her. "Hank hasn't asked me to marry him and you're talking babies."

"He'll ask. I've never seen my son happier."

Frankie thought about the hot shower she'd stepped into last night after they'd returned to their cabin. Hank had joined her, sans his clothes this time. Their lovemaking had been so passionate under the warm spray that she felt her cheeks heat at the memory even now.

"He makes me happy too," she said and took another bite of pancake.

"I can tell," Dana said with a secret smile. "You're glowing this morning. If it wasn't too early, I'd think you were pregnant."

Frankie almost choked on her bite of pancake. True,

last night in the shower they hadn't used protection, but pregnant? She swallowed.

"Would that be so awful?" Dana asked.

She thought about it for one whole instant and smiled. "Not at all." The thought of her child growing up on this ranch made her happy. She and Hank had talked about the future last night after their shower. He'd asked how she'd feel about living on the ranch, if she would still want to work as a private investigator, if she wanted children, how she felt about dogs and cats and horses.

She'd laughed as she'd listened to his questions and grinned. "I'd love living on this ranch, I'd probably want to be involved in ranching with you rather than continue working as an investigator, I do want children, and I love dogs, cats and horses. After that horseback ride with you, I'm hooked."

"Was it the horseback ride or me that got you hooked?" he'd asked with a grin.

"By the way, where *is* my son?" Dana asked, interrupting her thoughts.

Frankie helped herself to a slice of ham and just a couple more pancakes. "He went to say goodbye to Naomi."

HANK PARKED IN the pines beside the Gallatin River as he'd done so many times before. This time he was anxious to reach the water. He climbed out and wound his way through the tall pines. A breeze swayed the tops of the boughs, whispering. The sound of the river grew louder. He could feel the sun as it fingered its way through the pines. He breathed in the scent of pine and water as if smelling it for the first time.

Ahead, he got his first glimpse of the cliff. It was dark and ominous-looking, shadowed this morning until the sun rose high enough to turn it a golden hue.

It seemed strange to make this trek after everything that had happened. He wasn't sure he could ever forgive Naomi for what she did. He and Frankie had almost gotten killed because of a bag full of money. He still couldn't believe that she'd died protecting it.

He broke out of the pines and stood for a moment at the edge of the trees. The breeze was stronger here. It rippled the moving surface of the river and ruffled his hair at his neck. He took off his Stetson and turned his face up to the breeze, letting it do what it would with his normally tousled dark hair. He couldn't help but think of Frankie's fingers in the wet strands last night as she pulled him down to her mouth. The memory of the two of them laughing and making love in the shower made him smile for a moment before he dropped down to the edge of the river.

He listened to the gentle roar of the water as it rushed over the rocks and pooled at his feet. The breeze lifted his hair as he looked up. The ledge was a dark line cut across the rock surface. For three years it had lured him back here, looking for answers. Now he knew it all.

He thought of Naomi standing on that ledge that night with Tamara. He'd always thought of her as helpless, defenseless, fragile and delicate. He'd always felt he had to protect her—even her memory. He could almost see her teetering on that ledge. Would they have let her live if she'd given them the money? They would never know. But he knew now that she was willing to die rather than give it up.

Hank hated what that said about her. He thought of her mother working all those years to support herself and her daughter. Was that what had made Naomi think she had to steal? Or was it a sickness that had started with shoplifting and had gotten away from her?

Naomi's mother had made a life for herself with a man who loved her. Lillian would survive this since he suspected she knew her daughter much better than he ever had.

He waited to feel Naomi's spirit, to see a ghostly flash of her. He expected to feel her presence as he had so many times before. He'd always thought she was waiting here for him, pleading with him to find her killer.

Now he felt nothing but the summer breeze coming off the cool surface of the river. He stared at the ledge through the sunlight, but felt nothing. Naomi was gone—if she'd ever really been here.

As he settled his Stetson back on his head, he realized it was true. Naomi's ghost had been banished for good. He felt lighter. Freer. The cliff no longer held him prisoner. Neither did Naomi.

"Goodbye," he said, glancing once more at the cliff before he started back to the pickup. He realized that he could walk away without ever looking back, without ever coming back. It felt good. *He* felt good. He couldn't wait to get to Frankie. They were leaving today, but they would return.

He drove toward the ranch, excited about life for the first time in three years. He couldn't wait to see Frankie. But first there was something he had to do.

HUD LOOKED UP to find his son standing in the doorway of his office. "Is everything all right?" he asked, immediately concerned. Hank had an odd look on his face.

"I need to ask a favor."

He and Hank hadn't talked much since everything had happened. His son's statement about what had transpired at the cabin had filled in a lot of the blanks. He'd wondered how Hank had taken the news about Naomi and if he would finally be able to put the past behind him—with Frankie's help.

"Name it. If there's something I can do…"

Hank came into his office and closed the door behind him. His son seemed nervous. That, he realized, was what he'd been picking up on the moment he saw him standing in the doorway. He'd never seen him nervous. Angry, yes. But not like this. He realized that whatever his son had to ask him, it was serious.

"When I asked you for Grandmother's ring—"

Hud swore. He'd forgotten the day that his son had come to him and asked for his grandmother's ring. Since he was a little boy, Hank had been told that his grandmother Cardwell's ring would go to Mary, but that his grandmother Savage's ring was his for the day that he met the love of his life and asked her to marry him.

But when Hank had asked for it, saying he was going to marry Naomi no matter what anyone thought because they were all wrong about her, Hud had turned him down.

"I'm sorry, son. I can't let you give Naomi the ring." He and Dana had discussed it numerous times in the days before Hank had come to him. They'd seen that

Naomi was pushing marriage and could tell that their son wasn't ready. Add to that Naomi's…problems, as Dana referred to them.

"She's a thief," Hud had said. "Not just that. You know she's pressing Hank to leave the ranch to work for her stepfather."

"Maybe it's what he wants."

Hud remembered being so angry with his wife that he'd gotten out of bed and pulled on his jeans, had left. He and Dana seldom argued. But that night he hadn't been able to take any more. He'd driven up to Hebgen Lake to see his father, Brick, an old-time lawman. Hud had named one of his twin son's after his father; the other one after Dana's father, Angus.

He and his father had often been at odds, and yet that night, the old lawman was who he'd gone to for help. It was the same year that Brick had passed away. He remembered waking him up that night. Why he chose his father was a mystery since the two of them had spent years at odds.

But Brick had given him good advice. "Stick to your guns. He's your son. You know him. He won't love you for it. Quite the contrary." He'd seen the gleam in his old man's eyes and known that he was talking about the two of them and the years they'd spent knocking heads. "You're doing him a real disservice if you just give in to keep the peace."

He'd stayed the night, driven back the next morning and told Dana that he wasn't giving Hank the ring if he asked for it again. She'd been furious with him, but he'd stuck to his guns, even though it had cost him dearly both with his wife and his son. He'd never known if Hank would have married Naomi anyway if she'd lived.

"When you'd asked for my mother's ring, I thought you were making a mistake," Hud said now. "I didn't want you giving the ring to the wrong woman and later regretting it when you met the love of your life."

Hank shook his head. "It was your decision since my grandmother apparently put you in charge of it."

"Actually, it was your grandpa Brick," he said.

"Did he also advise you to not give it to me?" Hank asked.

Hud wanted to be as honest with him as possible. "Your mother and I argued about it. I had to leave, so I drove up to your grandfather's place and asked him what I should do."

Hank's eyes widened. "You actually asked your father for advice?"

"It happens," Hud said and smiled. "Admittedly, it took years before I found myself doing that."

With a grin, his son said, "It's hard for me to admit that you were right."

"I understand."

"But I'm back. I want to give Grandmother's ring to Frankie, and I'm not taking no for an answer this time. Rightfully, it's my ring to do—"

"I totally agree." Hud reached into the drawer where he'd put the ring after meeting Frankie.

"You have it here?"

"I had a feeling you'd want it," he said.

Hank shook his head as he took the small velvet box. "I will never understand you."

"Probably not." He watched his son lift the tiny lid

and saw Hank's eyes light up as he stared down at the diamond engagement ring.

"Do you think she'll like it?" The nervousness was back.

"She'll love it because she loves you."

FALL WAS IN the air that late day in August. The seasons changed at will in Montana and even more so in the canyon so close to the mountains. One day would feel like summer, the next fall, and in the blink of an eye snow would begin.

Dried leaves rustled on the aspens as Frankie rode her horse out of the pines and into the wide meadow. She breathed in the crisp, clean air, reined in her horse and dismounted at the edge of the mountain to wait for Hank. He'd been acting strange all day. She knew it had to be because they would be leaving here—at least temporarily.

Last night they'd lain in bed, wrapped up in each other after making love, and talked about the future.

"Are you sure you'd be happy at the ranch? Because if not, we could—"

She'd kissed him to stop the words. "Hank, I love the ranch. I can't imagine living anywhere more…magical."

He'd eyed her suspiciously. "You aren't just saying that because you're crazy in love with me."

"I am crazy in love with you, but no, I wouldn't lie to you." He'd told her that the ghost of Naomi was gone, but she wondered. He still thought that because Naomi could never be happy at the ranch, neither could any other woman. She knew it would take time for him to realize that she was nothing like Naomi.

"Look at your mother, Hank. She loves this ranch just like her mother did. Isn't that why your grandmother left it to her, passing on the legacy? And all the women your uncles are married to. They're all happy living here," she continued. "Isn't it possible I'm more like your mother than…?" She wouldn't say "Naomi." "Than some other woman might be?"

He'd nodded and smiled as he kissed her. "I feel so lucky. I keep wanting to pinch myself. I guess that's why it's so hard for me to believe this is real. I never dreamed…" He kissed her again. "That I could be this happy."

Now, as he rode up beside her, his Stetson hiding much of his handsome face, she felt almost afraid. He'd been so quiet all morning and it wasn't like him to hang back on his horse the way he had. As she watched him slowly ride toward her, her heart fluttered. She was crazy in love with this man, just as she had told him. And yet maybe this was too fast for both of them.

She thought of J.J. and quickly pushed it away. Hank wasn't J.J. Whatever was going on with Hank—

At a sound in the pines, she looked past Hank to see Hud and Dana come riding out of the trees. Behind them were Mary and Chase, and behind them were Stacy and the rest of the family.

Frankie blinked. "What?"

Hank looked up and grinned. "I am terrible at keeping secrets, and this one was killing me this morning," he said as he dismounted and took her in his arms. "I hope you don't mind."

Mind that he'd invited his entire family on their horseback ride? She felt confused, and yet as everyone rode toward them, they were all smiling. One of the uncles brought up the rear with a huge bunch of helium balloons.

"Hank?" she asked. He only hugged her tightly. She could see the emotion in his face and felt her heart take off like a wild horse in a thunderstorm. "Hank?" she repeated as they all began to dismount. His uncle was handing out the balloons. "I think you'd better tell me what's going on."

The family had formed a circle around them and seemed to be waiting, just like Frankie. Hank turned to her, taking both of her hands in his.

"I know this is fast, but if I've learned anything, it's that when things are right, they're right," Hank said and cleared his voice. "You are the most amazing woman I've ever met. You're smart, talented, independent to a fault, stubborn as the day is long, courageous—way too courageous, I might add—determined and…beautiful and loving and everything I could want in one unique woman."

She tried to swallow around the lump in her throat. "Thank you, I think."

A murmur of laughter rose from the group gathered.

"You saved my life in so many ways," Hank continued. "I can never thank you enough for that. And you've brought just joy to my life when I never thought I'd ever feel again. Frankie…" He seemed at a loss for words.

"Come on. Get on with it," someone yelled at the back of the group, followed by another burst of laughter.

Hank laughed with them. "They all know that I'm like my father, a man of few words." Yet another burst of laughter. "But if I forget to tell you all of these things in the future, I wanted to be sure and say them today. I love you, Francesca 'Frankie' Brewster, with all my heart."

She watched him drop to one knee to the applause of the group.

He looked up at her, his blue eyes filled with love. She felt her own eyes fill with tears as he asked, "Will you do me the honor of marrying me?"

The tears overflowed and cascaded down her cheeks as she nodded, overwhelmed by all of this.

He reached into his pocket and pulled out a small velvet box. "This ring was my grandmother Savage's." He took it out, held her left hand and slipped it on her finger.

She gazed down at it. "It's beautiful," she said as he got to his feet. Looking into his handsome face, she whispered, "I love you," and threw her arms around him.

As the two of them turned, his family let out a cheer and released the balloons. Frankie looked up toward the heavens as dozens of colorful balloons took flight up into Montana's big sky. She'd never seen a more beautiful sight because of what they all represented.

Hank hugged her and then everyone else was hugging her, the meadow full of love and congratulations. "This is only the beginning," he said with a laugh. "You always wanted a big family. Well, you're going to have one now."

"I never dreamed..." she said and couldn't finish. How could she have dreamed that one day she'd meet a cowboy and he'd take her home and give her a family?

* * * * *

THE STRANGER
NEXT DOOR

DEBRA WEBB

This book is dedicated to my brothers and sister.
Thanks for being my family!

Chapter One

Winchester, Tennessee
Friday, August 2

Murderer. Cecelia Winters stared at the ugly word scrawled in red paint across the white front door. She glanced back at the taxi that was already speeding away down the dusty road. She sighed, dropped her backpack onto the porch.

Her brother Levi was supposed to have picked her up at the prison when she was released. Evidently something had held him up. She went up on her tiptoes but still could not reach the ledge above the door. Surveying the porch, she decided a chair would work for what she needed. The two ladder-back chairs and the swing had been a part of her grandmother's front porch for as long as Cecelia could remember. The wicker plant stand that stood between the chairs was empty and in serious need of painting. Tiny flakes of faded white paint lay on the floor around it.

"Falling apart like everything else around here," she grumbled as she dragged the chair to the door and climbed atop it.

The key lay on the dusty ledge just as it always had.

It would be a flat-out miracle if the house hadn't been vandalized and cleaned out of anything worth taking. But Cece, as she had always been called, wasn't complaining. Her grandmother had left her this old house with the ten acres that surrounded it. The walls were still standing and the roof appeared in reasonably good condition. Anything over and above that would be icing on the cake. Cece was enormously thankful to have a place to stay at all. What was left of her family had turned their backs on her a long time ago.

Except for her grandmother, her momma's momma. She had never believed the lies. And Cece's little brother—at least, she had thought her brother had not turned on her. He had not shown up to pick her up when she was released so she could not be certain. Last month he had visited her at the prison. He had seemed fine and, frankly, over the moon that she would soon be free.

No one was happier about that than Cece. She had served her time.

She stared at the red letters of the word painted on the door once more before opening it and stepping inside. No matter that it was barely two in the afternoon, gloom filled the house that had always been Cece's refuge growing up. The shades, she realized. Moving from window to window, she tugged gently on the old roller-style shades, causing each one to slide upward and allowing sunlight into the house. Dust floated in the air, filtering through the rays of light like a thousand miniscule snowflakes in an old snow globe with yellowed glass.

Emily Broward had died one year ago. The house had sat empty, awaiting its new owner's release from prison. Levi had sworn he had checked in on things from time to time but Cece could not be sure he had done so. The house was neat and clean—other than the dust—so she supposed he had dropped by on occasion. Her grandmother had been an immaculate housekeeper, so the neatness wasn't surprising and likely had nothing to do with Levi's drive-bys.

The house was small. A living room, eat-in kitchen, two bedrooms and a bath. There was an attic and a tiny brick-walled and stone-floored basement that was more a root cellar than anything else. The house was plenty roomy enough, her grandmother had always said. The furniture was the same as Cece remembered from her childhood. Emily Broward had been far too frugal to spend money on new furniture when what she had remained serviceable.

Which, Cece imagined, was how she had hung on to what was left of this small family farm for nearly half a century. Emily's one and only child, a daughter and Cece's mother, had died more than twenty years ago. So the place now belonged to Cece. In truth, if not for this house, she would never have come back to the Winchester area. She had sworn she wouldn't be back. Ever.

But here she was.

Really, what else could she do? She had nothing but the clothes on her back and the backpack she'd had with her when she'd been arrested nearly nine years ago. She had nothing. No money. No job. No family—unless you counted her no-show younger brother, the sole sibling who hadn't disowned her.

Still, there was the matter of the truth. No matter that she had told herself a thousand times that she did not care, she did. Somewhere in this town, someone knew the truth and she wanted to find it. To prove she was not a cold-blooded murderer. To show whoever cared that she was the good girl her grandmother Emily always believed her to be.

Pushing away the overwhelming and painful thoughts, Cece decided what she needed at this moment was paint. Didn't matter what color. Anything to smear over the ugly word slashed across the front door.

Paint and tools were in the old smokehouse. Her grandmother had stopped using the smokehouse for its original purpose years ago, after Cece's grandfather passed away. She had turned it into a gardening shed. Flower and vegetable gardening had been Emily's favorite thing in the world.

Cece headed out the back door. The smaller rear porch was a little less stable than the front. South facing, it weathered the harshest elements. She would need to have a closer look at its condition soon. Her grandmother had been one of those women who refused to be helpless in any way. She had learned how to wield a hammer and a shotgun with equal skill. Cece would just have to do the same since she had no resources.

But first, she would need a job.

She opened the door to the smokehouse and peered into the dark interior. She shuddered, wondered if her grandmother's shotgun was still in the same place. Probably in her closet or under the bed. Deep breath. She stepped inside, reaching overhead for the string that would turn on the light. Her fingers found it and she pulled. The bare bulb glared to life, spilling light over the dusty, cobweb-infested space.

It took some doing but she found an old bucket of white paint. When she had opened it, removed a hard skin from over the top and vigorously stirred the contents, it appeared to be enough for her purposes. Hopefully.

With a serviceable brush rounded up, she turned off the light and closed up the smokehouse. There was a good deal of cleanup she needed to do. Someone had been keeping the yard cut, which was a really good thing. Augusts were generally as hot as Hades and rain was typically scarce. Snakes would be actively searching for water sources. About the only thing she disliked more than snakes were spiders. Banishing the idea of creepy, crawly things, Cece scrubbed a coat of paint over the graffiti. It would take several coats to cover the red, or maybe she would have to pick up a stain-blocking product to help make the glaring reality go away.

You need money for that, Cece.

After cleaning the brush and pressing the lid back onto the paint can, she decided to have a look in the bedroom she had used before ending up in prison. She left the front door ajar with its wet paint and headed that way. Her father had kicked her out of the house when she was sixteen. At the time she had been only too happy to go. She wouldn't have stayed that long if not for her younger sister. She had worried about Sierra, who was four years younger, but she had learned the hard way that her little sister was quite capable of taking care of herself.

Her grandmother had warned her, but Cece had not wanted to see it. Sierra had turned into a selfish, belligerent teenager. As a little kid she had looked up to Cece. Hung onto her hand every chance she got. Crawled into bed with her when she was scared. They had both been so young when their mother died, but especially Sierra. She had only been two years old. Cece had tried to be more than just a big sister. Fat lot of good it had done her.

Sierra and Marcus, their older brother, were fanatical just like their father had been. According to Levi, Marcus had taken over her father's church—cult was a better description. And Sierra was his right hand.

Another reason Cece would rather have been anywhere than here.

Regardless of how she pretended, she could not leave. Not until she found the truth. In the final letter she had received from her grandmother before Emily passed away, she had told Cece that her trusted attorney, Clarence Frasier, had hired a private investigator to help find the truth.

Unfortunately Frasier had died two months ago without passing along any new developments in the investigation. His partner had sent her a letter saying he would not be able to pursue her case or represent her. Her file was available for pickup should she choose to do so. Additionally, in his letter, he had confirmed her fears about the private investigator's inability to find anything new.

Probably she would pick up the files in a day or two. For now, she just wanted to be alone and enjoy being outside those gray prison walls. A nice hot bath or shower in private was very high on her list. Planning her own menu and picking out what she would wear. No one realized how important all those little decisions were until the right to make them was taken away.

The clothes she had owned before she was arrested still hung in the closet. Underthings and pajamas were neatly folded in drawers—her grandmother's doing, no doubt. Cece had never been that organized. Her heart squeezed at the memory of how she had begged to be allowed to visit her grandmother in the hospital those final days of her life and, when Emily was gone, to be able to attend her funeral. Cece's persistence had landed her in isolation for a week.

She would visit the cemetery soon. Take flowers, as soon as she had money to purchase something nice.

At the dresser, she hesitated before turning away. A framed photo of her mother and her grandmother from twenty-five years ago captured her attention. Cece had the same curly red hair as her mother and her grandmother. She was the only one in the family to inherit the red hair and green eyes. Marcus and Levi had dark brown hair with brown eyes, like their father. Sierra's hair was even darker, as were her eyes. Her coloring was a fact Cece's father had held against her. He had sworn her red hair was the mark of the devil. She remembered him telling her mother the same thing. Her mother had died when Cece was six years old but she remembered those cruel words.

Her father had been a mean man, and harsh, hurtful words and actions were the only memories Cece had of him. She hoped he was burning in hell.

Her grandmother would pat her on the hand and assure her he was, indeed, roasting in hell. She had hated Mason Winters. Her daughter's—her only child's—marriage to him had broken her heart.

Cece shook off the painful memories. There was a lot she needed to do. Starting with stocking the kitchen. Though food wasn't exactly a priority for her, she had to eat. The attorney had said in his letter that a credit of five hundred dollars awaited her at the market in town. Frasier's doing, no doubt. He had felt sorry for Cece and had adored her grandmother. Cece had often wondered if he had been in love with her grandmother. He had certainly seemed to be. He had been a widower, she a widow, but to Cece's knowledge their relationship had never been anything other than friendship.

Cece closed the front door and locked it. She tucked the key into the pocket of her jeans and went to the kitchen to see if her grandmother had still kept her truck keys in the drawer by the back door. She pulled the drawer open and there they were. She snatched up the keys and headed out to the side of the barn her grandparents had used as a garage. She raised the crossbar and the double doors swung open. She climbed into the blue truck that was twice as old as she was and inserted the key.

She said a quick prayer in hopes that Levi had done as he had promised and kept the truck in running order. Her grandparents had maintained it in immaculate condition, but after Emily's death the battery would have died if the truck wasn't started regularly, driven around a bit. Levi had promised to drive it once a week until Cece came home.

Holding her breath, she turned the key and pumped the accelerator.

The engine purred to life as if she had just driven the vehicle off the showroom floor.

Relieved, she slid the gearshift into Reverse and backed out of the garage. Her grandmother had taught her to close the garage doors whenever she took the truck anywhere. No one who passed would realize she was gone as long as those doors were closed. Even in a small town, run-of-the-mill thieves could be found.

Far worse could be found, as well. The really bad ones just knew how to hide better than the others.

THE DRIVE TO Ollie's in Winchester took scarcely twenty minutes. The first few miles were easy. Driving was like riding a bike, her grandmother had said in her letters. You won't forget how whether you haven't driven for eight years or eighty. She had been right about that part.

But the traffic—even in a small town—had Cece's heart pounding, her fingers gripping the steering wheel and sweat beading on her forehead. The fact that it was ninety-five degrees did not help. The old truck didn't have any climate control features. Her grandfather had insisted the windows were control enough. *You either let the climate in or you do not,* he would say.

All the noise—from the many different sounds blowing in through her window to the other vehicles on the road—had Cece on edge, as well. Not that she was complaining. It would just take some getting used to.

Cece did not breathe easy until she had braked to a stop in the lot at the market and thrust the gearshift into Park. For good measure, she engaged the emergency brake before climbing out. She pocketed the keys but didn't bother locking the doors since there was nothing in the truck worth stealing. The bench seat was a little on the worn side and the rubber-coated floorboards had never been covered with mats as far as she recalled. Just a plain old truck. No rust or dents but very basic. The automatic transmission was the one upgrade, and that had been added only because her grandmother pitched a fit about it back when her grandfather decided to buy a truck.

The asphalt steamed as she crossed to the store entrance. With only a handful of cars in the lot, she was hopeful that she wouldn't run into anyone who remembered her. Eight years was a long time. If she were lucky most folks would have forgotten her by now.

Yeah, right. Like people forgot when a girl was charged with murdering her father.

She would never live that down—no matter that she was innocent.

Her fingers curled around the handle of the shopping cart and she started with the aisle closest to the entrance. The store looked different now. At some point over the years it had been remodeled and she had no clue where anything was anymore, but she would leave empty-handed before she asked for help and drew attention to herself.

Mostly she only needed the basics. Bread, milk, cheese, eggs. Maybe some peanut butter and crackers. The fruit department spread out before her and she decided fruit would be nice, as well. She grabbed apples, berries, oranges and bananas before stopping to think that she had no idea how much this stuff cost anymore. Since she only had a limited amount of credit, she had to be careful.

Keeping the apples and bananas, she put the berries and oranges back and moved on. Next time she would have those. When she reached the coffee aisle, she realized she could not live without a caffeine fix every morning. Since her grandmother had preferred hot tea and only bought instant coffee for guests, there was no coffee maker. Cece grabbed a jar of instant and moved on. Resisting the snack aisle, she strolled on to the dairy department. When she had mentally checked off the items on her list and deposited each one into her cart, she headed for the checkout counter.

Fortunately, the cashier was young, maybe seventeen or eighteen. She wouldn't know Cece.

When she had rung up the final item, she looked at Cece. "That'll be sixty-two fifty-eight."

Uncertainty seared through her. How did she explain the credit? "Is there a manager on duty?"

The girl stared at Cece, impatience written all over her face. "Sure." She called for the manager over the loudspeaker.

Cece ignored the people who glanced at the register and her. What if the manager on duty had no idea about the credit? Her stomach twisted into a thousand knots. She should have called the attorney's office before coming here.

"She has a question," the cashier said, yanking Cece's attention to the man who approached the checkout.

He was older, fifty or so, and looked vaguely familiar. Tension banded around her chest making a breath near impossible. When he frowned, her anxiety escalated.

"Cece?"

She nodded, the move jerky.

A smile propped up the corners of his mouth. "Make a note of the amount," he said to the cashier. "The lady has a credit that will take care of the total." To Cece he said, "Whenever you come in, just have them write the total and my name on the back of the receipt and tuck it into the till."

Cece searched her memory banks but his name was lost to her.

"Thanks, Mr. Holland," the cashier said, saving Cece from having to ask.

She nodded. "Yes, thank you."

Holland sent her an answering nod and returned to whatever he had been doing before the cashier had summoned him to the front.

By the time the cashier had written Holland on the back of the receipt and deposited it into the till, a short line had formed behind Cece. She had her bags in her cart and was ready to run a good five seconds before the girl glanced at her and said the words that would allow her to feel comfortable making her exit, "Thanks. Come again."

Cece was almost to the door when a female voice called out behind her, "Aren't you that girl who killed her daddy?"

Cece did not look back, just kept going. Her focus narrowed to the old blue truck waiting for her in the parking lot. All she had to do was reach that truck, load her stuff into the passenger seat and drive away. When she had money of her own, she would go to Tullahoma or some other nearby town where people were less likely to know her. Then again, even if she had had money, the fear of her driving skills being too rusty would have kept her close to home today.

She remembered well how it was here—the way it was in most small towns—news of her return would rush along the gossip grapevine like a fire devouring dry leaves. Passenger-side door open, she placed her bags in the seat and floorboard. With the task complete, she ordered herself to breathe.

Slow, deep breath. She was okay. She would be in

the truck and on her way in a minute. This first foray into public was nearly over.

For a second she considered leaving the shopping cart sitting in the middle of the lot, but the manager had been nice to her, and she shouldn't repay him by leaving the cart where it might hit a parked vehicle or roll out onto the street and cause an accident. Besides, the cart corral was only a few steps away. The clash of metal as she slid the cart into the line of others already in there made her cringe. She wasn't sure when the fear that someone would attack her would diminish. Learning to be on guard at all times was necessary to survival in prison. Many things had been necessary to survival—things she wanted to forget.

"Murderer!"

Cece turned around to face the woman who shouted at her…a different one from the voice that had called out to her in the store.

This woman wasn't alone.

Cece's heart stuttered. Three women and four—no, five—men spread out between Cece and her truck. She didn't know any of them, but she recognized the clothes they wore. Plain, overly modest, drab in color. Salvation Survivalists. Members of her father's following. She refused to call it a church. These people had nothing to do with God.

"We shall purge this evil from our midst!" one of the men shouted.

Cece stood perfectly still. If she ran they would only chase her. If she called out for help she would be wasting her time since there was no one to hear her.

The woman who had spoken first drew back her right arm and flung something at Cece. It struck her in the side, making her flinch at the sharp pain, before bouncing onto the asphalt.

Rock?

Memories of rocks being thrown at a helpless woman whispered through her mind.

Another rock flew at her. Hit her shoulder.

She backed up, bumped into the line of carts.

"Stone her for her grievous sin!" one of the men shouted.

Cece turned to run. She had no choice. Stones hit her back, her legs, her shoulder. When one hit her on the head, she bit her lip to prevent crying out.

Before she could take off running, a man blocked her path. Tall, dark hair…dark eyes.

She opened her mouth to scream.

He grabbed her and pulled her behind him.

"Back off," he growled at the mob. "The police are on the way. Unless one or all of you wants to be arrested, you had better get the hell out of here."

Cece dared to peek beyond one broad shoulder. The stones had stopped flying but the group still stood there lurking like something from a bad horror movie.

"We're not finished," the woman who had spoken first said, her hate-filled gaze on Cece.

The siren in the distance had the group dispersing.

Cece watched as they climbed into two SUVs and sped away. The woman—the one who appeared to be in charge—stared at Cece as they drove away.

The woman's face didn't trigger any memories, but she certainly knew Cece.

The idea that they had all come together suggested that the attack against her had been planned. Anger, hurt and frustration twisted inside her.

"You all right?"

Cece looked at the man who had come to her rescue and nodded. She wanted to ask his name. She wanted to ask why he had come to her aid. But she couldn't seem to put the words together and force them beyond her lips.

The Winchester Police Department cruiser came to a rocking stop a few feet away and Cece was grateful the stranger took the initiative and explained the incident to the officer. By this time Mr. Holland had come out to the parking lot.

"Are you okay?" he asked Cece.

"Yes." She relaxed the tiniest bit.

The police officer approached her then. "Miss Winters, would you like to come to the station and fill out a report?"

Cece shook her head. "I just want to go home, please."

Holland turned to the officer. "I think that's a good idea. She's had enough excitement for today."

The officer nodded. "I'll let Chief Brannigan know you're home, Miss Winters. He'll check in on you. Be sure to let us know if you have any more trouble. The chief doesn't tolerate nonsense like this."

Cece found the wherewithal to thank him.

"I'll follow her home. Make sure she gets unloaded without any trouble."

She stared at the stranger. Why would a man she had never met go out of his way?

"Good idea, Ross," the officer said. He turned to Cece. "Miss Winters, Mr. Ross lives just down the road from you. He bought the old Wilburn place."

The Wilburns. She remembered them. "I'm sure I'll

be okay now, Mr. Ross." She met the stranger's gaze. "Thank you for your help."

All she wanted to do was get into her truck and drive away. Before anyone could attempt to change her mind, she rushed to her truck and climbed in. She left without looking back. She made it all the way to the city limits before the tears defeated her. She swiped at her eyes, frustrated and angry…mostly at herself.

She was back, and by God she was not going to be run out of this damned town until she had the truth.

Chapter Two

Deacon Ross stood at the edge of the woods, watching the house. Cecelia Winters had carried in her supplies a couple of bags at a time. She had not purchased all that much. Her funds were limited. He suspected the attorney—Frasier—had made some sort of arrangements before his untimely death.

It seemed that no matter how guilty most folks in the town thought Cecelia was, there were a few who wanted to look out for her best interests. The attorney he could understand—that was his job and he had been an old friend of her grandmother's. The chief of police and the county sheriff going out of their way to keep her safe infuriated Deacon, but, like the attorney, that was their job.

Chief of Police Brannigan and Sheriff Tanner had taken extraordinary measures to ensure no one learned the date she was coming home. If it had not been for Deacon putting the word out, she would have reappeared in Winchester with no fanfare at all.

He could not allow that to happen.

Fury fired through him. Made him flinch with its intensity.

The murder of her old man wasn't the only crime

Cecelia Winters had committed. Another man, a man who meant a great deal to Deacon, had disappeared around the time of that murder. It had taken years to narrow down the possibilities, but a year ago Deacon had discovered reason to believe Cece was involved. He had been digging into her past and her family since. If it was the last thing he accomplished in this life, he intended to find out what she knew about his friend's disappearance. As the date for her release from prison neared he had reached an important conclusion: the only way to find the facts he needed was to get close to her.

Eight years, seven months and nineteen days had passed since her arrest and she had not once changed her story. She was innocent, she claimed. She had not killed her father. When her appeals were exhausted, she quietly served out her time. Due to the circumstances surrounding her childhood, the judge had been lenient in his sentencing. The crime that should have earned her twenty years had garnered her only eight.

But the disappearance—probable murder—of Deacon's partner would be a different story. If she had played any role in his death, he intended to see that she was charged, found guilty and sentenced to the fullest extent allowed for that heartless crime. More of that fury ignited deep in his gut.

Jack Kemp had been a good man. A good man as well as Deacon's mentor and partner. Deacon blamed himself in part for not being here to provide backup for Jack. But the Bureau had wanted one of them to stay on the case in Gallatin. The investigation there had been on the verge of busting wide open. In the end, half a dozen people had died in Gallatin—all part of the extreme survivalist cult known as Resurrection. Since he disappeared, Jack had not been able to prove it but he'd believed the survivalists in Gallatin were connected to the ones in the Winchester area. The church—more a cult than a church—the Salvation Survivalists, was somehow serving as a liaison between the two branches.

All those years ago, Jack's investigation had been buried under a mountain of red tape. The powers that be hadn't wanted to acknowledge that Resurrection's reach was so wide and deep. The information had been suppressed for years. Deacon wondered if the truth would have ever come to light if he had not pushed so hard for so long. Jack's family had a right to know what happened to him. Deacon intended to see that he or his body was found and the mystery surrounding his disappearance was solved.

The death of Mason Winters nearly nine years ago had caused the group to close ranks even tighter. In all this time, no one had gotten close to infiltrating the group and several had tried. Despite the Bureau's attempt to conceal what went wrong with Jack and his investigation, they continued to tap any resource that could be found. Except, in Deacon's opinion, they were looking in all the wrong places.

Now he had a loose thread at ground zero—Cecelia Winters. He would learn all her secrets as quickly as possible. Time was not on his side. If she knew things, as he suspected she did, someone would tie up that loose end. *Soon.*

She knew what had really happened. He was certain of it. She was a part of the family Jack had been investigating. She was the only one who had the proper motivation to tell the truth. Her family had turned on her, which gave her every reason to no longer have any loyalty to them. Deacon would find the truth before he was finished here, no matter how long it took and no matter what he had to do to make it happen.

Everything had been set in motion. All he had to do now was watch and take advantage of the opportunities to get close to her. The people in this community who despised her would take care of the rest. Cecelia Winters had no idea how much her father's followers hated her. She had killed their messiah, their leader. Those who rose to power after his death were even more heinous—particularly her brother Marcus.

Before this was over she would wish a thousand times she had stayed in that hellhole of a prison. She would want to run—to get away from the past that haunted her. But she wasn't going anywhere until Deacon had what he'd come for.

He turned away from her and walked back through the stretch of woods that separated the place he had bought from the one she had inherited. He'd set up a stand of trees near her house so that he could watch her. Anyone who stumbled upon it would believe it was a hunter's blind. Hunting season was still a way off but hard-core hunters started prepping early.

When he reached the clearing in front of his house, he hesitated. A truck had pulled into his driveway. A moment or so later, the driver emerged. He crossed the yard and climbed the porch steps.

Sheriff Colt Tanner.

Deacon skirted the rear yard and headed for the back door. He had no idea why Tanner would visit him. Maybe to follow up on the incident in the Ollie's parking lot. Deacon had given a statement. He didn't see the need for additional questioning. But the sheriff had been somewhat skeptical of him since his move to the Winchester area. No surprise there. The man had good instincts.

Following the disappearance of his partner, Deacon had been ordered to stay away from the investigation. He had been forced to do his digging quietly and under the radar of his superiors. The decision made no sense to him. He should have been the one ferreting out the facts about Jack. The Bureau had not seen it that way. Too personal, they had argued. Deacon was ordered to leave Winchester and to keep his nose out of the investigation. He had done as he was told—until one year ago. When the case had been closed, his partner legally declared dead.

Deacon had started his own off-the-record investigation. In Winchester, Logan Wilburn had gotten himself murdered and his property had gone on the market. Deacon had bought it sight unseen only because the closest neighbor was the mini farm Cecelia had inherited.

With those steps in place, Deacon had taken a leave of absence from the Bureau and moved here to set up his cover. He had learned who was who, burrowed into the community, and then he had waited. But Colt Tanner had kept a wary eye on him.

He imagined that was what this visit was about, more so than the nasty mob at Ollie's.

As Deacon moved through the house, a firm knock echoed in the living room, most likely the second one since the sheriff's arrival. Deacon tossed his hat onto the side table near the door, unlocked and opened it.

"Sheriff," he said by way of a greeting.

"Ross," Tanner replied. "You have a few minutes?"

"Sure. Come on in." Deacon opened the door wide and waited for the other man to step inside.

Tanner paused in the center of the living room and removed his hat. "You've done a lot of work around this old place."

Deacon closed the door and faced him. "Not so much." He glanced around. "Paint mostly. Some maintenance that had gone by the wayside."

"Looks good."

Most of what Deacon had done around the place had been merely a part of building his cover. A necessary phase in establishing credibility. "I'm sure you didn't drop by to check out my DIY skills. How can I help you, sheriff?"

"First, I want to reiterate how much Chief Brannigan and I appreciate you stepping in to help Miss Winters today."

Brannigan had already said as much. Deacon was fairly confident this visit wasn't just so Tanner could pass along his appreciation in person, as well. "It was the neighborly thing to do."

Tanner held his white hat in his hands. Like the rest of the men in power around here, he sported a cowboy hat, boots and well-worn jeans. Deacon had chosen the same sort of attire, not because he actually considered himself a cowboy but because he wanted to fit in with the majority of the other "good" guys around the Winchester area. When Cecelia looked at him, he wanted her to see an image that reminded her of the sheriff or the chief. Someone she could trust.

Psychology 101. Play the part.

"Those folks were part of her dead daddy's church," Tanner said. "The whole group is up in arms. I don't know what part of the Bible they think makes it a Christian thing to do—going after a woman like that. I spoke to the leader, Marcus Winters, who is also Cece's brother. He's assured me there will be no more trouble but I don't trust him to follow through with that promise."

Deacon was well aware of who the people were. He was also thoroughly acquainted, if only secondhand, with the older brother. The man had stepped into his dead daddy's shoes as if he had planned the event. It was possible he and Cecelia had plotted the old man's murder together. Then again, the fact that Marcus and the younger sister, Sierra, had basically disowned Cecelia seemed to indicate otherwise.

Then there was the wild card, the younger brother, Levi. He had visited his sister in prison on a regular basis but then he had not picked her up when she was released. Had not dropped by since she arrived home.

"I'll do what I can to keep an eye out around here," Deacon said. Though he wasn't convinced the sheriff had paid him this visit to elicit his help in providing backup where the Winters woman was concerned.

"Do you know Cece's younger brother, Levi?"

The question surprised Deacon. "I know the name," he admitted. "I don't actually know him or any other member of her family." He shrugged. "I suppose I've seen him around."

"Strange," Tanner said. "About three weeks ago Levi caught me at home and went on and on about how he thought you might represent some threat to his sister. I asked him for details but he seemed reluctant to provide any."

Well, well. Levi had been watching him. Deacon had

thought he'd spotted the man once but he hadn't been sure. Now he knew. Deacon shook his head. "I can't imagine where he got an idea like that, sheriff. I don't know his sister or him, beyond the rumors I've heard."

Tanner shifted his weight ever so slightly. "I took the liberty of running a background search on you, Ross. I hope you don't mind."

Deacon chuckled. "'Course not. I have nothing to hide. I'm new in town. You have an obligation to the citizens of your county to look into potential trouble."

Tanner didn't comment on his reaction, apparently wasn't impressed or relieved. "You're an FBI agent. From Nashville. Not married. No family. What brought you to Winchester?"

"Real estate prices," Deacon said without hesitation. "Property in the Nashville area is crazy expensive. I was looking for a place to retire."

The sheriff was far from convinced. "You're thirty-five years old. Seems kind of young to be planning your retirement."

Deacon shook his head. "According to my invest-ment counselor you're never too young to start pre-paring."

Tanner nodded. "Well, I guess there's some truth to that." He placed his hat on his head. "I suppose you'll be returning to Nashville eventually, considering that's where you're assigned. You must have had a hell of a lot of vacation days accrued."

Apparently the sheriff wasn't going to be happy with Deacon's glossed-over responses. "I requested a leave of absence. I'm not sure if I'll be returning to field duty."

Tanner studied him from beneath the brim of that white hat. "Is that right?"

"I hit a wall, sheriff. I'm certain you can understand how that can happen. I'm just not sure of what I want to do moving forward. Peace and quiet, for sure. Beyond that, I can't say." That was as close to the truth as he was going. But the basic story was accurate. Accurate enough to get him through this, he hoped.

"Law enforcement can take a toll. I hope you'll feel free to look me up if you need anything." Tanner chuckled. "Keep in mind, we're always on the lookout for experienced lawmen in the sheriff's department. If you're interested in coming on board, drop by and we'll talk."

"I'll keep that in mind, sheriff. Thank you. As for Levi Winters, if he still feels I represent some threat, I'm happy to meet with the two of you and hash out the issue."

Tanner nodded. "If I find him, I'll tell him. It's the strangest thing."

Deacon braced for whatever the sheriff intended to say next.

"I haven't been able to find him since that day. According to the warden at the prison no one showed up to give Cece a ride home. I recall that Levi said he would be picking her up. I'm surprised he didn't. He's the only one in her family who didn't turn on her during the trial."

"Have you spoken to Miss Winters to see if she's heard from him?"

"I was about to head over there now. A tech from the phone company is coming to turn on the landline. I called in a request as soon as I heard she was being released. I don't want her out here with no way to call for help. I doubt she has a cell phone yet."

"The service out here is not that great anyway," Deacon pointed out.

"All the more reason to go with a landline," Tanner agreed.

"Hold on, sheriff." Deacon rounded up a notepad and a pen. He scribbled his cell number on the top sheet, tore it off and passed it to the other man. "This is my cell number—for what it's worth. If she needs to call someone in the middle of the night, I'm closer than anyone else. I haven't bothered with a landline. Maybe I should."

"I'm sure she'll appreciate that, Ross." Tanner folded the paper and tucked it into his pocket.

He headed for the door. When he reached for the knob, Deacon added, "I was serious when I said if her brother wants to talk I'm more than willing. Just give me a call."

"Will do."

Tanner left and Deacon watched from the window as he loaded into his truck and drove away. The sheriff was friendly enough, but he wasn't completely satisfied with what he knew or what his instincts were telling him about Deacon. At the moment he had no reason to pursue the issue, but he would be watching and maybe doing a little more digging. Deacon wasn't concerned. The Bureau would not turn over information regarding an agent to anyone just to satisfy his curiosity. The only aspect of Deacon's past or present that could in any way be related to his being here was his former partner's disappearance, which had occurred a long time ago, and Deacon had not even been a part of that investigation. Everything else he had told the sheriff could be confirmed with his direct supervisor if Tanner decided to push it that far.

Deacon waited a half hour or so, then he made his way back through the woods, a path he knew well now, and watched her house. Tanner had gone inside and the technician from the telephone company had arrived and begun his work. For the next half hour or so the man went through the steps of running a line to the house and doing the necessary installation on the inside. Ten minutes after he left, Tanner did the same. Deacon walked back to his house and got into his truck. He backed out onto the road and drove the short distance to his neighbor's home.

He parked only a few yards from the porch steps. By the time he reached those steps she had already peeked through the curtain to identify her newest visitor. He pretended not to notice, walked to the door and knocked.

The sound of the locks disengaging and then the creak of the door echoed before her face appeared. "Yes?"

She recognized him; he saw it in her green eyes. Not to mention he doubted she would have opened the door if she hadn't.

"I'm your neighbor," he said, choosing to go that route rather than bring up what happened in the parking lot. "Deacon Ross."

She nodded. "Thank you for doing what you did today. I'm reasonably certain no one else would have."

"You don't need to thank me, Miss Winters. I did what needed to be done."

"I'm grateful." She glanced beyond him, then managed an uncertain smile. "I put your number on the wall by the phone. I hope I won't have to call you, but I'll rest easier knowing there's someone I can." She shrugged. "I grew up here but I don't have any friends or…or family, none that still own me, anyway."

"I understand."

"I'm sorry." She backed up a couple of steps, opened the door wider. "I guess my manners are rusty. Would you like to come in?"

He had hoped she would make the offer. "Sure."

He stepped inside and she closed the door, though it was obvious she wasn't entirely comfortable doing so.

"If you prefer to leave the door open, feel free."

She looked up, blushed, her cheeks nearly matching her fiery red hair. "Am I that obvious?"

He smiled, forced a load of kindness he in no way felt into the expression. "Afraid so."

"I'll work on my presentation."

"I couldn't help noticing as I drove up, there's a couple of places on the roof that need some attention. You'll probably want to consider getting someone to do some caulking and painting around the windows and doors before winter, too. I've been doing a lot of that next door."

She nodded, her expression more worried than uncertain. "I can probably take care of those things myself."

"Maybe, but I can help if you'd like. I'm no expert but I'm reasonably handy."

She bit her lower lip for a second before she responded to his announcement. "I'm afraid this house has gone downhill since I saw it last. My brother—Levi—said he kept an eye on things but I'm not sure how much he would know about home maintenance.

And, to be honest, my grandmother always took care of things. She was a firecracker. I might have learned a lot more from her if I hadn't gone away." She stared at the floor a moment before meeting his gaze once more. "But I learn quickly. I can probably do most of it myself with some amount of instruction."

He nodded to the paint can and brush next to the front door. "Looks like you already have a start on things."

She tried to smile but didn't manage the feat. "Yeah. Some things can't wait."

She had painted over the unpleasant reminder of what she was labeled by some, but the vicious word still showed through her efforts.

"Is there anything I can help you with before I go?" He didn't want to overstay his welcome or push too far today. Slow, steady progress was the best plan.

She moistened the lip she had been chewing. "Well, I did notice that the stove won't turn on." She hitched a thumb behind her. "I was going to heat some water for coffee."

"I can have a look."

"That would be great. Thank you."

She led the way into the kitchen, not that he needed her to show him where it was. He had been through every inch of this house at least three times. She had a number of surprises waiting for her.

In the kitchen she gestured to the stove.

He turned a knob for a top burner, then the oven. Pretended to ponder the possibilities, then he said, "I should check your electrical panel."

She frowned. "The fuse box?"

He nodded. "If it was never upgraded to a breaker box then that would be it."

She shrugged. "I have no idea. My grandmother called it a fuse box."

"Let's have a look."

She guided him to what had once been a back porch but was later converted to a laundry room. A new, smaller back porch had been added. She gestured to the wall next to the door they had exited. "Right there."

The electrical panel in the house had been upgraded. Again, he took some time to look over the situation, then flipped a breaker—the one he had flipped to the off position a week ago. While he was at it, he took care of the one for the water heater, as well. That one, he supposed, had been turned off by whoever closed up the house after the grandmother passed away.

"I turned on the water heater, too." He tapped the breaker he meant. "If for some reason it doesn't work, flip it back to the off position and let me know. Let's see if that did the trick for the stove."

Back in the kitchen, he turned the knob that controlled the burner beneath the kettle and the light next to it flared red.

She smiled. "Thank you. I would not have made it through the morning tomorrow without coffee."

"If you need anything else, just let me know." He turned and strode back toward the front door. She followed. At the door he looked back to her. "Call if you hear or see anything that makes you feel uncomfortable. I'm a minute away."

"Thank you again." She frowned. "I don't mean to sound ungrateful, but why are you doing this?"

He searched her eyes, wondered what she would say if he told her the truth.

"I don't know what happened to you, but you seem like a person who needs a break."

He left before she could say more. No need to risk allowing her to see the truth in his eyes.

She watched from the door as he backed up and turned around. When he stopped at the road to see that it was clear, he glanced in his rearview mirror to find her still watching.

The lady was lonely and afraid. Good.

That was exactly the way he wanted her.

Chapter Three

Cece prowled through the closet she had used as a teenager. She could not believe her grandmother had not thrown this stuff away. But then, her grandmother had been the only person who believed Cece was innocent and who hoped she would come back home one day.

Home.

She glanced around the room. This really was home. God knew she had spent most of her childhood here. After her mother died, her father had dumped her and her sister here more often than not. He had always dragged the boys along with him, as if they were more important than the girls.

Of course he had thought that way. Females were a lower life-form as far as he and his church creed were concerned.

Church. Cece felt certain it was wrong to call the following her father had created a church. It was a cult. One with harsh rules and absolutely no compassion. How had it survived nearly nine years without him? She could only assume Marcus had stepped fully into his shoes and used his murder as a platform for his own selfish purposes.

No surprise there. Marcus had always been cunning

and self-absorbed. Sierra, too, for that matter. At least, once she passed the age of twelve. Cece and Levi had been the ones who were different. They were like their mother, her father had often accused as if it were a bad thing. All those times he had tossed Cece and her sister to their grandmother, poor Levi had been forced to go along with him and Marcus. She had heard her brother crying at night after many of their outings. When she had asked him what happened, he wouldn't talk about it. She could only imagine what Levi had suffered in the name of their father's twisted beliefs.

Levi still had not come to see if she made it home okay. She hoped nothing had happened to him. Maybe he had decided that staying on her side wasn't worth the trouble. If he had, she wouldn't blame him. Marcus and Sierra and their followers would make it especially hard on Levi for having any association with her.

Cece grabbed a nightshirt and panties from a drawer and made her way to the bathroom. She looked forward to the luxury of a long, hot soak.

She found a towel, soap and shampoo, and placed them on the edge of the tub. After setting the water to the hottest temperature she could bear, she stripped off the clothes some organization had donated to her since she had had nothing to wear when she left the prison. She spotted a couple of bruises from the stoning incident. She shuddered, tried to block the memory of another event like that one from long ago. She had been around ten and the members of her father's following had decided one of their members had stolen something from a fellow member. They had dragged him outside the barn they had used for meetings back then and thrown stones at him.

The man had eventually managed to run, escaping their torture, but Cece had never seen him again. She wondered if they had found him and finished him off. She had no proof that her father or any one of his followers had ever killed anyone, but the hatred and evil they spewed was so extreme, she couldn't help believing them capable.

She eased into the hot water and sighed. A bath had never felt so good.

Until the water started to cool, she was content to simply lie there and soak. Her muscles relaxed fully for the first time in what felt like forever. Eventually she washed the stench of prison from her hair and skin. Even the soap and shampoos used in the prison carried a distinct scent she would never forget.

When her skin felt raw from scrubbing, she pulled the plug and climbed out. The towel was clean but smelled a little stale from being folded up in the old linen cabinet for so long. She would need to wash all the linens, maybe hang them on the clothesline for airing out. Probably be a good idea to do that with her clothes, as well.

Dressed and feeling more comfortable than she had in nearly a decade, she draped her towel across the side of the tub and then marched out back to throw the clothes she had worn out of the prison into the trash can. She never wanted to see or touch anything from that place ever again.

She made herself a sandwich and wandered into her grandmother's bedroom. Her hand slid over the pink chenille spread as she sat down on the side of the bed. Pink had been her grandmother's favorite color. Cece wished she had all the letters her grandmother had written to her over the years. Always on pink stationery tucked into a pink envelope. Two weeks after her grandmother passed away the letters had been taken from her prison cell and she never saw them again. No matter how many times she asked about them, she never received a straight answer.

Cece had finally given up.

Her grandmother had told her repeatedly in the letters that if, for some reason, she wasn't here when Cece came home, for her to be sure to go to their special place for a visit. She looked around the space, rested her gaze on the bookcase next to the window on the other side of the room. A fainting couch sat next to the bookcase. She and her grandmother would relax there for hours and read. When Cece had been too small, her grandmother had read to her. Later, they read their own books silently, but together. That reading nook was their special place.

Cece finished off her sandwich and walked over to the bookcase. She pulled out the well-worn copy of *Little Women*. The weight of the book and the beckoning scent of the pages made her smile. This had been one of their favorites. Cece had lost count of the number of times she'd read it.

Something slipped from between the pages and drifted to the floor.

She crouched down to feel for it beneath the edge of the couch.

Money.

A one-hundred-dollar bill.

"What in the world?"

Taking her time, she flipped through page after page in volume after volume. By the time she was finished, there was five thousand dollars stacked on the flowery sofa. What had her grandmother been thinking, leaving all that money in the house? She had a bank account. Mr. Frasier had said there was some amount of money in the account, but Cece would need to go to the bank and do the necessary paperwork to access it. She doubted there would be much but she genuinely appreciated whatever was there.

But why leave this cash here where anyone who wanted to break a window or bust open a door could stumble upon it?

Had her grandmother been afraid someone else would get their hands on the money in the bank account? Or was this her mad money? She had often spoken of her kitty. A little secret stipend she kept tucked away for emergencies, she'd always said.

Cece kept a couple hundred dollars in her hand but she climbed up on the chair and put the rest on top of the bookcase where no one would see it. Her grandmother had thought of everything, it seemed.

Her grandmother had been smart that way long before being prepared became a lifestyle of the slightly overzealous.

With no television to watch, she dug out the family photo albums and entertained herself with a walk down memory lane. Whenever she and her grandmother had looked at the albums, Emily always told the story behind each photo. Cece remembered most of them. There were lots of photos from the era before her mother died. Photos of Cece's grandparents with the whole family, even their father. But after her mother died, her father had drawn deeper and deeper into the cult that eventually became his own personal kingdom of followers.

He had pushed her mother's parents away and focused solely on the *church*.

Cece sneaked over to see her grandparents after school whenever she could. Marcus always told on her if he saw her. Levi and Sierra mostly did whatever Marcus said to do. But Cece had never conformed. She and her father had fought often—until he kicked her out at sixteen. The whole family had shunned her at that point. Eventually Levi had started to sneak opportunities to see her. Marcus and Sierra wanted nothing to do with her. Their father's approval was far too important.

She traced her fingers over a photo of her younger brother. Why had he not come to pick her up the way he promised?

Cece hoped he was okay. She had no way to call him—even though she now had a house phone. She didn't know what cell number he used or even if he owned one. He hadn't owned one when she was arrested. Her father had not allowed them to have cell phones. Cece had bought one after she moved in with her grandmother. She had no idea where it was now, not that it would still work since her contract had long since run out. Knowing her grandmother, if it had been given back to her, it would be here somewhere. The police may have kept it as part of their evidence. Images of being questioned, of all the blood, flickered one after the other through her head.

The memories were taking a toll on her emotions. "Enough for today."

She put the albums away and decided to tug on a pair of jeans and a tee and walk around the yard. It wasn't dark yet. Plenty of time for a leisurely stroll. She was relieved when the jeans she had worn at twenty still fit.

She spotted a pair of flip-flops under the edge of the bed and pulled them on. The screen door whined as she pushed through it. The heat had finally started to ease a little as the sun brushed the treetops.

The yard was well maintained. She supposed the lawyer's office had someone cutting the grass. She had noticed the old lawn mower when she backed the truck out of the barn. If there was a gas can in there she would be in business. She could cut the grass when it needed it again. She had done it plenty of times when she lived here. Her grandmother had been old-school when it came to the distribution of chores. There were certain things that she considered man's work and cutting the grass was one of them. Cece had ignored her warnings about spending too much time out in the sun or making calluses on her hands and done most of the chores that had been her grandfather's.

On Monday she would need to get out there and look for a job and report in to her parole officer. As thankful as she was for the cash she had found, it wouldn't last forever. Though the house and the truck were paid for, there were insurance and property taxes, utility bills and food.

The idea that her driver's license was expired occurred to her. She would need to get that taken care of next week, as well. She did not want a ticket. Having an accident without insurance was not something she wanted to experience, either. If she wanted insurance, she had to possess a valid driver's license.

Crunching gravel echoed through the trees. Someone had turned into the driveway. Cece hurried into the house through the back door, locked it up tight and rushed to the front window to peek beyond the curtains to see who was arriving.

She didn't recognize the car. Older. Green. The driver's-side door opened and a man emerged. He turned toward the house.

Levi.

She grinned and hurried to the door, threw it open and rushed out to meet her little brother. He stared at her as she threw her arms around him. He seemed to have grown a foot since she saw him last month.

"I was beginning to think you had hit the road and didn't tell me," she said, squeezing him tighter. She was so glad to see him. "Especially after you didn't pick me up."

His body felt stiff beneath her touch. His arms were around her but weren't really hugging her. She drew back. "What's wrong, Levi?"

That was when she noticed his clothes. Plain, dark indigo jeans, plain white shirt. Work boots. Hair cropped short.

He was one of them.

"No." She shook her head. Searched his face, his eyes for some explanation.

He stared at the ground for a moment before meeting her gaze. "It was a long time coming."

No. No. No. "Levi, how many times have we talked about what they are? You can't be one of them!" Her entire body seized with the agony of it.

His hands braced against her arms, kept her at bay as if he could not bear to have her hug him again or get too close. "It was the right thing to do. Marcus and Sierra want me in the family."

She shook her head. "I don't care what Marcus and

Sierra want. All that matters to me is what you want."
She stared straight into his eyes. "Is this what *you*
want?"

"It's what Daddy would want. What God wants."

Cece shook her head. She wanted to tell him that God
had never been a part of this, but he knew without her
having to lecture him. He knew all too well.

"I just wanted to make sure you made it home all
right since I couldn't come pick you up." He dared to
look at her then. "I love you, Cece. In time you'll understand this was the right thing to do."

Before she could argue, he turned and climbed back
into the car. She wanted to stop him, to argue with him,
but she couldn't find the wherewithal to fight. If he had
left town without telling her, run off to marry his latest
girlfriend, gotten arrested for some small-time crime,
she would have been far less devastated.

She watched him drive away and she understood
with utter certainty that she had no one left.

No one. She was completely alone now.

Why bother staying in this damned place to prove
her innocence? To find the truth?

What would it matter?

Who was left to care?

No one.

Cece wasn't sure how long she stood there but dusk
had settled heavily by the time she made herself stop
waiting for Levi to come back and tell her he'd changed
his mind or that he had only been joking. She turned
away from the empty driveway that was being over-
taken by darkness and walked back to the house.

Inside it was dark enough to need the light on. She
felt for the switch, flipped it up.

Nothing happened.

"For Pete's sake, what now?"

In the kitchen she found the flashlight her grand-mother had kept in the tool drawer for as long as she could remember. She prayed the batteries weren't dead. She slid the switch and light gleamed across the room.

She breathed a sigh of relief and made her way to the laundry porch. She opened the door to the panel box and shone the light over the breakers. Everything looked to be as it should. Then why did she not have any lights?

Using the flashlight, she checked the lights in the other rooms. Nothing worked. Not the overhead lights, not the lamps.

She had no desire to be stuck out here all night with no electricity. The flashlight was handy but it was not the same thing as having a well-lit room. She went back to the kitchen and found the note with the stranger next door's name and number. Thankfully the telephone was connected through one of those regular old landlines and the phone was an ancient push-button, so it had its own source of electricity.

Two rings sounded before he answered. She took a breath and did what she had to do. "Mr. Ross, this is Cecelia Winters next door. I'm sorry to bother you but I have no lights. Nothing is coming on. I checked the panel box but I couldn't see the problem."

He assured her he would be right over. Cece thanked him and hung up the phone.

She pressed her forehead to the wall and hissed out a weary breath. She had been scarcely more than a kid when she went to prison. Growing up she had had chores and certainly she had helped her grandmother out when she lived here. But she had never been responsible for an entire house. She had no idea what things she needed to know, much less do.

Too bad they hadn't taught this kind of thing in prison. She could have used lessons for practical living.

However frustrating all this was, she reminded herself as she moved to the front window to watch for her neighbor, she greatly appreciated having a home to which to come. So many of the other women she had met in prison had nothing or no one waiting for them. Cece might not have any family left, but she had this small house and land. She had a little money.

She would manage.

If proving her innocence turned out to be impossible, she could always sell and get the hell out of Winchester.

Without Levi, there was nothing else keeping her here.

Headlights bobbed in the distance as a vehicle navigated the long driveway. She tightened her grip on the flashlight and hoped it was Mr. Ross. Being stuck here in the dark was less than reassuring. She should have already taken the time to find her grandmother's shotgun and the ammunition required to use it.

The driver's-side door of the truck opened and the interior light allowed her a glimpse of the man behind the wheel.

Deacon Ross.

Cece unlocked and opened the door. When he reached the porch, she offered, "I really am sorry to bother you again."

She felt confident the man had not expected to be taking care of a neighbor recently released from prison when he bought the Wilburn place. She kept the flash-

light aimed at the floor to provide the necessary illu-
mination without blinding either of them.

"No problem. You saved me from another bad epi-
sode of what used to be my favorite TV show."

He smiled and she relaxed. "I haven't watched much
television in a while."

Prisoners were allowed some amount of television
time but she had preferred to read. Reading allowed
her to ignore the others. Maintaining a low profile had
helped her to avoid trouble more than once.

"Trust me," he offered, "you haven't missed much."

She held out the flashlight. "You'll need this."

He took the flashlight, headed for the laundry porch
and she followed. He was tall. Six-two or six-three,
she estimated. Far taller than her five-three. Her lack
of height was something else she had inherited from
her mother and grandmother. Unlike her, her sister Sierra was dark haired and taller, more like their father.
Marcus and Levi were the same. However much grief
she had put up with as a kid being called "ginger" and
"red," she was glad she wasn't like them.

The lights came on. "How did you do that?"

She wasn't sure how she would ever truly show her
appreciation to this man.

"Have you been away from the house without locking the doors?"

She shook her head. "I took a bath. Took a walk
around outside." She frowned. "And my brother Levi
stopped by. I stood outside talking to him for a few minutes. Not long, though." The wary expression he wore
unsettled her more than the question.

"Unless you have an electrical problem that's tripping the main breaker, someone came inside and flipped it to the off position."

She hugged her arms around herself. "Oh."

He turned off the flashlight and offered it to her. "Do you have a weapon, Miss Winters?"

"Cece," she corrected. "Call me Cece." She drew in an unsteady breath. "My grandmother had a shotgun. It's probably still in the house, but I'm not allowed to have a firearm."

She hadn't thought of that until this very moment. Legally, she could not possess a gun. She should have spoken to the sheriff about this when he stopped by. Now she felt like a total idiot.

"Let's not worry about the technicalities, considering you're out here all alone. I think you should keep it put away and don't mention having it until your rights to own a firearm are restored. If there's an emergency and you have to use it, a decent attorney could use the fact that it was actually your grandmother's and had been left in the house. You forgot about it. As simple as that."

It didn't sound simple to her but she didn't have any idea what else to do. "Okay."

"For now," he said, "let's make sure it's in good working order and loaded."

He was right. She should have done that already.

He followed her to her grandmother's room. Every light in the house was now on. The .410 was in the closet. A box of shells sat right next to it. She gestured in that direction. "She always kept it loaded."

Ross picked up the shotgun. He slid his thumb over the heart that had been carved into the stock.

"My grandfather carved the heart for my grandmother. He said this was the smallest shotgun he could get, making it manageable for her and yet still able to kick the butt of any trespassers."

"He was a smart man." Deacon racked the weapon and nodded. "Not much recoil. That click you heard was a round going into the chamber so it's loaded. We can take it outside and make sure it fires, if you want to be certain."

"Let's do that." At least she could protect herself if the need arose.

He led the way through the house and out the back door. Once in the yard, he took aim, not straight up but toward the treetops, and fired.

When the blast stopped reverberating in the air, he gave her a nod. "Fires and racks smoothly." He passed the shotgun back to her. "Keep one in the chamber and you won't have to waste time racking."

The rifle seemed to burn her hands and she couldn't wait to get back inside and put it away. "Thank you. I hope I won't have to bother you again."

"Like I said, call anytime."

She followed him back into the house. He hesitated at the back door. "Keep your doors locked, even when you're home and step out into the yard."

"Good idea."

At the front door she thanked him yet again and said good-night.

He studied her a long moment, then nodded and walked away.

She watched as he drove off and was grateful again for this stranger next door who had turned out to be a very good neighbor. She certainly hadn't expected sympathy or compassion or much else from anyone in this town.

With a shudder she quickly put the rifle away. She did not want any trouble, especially the kind that might get her sent back to prison.

What she understood with complete certainty was that the troubles she had experienced so far were only the beginning of whatever was coming. No one who had liked her father was going to be happy she was back. Most of them considered her vile…evil, something less than human.

There would be trouble. Her plan was to do what she had done in prison: keep her head down and search for the truth. It was the only thing left in this town that held any interest for her.

The hard part might just be staying alive long enough to find it.

Chapter Four

Midnight was only minutes away when Deacon finally decided to call it a night. He had been watching her house for hours. She had turned out the lights an hour ago. As a precautionary measure, he had set up motion sensors at the edge of the woods around the house, several directed at the driveway. No one was getting close to her without his knowing about it.

Cecelia Winters had a lot of enemies in this town. Deacon did not want one or more of them getting in the way of his plan. He had wanted her to feel the pressure of coming home—the hatred, the shame—that was true. But no matter what she was guilty of, he did not want anyone hurting her physically. Even he wasn't that heartless.

He had waited a long time to find the truth about his missing partner; he wasn't going to allow some redneck with a grudge to screw that up now. Jack had a widow, he had two grown children who deserved to have closure.

Deacon had scarcely taken two steps along the path toward home when he heard the voices. They were too low to determine if they were male or female but there was definitely more than one. He eased into the copse of trees on the right to ensure his presence wasn't picked up in the moonlight.

The figures moved out of the woods, into the backyard. With the help of the light from the moon he recognized they were male. One carried what appeared to be a large black box. No, he decided, not a box. A gas can. Since they moved toward the barn, the two obviously planned to torch it.

Bad idea in more ways than one.

It had not rained in more than a week. The grass, shrubs and trees were dry. A setting for disaster. Frustration and impatience mounted inside him. These bastards likely didn't care the extent of the damage they caused, only that they wreaked havoc for the woman.

Deacon slipped along the edge of the woods bordering the yard until he reached the back side of the barn. The two were getting cocky now, talking a little louder, making more noise as they moved about to execute their dim-witted plan.

The smell of gasoline filled the air. One of the bastards had started to splash gasoline onto the barn.

Enough.

Deacon eased up behind the one with the gas can and pressed the muzzle of his weapon against the back of his head. "Don't move."

The man—the air—everything stilled for just a moment. A single moment that Deacon knew all too well. The fight-or-flight response would kick in next.

"If your friend lights a match I'm putting a bullet in your head," Deacon warned.

The guy dragged in a breath and screamed, "Mac!"

"You pull that trigger," the second man, the one named Mac, apparently, cautioned, "I'm pulling mine."

"Either way," Deacon pointed out with a nudge to gas man's head, "sucks to be you."

A shotgun blast exploded in the night.

The guy with the gas can dropped it and ran.

Deacon held the other man's gaze. The light from the moon glinted off the barrel of his weapon. "You still have time to run."

He held his position.

"Who's there?"

Cecelia's voice.

The sound of her racking the shotgun cracked the air.

Deacon's tension moved to the next level.

"I've already called the sheriff!" she warned.

Another second of locked gazes and the man, Mac, broke. He ran for the tree line.

Deacon let him. Better that than a shoot-out. The two were obviously amateurs. Likely paid or otherwise influenced to set the fire to terrify the owner.

"It's me!" Deacon called out as he tucked his weapon away and then stepped from the shadow of the barn where the moonlight would give her a clearer view of him.

She lowered the shotgun and turned on the porch light. "I heard voices."

"You had company." He walked toward the porch, scanning the tree line as he went. "We need a water hose."

While they rounded up a hose he explained about her late-night visitors and how he had heard the gunshot and come running. Not exactly the whole truth but as close as she needed to know. She was safe and the would-be troublemakers were gone for now.

Deacon used the water hose to dilute and wash away

as much of the gasoline as possible. When he felt satisfied with the results, he put the hose away and followed her inside. She had dragged on jeans beneath the nightshirt. Her hair was a tangle of fiery curls. She still held onto the shotgun, but she had started to tremble. The adrenaline from the excitement was receding, leaving her shaken. Deacon took the rifle and put it away. Just in time, since two deputies arrived and took their statements, then had a look around. The abandoned gas can might provide fingerprints. The man who had been carrying it had not been wearing gloves. Just proved how cocky he was. He hadn't expected to get caught.

Deacon provided a detailed description of both men. He had not seen the vehicle in which they had arrived or departed. In fact, he had not heard one, either. Typically sound carried a fair distance in the dark, particularly in the country where there was little or no unnatural noise in the middle of the night. Obviously, they had parked a good distance away from their destination.

The deputies assured Cecelia they would do everything possible to identify the perpetrators. Deacon suspected that wouldn't happen unless the prints of the man carrying the gas can were in the system. He was betting they weren't, otherwise the guy wouldn't have been so careless. Men who had done time generally did not want to do more. Still, there was a chance. One or both may have been high or something, though Deacon didn't believe that to be the case.

When the deputies were gone, Cecelia stared at him for a long while before she mustered up the courage to say what was on her mind. "I still don't understand why you're doing all this."

He had been expecting that one. "We're neighbors. You want me to ignore the sound of a gunshot?"

She blinked, considered his explanation for a moment. "So you've decided that being my neighbor makes you my designated protector?"

She was angry now. This was a woman who wasn't accustomed to folks lending a hand to help. She was suspicious and rightly so.

"I guess I could tell you how my father raised me to be kind and helpful, particularly when a lady was involved."

Her expression warned that story was not going to cut it.

"When I bought the Wilburn place, I ran into your attorney, Frasier. He was here, checking on things. I stopped by to introduce myself to my new neighbor and he explained the situation. During the course of the conversation he asked me to keep an eye on you once you were released. I told him I would."

Her mask of skepticism slipped just a little. "He was a good man. He tried really hard to help me."

"I didn't know him that well, but I got the impression he was quite fond of you."

She relaxed visibly. "I think he was in love with my grandmother. I guess he felt compelled to see after me because of her."

"I know a little about your story," he said, choosing his words with care. "A lot of people appear to be angry with you."

Her arms hugged more tightly around her slim body. "I have no control over what people choose to think of me or how they decide to act on those thoughts."

"Do they have reason to be angry with you?"

Her chin came up in defiance. "Apparently they believe so."

"You didn't answer the question."

"I need a drink."

Surprised, he turned and followed her into the
kitchen. She reached under the kitchen sink and retrieved a bottle of bourbon. He had noticed it there the
first time he came inside and had a look around. He
figured her grandmother kept it around for therapeu-
tic purposes.

She poured shots into two glasses and handed one
to him. "Thank you."

He accepted the glass. "No thanks necessary."

With one swallow she downed the shot, grimaced,
then set her glass on the counter. "No matter that the
thought crossed my mind on far more occasions than I
care to name, I did not kill my father."

She exhaled a big breath, as if saying the words out
loud somehow released a massive weight she had been
carrying for entirely too long.

He downed his drink, wished for another but set
his glass aside, instead. "You took the fall for someone else."

She leaned against the counter next to the sink. "I
guess so. Not that I chose to or that I have any idea who
I did it for. Don't get me wrong, I was glad he was dead.
For a little while, I didn't even care who killed him. I as-
sumed that the law would prove I was innocent—since
I was. But that's not how it worked out."

To his surprise she reached for the bottle again and
poured herself another shot. She offered the bottle to him
but he declined. It was highly unlikely she had drunk

anything that contained alcohol in more than eight years; one of them needed to remain stone-cold sober.

"So, you waited." He leaned against the counter on the other side of the sink.

"But the police claimed that all the evidence pointed to me. I was always the black sheep of the family so I wasn't surprised when Marcus and Sierra came out against me. Levi was the only one who stood by me."

"Was there hard evidence or was it mostly circumstantial?" He knew the answer but he wanted to hear what she had to say on the matter. His knowing too much would only make her more suspicious.

"Those last couple of months before his murder we had several public disputes. During at least one of those occasions I said I wished he was dead. It was the truth. I did. I hated him. Hated him for making my mother so miserable. Hated that she was dead and he was still alive. Hated what he did to our family—turning us against each other." She shrugged. "Basically, I hated him, period."

"That's hearsay—the arguments, I mean. There had to be other evidence."

"He called. Said he needed to see me. My grandmother warned me not to go. She said he would just try and talk me into coming back into the family." She turned, braced her hands on the counter and stared into the darkness beyond the kitchen window. "I should have listened to her. She had told me the stories of the things he said and did to my mother."

A moment of silence passed with her lost in her memories. To prompt her, he asked, "Why didn't you?"

"I guess all the way until the bitter end some part of me hoped to see a different side of him. Levi was having a hard time with all of it. He despised our father but he needed him. He was really young and he needed that male role model." She shook her head. "Not that our father was the proper kind, but some part of Levi still loved him anyway. So I went. Thought maybe he might be reasonable."

"Someone got there before you."

She nodded. "When I arrived, he was dying. He had been stabbed more than a dozen times." She drew in a big breath. "I think the autopsy report said nineteen."

Deacon had seen the photos from the crime scene. It had been a bloody mess. Dozens of people had trampled the scene even before the law arrived, including Cecelia's older brother and numerous other followers from the church.

"No matter that I hated him, I tried to help. I tried to stop the bleeding. Tried to give him CPR when he stopped breathing."

She lapsed into silence once more.

"He didn't say anything to you?"

"He did, actually. Well, I don't know if he was speaking to me or just mumbling in general."

"What did he say?" The answer to that question was also in the case file.

That answer was the one thing in all of this that gave Deacon pause. Winters had been dead when the police and the others arrived. No one would have known what he said to her if she had not given that information in her statement. He wondered if she had regretted doing so.

"He said the same thing over and over." She turned to face him, met his gaze. "*You*. He kept saying *you*. It was like he had something to tell me or to accuse me of, but he couldn't get the rest of the words out."

"You had no idea what he might have wanted to tell you?"

She shook her head. "We weren't exactly on speaking terms. Mr. Frasier said he may not have meant anything. He was dying. It may have simply been the only word he could say, or he may have been disoriented and confused. He may not have been speaking to me. It's possible he didn't even realize it was me trying to help him."

"Who—other than you—had reason to want him dead?"

"That's the strange part." She closed her eyes a moment as if the bourbon had started to do its work. "His followers worshipped him. There were people in the community who disagreed with his religious beliefs, but as far as I know he had no enemies. Nothing was taken from the house. Someone walked in, stabbed him over and over and then walked out again."

"I'm sure the authorities at the time explained to you that the sort of murder you described was an act of passion. There was a great deal of emotion involved. The killer would have been in a frenzy. Not thinking clearly."

She appeared to consider what he said for a few moments. "I don't remember any one mentioning anything like that."

Deacon ignored the thought that crossed his mind. "When you walked in and found him, did you see any footprints in the blood around his body? A killer who goes off the deep end and commits a frantic act usually isn't thinking of anything else—like avoiding leaving evidence."

She rubbed at her eyes with both hands and then

ran her fingers through all those curls. Her face was clean, like a child's. No residue of makeup, not even leftover mascara. Fingernails were trimmed short and unpolished. She looked fresh and innocent. The woman standing before him didn't fit the image he had envisioned all this time.

"I didn't notice footprints. When I was being questioned, one of the deputies mentioned that there was no indication of a struggle. Nothing overturned. Nothing broken. He was just lying on the living room floor with blood all over him."

"No one found this strange?" The idea annoyed Deacon far more than it should have.

"If they did, no one said as much to me. Mr. Frasier said they believed I walked in with the knife hidden under my sweater and that my first blow was the one that put him down. He didn't struggle because he couldn't."

He saw her hands tremble before she crossed her arms over her chest, tucking them away from view.

"They found no prints," she went on. "No nothing that pointed to anyone other than me."

"Frasier seemed to believe the police didn't pursue a real investigation," he said, "because they already had their killer."

"That's exactly what they did." She met his gaze again, determination in her own. "I'm not saying they didn't do anything, but it wasn't enough."

"Cops are only human," he reminded her.

She frowned, as if she had only just thought of something she should have recalled already. "Did you know Mr. Frasier?"

He hesitated, for a moment considered not telling her. "I spoke to him a few times."

Realization dawned in her eyes. "Are you the private investigator he hired?"

That had been his first lie when he arrived in Winchester. He had made it a point to run into Frasier. Had told him he was interested in the Winters case. He had used the cover that he was a former FBI agent who had started his own PI firm and that he was interested in the case.

"I am."

"Why didn't you tell me?"

"Mr. Frasier died. That was the end of the investigation."

"Did the two of you find anything? Discuss anything or come to any conclusions I haven't heard about?"

She was annoyed that he hadn't told her this already.

"We didn't. What we did was talk over the case and how it was investigated eight years ago."

"You asked me all those questions to see what I would say." The statement was an obvious accusation.

"I did. Old habits die hard."

"You've already decided there's nothing I can do to find the truth."

Another accusation. "There's a lot you can do, Cecelia. The question is whether it will change anything."

In his opinion, it would not.

"I did not kill him."

As much as he didn't want to, he believed her. "Give me full access and I'll see if I can help you find the truth."

"What do you mean, full access?"

"Full access to you, to the case files."

"You haven't seen the files?"

"I haven't seen the files through your eyes."

She thought for a moment, the pulse at the base of her throat fluttering wildly. "All right. Where do we start?"

"Right now, we start with sleep. You've had a big day. I'll be over in the morning and we'll talk. See where we go from there."

"Okay."

"Good night, then. See you in the morning."

He had almost made it to the back door when her voice stopped him.

"Thank you."

He glanced back, studied the image of the woman who looked so alone, so worried and so damned innocent.

She could not be that innocent.

Chapter Five

Twenty-four hours.

She had barely been home twenty-four hours and already people had thrown rocks at her and tried to burn down her barn.

"You're wasting your time, Cece," she muttered to herself.

She clutched her coffee cup more tightly and turned away from the window over the sink. All those years she had spent in prison she had told herself over and over that it didn't matter what people thought. That she did not care if no one believed she was innocent. She couldn't care less what these people thought of her.

But it was a lie.

She had been lying to herself. The people in this town had known Cece her entire life. Certain teachers she remembered from school had made her feel smart and relevant. A couple had urged her to go on to college but she had known that could not happen. There was never enough money or opportunity. Still, deep down she did not want those teachers to believe she had murdered another human—even one like her father.

In the living room, she stared at her reflection in the mirror next to the front door. She looked older than her twenty-eight years. Tired. Weary of this life and she had barely begun to live it. What did a man like Deacon Ross see when he looked at her? A woman? Or a screwed-up kid who had nothing but this old house and the spot of land it perched on?

She blinked away the thought. He was a kind neighbor, a man who had made a promise to her grandmother's lawyer friend to watch after her. Probably he saw her as an obligation—one he likely regretted having accepted.

"Don't even start, Cece."

She turned away from the mirror and walked across the room to the corner where the desk that her grandmother had used for letter writing stood. Until the day she died, her grandmother had clung to the handwritten form of communication. She had insisted that cell phones and the internet would be the end of polite society.

Cece found a notepad and pen. No matter that a mere twenty-four hours had passed, she understood one thing with utter certainty: she needed a project besides the search for the truth. Her grandmother had entrusted her with this home—the home she had worked hard to keep all those years as a widow. Whether Cece stayed or left, she owed it to her grandmother to take care of the place. Anything she did to shape up the house would be an investment for later if and when she sold it.

The mere thought was like a betrayal of her grandmother. But Cece knew Emily would understand whatever she decided to do. She had told her so in letter after letter. Her grandmother had not expected her to stay in Winchester.

"Paint." Cece wrote the word, shifting her attention to the necessary.

Next she jotted down roof, exterior caulk and paint. Deacon had mentioned those things. He had also offered to help. She would do as much as she could herself before she went to anyone else. As a kid she remembered her father's church going to the homes of the elderly and doing things like painting and general maintenance. Funny, no one had come to do any of those things for her grandmother.

"No surprise," she muttered. The people who belonged to her father's so-called church weren't good people.

They were followers of his hatred and cruelty.

No matter that she did not kill him, she was glad he was dead. Grateful not to have to wake up with the worry of running into him or having him show up unannounced to torture her with his hateful words.

She opened the front door to step outside and survey the roof and siding as best she could. A van rolling to a stop in the driveway caused her to stall on the porch. Her heart had already started to pound by the time her eyes and brain assimilated the name of the delivery service printed on the side.

"Morning." The man in the uniform waved as he walked around to the rear of the van. He opened the doors at the back.

Cece walked to the edge of the porch and started down the steps. "Morning."

Who would be sending anything to her?

The man rolled a hand truck toward where she stood. Three boxes were stacked one on top of the other.

"Cecelia Winters?" he asked as he stopped at the bottom of the steps.

"Yes." She looked from the boxes to him.

"These are for you." He passed her a clipboard. "Just sign at the bottom."

She stared at the form. "Who sent the boxes?"

"Clarence Frasier."

Cece's gaze connected with his. "That's impossible. Mr. Frasier died two months ago."

The man shrugged. "You would have to call the office to get the details. They'll be open on Monday."

She nodded. Told herself it was possible his office had sent them rather than have her come by to pick them up. She signed the form and handed the clipboard back to the waiting man.

"Thank you."

He looked from her to the boxes. "Look, we're not supposed to go inside, but I can pull these up the steps and right inside the door, if you'd like."

She nodded. "I would appreciate it."

"No problem." He smiled, and the expression sparked in his eyes.

He did not know her, of that she was confident. If he did, he wouldn't have smiled so kindly or even have made the offer to go beyond what was required of him.

He pulled the load of boxes up the steps, rolled the hand truck across the porch and through the door— just across the threshold, as he had said. He scooted the load off the hand truck and was out the door and down the steps with the efficiency of someone who had been doing the job for a good long while.

"Have a nice day!" he called as he headed back to his van.

Cece watched him load up and go. She waited until he had turned onto the road before going inside and closing the door. On second thought, she locked it, as well. Deacon had warned her to keep her door locked at all times. Considering last night's visitors, she intended to keep the doors and the windows locked. Thank God for the air conditioning window unit and the ceiling fans, otherwise she would be burning up.

A few minutes were required to find something to cut the tape on the boxes. She slid the knife blade along the edges until the flaps opened. Inside each box was another box, the sort in which files were kept. She stacked one after the other next to the couch. Then she removed the lids. An envelope with her name on it sat on top of the folders inside one of the boxes.

She opened the unsealed envelope. It was a hand-written letter from Mr. Frasier.

Cecelia,
If someone besides me has delivered these boxes, then I am dead. I don't expect that my death was any sort of unusual event. Probably a heart attack. My doctor has been after me about my blood pressure for ages. I suppose I should have listened better.

First, your grandmother has left you a sizable savings at First Union. Last I checked it was fifty thousand and some change. She said you should buy something better than that damned old truck. You know she always hated the thing.

Cece gasped. Tears crowded into her eyes as she thought of the woman who had been more of a parent to her than the man who had boasted the title *father*.

Use it wisely. Since the house is paid for, this should tide you over for a bit. In addition, your grandmother left a scholarship fund for you to use for college. These funds cannot be used for any other purpose. She was quite sneaky about that. She knew how smart you are and she wanted you to have the opportunity to explore all possibilities. Don't let her down.

Lastly, these are my working files from your case. I only wanted you to have them so that you would understand the insurmountable odds that were stacked against you. You have served your time. Don't waste any more on this case. Move forward, put the past behind you. Proving your innocence will not give you those years back.

Your grandmother's greatest wish was for you to be happy. Grant her that wish, Cece. And your-self.

Sincerely,

Clarence Frasier

Cece swiped at the tears dampening her cheeks. College. She had not even considered college. Though she had taken a few random classes in prison, she felt too old for college. But she knew that wasn't true. Lots of people older than her went to college.

She drew in a shaky breath and placed the letter on the coffee table. She rubbed her palms against her jeans and reached for the first file in the first box. This one contained a copy of the arrest record along with her lovely mugshot.

God, she looked so young. She had been, barely nineteen. A kid. Flashes of memory detonated in her brain like tiny explosions. Her hands in her father's blood.

You.

He just kept saying that one word over and over.

And then nothing.

The police had arrived. Question after question was fired at her. Her father's closest followers had filed in, throwing around accusations, praying fervently, then accusing her some more. Marcus had shown up. He had ranted at her.

What have you done?

Then the handcuffs had gone onto her wrists. The deputy had recited her rights as they led her away from her father's house, his blood all over her.

She remembered being ushered into the back seat of the patrol car. The door closing with a thud of finality. The radio on the dash crackling with voices.

Codes and words she had not understood at the time but did now.

Homicide. Perpetrator. In custody. Numerous other words and phrases that meant just two things: a man was dead, murdered, and they had the killer in custody.

End of story.

Except it wasn't true. It was a mistake. A setup. A lie.

Fury tightened her lips. She would go to college, just like her grandmother wanted. But first she had a story to rewrite.

Her story.

DEACON STARED AT the screen of his laptop. Cece sat on the sofa, file folders spread over the coffee table in front of her. She alternately cried and swore.

Part of him hated that he had planted cameras in her house and now watched her at a private moment like this. He kicked aside that too-human emotion. He needed the truth. Sympathy for her—this damned attraction he felt for her—would do nothing but get in his way. He had to remember those cold, hard facts. Ten years he had been in the Bureau. Ten years of training and hard work. His training had taught him not to get personally involved.

But that training had not been able to stop him.

He had spent months reading every single thing about this woman. Watching her at the prison. The warden had happily agreed to allow Deacon to stop by and observe the prisoner any time he wanted to. He had been allowed to read the incident reports, to interview her guards and other inmates.

He was well versed in most things that had happened to her inside those damned walls. Of course, not every incident was reported. The inmates had their own code. Cece had eventually learned to play by their rules. It was the only way to survive and she was a survivor.

One of the female guards he had paid to keep an eye on her had told him about the male guard who tried to rape Cece in the beginning. Another inmate had come to her aid in the nick of time. As it turned out, the Good Samaritan inmate was someone the attorney, Clarence Frasier, had paid to see after Cece. Well, he had not actually paid the inmate, he had taken care of the woman's mother and two kids for the service she provided.

Frasier had been that convinced of Cece's innocence.

That was the part that bugged Deacon. The reports and the scarce evidence backed his conclusions, but the lawyer and his passion about her innocence did not fit neatly into the scenario the former sheriff had built about Cecelia Winters.

The last part had not mattered to Deacon, not in all these months. And yet, in the past twenty-four hours, his confidence had started to slip. She had somehow breached his defenses, made him want to believe she was innocent. His training, his instincts, had kicked in the moment he first encountered her face-to-face. All those months of watching her from a distance, of reading the files—the same ones she read now—had not prepared him for the up-close encounter with her.

She exuded an honesty he could not deny and he hated himself for recognizing it.

He scrubbed a hand over his jaw and looked away as she set her face in her hands and started to sob.

Where was the evil, conniving woman he had expected? The one he had seen stand up to other inmates in prison? The one he had watched scrape her way through the final months of an eight-year sentence?

How had he seen that woman and not this one?

He closed his eyes as the answer echoed inside him.

She'd worn that tough mask to survive. He should have known—should have recognized the tactic—but he had not wanted to. He had wanted to see the heartless killer he had imagined her to be.

He had watched the taped interview of when she was questioned about his partner. She had sworn she did not know him. Had never seen him before. But she had lied. Deacon had recognized the lie in her eyes.

Whether she was responsible for Jack's disappearance or not, she knew something about what happened to him.

By God, he intended to find out what that something was.

He closed the laptop, grabbed his hat and walked out the door. He should stop himself right there, turn around and go back inside to watch her from a distance.

But that wouldn't get the job done.

He had to get closer.

Rather than walk, he drove to her house. During the short ninety-second trip he arrived at the perfect excuse for stopping by. It was easy. He had come up with dozens during the long planning stages of his strategy. All he had to do was pick one.

He parked, climbed the steps and knocked on her door.

She was slow to answer. Probably wiping away her tears and attempting to gather her composure. When she opened the door, it was clear she had failed miserably.

"Morning. I was headed into town for supplies and I thought you might want some more paint." He nodded to the door next to her. The red letters of the word *murderer* still lingered behind the layer of white she had brushed over them, giving the accusation a ghostly appearance.

He had spelled out that word with the red paint he bought at one of those hardware supercenters two towns over. He had wanted her to come home to that message, to feel the shame and the guilt.

He had watched Cece paint over the graffiti and he had hated himself for what he'd done.

Now, she stood in that doorway, her eyes red from crying yet again, and he hated himself even more.

Worse, he hated himself for hating himself.

How screwed up was that?

She moistened her lips, propped them into an un-steady smile. "Sure. That would be great. White exterior paint, please. I have money."

She turned and headed inside before he could stop her. She had found the money her grandmother had hidden for her.

There was more. He wasn't sure she knew about it yet.

He had interviewed her grandmother. The woman had believed Cece walked on water. Had adored her grandchild. He had pretended to want to help. That he had lied to the kind, elderly woman gnawed relentlessly at his gut even now.

He had done a lot of things over the past year he shouldn't have. Twice he had tried to forget. Had walked away and said he was done with the whole thing. Then a week or two later he was back, watching her again, asking more questions. Searching for that elusive truth he could not find.

He was a fool.

She was back at the door offering him a one hundred dollar bill. "I have no idea how much paint costs now. I need the stuff that blocks stains, too."

Her hand trembled ever so slightly as he stared at it. Before he could stop himself he closed his hand over hers. "What's happened that has you so upset?"

That his whole body yearned to hold more than her hand deepened that self-hatred rotting inside him.

"I received the files from my attorney's office. I've been going through them and…" She shook her head. "Sorry." She swiped at the fresh wave of tears that slipped down her cheeks. "I don't know why I'm so emotional. I haven't read anything I didn't already know about." She shrugged her slender shoulders. "But reading the statements—word for word—that recount the things my sister and older brother said about me was…painful. More so than I expected. It's ridiculous, I know. I sat in that courtroom and heard them answer the questions from the district attorney. But that was so many years ago and some of that time is like a blur. There was no shock or denial to soften the ugliness this time."

"People—even the people we think we know—can hurt us in ways we don't anticipate."

She stared up at him. Her eyes wide with sadness and uncertainty. "I tried to be a good daughter, a good sister, but I couldn't be what they wanted." She dropped her head, shook it. "Not even for Levi. I left. Left him and Sierra with that evil bastard and they were just kids."

His thumb slid over the inside of her wrist. "You were just a kid, too."

"A kid." She made a sound that was probably a stab at a laugh but did not quite hit the mark. "I was accused of murdering my own father before I was twenty. Left my baby sister and brother to fend for themselves when I was sixteen. I must have been a very bad person, Deacon. This kind of stuff doesn't happen to good people."

He released her hand before he turned any stupider than he already had. "How about a brush? You need a paintbrush? Drop cloth? Anything else?"

She shoved the money at him again. "Guess so."

He held up a hand and backed away a step. "I got this."

Turning his back, he had almost made it to the steps when she stopped him with a question he could not ignore.

"Why are you really doing this, Deacon Ross? I know I've asked you already." She shook her head. "I guess I keep expecting a different answer. Some hidden motive I don't see coming."

If he had hated himself before, he genuinely despised himself now. He faced her once more, the depth of the porch between them. "You need someone to care." He shrugged, his gut twisting with the words he did not want to say but could not hold back. "Now lock your door. I'll be back soon."

When he climbed into his truck and started to back away, she still watched him.

He barreled out of her driveway and onto the road. Anger blasted through him. He had to find a way to get back on track.

He owed Jack better than this.

He didn't owe Cece Winters one damned thing.

Chapter Six

By the time Deacon returned, Cece had pulled herself together. Her eyes weren't red anymore and she didn't feel like such a complete idiot. What she felt was mad as hell. The things her sister and her older brother had said about her in those damned statements were lies—most of them, anyway—just like their answers in that courtroom.

She paced back and forth, the crumpled statements in her hand. Deacon's knock on the door reminded her that she needed to calm down. Sure she had the tears under control, but the anger was a whole new level of emotion. Her entire life she could not remember ever being this outraged. Not even when the jury found her guilty of murder. Those people had not known her. They had based their judgment on the evidence, which was completely against her, and an endless string of witnesses who had either embellished some semblance of the truth or flat-out lied.

Not even, she told herself, when the two deputies and the sheriff had treated her like a murderer. She'd had her father's blood all over her. The knife had been lying on the floor at her feet and though her prints weren't found on it, the district attorney suggested she had wiped away the prints.

This, she tightened her fingers on the wad of papers, was her kin. They knew her. Grew up in the same house with her. And they had lied.

Another knock echoed and she stopped pacing, drew in a big breath, let it out and strode to the door. Her fingers on the knob, she hesitated, reminded herself to make sure who was on the other side before she opened it. Just because she was expecting Deacon didn't mean it was him.

The man on the other side gave her a little wave and she told herself to relax. That did not happen. Her heart fluttered and she lost her breath all over again. She really, really was an idiot. This man was only being nice. The last time she had been touched by the opposite sex, the guy had been a boy—not a man—and that had been a very long time ago. And he was a jerk. She had been way too naive.

She forced her gaze down to the bucket in his hand. "Thanks."

"Looks like you've been working."

She followed his gaze to the coffee table and couch. Documents were spread all over the place. "Yeah. I've been...working."

"Why don't you get back to it and I'll take care of the door. This paint has a built-in stain blocker. A couple of coats should do it. When you're ready, you can walk me through what you have."

He smiled that smile that did not mean anything, yet her pulse still reacted.

She nodded. "Sure. That would be great."

Taking another deep breath, she returned to her piles.

She knelt between the coffee table and couch, settled the wadded statements there and attempted to smooth them out. She shouldn't have reacted so angrily. She wasn't a kid anymore. She needed to handle all these emotions like an adult.

On some level she still felt like that nineteen-year-old who hadn't experienced the world. She had lived in Winchester her entire life. Never been farther than Nashville to the north or Birmingham to the south. She had never even seen the ocean. Navigating all this— she stared at the mass of papers—was difficult. She smoothed at the pages some more. Didn't help.

"As long as you can still read them, that's all that matters."

Her attention shifted to the man who'd propped open her front door and placed a drop cloth on the floor beneath it. His hand wrapped around the handle of the brush and her gaze followed the long brush strokes. His method for applying the paint was not at all like the smear process she had used.

"I guess I didn't like what I read," she confessed.

"You want to start with that?"

He was a stranger. He didn't know her family beyond their fanatical religious affiliations. She supposed he could be a good sounding board. Objective. She could definitely use an objective opinion. And he was a private investigator. He was an experienced investigator. Frasier had trusted him. She should, as well.

"When I was arrested, the police interviewed a lot of people who knew me and my father." She sat back on her heels and let her mind drift back to that dark time. "The reviews were mixed. Most folks lumped the whole Winters clan into the same category of fanatical misfits."

"Human nature." He glanced at her. "People see what they expect to see. What they want to see."

She bit back the question on the tip of her tongue. She wanted to know what he saw. "I didn't hold it against them. Still don't. Like you said, they see what they expect to see. I guess I hadn't given anyone a reason to see anything different."

"You were a kid."

She nodded. "True."

Cece wondered how old he was. Maybe thirty-two or thirty-three. Smart. Probably went to college. Most likely had a nice family.

She did not have a nice family. Since they had all turned their backs on her, she didn't really have a family at all.

"My older brother…" Saying his name was like a knife to her chest. She wondered if any amount of time would make that hurt go away. "Marcus, he stated that I was unbalanced and angry. That I'd said I hated our father on numerous occasions."

"He lied."

Was that doubt she saw in his eyes. After all, surely one's own brother wouldn't say such things. "About most of it, yes," she clarified.

"Which parts did he lie about?"

He did not look at her this time, just kept painting. She expected any moment that he would start looking at her the way everyone else in town did. It was highly likely that she wouldn't be seeing as much of this new neighbor after today. But then he'd been over the case file with Frasier. She wasn't telling him anything he didn't already know.

"I've never been unbalanced in my life."

When he looked at her with surprise she had to laugh. "Like you said, I was a kid. I probably told the bastard that I hated him a hundred times. I did hate him. And I was angry, very angry. I hated what he had done to our family, particularly our mother. I hated everything about him." She sighed and then said the rest. "I had probably wished him dead a thousand times, maybe more."

"But your brother didn't know that part?"

Cece shook her head. "I'm sure he knew but he chose to use that information in a way that suited him. What Marcus said didn't surprise me. He and I weren't that close. It was Sierra who threw me under the bus. We were really close growing up. I told her how I felt. Usually when I was so angry I couldn't stop myself. She gushed the mean things I had said to the jury so tearfully, they were certain the words were tearing her apart. But that wasn't the case at all. I could see it in her eyes. She was enjoying the attention and she loved making me look bad. Even though I was the one who had helped her out too many times to count."

"You think someone was directing her? Maybe your older brother?"

"Possibly." Marcus had wanted Cece out of the picture permanently. "He knew there were people in the church who would listen to me if I decided to speak out against him."

"You never spoke out against your father?"

She shook her head. "My grandmother was afraid if

I did that something bad would happen to me. The way it did to my mother."

Cece stared at the crime scene photos of her father lying in all that blood. Her shoe prints in the mess. Blood all over her hands, her clothes. No matter that she had hated him—despised him for all those years—as he lay dying and unable to be cruel or hurtful, she'd felt pain. The little girl in her who had loved the man who was her father had felt fear, anguish, shock at seeing him in that condition. Her most basic instinct had been to help him. To cry out for assistance.

"What happened to your mother?"

Cece's attention snapped back to the present. "I'm sorry, what?"

"You said your grandmother mentioned something bad happened to your mother."

She frowned. Why in the world would she tell this stranger all these terrible things about her past? If Frasier hadn't told him that part, maybe she shouldn't. Even as the thought entered her mind, memories from more than two decades ago rushed into her head. Voices and sounds from that night. She had only been six. Her sister had just turned two; Levi was four. Marcus had been twelve. The screaming woke her. Cece remembered getting up but Marcus was there, in the darkness. He had ushered her back to bed. Sierra clung to her, crying. Levi was hiding in the closet. It wasn't until the abrupt silence that Cece realized the screaming had been coming from her grandmother.

The sun came up on the next day before she understood what had happened. Her mother had fallen down the stairs. Her father had tried to help her but could not. Her grandmother had arrived in the middle of it all. Cece did not really understand that part but her grandmother would never talk about it. She just said something terrible had happened and she did not want anything like that to happen to Cece.

"My grandmother believed my father killed my mother. I'm certain of it." Cece had never said those words to anyone else. Not even Levi.

Deacon asked her to start at the beginning, the morning before that night. It took a while for her to pull all the memories from the place to which she had banished them. Slowly, she pieced all the parts together. By the time she finished he had put his paintbrush down and joined her on the floor between the couch and coffee table.

"Did you ever confront your father about your memories of that night?"

How could he seem to care so much? Had she been locked away for so long she couldn't tell the difference between basic human kindness and whatever else it was she believed she saw in his eyes?

What she *wanted* to see in his eyes?

"I did. One morning when I was sixteen and it was just the two of us, I blurted out that I thought he killed her. That's when he kicked me out. He said if my grandmother was going to fill my head with lies, I could just go live with her."

"But she never confirmed your belief?"

She shook her head. "No. But I saw the truth on her face. She was afraid of him. I'm sure he threatened her that night."

"What about your grandfather? Was he still alive then?"

"He was, but he was blind and confined to a wheelchair." She closed her eyes against the memory of her grandfather sobbing at her mother's funeral.

"You've been through a lot."

His words drew her back to the present. "Mine was not a pretty childhood."

"What about Levi? You didn't mention his statement to the police."

With him sitting so close she saw the lines at the corners of his eyes. He looked genuinely interested in knowing what happened. Was she so desperate for an ounce of human kindness that she would imagine his concern?

"Levi insisted I wasn't capable of murder. He believed it was Sierra. She was acting all weird about our father. Possessive and at the same time rebellious against his rules. He told the police as much in his statement. But it didn't change anything. Sierra had an alibi."

"Don't tell me," Deacon said. "Her alibi somehow involved Marcus."

"Her car had broken down and he went to her rescue. Sierra's boyfriend, who was a mechanic and a member of the church, helped, too."

"Convenient."

"Very."

They sat in silence for a long moment until he finally asked, "So, what's the plan?"

She laughed. "Who says I have a plan?"

"You were in prison for eight years. You had a lot of time to plan what comes next."

Relaxing against the couch, she decided maybe he did care. Not everyone in the world had a hidden agenda. Some people were genuinely good. "At first I mostly just concentrated on surviving. Eventually—

when I was more confident that I might live through being there—I started to think about when I got out."

"And here you are." He smiled, glanced around the room. "Ready to find some answers."

"I thought about not coming back."

She had made up her mind to come back and stay with her grandmother until she passed away and then move on. But her grandmother had died before Cece was released so she didn't get the chance. Why bother coming back with her grandmother gone? It would have been so easy to just never return. To forget this place. It should be even easier to leave now that Levi had abandoned her, too.

But life had never been easy for Cece and the trouble in the walking-away scenario was the idea that her grandmother had still been trying to prove Cece was innocent when she died. That reality changed something deep inside her. Cece needed to finish what her grandmother had started.

When she had finished relaying all this to her neighbor, he said, "Revenge is a very strong motivator."

If he only knew. "I guess so."

More of that silence settled between them.

She should probably say something but the quiet felt too comfortable to interrupt. Not at all like the noisy environment at the prison. So noisy and yet she had felt utterly isolated. Alone. There had always been the fear that the other shoe was about to drop…that something bad would happen at any second. Most of the time it did.

"I'll clean up that brush and have a look at the roof before I go. If you need anything, I can pick it up next time I'm in town."

"Sounds great. If you're sure you want to be that neighborly."

He got to his feet. "I'm sure."

Cece scrambled up and followed him to the door. "I have money. I can pay you."

He stared at her for a long moment. She couldn't quite label what she saw in his eyes, but it made her wish she had not said anything.

"I don't want your money." He reached for the brush and the bucket of paint.

She really was out of practice with how to read and to communicate with everyday people. "Okay. Sorry. I didn't mean to offend you."

When he met her gaze again, the strange look was gone. "It's all right, really."

But the tension she sensed in him told her it wasn't all right. That moment was the first time she had felt uncomfortable in his presence. It was as if the neighborly stranger had suddenly disappeared.

Had she made another mistake trusting this man?

JUST BEFORE MIDNIGHT one of the many alarms he'd put in place went off. Deacon straightened away from the files he had been reviewing. Checked the monitor and didn't see anyone outside the house. Cece had gone to bed. He grabbed his handgun, tucked it into his waistband and headed out. Could be an animal, but he preferred not to take the chance, particularly after last night.

He knew the path between their properties so well he didn't need a flashlight. A thin sliver of moonlight managed to cut between the trees every few yards, enough to ensure he didn't veer from the path. By the time he reached the tree line the sound of engines was loud in the air.

One was a four-wheel-drive truck, the sort with lifts that caused it to sit chest-high off the ground. The other was an SUV. Both dark green or black. Both blasting music and filled with drunk or just plain rowdy scumbags.

His cell vibrated in his pocket. It was her. He answered with, "I'm here. Call 911."

This wasn't going to be like the jerks last night. Those two had been sober and fully capable of being scared.

The ruckus these guys were causing just climbing out of their vehicles warned that the bastards wouldn't be scared of much. Not in their condition.

Never a good thing.

If Deacon could get the drop on one, he would gain the upper hand. He moved through the shadowed tree line. Counted heads as he went. Four. All sounded drunk or high and ready to cause trouble.

"Come on out here, Cece Winters!" The one who appeared to be the leader shouted.

He stood at the bottom of the porch steps.

The porch light flared to life and the front door swung open.

"Oh, hell," Deacon muttered.

She stepped out onto the porch, the shotgun in her hand aimed at the SOB at the bottom of the steps.

The commotion that followed sent Deacon's tension skyrocketing. Three weapons—looked like hunting rifles—suddenly appeared in the hands of the man's buddies, all aimed at Cece. Deacon palmed his gun.

Anything he did at this point could cause one of these drunken fools to pull the trigger.

"I called Sheriff Tanner," Cece warned. "He and his deputies are on the way right now."

"Good," one of the idiots said. "They'll get here just in time to pick up the pieces of your skinny ass from all over that porch."

The man at the bottom of the steps twisted around to face his friends. "Show some respect. Put those damned guns away. Right now, damn it!"

"She's got a shotgun aimed at you!" one of the three said. "Hell, man, she killed her crazy daddy. What's to keep her from killing you?"

"Hell, I ain't afraid of Cece. We used to be sweethearts. Now put your guns down and get back in your damned vehicles while I talk to the lady."

So this was the one boyfriend she'd had before going up the river. Evidently he wasn't any smarter than he'd been all those years ago.

The three weren't too happy, and they let it be known, but they did as their leader instructed. All three climbed into their vehicles and turned the music even louder. If Deacon was lucky the sheriff would get here before things got too interesting.

Deacon moved back through the tree line until he was parallel with the porch. The best he could tell, the man wasn't armed, but he could be carrying a piece in his boot. No way to make a firm determination.

"I just came to talk to you, Cece," the man said. "You should have called me when you got home. I can't believe I had to hear it on the street."

She laughed but didn't lower her shotgun. "Ricky Olson. Now why in this world would I call you? You never came to court to see how my case was going even once. You never even wrote me a letter all those years I was in prison."

"You're right." He nodded, grabbed the handrail to steady himself. "I was a total jerk. I should have come to see you before it was too late. I should have written."

"What do you want, Ricky? Like I said, the sheriff is on the way."

He climbed a couple of steps. "I just want to talk."

Deacon braced to move.

"We have nothing to talk about. You're drunk, Ricky. You should go home."

To her credit, she held her aim steady.

He climbed the final two steps. "I need to show you how sorry I am." He pounded a fist against his chest. "I should have taken better care of you. What happened was partly my fault. Your daddy was a piece of garbage and I should have testified on your behalf. It was the least I could do. That lawyer of yours asked me to, but my folks didn't want me to get involved. We were kids. You know, we did what our folks told us." He shrugged. "Most of the time, anyway."

"Well, I appreciate your apology, Ricky, but that's all water under the bridge. I've moved on. You should, as well."

He walked right up to her, allowing the muzzle of her shotgun to bore into his chest. Deacon gritted his teeth. This was going to get ugly.

"I want to make it up to you, Cece, baby."

"Go on, Ricky," Cece warned.

The music in the vehicles abruptly went silent. Whatever was about to happen, the guys with this asshole were anticipating a move.

Deacon had one chance and this was it.

He bolted out of the clearing at a dead run and was on the porch next to Ricky whatever-the-hell-his-name-was before the other guys could react. The barrel of his Glock bored into the man's temple. "Back off, Ricky."

Doors opened and curses swarmed in the air.

"In the house," Deacon ordered Cece.

She hesitated. Her eyes round with fear.

"Now," Deacon roared.

He wrapped his forearm around Ricky's throat and whirled him around, using him as a shield from the others. He stabbed the muzzle a little harder into his temple. "Tell your friends to back off, Ricky, and we won't have a problem."

Rifles were aimed at Deacon's head. He split his focus between the three approaching the steps and the idiot backed against his chest.

"I guess we've got a problem," Deacon threatened as he gouged the barrel a little harder.

"Hold up." Ricky held out his hands to his friends. "Let me and this gentleman talk for a minute, boys. We seem to have a little misunderstanding."

The three stopped in their tracks.

"You better hurry up, Ricky," the tallest of his buddies reminded. "She said she called the sheriff."

"Go on now," Ricky urged. "Get in the truck. Let me handle this."

When the three did as he asked, he spoke again. "You put your weapon down and I'll be on my way. I didn't come here for trouble. I just came to see her."

Deacon lowered his weapon but he didn't tuck it away. "Don't come back, Ricky. She doesn't want to see you."

Deacon dropped his arm from the other man's throat.

And then the dumbass went stupid.

Rather than walk away, he twisted and socked Deacon in the jaw.

Cheers went up from inside the parked vehicles.

The guy got in another punch before Deacon could get his weapon tucked away, then he leveled old Ricky with one solid cross.

Two seconds of silence echoed from the vehicles before the doors flew open. The three sidekicks rushed forward, rifles aimed.

Deacon knew better than to reach for his own. Instead, he raised his hands in surrender.

The door behind him opened and Cece was suddenly standing in front of him, her shotgun aimed at the threesome.

"Back in the house, Cece," he ordered.

She ignored him. "Get the hell out of here," she shouted to the three and then she shoved Ricky down the steps with her foot. "And take this piece of trash with you."

Blue lights throbbed in the darkness. Two patrol cars skidded to a stop between the trespassers and the porch. Deacon took the weapon from Cece.

Tanner and his deputies cuffed and loaded up Olson and his friends. Tanner took Deacon's and Cece's statements and then assured her that wreckers would arrive shortly and haul the trespassing vehicles away.

Tanner studied Deacon a moment before he left. There would be questions from the sheriff. He was suspicious of Deacon. Smart man.

For the first time in all these years, Deacon wondered if he was any better than the scumbags the deputies just hauled away.

"You need some ice for that jaw."

Deacon turned from the window and faced her. "It's not that bad. A lucky swing."

She laughed. A real laugh. The sound startled him. Free and relaxed, sweet.

"It is that bad," she countered as she reached up and touched his jaw.

He flinched and drew away.

She dropped her hand, obviously confused by his reaction to her touch. "Sorry. Let me get some ice."

He watched her walk away. It was only at that moment that he realized she was wearing just the night-shirt. No wonder Tanner had eyed him so speculatively.

Damn.

When she returned with ice wrapped in a hand towel he hadn't moved from the spot where he was standing when she left him.

She offered it to him. "I really am sorry about all this. I shouldn't have called you."

He clenched his fingers in the towel lumpy with ice. "I hope you're not serious. I think you can likely imagine what would have happened during the twenty minutes or so it took Tanner and his deputies to arrive."

He exiled the images from his mind.

When she said nothing, he added, "Your old friend came here to hurt you."

She nodded. "I'm well aware of his intentions and I genuinely appreciate your help." Her arms went over her chest. "But this is not your problem. It's mine. You've been a really good neighbor. Gone above and beyond the call. But it's not fair that my tragic life is doing all this…" she gestured to his face "…to you."

"Life isn't fair sometimes." He jammed the ice against his throbbing jaw.

She stared at the floor as if she wasn't sure what to say next. He understood perfectly the juncture where things had gone wrong. Damn it.

He reached out to her, touched her arm. She stared at his hand.

"I overreacted when you touched me. I'm sorry for that. I just don't want you to get the wrong impression."

She looked up at him. "That you want to take advantage of me somehow because I'm this helpless woman who's all alone?"

He hoped she didn't see the guilt in his eyes. He was the one dropping his hand away. "I—"

"First, I'm not helpless. Second, do you know how long it's been since someone who wasn't wearing a prison uniform touched me?"

The air in the room suddenly seemed too thick to draw into his lungs. "I'm a little unclear on what you might want me to say to that."

She shook her head. "I don't want you to say anything. I want you to touch me." She took a step closer. "I want you to kiss me. I want you to make me feel something besides anger and resentment."

He told himself not to touch her—to walk away. He couldn't do it. He reached out, cupped her cheek in his hand, slid his thumb over her bottom lip. His body tightened with need and he hated himself for it.

"One day you'll look back and be glad that I chose this moment to say good-night." He lowered his hand and turned away.

"Please don't go."

Despite his every effort to keep walking, he stopped. Cursed himself for the weakness.

"I don't want to be alone. I feel like I've been alone forever."

Somehow he found the strength to face her once more without grabbing her and kissing her into silence…and doing all the things that were suddenly rushing into his head. "I'll stay." He pointed to the sofa. "Right there and you'll be in your room."

She nodded. "Fair enough."

He felt guilty about that, too.

There was nothing remotely fair about his motives.

Chapter Seven

Sunday, August 4

She was going to church.

It was Sunday, after all. She had as much right as anyone else to do so.

Cece checked her reflection in the mirror over the dresser. Her skin was way too pale to wear this sundress but she didn't care. Prison did that to a person. She wanted them to see what they had done to her with their lies.

Would it matter?

No. They wouldn't care.

She took a breath and turned away from the mirror. Whether it mattered to them or not—whether it made the slightest difference, she wanted all of them to know. She wanted them to hear what she had to say.

They being her older brother and her sister.

Maybe she should include Levi. After all, he was one of them now. What could have happened since she saw him last month? In all this time he had never mentioned going to the other side.

He'd always hated the church and their father's followers.

What could Marcus have on Levi that had suddenly caused such a turnaround?

Evidently enough to keep him away from her beyond that brief drive-by. Maybe Marcus had made some threat that backed Levi off. Her little brother had always yearned for his older brother's approval, even when it was wrong.

Eight plus years ago they had all had their say.

Today she intended to have hers. She opened her bedroom door and the smell of fresh-brewed coffee filled her lungs, reminding her that *he* was here.

Deacon Ross. Warmth spread through her despite the cold that lingered with thoughts of the family who had abandoned her. Just as quickly she went cold again. She had practically begged him to kiss her and do anything else he might want to do. She closed her eyes and shook her head. How would she ever look him in the eye again? He no doubt thought she was every bit as pathetic as the rumors suggested.

She opened her eyes and faced the facts. She was. Pathetic, that was. As embarrassing as it was to confess—even to herself—her one sexual experience had been with the jerk who showed up drunk on her porch last night. In fact, the only boy who had ever kissed her was that same knucklehead. Unless she counted the guard who had forced his mouth over hers and would have raped her if not for the interference of the one inmate in the whole prison who had cared enough to step in.

Such a sad, miserable life.

Her grandmother had left her a college fund and some money. She should just leave now and never look back.

But she couldn't. She owed it to her grandmother to

do this. Besides, if she didn't, this would haunt her the rest of her life. Her education, any career she attempted, would all be impacted by her record as a convicted murderer—a killer.

She had told herself a million times that it didn't matter. She didn't care what anyone else thought. But that had been a lie. She wanted people to know the truth, especially the people in this town who had been so quick to condemn her. No one had cared enough to save four kids from a fanatical, no doubt insane father when their mother died. Everyone had just looked the other way and allowed him to drag them into his obsession.

Those same people had jumped at the chance to condemn her after his murder.

One way or another she was going to show them all. She was innocent.

For the first time since she'd realized that she was going to be released, she knew what she wanted.

She wanted them to know her grandmother had been right about her. She wanted her life back.

The one someone in this town had stolen from her.

With a renewed sense of determination, she went to the kitchen where Deacon leaned against the counter with a mug of steaming coffee in his hand. She stilled, thought of the way that hand had felt against her cheek.

"Good morning." He lifted his mug. "Coffee's hot and strong."

A glance at the clock told her she had slept until past eight. She could not remember when she had last done that. Of course, they had been up most of the night. She was glad to see his jaw wasn't swollen and the bruise was so small it was hardly noticeable.

"Good morning. Wait." She stared at the coffeepot on the counter. "I don't have a coffeepot."

"I went next door and got mine."

"Oh. Well, thanks." She crossed to the pot and poured herself a cup.

"I take it you have plans this morning." He nodded to the dress she wore.

She braced her hip against the cabinet and sipped the hot coffee, mostly to buy time. When she had savored the bold brew, she said, "I'm going to church."

He set his mug aside and leveled his gaze on her. "Unless you're going to First Baptist or over to the Methodist one, I would think long and hard about taking that step. I don't think anyone's going to welcome you with open arms."

She downed another swallow, scalding her throat. "It's a free country. I'm a free woman. I can go wherever I want."

He shrugged one broad shoulder. "That's true. If that's what you really want to do, I suppose there's nothing stopping you."

"Nothing at all."

She focused on the coffee until she had finished it. He did the same. Rather than go for more, she rinsed out her cup and announced that she was ready to go.

"Would you like to come with me?" She had not actually planned to ask that, but there it was…hanging in the air between them.

"Do you want me to come with you?" Those brown eyes of his watched her steadily, assessing her motives.

He did a lot of that assessing. She didn't actually mind. She had lived with deceit for so long she very much preferred straightforward. Other than that one off moment, this man had been more straightforward with her than anyone she knew.

"I was thinking it might be a good idea in case I run into those guys from last night." She hadn't really thought about that at all, but it sounded as good as any other excuse that popped into her mind.

"I think maybe you're right." He rinsed his mug and sat it on the counter next to the sink. "What time does the service start?"

"Not until nine, but I want to speak to the *reverend* before the crowd arrives." Marcus was about as much a reverend as she was…as their father had been.

"I'll drive."

"Thanks." Relief filled her. She hadn't been looking forward to facing Marcus alone. But she would have done exactly that if necessary. She wasn't going to permit fear to paralyze her.

She locked the door, checked to ensure the lock engaged. Deacon waited for her at the steps. They walked to his truck together. He opened the door for her and she climbed into the passenger seat. He closed the door and walked around the hood. It occurred to her that she really knew very little about this man. He was her neighbor. Relatively new in town. That first day, in the parking lot at Ollie's, the police officer seemed to know him. Surely that was a good sign.

Hadn't she already decided she could trust him?

When he slid behind the wheel, she asked, "Where did you live before you bought the Wilburn place?"

He started the engine, his gaze locked on hers. "A few places. Nashville, Louisville, and a couple of years in Mobile. But most of my time has been spent in Nashville."

"Where did you go to school?"

He checked the road in both directions before pulling out of her driveway. "UT."

The University of Tennessee. She was impressed. "What was your major?"

He glanced at her before refocusing his attention on the road. "You nervous or did you suddenly decide you needed to know me better?"

Her cheeks flushed. "Both, I guess. I woke up this morning and realized I don't really know very much about you. What I do know is good, but…" She shrugged. "You know."

"I do. What else would you like me to tell you?"

"What do you do? Besides rescue needy neighbors, I mean."

He flashed her a smile. "I'm an employee of the federal government but I'm currently on leave. I'm considering a career change. Maybe I'll go into the private sector and stick with private investigations."

Federal government could mean any number of things. She supposed he didn't want to talk about it and she certainly had no right to demand an explanation.

"I thought maybe you were already a private detective." He'd said he'd helped Frasier with her case, hadn't he? She had thought his being a private investigator and working for her attorney explained his dedication to helping her out of all those tight spots she'd found herself in since her release.

"Only on occasion."

Before she could ask anything else, he made the turn onto the road that ended in a graveled parking area surrounding an old-fashioned church. It was only about twenty-five years old but it had been built to look as if it were an original structure from the town's settlement.

Inside was nothing more than a huge room of worship and two bathrooms that were tucked behind the stage-like pulpit. Between the bathroom doors were the stairs to the basement.

The white building with its plain, handmade wooden cross looked exactly the same as it had when she exited those doors for the last time nearly twelve years ago. She had walked out on one of her father's sermons when she was sixteen and she had not set foot back inside those doors since. Two entwined S's stood above the double entrance doors.

Salvation Survivalists.

Walking God's path of readiness.

All of it was based on lies.

"Do you know if he's here?"

Cece pushed aside the troubling thoughts and studied the SUV parked to one side of the building. The emergency exit was on that side. Her father had always parked there, choosing to enter by the side door rather than the front. But when it was time for his followers to arrive, he would be found standing on that stoop, front and center, with the double doors open wide.

Cece's stomach cramped. How she had hated the man. No matter that he was her biological father, he had been a devil.

She shook her head. "That SUV is parked where my father always parked so I'm assuming that's Marcus." She reached for the door handle. "I'll know soon enough."

Deacon put his hand on her arm, waylaying her. "I can go in with you."

She shook her head. "He won't say what's really on his mind in front of anyone but me. A good liar never reveals his true self in front of anyone he can't discredit or control."

At least that's the way it had been when they were kids. She stared at the building that should be the setting of a horror flick. They weren't kids anymore. She had not laid eyes on Marcus or Sierra since the day she was pronounced guilty, more than eight years ago. To some degree she could almost understand what made Marcus do the things he did—he wanted to be like their father. He wanted all that their father had built. Sierra was a different story. When they were little, he'd treated Sierra no differently than he had Cece. By the time she was a teenager, she could do no wrong. He'd treated her like a little princess.

"I'll be standing outside the truck. Scream if you need me."

She shook her head, could not stop the smile. "Will do."

The gravel crunched under her sandaled feet as she slid out of the truck and closed the door. She was truly grateful her grandmother had kept all her stuff. She hadn't had much but she was thankful for it now.

She stared at the closed double doors a moment, perspiration beading under her arms and on her palms. She had forgotten how hot even the mornings in August were. Spending most of her time in one of the few Tennessee prisons with air-conditioning, she had forgotten a lot about being outside. Like how the air smelled when it wasn't surrounded by a towering fence. How different the sky appeared when you viewed it from between trees instead of from behind the bars of a tiny window.

As she had known it would be, the double-doored entry to the church was unlocked. She opened one side and walked in. The air was cooler. Apparently air-conditioning had been added since her last visit.

But the smell had not changed.

Old, dank. Her father had bought the pews from a salvage place. The seller claimed they came from a two-hundred-year-old church in northern Tennessee.

Marcus was doing the same thing she had watched her father do a thousand times, ensuring the hymnals and Bibles were tucked into the racks on the backs of the pews. No one who needed one or both should be without. Not that her father had ever preached straight from the Bible. Instead, he had twisted the words to suit his own purposes. Funny how no one ever seemed to notice.

Or maybe they were simply afraid to mention it.

She had mentioned it plenty of times. Likely another of the reasons her father had hated her so.

The floor creaked with her first step inside as if the building itself was offended by her presence.

Marcus looked up. The pleasant expression he had been wearing vanished.

"Blasphemy," he bellowed.

She kept walking toward him. "Probably." She glanced up. "I expect the roof to fall in any second."

"Leave this church!" He pointed to the door. "I will not have the likes of you desecrating this house of God."

Cece laughed, could not help herself. "God has never been any part of this, Marcus."

He began to move toward her then. Cece stilled. Let him come. She refused to be afraid.

"You murdered our father." His tone simmered with hatred and disgust.

"You know I did not. You lied and so did Sierra. The

only thing I want to know is why? Both of you hated him as much as I did. If you say you didn't, you're lying."

Fury twisted his lips. "You are the liar. Father knew what you were when he cast you out."

This man was her brother. How could he look at her with such sheer hatred and not the slightest flicker of basic human compassion?

"What've you done to Levi?"

"Levi has finally come to God." Marcus was close enough that he towered over her and had to glower down at her to look her in the eye. "I will not allow you to alter his course. Go back to the devil where you belong."

Cece peered up at him. "You know what I think? I think you killed our father. Look at all you had to gain. His church, his house. You came out with everything, Marcus. I wonder why the police didn't consider that."

"Foul bitch," he snarled. "You know Sierra and I had confirmed alibis."

"You two fooled everyone back then—except me. I'm going to set the record straight, Marcus. I will find the truth. This time you and Sierra won't be able to stop me."

"What is she doing here?"

Cece's gaze flew to the woman walking down that long center aisle. *Sierra.* Cece tried her best not to show how seeing her sister sucker-punched her, but she wasn't entirely successful. Some betrayals couldn't be so easily forgotten.

"Sierra." Cece drew in a big breath and steadied herself. "I was just telling Marcus how I'm looking for the truth. Why don't you help me find it?"

Sierra glared at their older brother. "What is she talking about, Marcus?"

Inside, where no one could see, Cece smiled.

"Get out," Marcus roared. "I won't have you here when the followers start to arrive."

"You shouldn't have come back, Cece," Sierra warned. "No one wants you here."

"When I find what I'm looking for," Cece said, "I'll be out of here so fast your head will spin. But I'm not going anywhere until then."

"Watch yourself, sister," Marcus mused with fire in his eyes. "There are many who wish you ill. I work diligently to keep my followers on the right track but I can't be expected to keep them all on the proper path."

"I'm aware," Cece assured him. "But your followers aren't going to stop me."

"God will take care of you, Cece," Sierra warned. "If I were you, I would be very afraid."

"Funny," Cece tossed back. "I'm not afraid at all."

She turned her back on the two and started toward the door.

Let them stew on that for a while.

Her brother started to pray. Sierra did the same.

Cece rolled her eyes.

DEACON PACED BACK AND FORTH, his gaze hardly leaving the entrance of the so-called church. He should never have allowed her to go in there alone. But she was right, her brother was far more likely to talk to her without an outsider around.

How had he stumbled so badly so far? He had been trained never to allow a civilian to walk into danger. Keeping her safe should have been a priority above all else—including solving the case. But it wasn't because he wanted the truth no matter the cost to her or anyone else.

She'd been found guilty of killing her own father. A woman like that wouldn't think twice about killing Deacon's partner.

Except now he wasn't so sure she had killed anyone.

He had waited a long time for this opportunity, had put his career and life on hold. Now he was riddled with second thoughts and uncertainty.

A car pulled into the lot, then another. He scanned the faces, shot another look at the door. What the hell was she doing in there? If the place filled with the older brother's followers anything could happen.

Before the thought fully formed in his brain Deacon had started for the entrance.

He was about to take the two steps up to the stoop when the door flew open and she stormed out.

"I'm done here," she said to him.

He nodded. "Okay."

They walked back to his truck amid curious stares from the ones who did not recognize Cece and hate-filled glares from those who did. He opened her door and waited for her to settle in the seat before he went around to the other side and climbed in behind the wheel.

"You recognize any of these people?"

"Some of them," she said as he backed away from the growing cluster of vehicles.

"Did you see Levi?"

"No. I think they've got him hidden away some-where. Probably at the house."

"Do you mean against his will?"

She waited until he had pulled out onto the road and turned back to her before she nodded. "I believe so. I know Levi. He wouldn't become one of them. Not for any reason. He might pretend if he had to, but he would never do it for real."

"You think we should talk to Sheriff Tanner?" He asked this knowing full well she would say no. Like him, her plans didn't include playing by the rules. Involving the authorities required playing by the rules.

"Tanner can't help with Marcus." She stared out the window at the passing landscape. "Marcus and his followers consider themselves above the law. They answer only to God and to their interpretation of his word. Besides, they're too careful to make a mistake in front of anyone like the sheriff."

He braked for the stop sign at an intersection. "Like I told you before, I'm ready to help. What would you like to do next?"

She stared at him for a long moment. Guilt assaulted him again at the idea of how young she looked…how innocent. But she wasn't innocent. Was she? He had totally lost his perspective during the past forty or so hours. He wasn't sure how to get it back.

"I want to go to the house."

"Heading there now." He flipped on the left turn signal and checked for oncoming traffic.

"No. I mean the house where I grew up."

He pushed the turn signal back to the neutral position. "To go onto your brother's property would be trespassing."

She shook her head. "It'll be breaking and entering because I'm going inside the house."

Deacon opted not to try and talk her out of the decision.
But one thing was certain—if she was going in,
so was he.

Chapter Eight

The house where Cece grew up was a large two-story farm-style home set back in the woods on a forty-acre piece of property her father had inherited from his father. About five acres around the house were cleared for the yard and a massive garden. Their family had never raised their own livestock. Fresh milk, eggs and meat had been purchased from local farmers or provided by followers. Her father had lived by the philosophy that a man should focus on what he was good at and leave the rest to someone else.

Mason Winters had never been good at anything but conning people into believing the garbage he doled out as gospel. In Cece's opinion, it was a miracle no one had killed him long before she was supposed to have done the deed.

Right around this bend in the mile-long drive would be the house. If they drove any closer, anyone at the house would see them. To the right, just through those woods, was the church. It seemed farther when driving from the house to the church or vice versa, but through the woods it wasn't far at all.

She turned to the man behind the wheel, who so far had gone along with her scheme without balking.

"You should probably stay in the truck. Me deciding to break the law is one thing, but I can't expect you to do the same."

Deacon stared at her as if she had lost her mind. Quite possibly she had. This was a risk. If Marcus caught her here, he would have her stoned or tortured in some other heinous manner rather than call the police. He would swear she had done something terrible and that he was only defending himself. She would either be dead or back in prison.

Which meant she could not get caught.

"Listen to me."

Deacon's words pulled her attention from those troubling thoughts to the man who'd spoken. This was the moment when he would tell her that if she went any further he was out. Completely understandable. He wasn't an outlaw or ex-con and she was. Her reputation was already a disaster. She had little to lose.

"The house," he went on, "belongs to Marcus now, right?"

She nodded. "He inherited it, yes. The house and the church. The one contingency is that he must always take care of his siblings—as long as they stay in the church. Levi and I were out of luck. Not that I wanted any of it. If I had inherited the place, I would have burned it down."

Before this was over, she might anyway.

"Did your father have guards when he was alive? Anyone who watched after the house when he was away?"

"Not as far as I know."

"All right." He looked around. "I'm going to back into

that narrow side road over there. I can park out of sight from the house or anyone who turns onto the driveway."

The side road he meant wasn't really a road. It was just a track that had formed over the years from the people who turned around in that spot when they realized they had taken the wrong road or changed their mind about visiting Reverend Winters. Cece had used that spot a few times herself. Usually when she needed to sneak back into the house for something she had left behind.

Once Deacon had backed into the clearing, he said, "I'll follow you as you approach the house, but I'll stay in the woods out of sight."

Considering all that Marcus had said to her in the church it was probably a good idea. He hated her. Sierra did, as well. It made Cece furious that she felt sad at the idea. She shouldn't care and somehow she still did. Wouldn't it be nice to cut them out of her heart entirely?

"Okay, if you think that's the best way."

"I do. What're you looking for, besides Levi?"

"I'm not sure. Maybe nothing beyond Levi. It's not like I think they'll have evidence of my innocence lying around. Or evidence of their own guilt, for that matter. I just need to look."

Her instincts wouldn't let go of the idea that there was something she needed to see.

She reached for the door handle.

"Remember, if you run into trouble—"

"I know," she said as she opened the door. "Scream."

"You got it."

Cece reached down deep for her courage, stepped out of the woods and started toward the house. As she rounded that curve and the house came into view, she immediately spotted two men. Both wore jeans and Salvation Survivalists tees. She didn't recognize either one. Well, well, her brother had decided guards were necessary.

The only reason to hire guards was if there was something worth guarding.

Had Marcus found out Levi visited her and decided to imprison him?

Deacon was trailing her. She felt confident he had spotted the guards, as well.

Standing on the porch, the two watched as she approached. They were armed. Rifles hung from straps draped over their shoulders. Thankfully, the rifles stayed on their shoulders as she approached. She had no desire to get herself shot.

When she was ten or so yards from the porch, she waved. "Hey. Is Levi home?"

The two men stared at her as if they weren't sure they should acknowledge her existence, much less speak to her.

"Marcus said he had stayed home sick today. I thought I'd check on him."

The taller of the two looked at his watch. His instinct, she suspected, was to call Marcus. But he couldn't. The church service was already underway.

"I'll ask him," the other guy said. "See if he's feeling up to company."

Anticipation seared through her veins. She was going in. At least, as long as Levi was there, and the man had basically said he was. "Thanks, I appreciate it."

The one who had checked his watch stayed on the porch and watched her while the other one went inside. She reminded herself to breathe but her lungs wouldn't cooperate. The service lasted a couple of hours, considering confessions and healings and all that other nonsense, so she had some time.

All she needed was inside.

Maybe she would have a chance to talk some sense into Levi.

As if the thought had summoned him, he appeared at the door, the guard behind him. He stared at her for a moment before he moved. Then he stormed across the porch and down the steps. He did not stop until he was standing toe to toe with her.

"What're you doing here?" he demanded.

She flinched. His voice was hard and unforgiving.

"I came to see you."

He stuck his face in hers and whispered fiercely. "Meet me at the shack in twenty minutes." Louder, he added, "You cannot be here! You are not one of us anymore." He backed up a step. "Leave and never come back."

Cece hesitated, her brain reluctant to absorb what was happening.

"I said get out of here!" he shouted.

She fell back a step.

Levi turned back to the house. To the guards he said, "If she ever tries to come back here again, escort her to the road."

Cece could not bring herself to turn around until Levi disappeared into the house once more. Then she turned and ran. No matter that he had told her to meet him at the shack, the rest of his words shook her to the core.

He was the one person in her family she had always

been able to count on. Was it possible he really was one of them now?

She thought of the shack and how he had said to meet him there.

Maybe not. She could hang onto hope for a little while longer.

Deacon was already standing at the truck when she made it back there.

"Let's get out of here," he said, his face dark with fury.

If he had not heard Levi's message about meeting him at the shack, hopefully the others hadn't either.

"We have one more stop." She explained what Levi had whispered to her as they climbed into his truck.

"Where?" He didn't sound entirely convinced.

"It's an old tumbledown shack where we used to play as kids. I think it's actually on the neighboring property, but that never stopped us from using it."

After a couple of false starts she finally directed him down the right dirt road. Narrow, crowded on both sides by the forest, the road only led as far as the branch of the creek that crossed a portion of both properties. Fed by an underground stream, there was always water running in the creek—even during the hottest part of the year, like now.

The sound of the trickling water was soothing to her frazzled nerves. She had loved exploring these woods as a kid. They were the only pleasant memories she had after her mother's death. Deacon locked up his truck and moved along the side of the creek with her.

"There's a point where we have to cross to the other side." She hoped that fallen tree trunk was still sturdy enough to act as a bridge or they would be getting wet.

"You have any reason to doubt his motives for meeting you here?"

"No. If he had wanted to hurt me he would have had the guards take me in the house and keep me until Marcus came home."

"Valid point."

It was a good half mile before they reached the crossing point. Neither she nor Deacon had spoken after that initial burst of conversation. Sound carried in the woods. No one wanted to end up a target.

"I'll go first," Deacon suggested. "If it'll hold me, it'll hold you."

"If you're sure." She seriously appreciated his need to play the part of the gentleman. Part of her worried about him tiring of seeing after her. She was really starting to like his company for far more than his gallantry.

So not smart, Cece.

He adjusted his hat and stepped up onto the old log. About midway across it shifted and Cece's breath caught. Then he was on the other side.

"You think you can handle the pressure?" he asked.

"Get real. I did this a million times as a kid."

She took a breath and stepped up onto the log. Without hesitating, she moved across the length of it and hopped down on the other side.

"What did I tell you?"

He grinned. "Like riding a bike, huh?"

"Exactly." Speaking of that, she had to get her driver's license renewed. Tomorrow, she decided. No putting it off. Her job search had to start tomorrow, as well as reporting in with her probation officer.

The shack wasn't far once they were across the creek. It looked deserted and ready to fall in. Funny, when they were kids it had seemed so big and so cool. Like a pirate's stronghold or a gangster's hideout.

"Is that it?"

She nodded. "It's been a while since I was here."

Before she reached the shack, Levi stepped from behind it. He glared at Deacon and then at her. "What the hell are you doing, Cece?"

"I could ask you the same thing." All the anger she had been holding back since walking through those gates at the prison and finding no one waiting for her ignited inside her. "You were supposed to pick me up. Do you have any idea how it felt to wait and wait and finally realize that no one was coming?"

"I'm sorry. Marcus wouldn't let me."

"Oh, so Marcus is your lord and master now?" She shook her head. "How did this happen, Levi?"

"First…" Her little brother glowered at her. "Who the hell is this?"

"A friend." She refused to tell him anything else. He had no right to demand anything from her.

"You think I'm going to talk in front of this *friend*?"

She was grateful Deacon kept quiet. "I trust him completely. You can trust him, too. He's helping me." When Levi would have argued, she added, "He kept Ricky and his friends from doing no-telling-what to me last night." She pointed to Deacon. "He stopped the two guys who planned to burn me out the night before. Oh, and did I mention that he kept a herd of Marcus's zombies from stoning me outside Ollie's?"

It wasn't until that moment, standing there staring at her little brother and recounting all that had happened in less than forty-eight hours, that the landslide of emotions hit her. She started to cry and she couldn't stop.

No matter that she wanted to. No matter that she was embarrassing the hell out of herself. No matter that she hated the weakness. She. Could. Not. Stop.

"Cece, I'm sorry." Levi wrapped his arms around her. "I am so sorry. I messed up again."

She shuddered with the sobs rocking through her weary body. She was so tired of all of it. She should just leave and never look back.

But then she would never be free of this millstone. And all her grandmother had done would be for naught.

Levi drew back from her, held her by the shoulders. "After I came to see you the last time, I decided I was going to try and find the truth to save you the trouble. I know how much you want to prove your innocence." He exhaled a big breath. "It's just taken me longer than I expected."

Cece swiped at her eyes. "What're you talking about? This is too dangerous. You shouldn't be trying to fool Marcus. He's capable of anything, including killing you, you know that."

"I'm getting close, Cece. I heard him and Sierra talking the other night. She was telling him that he had to do something or you would figure it all out."

The words gave her pause. "Figure out what?"

"I don't know yet. For the first couple of weeks I was there they were real careful not to say anything around me or to leave me alone at the house. But they're loosening up now. Today was the first time I was ever able to stay at the house alone."

"What about the guards?"

He shook his head. "They don't come inside. I'm going through the house one room at a time looking for whatever I can find."

"It's too dangerous. Just forget it and come home with me." She did not want to lose her little brother. She had lost everyone else she cared about. She could not lose him, too. Nothing else was as important as his safety.

"Just let me do this. Let me keep listening and looking. When I have something, I'll come to you. Until then, you stay away from Marcus and Sierra. They're crazy, Cece." His eyes were wide with worry. "I mean, like, freaky crazy. I think Sierra might be on some sort of drugs. All she talks about is how she was daddy's princess and everybody better start treating her like one."

Obviously there was no talking him out of this. "Just be careful. Don't do anything too risky."

"I won't. I'm careful, I promise."

Cece hugged him hard. "I can't lose you," she whispered against his ear.

"I better get back." He drew away and smiled at her. "You look good, Cece. A little pale, but good."

She slugged him on the shoulder. "You know how to sweet-talk a girl."

He glanced at Deacon. "I don't know about this guy, though."

"I do," Cece assured him.

They hugged some more and then went their separate ways.

Cece could not talk as she and Deacon walked back to his truck. Her emotions were too raw. Too full, pressing against her breastbone.

When they were on the road headed toward home, she could not hold back anymore. She started to cry again. God, how she hated blubbering this way.

This time it was Deacon who held her. He pulled over to the side of the road and pulled her into his arms. He held her until she had cried herself out. Until there were no more tears left.

And then he took her home.

"YOU REALLY DID not have to go to all this trouble."

Deacon grinned. "I'm not exactly a chef but I always prided myself in making a hell of a grilled cheese sandwich."

She nibbled another bite. "The extra cheese is perfect."

Deacon picked up his glass of iced tea and took a swallow. "I'm glad you were able to see Levi today. I know you were worried about him."

He had considered several ways to bring up the subject again but he had put it off. She had been so torn up after the visit with her younger brother, he'd felt damned sorry for her.

He wasn't supposed to. Hated that he did, but he wasn't heartless.

Apparently, the girl he had thought was fully capable of killing another human wasn't entirely heartless, either. No one without a heart could cry like that.

"Me, too. But I'm worried about him. He wants to be my hero but I'm so worried he will get himself killed."

"You believe Marcus and his followers are capable of murder?"

She nodded and stared down at her sandwich.

"Cece? What's going on?" The lady had something on her mind. Something she was worried about telling him. Anticipation drummed in his chest. "You should know by now you can talk to me. I'm on your side in all this. You can trust me on that one. I won't let you down."

Three lies in a row. He was on a roll.

Funny thing was, they didn't *feel* like lies.

"There was a man." She clasped her hands together, her forearms braced on her knees. "Back when everything went to hell. His name was K.C., you know, like the initials."

Shock radiated through Deacon. K.C. was the cover name Jack had been using. K for Kelley and C for Charlie, his kids.

"He came around my grandmother's house a few times asking questions. I think he was some kind of undercover agent or..." She shrugged. "I don't know. Anyway, my grandmother wouldn't talk to him. She warned me not to, either. She said he was trouble and that we did not need any trouble. She was trying to keep a low profile because my father was on one of his rampages."

"Rampages?" It was all Deacon could do not to grab her and shake her. He needed answers and it felt as if he was so damned close.

"Every so often he would decide I was his daughter and he wanted me back. He would give my grandmother hell. I suspected she was giving him money to get him to stay away from me, but she would never admit as much."

"So you never spoke to this K.C.?" He reminded himself to breathe. To keep the tension inside where she couldn't see.

"He caught up with me once at the diner where I worked as a waitress. It was the only time he tried to talk to me. I guess my grandmother put the fear of God in him because he never approached me before or after that day."

"What happened?"

"He asked me if I was ever aware of my father being involved with a group known as Resurrection. I had heard of them. A secret society of preppers—you know, the doomsday people. I told him the truth, that if my father had anything to do with them, I knew nothing about it. The members don't want anyone to know who they are, you know? I heard my father say once that it was because when Armageddon comes they don't want the fools who aren't prepared to come to them for help."

"Did this K.C. seem okay? Upset or angry by your answer?"

"He was nice. Kind, you know, in a fatherly sort of way. Not that I had ever had a role model to go by, but he was very nice. I didn't understand why my grandmother was so afraid of him. Anyway, I never saw him again after that. I guess I couldn't give him what he needed so he moved on. He seemed really intent on learning about my father's connection to that group."

"You're certain your father wasn't part of them?"

"I don't think so, but I really tried to stay clear of him. Even before I left home, I avoided him like the plague. We hated each other."

"Would Levi know? He stayed home after you left, right? You think he was approached by this K.C. guy?"

She searched his face, his eyes. "I don't know. He never mentioned the prepper stuff or the man. Do you know him?"

This was the moment. If he lied and later she found out—and she would—she wouldn't forgive him. If he told the truth, she could balk here and now.

He was too close to take the risk.

"I'm just looking at all the possibilities." When she still looked suspicious, he posed a question that he thought would erase that look from her eyes. "You think this K.C. could have had something to do with your father's murder?"

She frowned. "I don't know. I never considered the possibility. I guess it's possible." She turned back to Deacon. "But he was really nice, so I don't know."

Nice.

Really nice.

The realization that this woman—the woman he had studied and obsessed over for months—knew nothing about Jack or his disappearance hit him square between the eyes.

She wasn't the one.

He had despised her for so long. Hated her, actually. Dreamed of taking her down. Those people who had thrown stones at her that first day were likely there because he had leaked the date and time of her exit from prison. He had wanted her to be humiliated, shamed.

And he had been wrong.

"I'm sorry." The words choked out of him before he could stop them.

She blinked. "Why are you sorry?"

Before he could answer, she reached for his hand and took it in her own. "You've been so nice to me, Deacon. I'm not sure how I could have gotten through all this without your help. Thank you."

He managed a smile though he felt sick—sick at what he had done. "You don't need to thank me."

"I know you didn't want to kiss me when I asked.

But is it okay if I kiss you? On the cheek, I mean? To show my appreciation."

"Sure."

She stretched toward him and kissed him on the jaw. Her lips were soft, like a butterfly's wings against his skin.

She drew away quickly, shot to her feet as if she intended to run. "I should clean up the mess in the kitchen."

"I'll help." He stood, reached for his plate.

"You did the cooking," she argued.

"At least let me watch."

"Fine." She picked up her plate and glass and led the way over to the sink.

He watched as she filled it with hot water. There was no dishwasher. When she'd wiped down the counter and the stovetop, he decided to dig a little deeper into the older brother.

"Based on what I know about Marcus, he never married. No kids."

She paused, her hands deep in the sudsy water. "There was a girl back when he was in high school, but they broke up and as far as I know there wasn't another serious relationship."

"You think he has been too focused on building his followers? Or maybe what he really wants, he can't have because of his beliefs. Maybe he fell for someone who isn't a follower?"

"It's possible, I guess, but Marcus is so uptight. I can't see him doing anything like that. He would die first. He's just a loner, I think. He stopped having friends and participating in extracurricular activities at school when he was really young, like twelve or thirteen. He was that devoted to following in our father's footsteps.

"He was the only teenage boy I knew who spent all his free time with the elderly of the congregation. Every time one of them would pass away he would lock himself in his room for days. Maybe he used up all his compassion when he was young and had none left by the time he was an adult. He certainly never had any for me."

Deacon picked up a tea towel and reached for the plate she had rinsed. "What about Sierra? Was she similarly devoted?"

Cece shook her head. "When we were little kids, she adored me. The three of us, including Levi, played all the time and we were happy. As happy as kids in our situation could be. But then about the time our father kicked me out, she changed. It was like she suddenly hated me. She hardly left the house. It wasn't until she finally had a boyfriend that I started to see her around town again. She still had nothing to say to me, but at least she acted somewhat normal. Whenever I'd ask Levi he would only say that she was nuts. He thinks she was taking drugs even back then."

Her family had been devastated after their mother's death. Deacon was beginning to think it had more to do with Marcus and Sierra than it did with the father.

He watched her rinse the sink and dry her hands.

When had this investigation become about her and her family instead of his partner?

Chapter Nine

Monday, August 5

Cece watched as the number on the digital readout changed from 21 to 22, then she stared at the blue tag with the number 25 in her hand.

Apparently the first week of the month was the busy time at the driver's license renewal office. She sighed. She still didn't feel comfortable driving, but she supposed that would come with time. Living in the small-town South, it was necessary. There were no handy buses or trains to take you around town.

Deacon had offered to bring her but she had decided she needed some time alone. She glanced around the crowded lobby. Not that she was alone, by any means, but so far no one had recognized her. Basically she was alone. Everyone in the lobby was either scrolling on their cell phones or chatting with their neighbor in the next chair.

Since Cece had no cell phone and didn't know either of the older men seated next to her, she just sat there. If she was very still maybe they wouldn't notice her and strike up a conversation. It was human nature to ask about school, jobs, kids, the everyday sorts of things.

Telling anyone she had spent her college years in prison and had no boyfriend, much less a husband and kids, was not exactly an acceptable icebreaker. The person asking would no doubt regret having done so.

Her mind drifted to the new images imprinted in her memory of her neighbor lingering in her kitchen, staring out the window over the sink, a steaming cup of coffee in his hand. She had stared at him a good long while before making her presence known this morning. The way the jeans he wore molded to his body. The way his shirt stretched over his shoulders. His shaggy brown hair curled around his collar.

Some part of her wondered why this stranger would go so far out of his way to help her. Did he have nothing better to do? Was he simply bored? She wanted him to be exactly what he appeared to be—the stranger next door who liked playing the role of Good Samaritan.

But another part of her worried that she was making a mistake. She didn't really know him. Did not know his true motive.

Yet she wanted to know him…wanted to do things with him. She felt heat rush up her cheeks. She covertly glanced at the people around her as if she had said the words out loud rather than thought them.

It was true, though. She wanted to kiss him, to be kissed by him. She wanted him to touch her, to show her all the ways a man could pleasure a woman. Her one and only sexual experience had been awkward and bumbling with that jerk Ricky Olson. Just kissing Deacon on the cheek had made her pulse race.

That he genuinely seemed interested in helping her with her search for the truth just made the idea of—

"That's you."

Cece jumped. The man to her right gestured to the number she held and then to the display. She forced her lips into a polite smile. "Oh, thank you."

She hurried to the counter and presented the required documentation. The clerk informed her that since her license had been expired for so long she would need to retake the driver's test. This was not something she had come prepared to do, but there it was. She could either do it now or come back.

Now was as good a time as any.

Once the written part was over, the administering officer climbed into her truck and advised her of the route for the road test. Cece drove. She made the turns he requested and parallel parked as best she could in front of the federal courthouse. The officer said little else to her, only giving her the directions. By the time they returned to the office, her nerves were shot and she had no idea if she had passed his test.

He led the way back to the counter and gave a paper to the clerk who had waited on her when she first arrived. The woman smiled. "Congratulations, Miss Winters. You passed. Stand right over there on that red X and I'll take your picture for the license."

The photo and remaining paperwork took only a couple of minutes. Cece left with a paper version of her new license. The final version would arrive in the mail in ten to fourteen days.

Cece stopped by the insurance office and updated the information in her file with her new driver's license number. Next was the visit to her parole officer. That part was surprisingly easy. The man, Mr. Berringer, was nice. He was older, sixtyish, and very kind. He made Cece feel as if she was a real person who mattered, not a recently released murderer. She was grateful. Funny how she found that sort of kindness in the least-expected places. The sheriff, the chief of police, they had all been exceedingly nice to her. Like the man next door.

Afterward, rather than going straight home, she decided to stop by the cemetery to visit her grandmother's grave. She made a quick stop at the florist and bought her grandmother's favorite roses.

At the cemetery she walked through the aisles of headstones until she found the right one. Though she had not been here for her grandmother's funeral, she had been present for her grandfather's. Emily Broward was interred next to the man she had loved her whole life.

Cece knelt down and placed the flowers against the headstone. "Hey, Gran."

Emily Broward had preferred Gran to Grandmother. Cece smiled as she thought of how her grandmother had never failed to look less than perfectly put together. Her hair was always just so, the makeup, the outfit. Even when she was gardening she looked ready to drop everything and run to the country club. The one person in the world she had loved as much as her husband was her only child, Cece's mother. She had always said her grandkids came in a close second, especially after Cece's mother died.

For as long as Cece could remember, everyone believed that Emily Broward was partial to Cece because she looked so much like her mother, but that wasn't the real reason. Cece was the one who spent the most time with her. She took every possible opportunity to be with her grandmother. Helped her in any way she needed.

Then Cece had moved in after her father kicked her out. Of course they were close. Her grandmother had not chosen Cece over anyone else; Cece had chosen her.

Movement a few yards away drew her attention. The blonde woman walking the cemetery with her German shepherd looked vaguely familiar. Cece watched her until she was close enough to get a good look at her face.

Rowan DuPont. The undertaker's daughter.

Cece didn't really know her—not personally. But she had seen her on the news. First because she'd published a book that gained her national attention. Seemed funny to know someone from her small hometown who was so famous. Then she had seen the news about Rowan's father being murdered by a serial killer who was a close friend. Cece vividly remembered Mr. DuPont. He had taken care of her grandfather. He'd also taken care of her mother, but she didn't remember as much about that funeral. She'd only been six at the time.

Rowan's mother had died when she was young, too. She had hung herself right there in the funeral home only a few months after Rowan's twin sister drowned.

Their gazes collided and the other woman smiled. Cece smiled back. They both had plenty of tragedy in their histories. If Rowan DuPont could pick up the pieces and move on, maybe there was hope for Cece.

Rowan and her dog walked out of the cemetery and disappeared down the block. She, too, had come back to Winchester after a great tragedy. Somehow she had found a way to survive the rumors and the gossip.

Cece wasn't sure she wanted to try. She just wanted the truth. Then she wanted to be anywhere but here.

"You always could fool her."

Cece's gaze shot up to meet her sister's. Sierra stood six or seven feet away, her face full of accusation.

Pushing to her feet, Cece held her contemptuous glare. "Fooling people is your specialty, Sierra, not mine. I guess you never outgrew that childish habit."

Sierra glared at her, her raven-black hair and equally black eyes so unlike Cece's own pale coloring. "You should move on, Cece. You can't change the past. You did what you did and no one is ever going to believe your lies claiming otherwise. You took him away from all of us."

Cece took a step toward Sierra. She refused to allow her little sister to use her intimidation tactics anymore. "I did not kill him, Sierra. Maybe it was you. You were the one still stuck under his thumb. The princess he doted on all the time. The one who did everything he said. Maybe you got tired of his rules."

Hatred filled Sierra's black eyes. "You couldn't possibly understand how much I loved him. He was everything to me."

Now that was about as far from the truth as could be gotten. "Liar. You hated him as much as I did."

Sierra laughed. "Whatever my true feelings, I was so much smarter than you, sister. I did not go around telling people how much I hated him the way you did. Even if you hadn't been found with blood all over you, everyone would still have believed you killed him."

"Maybe it was Marcus. He was the one who had the most to gain. He took over the house, the church. It's all about him now."

"I'll be sure to tell him you said so." Sierra stepped toward her now. "You know he hates you for killing our father. He loved him so. Worshipped him, really.

He never wanted you to get out of jail. He still hasn't forgiven you. We both know how Marcus always took care of the sick and dying of Father's flock. Maybe he'll take care of you when your time comes, Cece. I would watch my back if I were you."

"Well…" Cece wasn't surprised in the least about her brother's feelings. Marcus had always been obsessed with their father. "You give him my best. And don't worry. I will be watching. I'm watching you both."

"Maybe it's Levi you should be worried about. He would have done anything for you. Maybe he killed Daddy and you took the fall for him." Sierra smiled. "I wonder if Marcus has ever considered that possibility. It is rather strange that Levi finally wanted back in the fold when it came time for you to be released. Maybe he's afraid the truth will finally come out."

Cece moved in toe to toe with her. "You leave Levi out of this. He had nothing to do with what happened to that old bastard. I'm just glad he's dead. I wish it *had* been me who shoved that knife into his loathsome chest over and over."

Fury whipped across Sierra's face. "I guess prison didn't rehabilitate you at all. You're still the same heartless bitch you were when we were kids."

"I'm not heartless, Sierra, I'm just not a fool. Mason Winters was a con artist and a pathetic excuse for a father. I'm glad he's dead."

"Maybe you'll join him soon, sister. I know a lot of people want to see the end of you."

"Maybe," Cece allowed. "But I will know the truth first. You can't stop me from finding it." She held her thumb and forefinger an inch apart. "I'm this close."

Sierra turned to go but then hesitated. "Just so you

know, no one is going to bring you flowers when you're in the ground next to her." She glanced at their grandmother's headstone and then walked away.

Cece hugged her arms around herself and pressed her lips together. Nothing she could say or do would change how her sister felt. Didn't matter. All those years ago Cece had been so worried about her sister and her brothers and what was going to become of them.

She wasn't worried anymore. They could go to hell. Every damned one of them. All she wanted was the truth.

She said her goodbyes to her grandmother and headed back to the truck. When she rounded the cemetery gate and started up the sidewalk, she stalled. Her truck sat right where she had left it, at the curb next to the sidewalk. But the tires were flat. She hurried the last few yards and walked all the way around the vehicle. All four tires had been slashed. If she had not been so damned mad she might have cried.

Fortunately, the local co-op was able to take care of her tires. They were slashed—probably with a knife—in such a way that they couldn't be repaired. Cece used a portion of the money she had found in the books to have a new set installed and aligned. She had the oil changed while she was at it.

After she left the co-op, she stopped by a local staffing firm and filled out an application. Mr. Berringer had warned that having and keeping a job was not optional. It was required. However long she would be here, she had to try and proceed with a normal life.

She laughed as she drove home, the sound flowing out the open window as she drove. There was nothing normal about her life. Never had been, probably never would be.

By the time she arrived it was well past lunch, and she was hungry and emotionally drained. She grabbed the mail from the box and rolled the rest of the way down the drive. When she had parked she sifted through the mail. An envelope from the tax assessor's office snagged her attention. She opened it first.

Delinquent taxes. Lien.

A lien had been taken out against the house because of overdue taxes. This was the third notice.

She wanted to lay her head against the steering wheel and sob. She really did. This had been a really horrendous day. Instead, she twisted the key in the ignition to start the engine. She might as well go back to town and take care of this now.

The engine failed to turn over. A frown furrowed her brow. She tried again. Nothing but a *click, click, click*.

She dropped her head back against the seat. What now?

The only choice she had was to call Deacon and see if he was interested in coming to her rescue yet again.

Funny how the stranger next door had turned out to be the best neighbor she could possibly hope for.

A real hero.

CECE WAS SITTING on the top porch step when Deacon pulled into her driveway. She looked as if she had lost her best friend, except he knew she didn't have any friends. For all intents and purposes, she was completely alone in the world. An outcast.

One he had been certain was guilty of far more than she had gone to prison for. He worried now that he had made a mistake, but he wasn't ready to give her quite that much grace just yet. There were still questions. Questions for which he intended to have answers. At this point he was relatively certain she wasn't guilty of murdering her father or having anything to do with his partner's disappearance. But she had information. Information he needed to solve that mystery once and for all.

"Nice tires," he said as he walked around her truck.

She pushed to her feet and descended the steps as if she were walking to the gallows. "Now if only the engine would work to roll those nice tires down the road."

"Sounds like the battery. Let's have a look." He raised the hood; she joined him as he surveyed the engine compartment.

"Let's clean these connections up a little and see if that helps." He went back to his truck and grabbed his toolbox.

"You think that might do it?"

"It can't hurt." He scraped the buildup from the connectors, one by one, and tapped them back into place. "Try starting it now."

She climbed in and did as he asked. The engine turned over but too slowly to start. She made a face and groaned.

"Let's go get a new battery. That'll most likely take care of the problem."

"What if it's not just the battery?"

He removed the connectors again, removed the battery. "Could be the alternator, but judging by the looks of this battery, this is likely the source of the trouble. They can test it to be certain."

After putting the battery in the back of his truck,

he opened the passenger-side door and waited for her to get in.

"Can we stop at the tax assessor's office first?" She held up a letter. "I guess no one remembered to pay the taxes."

"Should be an easy fix, as well."

"That might just salvage this really crappy day. Stopping by the cemetery turned out to be an unpleasant decision."

She looked so hopeful, he couldn't help the smile. "Hop in."

They were a mile or so down the road when she asked, "How has your day been?"

"A lot more boring than yours, apparently." He shot her a grin. "So tell me what happened at the cemetery."

She told him about her sister's visit. "You think she slashed your tires?"

"It was either her or a friend of hers."

"Do you really believe she or Marcus killed your father?"

"It wasn't Levi," she answered without answering his question. "He couldn't have done it. Based on what Sierra and Marcus said about me at trial and what I've seen since I got back, I wouldn't put anything past either of them."

"But it could have been another member of his following," Deacon countered. He had been thinking about that today. More than a few of his followers had fallen out with Mason Winters around the time of his murder. The man's popularity had been on the decline. The trouble was that many of his followers wanted to cling to him because he had started the church.

Those were the ones who would have gravitated to

his son over anyone else. The son had, from all accounts, turned things around. Membership was on the rise and his congregation appeared to be loyal to a fault.

"Probably. I had been out of the church for a while at that point so I wasn't privy to the ongoing politics. The police investigated the possibility but not really well. I think they were satisfied that I killed him and didn't want to waste time."

She was likely right. "I was thinking about the man, the K.C. that you mentioned. I think you should talk to Levi about him. There may be a connection to who killed your father. Maybe his murder had something to do with that Resurrection group you were telling me about."

"It's worth a shot. Some of those extreme preppers are very territorial."

The quiet that followed warned him that she had something else on her mind.

"Have you ever been married, Deacon?" She made a face. "If you don't mind me asking."

"Never been married."

She looked surprised.

Before she could ask, he went on, "I guess I'm like your older brother. I never took the time to nurture a relationship."

"No kids?"

He shook his head. "My parents live in Nashville. I have a sister. No brothers. Several cousins and a half dozen or so aunts and uncles."

She smiled and he liked the way it made her green eyes sparkle. "Do you have big family get-togethers for the holidays?"

He slowed for a turn. "Sometimes."

"We never had those. My mother was an only child and my father had no association with any member of his family. One of his brothers came to his funeral. I think they're all in Memphis."

"Your father didn't approve of the holiday dinners and celebrations?"

"Not the way the average person does. His idea of a family get-together was him preaching some hellfire and brimstone sermon while we sat and listened avidly. If we blinked or looked away we were punished."

"Sounds like a great guy." Some people shouldn't have children.

More of that quiet.

"You can ask me whatever you like." Might as well let her off the hook.

"Have you decided what you're doing next? Is there a chance you'll be going back to Nashville or someplace like that?"

He pulled into a parking slot at the courthouse. "I'm not sure yet. Just taking my time and considering my options."

"Hopefully this won't take long." She reached for the door.

"Why don't I go with you?"

She searched his face for a moment. "Okay."

He got out and met her at the hood. There was a distinct possibility he was taking the protective thing too far. He opened the entrance door and followed her inside. A chance he was willing to take. In light of the trouble that kept showing up, he wasn't ready to let her out of his sight. He knew who had slashed her tires because he had been watching. The question was, why would her brother do that?

Levi was supposed to be the only one who cared about her.

Deacon watched as Cece showed the letter to the lady behind the counter. He noted the way the other woman looked at her, as if she were nothing—not worthy of standing in their midst. If Cece noticed she pretended not to. The clerk seemed reluctant to accept the cash Cece placed on the counter. Maybe she feared she had just printed it or earned it on the street corner selling drugs or herself.

By the time Cece finished her business and they walked out, he was fire-breathing angry on her behalf.

"Anything else you need to do while we're here?" He had to work at keeping his tone even.

"I think that's it other than the battery."

"There's a new diner in town. I've heard good things about it. After we pick up the battery, why don't we go for a late lunch and celebrate?"

"What're we celebrating?"

She looked so uncertain and yet so hopeful. He wanted to pull her into his arms and promise her it would all work out just fine.

What the hell was wrong with him? He had lost all perspective. But the real problem was that he no longer cared.

"Surprises," he offered. "Life is full of them."

Chapter Ten

The diner wasn't really new. It was the same one that had been in Winchester as long as Cece could remember. She had worked here when she was a teenager... before she ended up in prison. Of course Deacon had no way of knowing that. The place had shut down ages ago and only recently reopened under new management.

When they had placed their orders, Cece said as much. "Working here was my first job."

He surveyed the place. "Well I'll be damned. Here I thought I was bringing you to someplace new."

The shiplap walls were white now instead of the stained wood color they had been when she was a kid. The red booths with the gold-speckled white tables were the same. The black-and-white tile floors were a little shinier. The long counter that served as a bar was still fronted by red leather-topped stools.

"It's the thought that counts, right?" She lifted her soda and took a sip. Tried to relax but that wasn't happening. Part of her worried that someone who remembered her would walk up to their table and make a scene. If it hadn't meant having to face the public every hour of every work day, she would have asked if waitresses were needed. Picking up where she'd left off would have been easy enough and maybe even allowed her to work her hours around a class schedule at nearby Motlow College.

"You started working here when you were in high school?"

He had the brownest eyes. Kind eyes. Not dark and cruel like her father's had been. She blinked away the thought. "Yes. My dad kicked me out and I didn't want to take advantage of my grandmother's kindness so I got a job here after school and on weekends. Bought my own clothes. Paid for my lunch at school. She said it wasn't necessary but that it was a good idea since staying busy would keep me out of trouble."

Too bad that part hadn't worked.

"Sounds like your grandmother was a really cool lady."

"She was. A fiery redhead like me and my mother. Green eyes, too." Cece smiled, remembering. "Smaller than me. She swore she was five feet tall but she wasn't. Maybe four-eleven. But she wasn't afraid of anything or anyone."

Except her father. Cece knew her grandmother had worried about the bastard trying to drag Cece back home before she turned eighteen. Two tough years. Cece hated that she had been the cause of those worrisome weeks and months for her grandmother. But Emily Broward had sworn she wouldn't have it any other way. She wanted Cece with her. To hell with the rest if they didn't recognize what an evil snake their father was. Her grandmother had truly been one of a kind.

As much as it pained her, she had thought Marcus was just as evil as his father. Sierra was too young and too much of a follower to understand, her grandmother had insisted. Levi waffled between sleeping over at their grandmother's and crawling back home. Cece had understood. He'd wanted the approval of his father and his older brother. Most young boys did. He hadn't recognized what they were. She hoped he did now.

She didn't want to lose Levi, too.

"I have a feeling you're a lot like your grandmother," Deacon said.

Cece smiled. "Maybe. Either way, I consider that a compliment."

"You said this man, K.C., came to your grandmother's house. Do you think she knew him? Maybe he talked to her when you were at school or at work."

She hadn't considered the idea. "It's possible, I guess."

"It seems too much of a coincidence that he was coming around about the same time your father was murdered. He may be related somehow to what happened."

She had wondered about that since she'd suddenly remembered him showing up those times. "I should start going through more of the files my attorney sent."

"I can help with that, if you'd like."

He had made the offer to help before. He certainly gave the impression of being sincere about it. But he still hadn't told her what he did for the federal government. Was it possible he did the same thing that man—the one who went by the name K.C.—did?

"Do you know that man? K.C.? Is that why you're asking about him?"

He held her gaze for a long while before answering. Cece felt her world shifting. She needed this man—this stranger—to be the real deal. A nice guy who lived next door. She absolutely did not want to learn he was some kind of creep or just some investigator using her for his own purposes. He'd admitted to having done some private investigations. Uneasiness started a slow crawl through her.

"Maybe. We have reason to believe he was someone else. A man we've been trying to find for a very long time."

There it was. The cold, hard truth.

"Is that why you've been so nice to me? So helpful?" Her heart pounded twice for every second that elapsed before he smiled and shook his head.

"Cece, I had no idea you'd ever met the man until you brought him up."

She closed her eyes and shook her head. "Sorry. I'm just so used to being let down."

He reached across the table and covered her hand with his own, sending warmth firing through her. "I'm sorry I didn't tell you I was looking for him when you first mentioned his alias."

"Alias?" She felt suddenly cold despite the warmth he had elicited.

"K.C. is an alias he used for going undercover."

"What's his real name?"

"I'm afraid I can't tell you that."

"But you think he was working on something related to the Resurrection doomsday preppers or whatever they are?"

He nodded. "We think so. Whatever he was doing, he's been missing since around the same time your father was murdered."

"Wow." She tried to remember the man's face, the words he'd said. "Do you think he's dead, too?"

"That's what we need to find out."

The waitress arrived with their burgers and fries. Deacon drew his hand away and Cece wished he was still holding onto her. The idea that she was in way over her head had her digging into the food in hopes of ignoring the new tension flooding her. Honestly, she hadn't realized how hungry she was until she smelled the food. She poured on the ketchup and devoured the fries first.

She caught Deacon watching her and felt embarrassed. "Sorry. I was starving and maybe trying to comfort myself."

He grinned. "Nothing wrong with that." He popped a fry into his mouth and chewed. "We all need a little comfort now and then."

She was suddenly afraid. Three days. She had known this man for three days and already she felt close to him, dependent on having him back her up. On him being here...with her.

She was a complete idiot.

She stared at her burger and suddenly felt sick. What if he wasn't who she believed he was? What if he was lying to her? Everyone except her grandmother had lied to her. She knew better than to trust.

And yet, somehow she trusted this man.

Not smart, Cece.

Apparently she had never been as smart as she should have been, otherwise she wouldn't have ended up spending most of her adult life so far in prison.

She watched Deacon as he bit off a chunk of his burger. He had great lips for a man. Classic square jaw. Perfect nose, not too big, not crooked. He was handsome and sexy and so nice.

Really nice.

Her grandmother had always said when something seemed too good to be true, it usually was.

Was this man another mistake? He surely seemed too good to be true.

DEACON SHUT OFF the engine and climbed out of Cece's old blue truck. "You are good to go." The new battery had taken care of the problem. According to the gauge on the truck, the alternator was charging. "You shouldn't have any more trouble."

"The guy at the tire shop said the brakes were still good." She stood watching him, her arms crossed over her chest.

He closed the driver's-side door and moved toward where she stood just outside the entrance to the makeshift garage that was actually a part of the barn. "You got something on your mind?"

"I was thinking we should go through those files. If your offer to help is still on the table."

He moved beyond the doors, pushed them shut. "Sure." He dropped the crosspiece into place that held the doors closed. "If you're certain you want me to help. I feel like you might have some doubts or misgivings about me."

No point allowing her uncertainty to build. He had made a couple of missteps and he needed to rectify the situation while it was still salvageable. Whatever else he thought about this woman, she was still his only connection to Jack. She could very well be one of the last people to see him before he disappeared. If she or anyone she knew had information that would help find him, Deacon had to pursue that route. No matter the cost.

That last part didn't sit right in his gut. He didn't want to be another of the people who'd hurt this woman.

"I trust you, Deacon." She smiled and he hated himself a little more. "I'm grateful for any and all help."

"Okay. Let's get to it."

She led the way inside the house. That he watched her hips sway with far too much interest was another reason to hate himself. But he was human. She was a gorgeous woman. Petite with soft curves. All that red hair that made him long to tangle his fingers in those silky curls. He wasn't alone in his fascination. She looked at him with a similar yearning. He had thought as much, but the way she'd stared at him in the diner had confirmed his instincts. She was attracted to him.

But then she was lonely. To let this mutual attraction go any farther would be taking advantage of her vulnerability and he did not want to go there. In his ten-year career he had never used sex as leverage or influence.

This was the first time he'd ever longed to do exactly that, whether it proved beneficial to his investigation or not.

In the living room, she settled on her knees next to the coffee table. "He had a copy of everything as far as I can tell. Arrest record. Witness interviews. Not that there were any actual witnesses to the murder, but people who knew him and who knew me."

"Character references and situational witnesses. That's the usual procedure when no one saw what really happened. The police build a scenario based on what they can find out about the people closest to the victim. In your case, you were at the scene—covered in his blood—so they started with you."

"Since they found what they wanted, they didn't look any further," she suggested.

He nodded. "From what you've told me and what Frasier showed me, it certainly seems that way."

She stared at the pages and pages lying on the table. "How can any of this tell us anything if it only shows what we already know?"

"There's always the chance that something someone said in an interview will mean something different to you than it did to the investigating officers or to Frasier or me." That was his only thought when he'd first reviewed the file with Frasier. The notes and statements provided little else in the way of support for her version of events.

"Oh." The frown that had creased her forehead relaxed. "I see. I think."

He wasn't so sure she did. "Let's make a list of people you would consider suspects in the murder of Mason Winters."

Cece shuffled the pages around and found the notepad she had been using. A pen and a pencil lay amid the pages. She grabbed the pencil and wrote *Suspects* across the top of the page. Her strokes were neat and fine with a dash of unique flair, the way a teenage girl would write. The reality that she'd never had the opportunity to move beyond the writing style she'd developed in high school was another reminder of what she'd lost. Eight years of learning, of becoming who she would be.

He forced away the thoughts and focused on the task at hand. "Who would you put at the top of the list? The person you believe had the most to gain by his death."

She hesitated only a moment before she wrote *Marcus Winters*. "He gained the church and most of our father's followers. He got the house. He has the power now. The admiration and respect."

"Okay, that's a start. Who's next?" He had his own ideas about that one but he wanted to hear her conclusions before he gave his own.

Another of those worrisome frowns lined her brow as she considered the question for a bit. "Sierra. She was a little wilder than me. She didn't like all his rules, but they had this bizarre daddy–daughter relationship. She was his princess and it was like sometimes she adored him and wanted his attention and sometimes she didn't. You never knew which Sierra you were going to get." She wrote her sister's name next.

Sierra would have been his second choice, as well.

"Was there anyone else among his followers who might have hoped to gain control of the church?"

"I don't think so." She tilted her head as if reconsidering. "There was this one man who came every Sunday and sat in the back. He never spoke to anyone. My father made it a point to know all of his followers. He was like a politician, he pretended to be friends with everyone. The fact that he never exchanged so much as a hello with the man was unusual. I told the police about him, but Marcus claimed I made him up."

"Do you remember his name?"

"I never knew his name, but he came into the diner once. It was the only time I ever saw him in town. He sat at one of my tables."

She fell silent, remembering.

"He ordered hot tea," she finally said. "No food, just the drink. He sat there for half an hour or so and watched me."

"Did you tell the police about this incident?"

She nodded. "I did but they blew it off." She shrugged. "I suppose it did sound as if I had made him up. I didn't know his name, and Marcus and anyone else they asked—assuming they asked anyone else—had no idea who or what I was talking about. It was an easy jump to conclude I was trying to shift focus from me."

"What did he look like?"

"Old. Maybe sixty-something. Heavy gray beard. Gray hair. Medium height, thin."

"How did he dress?"

"Overalls and plain plaid shirts, the button-up style. Boots. The hiking kind, not cowboy boots like you wear. That was another thing that made him stand out at the meetings. The followers wear very plain clothes, solid colors. The plaid shirt said all that needed to be said. He was not a follower."

"No hat?"

Her gaze narrowed. "There was a hat. Not a cowboy hat or straw hat. One of the felt kind, like a fedora. A really old one, like you see in those black-and-white movies."

"Eye color?"

She shook her head. "I don't know. I never looked that close. He made me nervous, sort of."

"He didn't say anything to you that time in the diner?"

"Just gave me his order."

"Was that close to the time your father was murdered?"

"Maybe a week before. I can't be sure. It didn't seem significant at the time and by the time it did, it was too late."

A thought occurred to Deacon. "Are there photo-

graphs from the trial in these files?" The files Frasier
had showed to him hadn't contained any pictures. Deacon couldn't be sure, but by the time he'd started to in-
teract with Frasier, his health had been seriously going
downhill. There were times when his mind didn't appear to be working properly. Deacon worried that Frasier hadn't told him everything, certainly might not
have shown him everything.

"I haven't seen any yet, but we can look."

Deacon moved to the boxes and began to go through
the files. Cece did the same.

"Are you thinking he may have come to the trial to
watch?"

"Yes. Killers do that sometimes. As do others who
have an interest in how something turns out. If there are
photos, we should go over every face present."

There were no photos in the file except the crime
scene photos. "We should try the newspaper," Deacon
suggested.

"The woman who runs the newspaper, Audrey Anderson, came to see me at the prison last month. She
wanted to do an interview." Cece shrugged. "But I said
no."

"Maybe you should call her. See what she has. Tell
her you're reconsidering her interview."

A smile tugged at her lips. "I was just thinking the
same thing."

She used her grandmother's old telephone book to
look up the number for the newspaper office and then
she made the call. Deacon listened as she played her
part, offered to reconsider the interview and then asked
for any photos.

"I would really appreciate that." She smiled at Deacon. "When could I pick them up?" She listened for a moment. "Perfect."

When she hung up the phone she said, "She needs an hour to pull the file. The reporter who covered the case has an entire file of interviews he did and a ton of pictures. She said I could see everything."

"We should put these files away before we go."

She surveyed the scattered pages, then looked at him, startled, as if she had only just realized that someone could break in and steal the files or, worse, burn the house down. After what happened with the electrical box, she certainly should have thought of that.

"We could take them to my place, if you'd like."

"Good idea."

They packed the pages back into the folders and the folders into the boxes. By the time they delivered them to his house, it was time to head to the newspaper office. The *Winchester Gazette* building was one of the oldest in town. It sat just off the courthouse square. As soon as they walked through the door, the receptionist directed them to the conference room on the second floor.

The second floor circled the interior space of the building and opened in the center to the first floor. Glass and steel allowed for near complete transparency of the second floor offices.

Audrey Anderson met them on the landing. Deacon didn't know her but he had seen her face and name on the news and in the paper frequently since his move to Winchester. Audrey Anderson was a mover and a shaker in Franklin County. She knew everyone and made no bones about what she wanted when she went after something.

"Miss Winters." She extended her hand and Cece accepted the gesture and gave her hand a shake.

"This is my friend and neighbor, Deacon Ross."

"Mr. Ross." Anderson gave his hand a firm shake, as well. "It's very nice to see you both. Let's move on to the conference room."

"I appreciate you going to all this trouble," Cece said. "It's very kind of you."

Anderson led the way into the spacious room and gestured to the table in the center. "Thank you for saying so, Cece. May I call you Cece?"

"Of course. Wow." Cece stalled at the table and stared at the mounds of papers and photos.

"I wish I could claim that I was doing this out of the kindness of my heart, but I have a very good but selfish reason for helping you. I want your story."

Cece nodded. "I understand. So you know, I have questions I'd like to find the answers to before I give anyone my story."

"You want the truth."

Cece looked from the other woman to Deacon and back. "Yes."

"Whatever I or my staff can do to help you find it—we are at your disposal." She gestured to the table. "Take your time. Any questions, my office is just down the hall."

Anderson closed the door as she left the room.

"You think she's serious about helping me?" Cece asked.

Deacon glanced toward the office where the woman had disappeared. "I think she recognizes there's a big story here and she wants it. She's a very smart newspaper publisher and she's interested in helping you so she can get an exclusive."

Cece's green eyes filled with emotion. "When I came back, I was certain I wouldn't find anyone who wanted to help me."

More of that guilt heaped onto his shoulders. "Let's get to it."

The photos taken were extensive. There were numerous glossy eight by tens of the courtroom and those present to view the proceedings.

"Take your time," Deacon reminded her. "Point him out if you see him."

He had already spotted a man that matched the description she had given. But there was more than one in overalls and with a beard.

"That's him." She tapped the one he had pegged.

"You're certain?"

She nodded. "One hundred percent."

"Maybe Ms. Anderson can track down his name for us."

"I'll ask her." Cece took the photo and headed to Anderson's office.

Deacon picked up another of the photos. As he surveyed the faces, he stalled on one, his heart stumbling. *Jack.*

His partner sat two rows back from the prosecutor's table. In front of Jack and slightly to his right was Sierra Winters. The photo had captured Jack staring at the young woman.

Deacon grabbed more of the photos and shuffled through them, his heart pounding now.

Two more photos showed Jack in the crowd outside

the courthouse, always near Sierra…near enough to reach out and touch her.

Jack was either watching Sierra or the two knew each other.

Chapter Eleven

The man in the photo was Rayford Prentiss but he no longer lived in the house at the end of Pleasant Ridge Road near Huntland. Audrey Anderson had tracked him down to that address. According to the man who lived there now, Prentiss had not lived there in around seven or eight years.

Convenient.

And frustrating.

Cece wanted to scream. Every time she thought she had found someone or something that might help, it or they turned out to be a dead end.

She glanced at the man behind the wheel. Deacon had been oddly quiet since they left the newspaper. Asking him if something was wrong seemed like the right thing to do but she was nearly afraid to open that door. The way her luck ran, whatever was wrong would likely be a travesty that involved her. For now, she decided to be content in the not knowing.

When he headed across the road from what used to be the Prentiss place, she asked, "Where are we going?"

"To check in with the man's former neighbors. Maybe some of them knew him and know where he is now."

"Assuming he's still alive," she offered forlornly. The way her luck was running, the man had disappeared without a trace.

"Assuming he's still alive," Deacon agreed.

The laneway to the house on the opposite side of the road was a long one, more than a mile. At the end of that lengthy drive, a farmhouse sadly in need of a fresh coat of paint sat nestled against the side of the mountain, trees crowding in around it. Beyond the thick woods were pastures. They had driven past those on the way here. The yard around the house had been left wooded, adding a layer of privacy most of the farmhouses along this road did not have.

"People who live off the beaten path sometimes answer the door with a shotgun." She'd decided to mention it because Deacon was still fairly new around here. Since he'd spent most of his time in the Nashville area, he might not run into that sort of thing too often. She didn't want him getting shot by some nervous homeowner.

"Do I look like a bad guy?"

Cece couldn't tell if he was kidding or not so she gave him a thorough once-over—the beard-shadowed jaw, the cowboy hat pulled down low on his forehead, well-worn jeans and scuffed cowboy boots.

"I should probably go with you." She reached for the door. "I look a lot more harmless."

He grinned. "All right then."

They climbed out of the truck, met at the hood. He asked, "You remember any of the folks who live nearby?"

"Maybe if I heard the names I might. But I don't remember any of the houses so far."

She'd never had any reason to be in this neck of the woods. Huntland had its own high school so she hadn't gone to school with any of the people from this area. Not that she recalled, anyway.

"Let's give a knock and see what we find."

As she had predicted, the woman of the house showed up at the door with her shotgun. "You lost? You don't look like those door-to-door Bible thumpers."

"Afternoon, ma'am," Deacon said, his voice and that smile charming as hell.

Cece shivered. Until that moment she hadn't noticed just how deep his voice was. Well, maybe she had noticed, but there was something about the way he said *ma'am* that made her shiver. The smile, well, that was the usual generous one that flowed so easily across his lips.

"My name is Deacon Ross and this is my friend Cece. We're trying to locate my momma's cousin, Rayford Prentiss. We lost contact with him years ago and I wanted to let him know she was real sick and might not be long for this world."

There was something else Cece noticed for the first time. The man could weave a tale way too smoothly. Another shiver went through her, this one for an entirely different reason.

"I think he moved away or died or something. Come on in and I'll ask Daddy. He'll know. He knows everything about everyone around here."

"I would sure appreciate that, ma'am."

"Geneva Harvey." She lowered the barrel of her weapon, tucked it under her left arm and thrust out her right hand.

Deacon shook her hand and then she offered it to

Cece who did the same. Cece was immensely thankful the lady didn't recognize her.

"This way."

Ms. Harvey headed deeper into the house. Deacon closed the door behind them and followed behind Cece. They moved through the living room and then the kitchen. The house smelled of cigarettes and the leftover fried okra sitting in the cast-iron skillet on the stove. Cece could not remember the last time she'd had fried okra. Her grandmother had loved it. Beyond the kitchen was a back hall lined with doors. The bedrooms, she imagined. One of the open doors they passed led to a bathroom, complete with claw-foot tub and vintage pedestal sink, both a little stained.

The woman knocked on one of the closed doors. "Daddy, you decent?"

"Why wouldn't I be? Come on in."

The voice on the other side of the door was rusty and gravelly. When the lady opened the door, cigarette smoked greeted them like a fog rolling in off the lake.

"Daddy, this is Deacon Ross and his friend Cece. They want to know what happened to Mr. Prentiss. You remember him?"

All this she said in a really loud voice. Apparently her daddy was about half deaf.

The man sat in a wheelchair. His bed was the type used in hospitals. His skin was more yellow than white. Even his fingernails were yellow, Cece noted, as he lifted his cigarette to his lips and took a draw.

Beyond the wheelchair and hospital bed, the room looked like most any other. A dresser and a door to what was likely a closet. The windows were raised, and a box fan sat in one, trying its best to draw in the air from outside. Overhead a ceiling fan twirled, dust hanging from its blades like fur lining the collar of a coat.

Next to his chair was a table with a glass and a bottle of Jack Daniels. Now that Cece looked more closely, the man's eyes were bloodshot and rimmed in red.

"Cancer."

Cece started when she realized he was speaking to her. He stared directly at her. Evidently he had noticed her sizing up him and his room.

"I got maybe two months left. The painkillers caused other problems so I decided to handle the discomfort on my own terms."

"I'm sorry." Cancer was not a pleasant way to go.

He laughed, the sound a hoarse throaty sound. "Don't be sorry, little girl. I brought it on myself. Smoked two packs a day my whole life. Drank like a crazy man and basically had a hell of a good time. Dying sucks but it was fun while it lasted."

"Mr. Prentiss, Daddy," his daughter scolded. "They want to know about the old man who used to live across the road."

"Rayford was more hermit than anything else," he said. "Those last few years he lived across the road he was busy building him one of them bugout places. God only knows where. He was into all that prepping stuff. A little over-the-top, if you ask me."

His daughter made a harrumphing sound. "Like you ain't."

He pointed a glare at her. "I'm not like them crazy ones," he snapped. "Rayford's one of them doomsday preppers. The ones that claim they'll rise up after the rest of us are blown to bits by a nuclear bomb or some such shit."

Cece caught Deacon's gaze. *Resurrection.*

"Do you know how we might find him or his friends?" Deacon asked.

Harvey shook his head. "You don't want no part of that bunch," he warned. "They don't like nobody in their business."

"I just want to see that he gets the news," Deacon assured the man.

Harvey's gaze narrowed. "They don't cotton to outsiders, Mr. Ross. You might as well tell your momma he's a lost cause. 'Course they'll probably be the only ones to survive when we all get poisoned by one of them pharmaceutical companies."

"Some of them still live openly," Cece countered. "They just don't tell anyone about what they do out in the woods."

Harvey nodded. "That's right. But then you have those who decide to make it a way of life. They sort of vanish. Nobody ever sees them again. They don't want to be seen. They refer to them as the *others*. No one talks about them."

"Thank you, Mr. Harvey," Deacon said. "If you happen to see Mr. Prentiss, let him know I'm looking for him. I bought the old Wilburn place."

Another nod and then Harvey looked directly at Cece. "You're Mason Winters's daughter. The one who killed him."

Cece froze. Not sure what to say. Finally she managed an affirming nod. "I'm his daughter, yes." No use arguing the other with him.

"No offense, but you did the world a favor killing that mean old bastard."

"Daddy," his daughter warned.

"It's okay." Cece managed a half-hearted smile for the other woman. "He's right. My father was a mean old bastard."

Harvey laughed until he lost his breath and started to cough. When he stopped coughing, he looked to Deacon. "I'll send your message, but don't say I didn't warn you."

Deacon thanked him again and Ms. Harvey guided them back to the front door. When they were in the truck and back out on Pleasant Ridge Road headed toward Highway 64, Cece turned to Deacon. "My sister had a boyfriend back then." Cece laughed. "She's actually had a few, according to Levi. But back when the murder happened, there was this one. Her first love, sort of. I think we should talk to him. He was at the house a lot with Sierra. He might be able to tell us anything he heard or saw around the house during that those final few weeks."

"Do you mean the guy who gave your sister an alibi?"

She nodded. "That's the one."

"What's his address?"

"I know where his parents live—where he lived back then."

"Close enough."

SLADE FAIRBANKS HAD BEEN married and divorced twice over the past eight years. He had three kids, none of whom lived with him. He rented a small place in a mobile home park just outside town. His younger sister was only too happy to tell all about her relationship-damaged brother. According to her, Sierra ruined him. He was no good after she was finished with him.

As they drove away, Cece confirmed that she didn't doubt the woman's claims for a minute.

As they neared the address the sister had provided, Deacon asked, "Is that him?"

Cece leaned forward and peered at the man in question. "I think so."

As they pulled into the small driveway she nodded. "Yeah, that's him."

He was attending to something on a small charcoal grill while sucking down a beer. The twenty-something man was shirtless and his jeans hung well below his waist.

Fairbanks stared at them as they climbed out of the truck. Recognition flared on his face when he realized who Cece was.

"Cece Winters! Well, I'll be damned."

He tossed the spatula he had been using into the chair behind him, threw his apparently empty beer can on the ground and started her way. He hugged her tight, for a good while longer than necessary.

"I heard you were out." He held her at arm's length and looked her up and down. "Damn, girl, you look good for a recently released ex-con."

"Thanks, Slade."

He glanced at Deacon.

"This is my friend, Deacon Ross. We wanted to talk to you for a few minutes if you have the time."

A frown tugged his thick eyebrows together. "What's this about?"

"Sierra."

"Oh, hell." He looked around, wiped his hands on his jeans. "Okay." He grabbed the spatula and shifted two burger patties from the grill to a plate. Then he hitched his head toward the trailer. "Come on in."

As he showed them inside, he talked about how his child support kept him from the lifestyle he had hoped for. "As my daddy says, you make your bed, you gotta lay in it."

Cece asked him about his children. He showed her photos on his phone. Deacon kept quiet and let them do the catching up thing. The man was more likely to talk if he was comfortable and felt as if he were in charge.

"You really do look good, Cece." Fairbanks shook his head. "I'm glad you got through that time with all that happened. I know it was hard."

"It was. Tough. Especially since I didn't kill anyone, much less my own father."

He looked away then. Stared at the floor.

"Sierra and Marcus said things about me that weren't true," she went on when he didn't look up. "You were close to her back then. Why would she do such a thing?"

His gaze met Cece's and for a half a minute Deacon was certain he intended to balk.

"You know how she was. Selfish, self-centered. She didn't care about anyone but herself."

"What happened to the two of you? You were so good to her."

Smart move. Deacon wanted to give her a high five.

"She dumped me like she did all the ones who came after me. You can't satisfy her."

"Was she cheating on you? That seemed to be what she did back then."

Deacon figured Levi had told Cece that part, as well. He nodded. "Oh, yeah. She had her an older guy.

I caught her with him right before…well, you know. The murder."

Deacon's instincts perked up.

"What old guy?" Cece asked. "I don't remember an old guy."

The fact that she completely passed over his mention of the murder and went straight to the cheating surprised Deacon.

"It was a big secret," Slade said with a heavy dose of derision. "He wasn't from around here. Pretty much no one knew she was involved with him. I found out totally by accident. Walked right up on the two of them in a car, all hugged up."

Deacon's thoughts had gone still at the "he wasn't from around here" part.

"Who was he?" Cece pressed.

Fairbanks shrugged. "I don't know his name. I saw him that once, though. Black hair, a little gray around the temples. I didn't get close enough to see his eyes."

His breath jammed deep in his lungs, Deacon opened the photo app on his cell phone and handed his phone to Cece. She looked at the image on the screen and then showed it to Slade. "Was it this guy?"

He stared for a moment, then his head started to bob up and down. "Yeah, that's him. Creepy old bastard."

Deacon flinched.

"Are you sure they were involved?" Cece asked. "Maybe they were just friends."

He laughed. "No. She bragged about it later. Said he was going to take her away from here. Give her the life she deserved."

"Did they break up? What happened to him?"

Deacon's voice sounded overloud in the room. Cece glanced at him.

Fairbanks stared at him a moment. "I don't know for sure," he said. "I only know that she moved on to somebody else. I never saw the guy again." He turned back to Cece. "You remember Tommy Woosier? She started going with him after that."

Deacon's brain was throbbing. Sierra had been involved with Jack somehow? He stared at Cece. Had he been blaming the wrong sister all along? Deacon lost track of the conversation for the next few minutes as he mulled over the potential facts he'd just had to face.

"I just have one other question, Slade."

Deacon shook off the disturbing thoughts and focused on the conversation between the man and Cece.

"Why did you lie for Sierra that day?"

He paled. "What do you mean? Lie about what?"

"You said you helped Sierra when her car broke down at the time our father was being murdered, but that isn't true because you just said she was cheating on you. You caught her before the murder. The two of you broke up. Why would you help her?"

Holy hell. She was right, Deacon realized. He'd been so stuck on the news about Sierra and Jack, he'd missed that part of the conversation. He couldn't wait to hear the man's answer to that one.

Slade shot to his feet. "Oh, man, you see the time?" He gestured to the clock on the wall. "I have to go. My oldest is expecting me to pick him up."

Cece stood more slowly. Deacon did the same.

"I'm not leaving until you tell me the truth, Slade. I've spent eight years in prison. I deserve to know why."

He held up his hands as if he could stop her words. "I know. I know."

"No, you don't know. You have no idea the things that happened to me in there. Now tell me the truth. You owe me the truth."

"Okay." He nodded about twenty times in five seconds. "But if you say I said it, I'll deny it. That brother of yours—Marcus—told me if I didn't tell the police that story, he would kill me."

Cece stared at Fairbanks, her expression one of utter defeat.

"Now go. I have stuff to do."

The drive back to Cece's place was made in total silence. It wasn't until Deacon parked that he spoke, disrupting the too-quiet space between them.

"You think he's telling the truth?" Deacon asked. She knew her brother. Knew what he was capable of, even if she hadn't wanted to see it.

"Yes."

"In that case, it looks like Sierra was way deeper into whatever happened than you thought." He twisted in the seat to look at Cece. She stared straight ahead. "Do you think she could have killed your father?"

Or my partner? he wanted to say.

"She was a few months from turning sixteen. Just a kid. More important, I never saw her react violently before." She turned to meet his gaze. "But Marcus could have."

"They set you up." The whole damned thing was so crystal clear.

"That's what I've been trying to tell everyone. I didn't know who was setting me up, but I knew for certain that I didn't do it."

Deacon reached to start his truck once more.

"Where are we going?" she asked, her voice suddenly shaking.

"We're going back to see your sister's old boyfriend. I intend to beat the rest of the truth out of him and then we're calling the sheriff."

That look—the one like a wild animal trapped in the headlights of an oncoming car—claimed her face, filled her eyes. "You believe me?"

Before he could stop himself he grabbed her face in his hands and kissed her. He hadn't meant to. Definitely had not meant to kiss her so hard and so deeply. Her lips felt soft beneath his. Her skin smooth and delicate in his palms. Every cell in his body started to burn. Her fingers touched his hands, trembled, and he wanted to pull her beneath him and do things she would hate him for when this was finished.

When he could control himself once more, he drew his mouth from hers but he could not let go…could not lose that contact. He pressed his forehead to hers. Closed his eyes and reached for reason.

But there was no reason.

Not in this.

Chapter Twelve

Tuesday, August 6

Deacon had spent the night on her couch again.

Cece had wanted him to sleep in her room. Well, sleep wasn't actually what she had wanted. She had wanted more of those hot kisses. She had wanted him to make love to her. Didn't matter that he was basically a stranger. She knew enough. She wanted him. Wanted to know all of him.

But he had talked her out of being in a rush. *There's time*, he had insisted. Time for her to be sure she wasn't making a mistake, he had explained. He had warned that he was a lot older than she was. That he had a history she didn't know and understand. He had even said she shouldn't trust him quite so much.

Then, this morning, he had explained that he had to run an errand and that she should stay in the house, doors locked, shotgun and phone handy.

She had a feeling he was going back to try and locate Slade. He had more questions for him. They hadn't been able to find him again yesterday.

Her mystery seemed to have become extremely important to Deacon. It felt as if he wanted the truth as badly as she did. Warmth spread through her. He cared about her. That was obvious. She didn't fully understand how it was possible given the short time they had known each other. A mere five days ago he had been just the stranger next door—the new neighbor.

But that had all changed now.

At least, for her it had changed.

She rinsed her coffee cup and decided to get back to finding the truth. There had to be something in those files that would help. Deacon had brought them back last night and they'd dug around some more—until it became clear they couldn't be in the same room alone together for another minute. Then she'd gone to bed and he'd crashed on the couch.

As she knelt next to the coffee table and picked up the copies of the photos from the courtroom that Audrey Anderson had provided, she wondered about the man. This K.C. who'd made all those promises to Sierra—at least, according to Slade. Seeing these photos of him certainly made Deacon unsettled. Did he know the man personally? Was that why he'd had to run errands this morning?

There was something…maybe he was right. Maybe she shouldn't trust him so completely.

Knocking at the front door made her jump. Fear slid through her veins. She got to her feet and went for the shotgun in the corner. It was loaded. Deacon had made sure. She moved quietly to the window to peek out to see who her visitor was. She held her breath as she moved aside the shade.

Sierra.

Cece scanned the front yard to ensure no one was with her. A car sat in the driveway. Not the same one

Levi had driven. She supposed it belonged to her sister. There didn't appear to be anyone else in the vehicle.

Still, she hesitated. Was her little sister capable of murder? Cece just wasn't sure. What if something else had happened? The possibility that Levi had been hurt and Sierra had come to tell her had Cece going to the door and unlocking it. She drew it open, the shotgun in her grasp.

"What do you want?" she demanded.

Sierra looked from Cece to the shotgun and back. "We need to talk."

"Is Levi okay?" Cece resisted the urge to shake her younger sister and demand to know why they couldn't start over and pretend none of this ever happened.

But it had happened.

Sierra had helped to steal Cece's life. God only knew what else she had done.

"I don't know. I haven't seen him. I was hoping you had."

Cece thought of her meeting with Levi at the shack. "No. I haven't seen him."

Sierra closed her eyes. "Oh, God." Her dark eyes suddenly flew open, hatred burning in their opaque depths. "Why did you have to come back? Why didn't you go somewhere else? Anywhere else? There's nothing here for you."

"This is my home as much as it is yours." Though Cece felt anything but at home in this place, she wasn't going to allow her sister to tell her where she belonged or did not belong.

"No one wants you here. Can't you see that? All you do is make everyone restless. Bad things happen when you're here, Cece."

The words hit their mark. All these years Cece had been certain her sister—or anyone else for that matter—could say nothing else to her that would hurt. But she had been wrong.

"Just go, Sierra. Just leave." Cece started closing the door.

Sierra stepped onto the threshold, preventing the door from closing. "I'm warning you, Cece. You should go before something really bad happens."

Cece studied her sister's face, searched her eyes. "Are you high? What kind of drugs are you taking?"

"It doesn't matter," Sierra snapped. "What I do hurts no one but me. I'm trying to help you."

Cece laughed. "You mean, the way you helped me during the trial? You and Marcus practically drove the final nails into my coffin. Why would I believe anything you say now?"

"Believe what you want. But if you're half as smart as you think you are, you'll go before it's too late."

"It's already too late, Sierra. Are you just now seeing that?"

This time her sister stepped back when Cece closed the door.

She locked it, propped the shotgun in the corner and collapsed against the door. She squeezed her eyes shut and fought back the tears. She had sworn she would never cry over her family again and here she was, blubbering like a fool.

Sierra did not care about her. Marcus sure as hell didn't. God only knew what was on Levi's mind these days. The one thing Sierra had right was that Cece should leave. She did not belong here. She should never have come back.

Except she wanted the truth.

She exhaled a breath. Would it change anything? No. Those eight years were gone. There was no getting them back. Would it prove she wasn't the bad person everyone around here thought she was? Maybe. Maybe not.

Then why didn't she just go? List her grandmother's house with a real estate agency and get the hell on with her life?

Because she could not.

She could not pretend the truth didn't matter.

The truth was all she had.

A knock on the door made her jump away from it.

She gasped. Put a hand to her throat. Damn Sierra. Why didn't she just leave?

Cece unlocked and yanked open the door. "What do you—?"

But it wasn't Sierra standing on her porch now. It was the sheriff.

Fear throttled through her. "What's happened?"

Please don't let Levi be hurt...or worse.

"Morning, Miss Winters. You mind if I come in a moment?"

"Of course. Come in, Sheriff Tanner." She considered that the shotgun was in the corner but opted to hope he wouldn't notice. "Sorry. I thought you were someone else."

He smiled as he stepped inside. "I understand. You've had reason to be a little jumpy."

Cece closed the door behind him. "I could make some coffee if you'd like a cup, sheriff. I don't have much else to offer. A glass of water?"

He removed his hat and held it in his hands. "I'm fine. Can we sit and talk for a minute?"

"Of course." She gestured to a chair. "Excuse the mess. I've been going through the files from my court case."

The pages were spread all over the coffee table and some on the couch. She felt confident the gruesome crime scene photos were nothing new to him.

"Your neighbor, Deacon Ross, has been helping you?"

Cece settled onto the couch, knowing the sheriff wouldn't sit until she did. "Yes." She smiled. "He's been very helpful. Kept me out of trouble a couple of times. He's a good neighbor."

The sheriff held her gaze for a long moment before saying more. "I'm afraid I have some potentially troubling information about Mr. Ross."

Fear stabbed deep into Cece all over again. She had been so worried about Levi. Maybe it was Deacon who had been hurt. "Has something happened?"

"Whenever a stranger comes to town and draws our attention in some suspicious way, Chief Brannigan and I try our best to check him out. Make sure the folks we're sworn to protect don't have anything to worry about."

The fear receded but something else, something dark and disturbing swelled inside her. "Is there something I should know about him?"

Tanner nodded. "I'm afraid so. Mr. Ross is an agent with the FBI."

Cece managed a jerky nod. "He told me he worked for the federal government."

A margin of relief trickled through her. Deacon had told her the truth, pretty much. That was good, wasn't it?

"There's more to the story, I'm afraid. I spoke to his

superiors again this morning. Mr. Ross has been on a leave of absence for a good while now. Apparently, he took that time off just to come and live here. Next door to you."

She frowned. "I don't understand."

"He bought the Wilburn place because he wanted to be close to where you would be when you came back after your release."

A wave of unsteadiness went through her. "You mean, so he could watch me?"

The sheriff nodded. "Back when your daddy...died, there was a man who went missing. The FBI was all over the county looking for him for a good long while. You won't remember that because you were..."

She nodded. In jail. Awaiting trial. He didn't have to say any of that.

"I didn't recognize Mr. Ross because he was on some deep cover assignment at the time. But this morning I learned that man who disappeared, Jack Kemp, was his mentor and friend. I believe Mr. Ross has come to Winchester because you're back. He may believe you had something to do with or knew his friend."

Her hand trembling, Cece picked up one of the photos Audrey Anderson had provided and handed it to the sheriff. "Is the man circled in that photo this Jack Kemp?"

Tanner studied the photo then nodded. "That's him." He passed the photo back to Cece. "Did you know him, Miss Winters?"

She shook her head slowly. "But my sister may have."

He stood. "I'm as sorry as I can be that I didn't have this information before now. Under the circumstances, I would be wary of Mr. Ross. I've got my deputies watching for him. When I catch up with him, he and I will have a talk. If you'd prefer, I'll tell him not to bother you anymore."

"He…" Cece stood. Betrayal twisted inside her like barbed wire. But the truth was the truth. "He hasn't bothered me, sheriff. In fact, he probably saved my life the other night. I don't know why he bought the farm next door and I don't know why he befriended me, maybe for the reason you said, but he hasn't done anything to hurt me. He's done exactly the opposite."

Tanner nodded. "All right. I'll still need to talk to him. If you hear from him, you let him know we need to iron out a few things."

She nodded. "When I see him again, I'll tell him."

At the door the sheriff hesitated. "Miss Winters, I wasn't part of the original investigation, but I want you to know that if you would like me to review the case, I'll be more than happy to do so. I'll do whatever I can to help. If you believe justice failed you, I would very much like the opportunity to help make it right. I'm certain Chief Brannigan would be happy to do the same."

Cece barely kept the tears burning in her eyes from sliding down her cheeks. "Thank you so much, sheriff. That means a lot to me."

When he was gone, Cece locked the door and pressed her forehead against the cool wood. All these years she had dreamed of the police realizing their mistake and helping her to find the truth but that had never happened. Then a stranger seemed prepared to do exactly that.

Except she couldn't be certain if he really wanted to help her or if he wanted to link her to whatever happened to his friend.

Either way, he had lied to her. What she'd told the sheriff was true. Deacon had probably saved her life and she appreciated what he had done. But he had used her. She had been used enough in this life. She had been lied to far too many times.

It would be better if she cut her losses where he was concerned.

DEACON WAS ONLY a few miles from Cece's house when blue lights flashed in his rearview mirror. He scrutinized the truck behind him.

Colt Tanner. The Franklin County sheriff.

Deacon slowed and eased to the side of the road, put his truck in Park and powered down his window. He watched as Tanner climbed out of his own truck, set his hat into place and then strode toward Deacon's door.

"Sheriff." He gave the other man a nod. "Was I speeding?"

Deacon doubted the sheriff had pulled him over for the five miles per hour over the posted speed limit he had been going. This was about something else. He wouldn't need three guesses to hit the right one. Tanner had been making calls. Deacon had gotten a heads-up from one of his colleagues.

"We need to talk, Ross. Can you follow me back to my office?"

Deacon assessed the man. "Any reason we can't talk right here?"

Tanner glanced up and then down the road. "I guess not. Mind if I join you?"

"Make yourself at home." Deacon pressed the button to unlock the doors.

The sheriff walked around the back of the truck and

climbed into the passenger seat. He sat for a moment before he said anything. Deacon recognized the strategy. He hoped to escalate the tension. No need. Deacon's tension was already sky-high and it had nothing to do with the man seated across the console from him.

"I don't think you've been completely up-front with me, Mr. Ross."

"Deacon," he corrected. "You should call me Deacon."

"Well, Deacon, I spoke to your supervisor up in Nashville and he seemed to think you might be on a mission down here—one that has nothing to do with purchasing less expensive property or helping out a new friend."

"You could say my mission here is twofold," Deacon admitted. "When I first came, it was for a singular purpose, but I realized I liked the area so I decided to buy land." He was wasting his time. The man knew why he was here, but that didn't mean Deacon had no choice but to spill his guts.

"I don't have a problem with a fellow lawman looking for the truth." Tanner shrugged. "Hell, if I thought a case hadn't been investigated properly or that stones had been left unturned, I would be all over it. Particularly if that case carried some personal significance for me."

"Jack Kemp was a good friend," Deacon said, deciding to play this a different way. "He trained me. There wasn't a better man in the Bureau. All I want is to know what happened to him."

"He disappeared around the same time Mason Winters was killed?"

Deacon nodded. "He was here investigating the group that calls themselves Resurrection. They're vastly different from the usual prepper folks. They're extremists with fanatical views. Jack was part of a joint task force with the ATF. I can't go into all the details because I don't know everything there is to know, but there was speculation that this doomsday prepper group was working with others across the country."

"Running guns," Tanner guessed.

"Among other things," Deacon allowed. "These people live in communities. They go the extra mile not to stand out, to blend in. No one knows who they are. They're careful and very hard to catch. Their one goal is to ensure the success of their mission."

"Their mission is?" Tanner asked.

"To be prepared to resurrect mankind when the rest of us destroy ourselves."

Tanner grunted. "Interesting. Your friend was attempting to infiltrate this group?"

Deacon nodded. "More than two decades ago, Jack lived here for months in hopes of finding a way into the group that had just started in your county. The belief is that he thought the church Mason Winters had started was connected. When the case went cold, Jack was reassigned. Nine years ago, he came back for a followup. He was here a few weeks and then he disappeared. I need to know what happened to him."

"You could have come to me," Tanner argued. "It's important to me that the residents of my county are safe. If this Resurrection group represents some threat, I'd like to know."

"That's the problem," Deacon said. "You could be one of them."

Tanner's face showed his unhappiness with that comment. "I'm not."

Deacon held up his hands. "I'm not accusing you, sheriff. I'm merely pointing out the dilemma involved with this kind of investigation."

"According to your boss," Tanner countered, "there is no investigation. The one your friend was a part of was closed years ago. Mr. Kemp was declared legally dead last year."

"There's no official investigation," Deacon admitted. He wasn't going to play games with the sheriff. "But I'm not finished yet."

After an extended stare down, Tanner nodded. "All right. I'm good with that as long as you keep me informed and don't do one damned thing that breaks the law."

Deacon nodded his agreement. "I can live with that."

"What do you believe happened to your friend?"

"My guess is, he got caught and he's buried around here somewhere. But he has a wife and a family who need closure. I want to find that for them."

Tanner considered his answer for a moment. "I got the impression your people don't want you stirring this particular pot."

"The joint task force doesn't exist anymore. The Bureau backed off and turned the investigation over to the ATF. Politics. Someone somewhere wanted to do things a different way and that was that."

"But you can't walk away?"

"It took me years to find out where he was assigned and what he had been doing. I still don't know all the details, but I know he was here. And then he disappeared."

"But you found him in those courtroom photos of the Winters murder case."

Deacon confirmed his assessment with a nod, not

that the sheriff needed his confirmation. He already knew the answers.

"Like I said, I'll be happy to work with you, Ross. See if we can figure out what happened to your friend. But you need to leave Cece Winters out of this. She's been through enough. She doesn't need you using her. She's been let down by everyone around her—except maybe her grandmother. She spent nearly nine years in jail and in prison. She came back here looking for the truth. She sees you as some sort of hero. If you can't be that hero, you need to leave her be."

"I'll talk to her," Deacon promised. He should have already. "Explain myself."

"Just so you know," Tanner explained, "I've already talked to her. She knows why you're here." He reached for the door. "I expect you to handle this properly. You have an obligation to protect and serve the same as I do. When you're ready, we'll talk strategy for this investigation of yours. I mean what I say, don't forget that."

He got out and walked back to his truck. Deacon waited until he had driven away before he did the same.

At Cece's driveway, he made the necessary turn. He parked near the house and climbed out. When this thing started, he'd anticipated telling her the truth. He had intended to come in, find what he needed and ensure she paid for the crime if she was responsible in any way for what happened to Jack. And then he would be gone.

Except nothing had worked out the way he planned. She wasn't the person he had thought she was.

Cecelia Winters wasn't a killer.

Like Tanner said, she had been let down by everyone she had counted on and she deserved better than what Deacon had given so far.

She opened the door before he knocked. She stared at him, the hurt in her eyes a punch to the gut.

"Did you have more lies you wanted to tell me?"

He removed his hat. "No. I've told you too many already."

Before he could apologize, she held up her hand. "Don't. I don't want to hear anything else you have to say. I appreciate that in some ways you've helped me. I truly do. But you came here to use me. I can't get past that." She shook her head. "Did you think I killed my father and your friend? What kind of person do you think I am?"

"I didn't come here to use you or to prove you..." He closed his eyes a moment. "I don't know. Maybe I did. But I was wrong."

"Why? Because you got caught? Would you have told me the truth if the sheriff hadn't told me first?"

"I want the truth, Cece. Just like you. I didn't come for anything else. Just the truth. I wasn't expecting things to become personal. But they did, and as sorry as I am for misleading you, I'm not sorry about anything else."

She looked away. "I wish I could believe you."

"I can't make you believe me, but I can urge you to let me help you with this. We're close. I know it and I think you do, too. Let me help you. You can trust me. You have my word."

"Your word isn't worth much, Mr. Ross. I started this alone and I'm pretty sure that's how it'll end. I'm not counting on anyone. Not anymore. You would think I'd learned that years ago but I still allowed you to lead me down that path. Don't expect me to be grateful you feel bad about it now. Goodbye, Deacon."

She closed the door.

He knocked hard. "Cece, please let me help you."

She didn't answer.

He flatted his hands against the slab of wood that stood between them and leaned his face there. "You shouldn't do this alone."

"I've always been alone."

The key turned in the lock and he didn't need X-ray vision to know she had moved away from the door.

He had screwed up and he wasn't sure he could fix it.

Chapter Thirteen

Cece washed her face, then stared at her reflection in the mirror. How had she allowed Deacon to fool her so thoroughly? Had she not learned anything?

Eight years in a damned prison should have taught her something besides how to be beaten and threatened and terrified.

Look at Levi. She had sincerely believed he was on her side and look what he had done. Even if there were moments when she thought differently—like Deacon saving her from Ricky—everyone she had counted on proved her a fool in the end.

"What the hell is wrong with you?"

She turned away from her reflection and went back to the living room. She checked out the window to make sure he was gone.

The yard was empty. The driveway was deserted.

She was alone again.

She shouldn't have expected anything different, yet she had allowed herself to hope. That kiss…that one damned kiss…shouldn't have made her dream of the possibility, but it had. She had dared to believe.

Damn it.

In the living room she stared at the stack of papers

and photos. She should take the whole pile out back and burn it. She should list the house and walk away. Never look back. Never, ever come back.

Sierra hated her. Marcus hated her.

Who knew what Levi was doing or thinking. Whatever was on his mind, it wasn't being there for her.

Why waste any more time? She was nearly thirty years old. There was the college fund. She had a chance at a real life.

Except the past would haunt her forever. She had realized this already. Pretending it wasn't so wouldn't change a damned thing.

A murder charge did not just go away.

She had to see this through. Either she would do it alone or she would take the sheriff up on his offer. She didn't really know Colt Tanner but he seemed sincere.

Then again, so had Deacon Ross.

The fact was that she just could not trust her instincts anymore. Apparently, she never could.

The phone rang, the trill echoing through the house. She jumped. If it was Deacon she was hanging up on him.

She picked up the receiver. "Hello."

"Cece?"

"Levi? Where are you? Are you okay?"

"I… I need you to come to the house. Marcus wants to talk to all of us."

Levi's voice sounded strange. Something was very wrong. "Are you all right, Levi?"

"Can…" He cleared his throat. "Can you come?"

"Of course. I'll be right there. I just need to know that you're okay."

When he didn't say anything else, she said, "Levi? Did you hear me? I'm coming."

Worried, she started to hang up but shouting stopped her. She pressed the receiver back to her ear.

"Don't come, Cece! Don't come! It's a trap!"

The line went dead.

Fear and fury exploded inside her. Damn Marcus. She'd had enough.

She stormed across the room, grabbed her shotgun and headed for the truck. She wasn't playing with him anymore.

Outside, she strode to the barn, opened the doors and climbed into the truck. She propped the gun against the seat next to her and took off. She didn't bother getting out to close the barn doors the way her grandmother had taught her. She didn't care anymore. Levi was in trouble and she intended to find out what the hell was going on.

The drive to the house where she had grown up only took fifteen minutes but that was fifteen minutes too long. There were no other vehicles in the driveway. No guards strolling around.

Maybe she should have gone to the church.

She got out, reached back in for her shotgun and walked toward the front door. Someone had to be here. If her grandmother's phone hadn't been so old she would have had caller ID and maybe she would have known for sure where the call came from. Guess it wouldn't have mattered since it was probably a cell phone. Everybody had them.

Except her.

She banged on the door. It flew inward. Since no one was standing there she figured it must have been ajar. Listening for the slightest sound, she stepped across the threshold. The house was as silent as a tomb. Goose bumps raised on her flesh.

"Levi?"

His name echoed in the silence.

Cece took a deep breath and moved beyond the entry hall and into the living room. The room was a mess. Books pulled off shelves and slung across the floor. Couch and chair cushions yanked out of place.

What the hell happened here?

Her heart bumped into a faster rhythm. "Sierra?"

No response. Nothing but her voice reverberating in the deafening silence. She moved on to the dining room. Broken dishes that had once been in the china cabinet were scattered over the wood floor. Chairs were upside down and silverware had been tossed out of drawers.

"Marcus?"

She walked through the kitchen that was in the same condition and prepared to take the three steps down to the family room her father had added on when they were kids.

Marcus stood on the other side of the room, one hand resting on the mantel of the fireplace. Sierra sat on the couch. Neither turned to look at Cece.

"Where's Levi?"

Sierra said nothing. Just sat there and stared as if she were in a coma.

"Marcus," Cece demanded, "where is Levi?"

"He's gone."

Still, he didn't look at her.

"What do you mean he's gone? He just called me and said I needed to come here."

"He made a mistake, Cece. The same way you did."

Marcus turned to her finally. He moved toward her and Sierra started to sob.

"What're you talking about? I know what I did. I stood up to that bastard. What did Levi do?"

"He turned against us. Against our family. The same way you did."

He kept coming. Cece tightened her grip on the shotgun.

"This family turned against me." She spat the words at him. "Have you turned on Levi now?"

"Family is all that matters. If we don't stick together, we're nothing."

Cece aimed the shotgun at his chest. "Where is he?"

"You should have stayed gone, Cece. We were fine. We had moved on. But you had to come back and stir it all up again."

"Stop right there," she warned. "Where is Levi?"

"He's gone," Marcus said again, his dark eyes boring into her like hot coals. "It was the only way to save him."

"What does that mean?" Rage roared through her. He was just like their father. Heartless and self-centered. Insane.

"But you—you can't just go. You keep coming back. We can't have that anymore, Cece. This has to be finished once and for all."

"You're just like our father," she accused. "Evil and full of yourself. You think you're God. Just like he did. You don't get to decide who goes and who lives or dies. Did you kill him? To take all the power for yourself? Is that what happened, Marcus? Did you stab our father for all the times he made you feel so small and insignificant?"

"Goodbye, Cece."

She shook her head and steadied the shotgun. "I'm not going anywhere. Not until you tell me what you've done with Levi."

The blow to her head came from behind her. She pitched to the floor like a rag doll tossed aside. The shotgun landed a few feet in front of her. She saw it lying there. Told herself to reach for it, but her body wouldn't respond.

Feet moved into her line of vision. Small, bare feet. A face was suddenly in front of hers.

Sierra.

"You should have listened to me, Cece. Now it's too late."

DEACON RODE OUT another hit.

Ricky Olson grinned. "Don't that feel good, buddy? Our time together was cut short the other night. I thought we would finish up tonight. Then I'm going over there and picking up where I left off with Cece."

Olson's two thugs had Deacon's arms pulled behind his back. In order to hold him the way their buddy had instructed, they'd had to put their weapons away. Olson, on the other hand, still had his in one hand.

Deacon stretched his neck. Licked his bloody lip. "Is that all you've got, Olson? I can see why Cece wasn't satisfied."

The snorts from the guys behind him helped Deacon out more than they would ever know. Fury claimed Olson's face. He jammed his nine millimeter into his waistband and prepared to throw his full attention and weight into his next punch.

That was Deacon's cue. With his right arm, he

flung the guy clamped around it toward Olson. Then he grabbed the one on his left with his newly freed right hand and twisted his head hard enough to nearly break his neck. When the guy jerked away, Deacon snagged his weapon.

He put the barrel in Olson's face just as he lunged for him. "Come on," Deacon urged. "Draw your weapon. Flinch. Something. So I can shoot your sorry butt."

Olson froze. Both his buddies did, too.

"On the floor," Deacon ordered. "Facedown."

When the three were nose down on the hardwood, Deacon took their belts and secured their hands behind their backs. He claimed their weapons as his own. He ripped off the first guy's sneakers and used his tube socks to secure his feet. Then he did the same to the other two. All three cursed and threatened the whole time. Deacon ignored them.

"Nice to see you again, gentlemen. I'll let the sheriff know you're here waiting for pickup."

Deacon rushed out the door. He had been watching Cece's house and saw her heading out to the barn in a hurry. She'd had her shotgun with her. He had rushed back to his place to get his truck and been met by Olson and his welcoming party.

He climbed behind the wheel of his truck and started the engine. Just in case the three got loose before he expected, he drove around their truck and fired a round into each tire. That should keep them here for a while.

As he drove down the road, he tossed their weapons into the ditch one by one. He pulled into Cece's driveway and barreled toward the house. The doors where the truck was usually parked stood open. He climbed out, rushed up the front steps and knocked on the door.

When she didn't answer, he gave the knob a twist. The door opened. He scanned the living room. The phone receiver dangled from its curly cord instead of resting on the base. He walked into the kitchen. The back door stood wide open. Wherever she had gone, she had been upset and it had something to do with a phone call.

Had to be Levi or Sierra. Maybe Marcus.

He bounded out to his truck and drove to the church since he passed its location first. The building and the parking area were empty so he drove to Marcus's house next.

Cece's truck wasn't in the driveway.

Damn it.

When he would have backed away, someone peeked out the window. The curtain fell just as quickly as it had moved aside.

His instincts started to hum. Maybe it was nothing. But there was no one else in this town who would go to the trouble to find Cece's new number and call her. She had no friends.

He shut off the engine and got out. He tucked his weapon at the small of his back and then closed the truck door. Listening for the slightest sound and scanning from left to right and back, he walked toward the front door.

It opened before he raised his hand to knock.

"Can I help you?"

Marcus Winters.

"I hope so." Deacon relaxed into the part of friendly neighbor. "I'm looking for Cece. She mentioned she was coming by to see Levi. Is she here?"

Marcus shook his head. "I haven't seen or heard from her in years. I hope I never do."

Deacon hummed a note of confusion. "That's strange. She said she spoke to you on the phone just a little while ago."

Something flashed in Marcus's eyes before he could conceal it. Oh, yeah. He had seen her.

"As you can see," he gestured to the driveway and yard behind Deacon, "her truck isn't here. Obviously she is not here."

"Maybe I should talk to Levi. Is he here?"

"He is not."

"Well, I suppose I can talk to Sierra. She's here. I saw her in the window."

The statement wasn't entirely true, but unless she actually wasn't here, this asshole couldn't know that.

"Very well." Marcus turned away from the door and walked to the bottom of the staircase. He shouted for his younger sister. Eventually Sierra came down the stairs.

"This man wants to talk to you." Marcus walked on into the house, leaving the two of them alone.

For a moment Deacon could not speak. This woman had been involved somehow with Jack. She could very well know what happened to him.

Focus. He was here about Cece.

"I was looking for Cece. She said she was coming here. Have you seen her?"

Sierra shook her head. "No. Haven't talked to her either."

She was lying. The woman was as transparent as glass. Deacon resisted the impulse to grab her and shake the hell out of her.

"Thanks for your time. I guess I misunderstood."

Deacon turned and started toward the door.

The shotgun propped against the wall next to the door stopped him.

He saw the carved heart on the stock.

Cece's shotgun.

Rather than confront the two, he walked on out the door. Whatever had happened, he was going to need help.

He climbed into his truck, turned around and drove off. Once he was on the road, he found a place to back into the edge of the woods and pulled out his cell. He called the sheriff's department and waited while the dispatcher patched him through to Tanner. Before Deacon had finished filling him in, Tanner had already ordered a unit to Cece's house just in case she showed up there. He assured Deacon he would join him ASAP.

"You should probably send a unit to my house," Deacon said as an afterthought. "I left Ricky Olson and his two pals tied up on the floor. I'll explain when I see you."

Deacon ended the call and focused on the driveway that led back to the Winters' home place.

The next eight or ten minutes were some of the longest in his life. Tanner pulled in and parked directly in front of Deacon's truck. The road was so narrow there wasn't room to park beside him.

Deacon met him between the two trucks and briefed him. "No one has gone in or come out. Unless there's another entrance onto the property."

"I'm pretty sure that's the only one," Tanner said. He searched Deacon's face for a moment. "You're certain about the shotgun?"

"Positive. It belonged to her grandmother. Look,

Tanner, I don't want to waste time. The bastard knows where she is. He's holding her hostage or—"

"I'm going over there to talk to him."

Deacon wanted to argue but the man was right. "Do what you have to."

"Stay put," Tanner warned.

Deacon nodded. He knew the drill. But that didn't mean he liked it.

He watched Tanner back out onto the road and head down the driveway across the road. He paced the length of his truck about a hundred times before Tanner came back. He parked, climbed out, shook his head.

"Damn it." Deacon knew Marcus and Sierra were lying.

"The shotgun wasn't by the front door anymore."

"I'm telling you it was there."

Tanner considered the situation a moment. "I know this family was torn apart by the father's death. Sides were taken. Seems like the whole bunch, except maybe Levi, turned on Cece, believed her guilty. But do you really believe Marcus or Sierra would do anything to hurt her? Physically, I mean?"

"Absolutely. Marcus Winters is a fanatic. You have to know that. Even Cece believes her sister is on drugs. Levi suddenly goes missing. Now Cece. Look, sheriff, you gave me this whole lecture about how she had been let down by everyone around her. Well, whatever you think of me, don't let her down because you don't trust me."

"All right. But we have to do this right. I'll get a search warrant for the shotgun. That'll give us legal cause to search the property."

"How long will that take?" Deacon did not intend to stand around here and wait.

"I know a judge. It shouldn't take long. A couple of hours."

Deacon shook his head. "No way am I waiting that long."

"No problem," Tanner said, his own anger tinging his words. "I can arrest you."

Deacon held up his hands. "How about I go into the woods over there and watch the property? I won't go near the house. I won't make a damned sound."

"Don't you approach that house, Ross. Don't you do a damned thing until you hear from me."

"Unless I see Cece, you have my word."

"Fair enough."

Tanner got back into his truck and drove away. Deacon ensured the road was clear and then he ducked into the woods. He moved carefully, watching, listening, until he reached a spot where he could see both the front and the rear entrances of the home. He ensured his cell phone was on vibrate and then he watched.

Whatever the cost, he was not going to let Cece down.

Chapter Fourteen

When Cece's eyes opened it was dark. She rolled onto her side. Her skull protested, the ache deep in her head threatening to expand. Somehow she forced herself to sit up. It was so dark.

Had she been unconscious that long? It had been early afternoon when she went to the house demanding to see Levi.

Sierra had hit her. Not Marcus.

Cece gingerly touched the back of her head. Why would Sierra protect Marcus?

They had ganged up on Cece during the trial and they were still doing it. Did they really believe she killed their father?

Is that why they hated her so?

Even if she had killed him—which she had not— why would they turn on her with such total aversion? Their father had been cruel and unforgiving. He had been particularly hard on Marcus. Marcus should have hated him more than anyone else.

Maybe he had.

Cece sat in the darkness, her head throbbing, and thought of all she had seen since her return five days ago. Marcus was in control. The church was his now, their father's followers were his followers. The family farm was his, too. And Sierra was his faithful disciple. When it came to motives, Marcus's had not been particularly clear eight years ago. He had been a loving son, one who only wanted his father's approval no matter how hurtful the man was to him.

Cece almost laughed. None of them had ever come close to having the bastard's approval.

She pushed aside the thought. But Marcus's motive was clear now. He was all-powerful now. He had everything.

It was him.

Cece crawled until she found what felt like a wall and she used it to lever herself upright. Slowly, she moved along that wall. Within a few feet, maybe six or eight, she hit a corner and another wall. She repeated this process until she had traced all four walls and discovered the door.

The door was locked. Did not move or rattle when she pushed against it with her entire body weight. There were no windows and the walls felt like stone.

Her head still aching, she closed her eyes and tuned out all thought. She focused on what she smelled. Dank. Musty.

Earth.

She lowered to her hands and knees again and felt the floor. Stone, she decided.

A basement.

There was a basement in their childhood home. That must be where they were holding her. Though she didn't remember a small, lockable room. Marcus could have built one. She squeezed her eyes shut and forced her mind to go back in time. She and Levi had played in the basement sometimes.

Brick.

The floors and walls had been brick. Not stone.

Maybe Marcus had had another room dug and used stone in it. She climbed back to her feet and moved to the door once more. She felt her way all around the perimeter, following the seam between it and the jamb. The knob wouldn't budge. She tried pushing again. No luck.

"Think, Cece."

She extended her arms and walked through the center of the room, using her arms as if she were doing a breast stroke to ensure she didn't run into anything.

Light suddenly filled the room. She closed her eyes against the brightness. Then blinked and looked around. Fluorescent lights overhead glared down at her.

The scrape of metal against metal warned someone was at the door.

Cece spun around.

The door swung inward.

Sierra.

Instinctively Cece stepped back.

Her sister wrung her hands in front of her, the chain of keys clinking as she did so. "I'm sorry I had to hit you, Cece. I was afraid of what he was going to do so I did something first."

Cece scrubbed her palms against her legs, felt the grit and dirt on her jeans from where she had crawled around on the stone floor. And it was stone. Floor, walls, ceiling. She could see that now.

"Why?" She decided to start there. "What did I do to make the two of you hate me so much?"

Sierra shook her head. "I've never hated you. It was Marcus. He's the one who wanted you to go away forever. He thought that would happen when you were blamed for the murder. But it didn't. You came back and he doesn't want you here."

Cece shook her head. "I don't understand. Why did he want me gone so badly?"

Not once in her life could Cece remember being mean to her brother. He was six years older. Maybe being the only child for so many years had made him resent her. He had never said anything. And what made her different from Levi or Sierra? They had prevented him from being an only child, as well.

Sierra leaned against the wall as if she were too tired to remain standing without assistance. "I don't know. But he wants you gone and this time I think he has something awful planned."

Cece ignored the way her heart started to pound, the way the fight-or-flight instinct roared inside her. "Where is Levi?"

Dear God, what if he had already harmed Levi?

Sierra shook her head. "I don't know. He left. He said he had something to do. He wouldn't tell me what. I think it had something to do with you or that man who moved into the Wilburn place."

"Deacon? Why would Levi have a problem with Deacon Ross?" Cece thought of Deacon's partner, Jack Kemp. She also thought of the photos of Kemp with Sierra sitting so near him.

How could all this insanity have happened with her so oblivious? School. Work. She had been pretty busy. She had been finishing up her senior year of high school and working every possible shift at the diner. Since she was living with her grandmother, she had been really out of touch with what was going on at home. Basically she had abandoned Levi and Sierra. But she had not wanted to. Her father had kicked her out. She'd had no choice.

"Did you know a man who went by the name K.C.? Dark hair and eyes." Like you, Cece realized. Sierra had those same dark eyes and the dark hair, far darker than that of their father and brothers.

Sierra looked startled. "He…he came around a few times. He said he knew Mom a long time ago. But they lost touch."

The idea of what that could mean—that Sierra was the only one in the family with that dark hair and those dark eyes—slammed into Cece. Levi and Marcus had hair that was brown with the slightest red highlights. A sort of cross between their mom and their dad. But Sierra, she was nothing like any of them.

Was it possible this K.C.—this Jack Kemp—was her biological father?

Wait, wait, wait. That did not make sense. Obviously the blow to her head had done far more damage than Cece realized. Her mother wouldn't have cheated on their father…would she? He *had* been a cruel and hurtful man.

Sierra blinked. "But no." She shook her head adamantly. "I didn't really know him."

She was lying. Cece could see it in her eyes. The eyes that did not belong to a daughter of Mason Winters.

"Tell me the truth, Sierra. That's the only way any of us are going to get through this."

Sierra stared at her for a long moment, her gaze bleary like an inebriated person's.

"What kind of drugs are you taking?" Cece asked.

"I'm not doing anything wrong," Sierra shouted. "I take what the doctor prescribes. For my anxiety and depression."

Cece nodded. "I see. I didn't know."

"Of course you didn't know. You've been gone. Far longer than eight years. You don't know the things he did to me."

"Do you mean the man, K.C.?"

"No!" That she shouted the word warned she did not want to talk about this mysterious man.

"Tell me, please." Cece moved closer to her. "I'm your sister. I want to know."

"He started doing things to me when I was twelve."

Cece could not speak. That would have been the year after their father kicked her out. "You mean, sexually?"

Sierra looked away. "Yes."

"Oh, my God." She started to demand why Sierra hadn't told anyone but she stopped herself. Of course she hadn't told anyone. She was ashamed and afraid.

"That day. The day he died. I told him I knew the truth. I knew he wasn't my father. I was going to the police. I decided I didn't care what people said or thought when the truth came out. I was going to make sure he paid. My real father had promised to take me away from here. He realized the first time he saw me that I was his daughter. The bastard took that from me."

Cece put her hand against the wall, her knees suddenly weak. "What did he do?"

"He laughed and said our mother was a whore and that if the devil who fathered me really wanted me he would have come back for me a long time ago."

"K.C.?" Cece's voice sounded hollow.

"His name was Jack. Jack Kemp. He was going to take me away from here. He had come to Winchester on some sort of assignment or mission but he said he didn't care about that. He had to get me away from the bastard raping me."

"What did you do when Mason said these things to you?"

"I told him I was going to find Jack and that I was leaving. I ran into the kitchen and grabbed his truck keys but he caught me before I could get out the back door. We struggled. The knife was in the drainer with the other dishes I had washed that morning." She stared at the floor. "I stabbed him."

Cece swallowed back the bitter taste of bile. "You had no choice."

"He staggered back and I kept stabbing him. Over and over and over."

"You didn't call for help?"

Sierra shook her head, the slightest movement. "I was going to, but Marcus came in. He said I would go to prison. That no one would believe the things he had been doing to me. Everyone always thought Daddy and I were so close. He said they would think I was a monster."

Cece forced air into her lungs. "That's when you decided to blame me."

Sierra's gaze collided with hers. "Marcus made me say it. He said if I didn't do what he said, he would make sure everyone knew the truth about me and that he would tell people how I planned the murder and…" She closed her eyes and shook her head. "He said you deserved whatever happened to you for deserting us. You never cared about anyone but yourself. He said because of all the public fights you and Daddy had that people would believe you killed him. He said you would get off on a self-defense plea, anyway. By the time I knew that wasn't going to happen, it was too late to change my story."

Cece swiped at a damned tear that rolled down her cheek. "I guess Marcus told you that, too."

"He said they would know I had planned the whole thing then. I would get the death penalty."

"You were fifteen years old, Sierra. You wouldn't have gotten the death penalty. You probably wouldn't have even gone to prison."

Tears poured down Sierra's cheeks. "I didn't know. I just did whatever Marcus told me to do. When he came in and saw what I had done, he made me swear never to tell a soul. He said everything would be fine. I just had to be quiet for a little while."

"Did you tell Jack?"

She shook her head. "Marcus said I could never tell anyone, so I didn't. Not until now."

"What happened to Jack?"

She shrugged. "I saw him at the trial a couple of times and he kept asking me questions about what happened. About you and everything…and then he just disappeared."

Cece felt ice slip through her veins. "Did you tell anyone about Jack asking you all those questions?"

"I told Marcus. I was afraid not to."

Dear God, what had her brother done? No more talking. They needed to get out of here. "Sierra—"

"I know what you're thinking," her sister said, cutting Cece off. "You're thinking Marcus killed Jack."

Cece had a bad feeling that was the case. "Is that what you think happened?"

She shrugged. "I don't know. Marcus has taken care of me all this time. He makes sure I'm okay."

"Did he take you to the doctor who gave you the medicine?"

Sierra nodded. "He's been a good brother to me." She looked to Cece then. "But what he did to you—what I did to you—was wrong. We have to fix that now."

"We should go for help," Cece urged. She took Sierra by the arm. "Sheriff Tanner can help us."

Deacon, too, she wanted to say, but she wasn't sure where she stood with him. He had misled her and she wasn't certain she could forgive him for lying to her.

"You go," Sierra said. "I'll stay here and take care of Marcus. He needs me. He doesn't have anyone else."

"Sierra." Cece took her by the shoulders and shook her a little. "We both have to go. We don't know what Marcus might do. He isn't well." A man who would do the things he had done couldn't be well. The sort of help he needed wasn't anything Sierra could give him.

"He's too close," Sierra argued. "We can't get away. If I distract him, you can."

Well, hell. "We'll figure something out," Cece argued. "I'm not leaving without you and then we have to find Levi."

She hoped Marcus had not hurt Levi.

"There's no way out," Sierra insisted.

"Wait." Cece held up her hands. "Explain to me where we are." She glanced around the room. "This doesn't look familiar to me."

"Marcus and some of the followers built a tunnel between the house and the church. There are rooms down here and…and things stored."

Things? There was no time for Cece to pursue the idea of what other things might be stored down here. She had been right; this was a basement of sorts. "Where was Marcus when you came down here?"

"He's at the church with his elders. They're discussing what to do." She lifted her gaze to Cece's. "With you."

"Then we'll go back toward the house." Cece ushered Sierra out of the cell-like room. "Which way?"

Sierra stalled. "If they find us, they'll give us to the *others*. No one comes back from the *others*."

"What's the *others*?"

"A place where you learn lessons you never forget."

Cece whirled around at the voice. *Marcus*. Thankfully he was alone.

"We just want to leave, Marcus," Cece informed him. "We don't want to be here."

"Do you want her to tell them what you did?" Marcus asked Sierra.

"She protected herself," Cece countered. "Protecting herself isn't against the law."

"Even if she killed a man in the process?" Marcus glared at her, his brown eyes glowing with anger.

"He was hurting her. You knew this," Cece accused him. "You let her believe she had done something wrong and you knew better."

He laughed. "You deserved what you got. More than you got," he sneered. "You should have died in that prison. Old and withered. You don't deserve a life."

Cece scooted Sierra behind her. She wasn't sure if her brother had a weapon or not but she wasn't taking any chances. "What did I ever do to you, Marcus? You turned on me for no reason."

He laughed even louder then, the sound filled with sheer hatred. "You honestly don't remember, do you?"

"I don't know what you're talking about." She eased back a step, ushering Sierra along with her. "What is it you think I did?"

"You found the hole I made in your wall."

What the hell was he talking about? "What hole?"

"The one I made so I could watch you. The same kind I made in the wall to Sierra's bedroom."

The memory of catching her brother touching himself while staring through a tiny hole in the wall rushed into her mind, pressed the breath from her lungs. "You mean, when you were watching Sierra take a bath? My God, that was when I was, what? Seven? Eight? I didn't even remember until you mentioned it just now."

"You were seven. I was thirteen."

"We were kids," Cece argued. "Young boys do stuff like that. Trade porn magazines and sneak peeks at any girl available—including sisters. It's hormones."

"Do you know what our father did to me?"

She didn't recall any particular punishment. "Did he beat you?" She vaguely remembered Marcus being ill. Had he been in the hospital, too? "I'm so sorry, Marcus. I was a child. I didn't mean to get you into trouble—"

"He and three of his followers said it was necessary to exorcise the lust from me. They kept me in a sweat room, beat me, prayed over me. For days they attempted to rid me of the evil they claimed had possessed me. Then they tested me."

Cece was terrified of what he meant by the last. "Tested you how?"

"They showed me photos of naked girls. When I grew aroused, they announced I had failed the test."

"Oh, my God. I didn't know."

More of that cruel laughter. "That was when they decided that extreme measures had to be taken."

What they'd already done wasn't extreme enough? "Marcus, you know he was evil. He was a sick bastard who damaged us all."

Marcus shook his head. "They castrated me. He said because I lusted after my own sisters I wasn't worthy of being a whole man. They had to cut out the wicked part of me. So they removed my testicles. All because you told him what you saw while I was still too young to fight him."

Dear God. No wonder her brother hated her. "He was the one who was evil, Marcus. Look what he did to Sierra. He threw me out when I was still a kid. He was the devil. He was the evil one."

"You were the lucky one, Cece," Marcus argued. "The one who looked like our whore mother. He couldn't stand it, couldn't bear to look at you. I remember the night he killed her. He pushed her down those stairs and let her lay there and die. He had realized that Sierra wasn't his child. He tortured her until she confessed and then he threw her down the stairs like a piece of trash. When I tried to call for help, he locked me in the basement. You see, Cece, you got away scot-free. You were the lucky one. How can you complain about a few years in prison, considering what the rest of us went through?"

"You're right." Cece decided the only hope she and Sierra had of surviving this big confession was to play along. To get as much information as possible. "I have no right to complain. What about that man? The one who started all this with our mother? If she hadn't cheated, maybe our father wouldn't have turned into such a monster. This is all her fault."

"He paid for his sins," Marcus assured her. "He was every bit as evil as our father. He didn't deserve to live, either. They both were sent to hell where they belonged."

Cece took Sierra by the hand and then reached for her brother's. "We are all we have left. Us and Levi. We should make a pact to take care of each other. God knows our parents didn't."

Marcus stared at her for a long moment. "You shouldn't have come back, Cece. You're not like us." He looked to Sierra then. "You know what has to happen."

Cece shifted her attention to Sierra.

"He's right," her sister said. "I tried to help you and now it's too late. You shouldn't have come back, Cece."

DEACON WAS THROUGH WAITING. If Tanner didn't arrive soon with that warrant and backup, he was going in alone.

Still no movement at the house. They could be doing anything in there. It had been better than three hours since he saw Cece leaving. He wasn't waiting any longer. His cell vibrated. Deacon snatched it from his pocket and answered.

"Where are you?" the caller demanded.

Tanner.

"I'm at the edge of the woods near the house. Did you get the warrant?"

"I'm coming in."

The call ended. Damn it. Why didn't he just answer the question?

Deacon waited for Tanner to reach his position. Two of his deputies were right behind him. "Do you have the warrant?"

"The judge was in court. We should have his signature any minute."

"That's a no," Deacon snapped. "I'm not waiting."

Tanner started to argue with him but reached for his ringing cell phone, instead. Deacon waited, hoped it was the warrant.

"Got it. Thanks." He tucked his phone away. "Warrant's been signed." He looked to his deputies. "Call it."

While the deputies took care of notifying the rest of the team Tanner already had in place that it was time to get moving, he and Deacon headed directly for the house.

No vehicles had arrived during the time Deacon had been watching. At the front door, Tanner did the knocking. After three attempts to get someone to the door, he went in, gun drawn.

They moved quickly from room to room, first and second floor. No sign of anyone. Then they looked in the basement. One large brick-floored-and-walled room. Empty beyond a few jars of canned goods and a couple of boxes that had been stored long enough to look vintage.

"No one came in or out of the house while I was watching," Deacon said, frustrated.

"Marcus and a couple of his followers are over at the church. My deputies should be finished going through the building by now." He reached for his cell.

"Wait. Did you say Marcus was there?"

Tanner nodded. "He is."

Deacon turned all the way around in the basement. "Then there has to be an underground tunnel because he was in this house and he did not leave by either of the exits."

They started with the walls, going over every square inch in hopes of finding a hidden passageway. They moved on to the floors. Nothing.

"Let's go back to the first floor," Tanner suggested.

Upstairs the deputies were moving through the house, looking for the shotgun Tanner had listed on his warrant. They went through each room, finally entering the only first floor bedroom, which obviously belonged to Marcus. Male clothes were in the closet. They moved the rug on the floor, the furniture, and found nothing.

Back in the closet, Deacon checked the floorboards. "Got something here," he said to Tanner.

A square of flooring lifted up, revealing a trapdoor. A metal ladder led downward into the darkness.

"I'm going first," Tanner said in no uncertain terms.

As much as Deacon would have liked to argue, the sheriff was right. This was his jurisdiction. Deacon followed, moving down slowly and as soundlessly as possible. When they reached the bottom of the ladder, Tanner used his cell as a flashlight and discovered a light switch. He turned it on, revealing a long tunnel lined with doors.

"What the hell?" Tanner muttered.

One by one they checked behind the doors and found nothing. Midway along the tunnel were two doors that were locked. When they couldn't get an answer from beyond the locked doors, Tanner left two deputies attempting to open them while he and Deacon moved on.

At the other end of the tunnel was another ladder. Tanner went up first. He raised the trapdoor carefully and climbed on out. Deacon did the same.

The room they found themselves in was small. Hooks for coats lined three of the four walls. The one window looked out onto the woods. They were at the church.

Voices.

Tanner moved to the door. Indicated for Deacon to keep quiet.

He listened a moment longer, then stepped back and prepared to open the door. Deacon leveled his weapon, ready to fire if necessary.

Beyond the door was the main worship hall of the church.

Marcus Winters, his sister Sierra and two other men looked up from the books they held.

"What is this?" Marcus shot to his feet.

"Where is Cece?" Tanner demanded.

Deacon moved through the room, went down a small hall behind the stage-like pulpit and checked both bathrooms.

Nothing.

Sweat broke out across his forehead. His pulse rate climbed higher and higher. She had to be here.

Marcus was arguing with Tanner about his sister.

"We haven't spoken in years," Marcus was saying.

The two older men sat silent, watching. Sierra stared at the floor or the book she held, presumably a Bible.

Tanner continued to pressure Marcus. Deacon zeroed in on Sierra.

"Where is she, Sierra?"

Sierra lifted her gaze to his.

"Don't allow him to intimidate you, sister!" Marcus shouted.

Tanner told him to shut up.

"Where is Cece?" Deacon pressed, moving closer to her.

"She's gone to be with the *others*."

Fear knotted in Deacon's belly. "Can you show me how to find where she is?"

Marcus started to yell again and Tanner pushed him into a chair and shoved his weapon into Marcus's face. "Not another word."

"Please," Deacon urged. "Show me where she is before it's too late."

He had no idea what kind of place she meant, but he innately understood it was not good.

She nodded and tossed the book aside.

Marcus dared to threaten her once more but Sierra didn't look back. Deacon stayed right on her heels. She went out the back of the church. By the time they reached the tree line, two deputies had joined them.

As they moved into the trees, Sierra hurried faster and faster. Deacon sensed her anticipation and her fear. A half mile or so into the thick woods, Sierra stopped. Deacon held up a hand for those behind them to stop.

She pointed. "There."

Cece was tied to a tree, a gag preventing her from screaming.

Deacon started around Sierra. She put a hand on his arm. "Be careful. The *others* could be out there."

Deacon looked to one of the deputies. "Don't let her out of your sight."

"Yes, sir," the deputy agreed.

Deacon and the other deputy moved forward. The

deputy kept watch while Deacon went to Cece. He removed the gag of tape and cloth first. She cried out.

"I've got you," he assured her.

The deputy had a knife and cut loose her bindings. Cece fell against Deacon, nearly too weak to walk.

"We have to get out of here," she whispered.

He grabbed her up in his arms and started back in the direction from which they had come. The deputy who had stayed with Sierra escorted her while the third brought up the rear, keeping watch.

When they reached the church, several more squad cars had arrived. Marcus had been arrested, as had the two followers who had been at the church with him.

When Deacon lowered Cece to her feet, she turned to her sister. "Thank you."

Sierra nodded.

Cece put her hand on her arm. "It's time to tell the truth now."

Chapter Fifteen

Thursday, August 8

Wednesday had passed in a blur of jurisdictional issues and frustration for Deacon. Marcus Winters had given Jack Kemp to these so-called *others* to ensure he never got the truth out of Sierra.

According to Sierra, no one knew who the *others* were. Deacon figured the whole story was something Marcus had made up to keep his sister in line. The Bureau had authorized ground-penetrating radar since there was a strong possibility there would be more remains than Jack's found somewhere on the Winters property.

One of the followers who was in the church with Marcus when the warrant was served had decided to help with the investigation for a chance at immunity. It was too early to say how much help his assistance would prove to be.

Cece had asked to stay with her sister while she gave her statement. Tanner had agreed. Which gave Deacon an opportunity to sit in on the questioning of Benton Syler, the follower who had agreed to cooperate with the investigation.

"Mason kept a tight lid on how he operated. Marcus worked a little more loosely with a couple of us."

"Mr. Syler," Tanner asked, "can we anticipate finding human remains buried on the church property?"

Syler nodded. "There's plenty. The killings go way back. As for Kemp, I don't know anything about him. That was a personal matter between Marcus and Sierra. It wasn't decided by the council."

Deacon wanted to reach across the interview table and shake the hell out of the man. They had learned that the council was a group of four followers who made decisions, with Marcus leading.

"Did the council make life-and-death decisions on a regular basis?"

Tanner didn't do a very good job of hiding his disgust when he asked that question. Syler noticed.

"I was only ever in on three. Not because I wanted to be but because I did as I was told, sheriff. I didn't want my family to end up on the agenda."

"Are you suggesting Marcus would have harmed your family if you didn't follow his lead?"

"I'm not suggesting anything, sheriff. I'm telling you that's the way it was. Don't get me wrong. I worked hard to get this position. I figured my family and I were safer if I was in a higher position. No surprises that way."

It never ceased to amaze Deacon how far one man would go to please another when it came to societal hierarchy.

"Most of our decisions were about who would be handed over to the *others* if they did wrong. I think the three who were stoned to death had something to do with a bad thing that happened to Marcus when he was a kid. But I don't know for sure and I knew better than to ask."

Sierra had said that Cece was to be given to the *others*. "Who do you mean?" Deacon asked.

Syler looked at him as if he wasn't sure whether he should answer. Tanner gave him a nod and he proceeded.

"The *others* are the most extreme wing of the Resurrection, an offshoot. Went off on their own years ago. We're talking way over the edge. Human sacrifices. You name it. Back when Mason first started the church, we had a couple of members go missing. Their mangled or cleaned-to-the-bone remains would show up eventually. Mason sent men into the woods looking for what he expected to be wild animals. Bears or mountain lions. Something like that. What he found was this extreme group. He figured out the only way to keep them from hunting among his followers was to supply them with what they wanted."

"You can lead us to these *others*?" Tanner asked.

"No one knows where they are. You mess around in those woods long enough and they'll find you."

A knock at the door sounded before one of Tanner's deputies came in. She whispered something in the sheriff's ear and hurried back out of the room.

Tanner stood. "Mr. Syler, we'll need to continue this at a later time. I have an emergency to see to."

Deacon followed Tanner out of the interview room. "What's going on?"

"The second warrant, that allowed us a more liberal search," he explained, "has found something I think your friends at the FBI and at the ATF will be interested in."

"Weapons?"

Tanner nodded. "A whole load hidden in that tunnel. I'm guessing Marcus was using the church as a neutral holding ground between the dealers and the Resurrection members."

"Sheriff." Another deputy hustled toward them. "You're going to want to come and listen to what Sierra Winters is saying about her brother Levi."

Deacon and Tanner followed the deputy to the observation room.

"Run that interview back," Tanner ordered the technician who was recording the interview.

"Right there," the deputy said.

The tech hit Play.

"Levi was working with Jack. He was helping him get in with the Resurrection. Until Jack figured out I was his daughter and then he got distracted."

Deacon's instincts moved to a higher level of alert.

"I think Levi has lingered on the fringes of those crazy preppers all this time. He's been very secretive about where he goes when he disappears for a few days. I believe that's where he is now. I don't know if they've figured out he's trying to bring them down or if they like him and want him in deeper. Either way, he's playing with fire. Those people don't play games."

The worry on Cece's face made Deacon's gut clench. He walked out of the observation booth and made a phone call. There was only one way this could end even remotely well.

He intended to do all he could to see that Levi was brought back alive.

For Cece. For Jack's family.

Levi would know more about Jack's last days than anyone else.

BY THE TIME the district attorney was finished interviewing Sierra, Cece was exhausted. Her head was still reeling at the idea of what her older brother had done. Dear God, what her father had done.

He had killed their mother. He had castrated his own son.

How the hell were any of them supposed to get past this?

Sierra would be in protective custody for now, so Cece gave her a hug before parting ways.

She had known her father was a cruel, evil man, but she had had no idea just how depraved he had been. The district attorney had assured Cece that the charge against her would be overturned. She could start her life over with a clean slate. She had been waiting to hear those words for most of her adult life.

In the corridor outside the sheriff's office, Deacon waited, one shoulder leaned against the wall as if he had been watching for her.

She smiled. Thankful to see him again. There was so much she needed to say to him. So much she wanted to ask him.

Mostly she wanted him to know she was very grateful.

"Hey." He searched her eyes as if unsure how to proceed.

"Hey." She smiled. "I am glad to see you."

His lips stretched into a matching smile. "I can't tell you how happy I am to hear that."

"We have a lot to talk about," she confessed.

He nodded. "We do."

"I'm really worried about Levi."

"You have every right to be," he agreed. "The good

news is, I made a call. The best retrieval expert in the Bureau has agreed to help find Levi."

Hope lit in Cece's chest. "That's great news. How soon will the agent be here?"

"She's on the way. She'll be here by morning. Her name is Sadie Buchanan. She's the best extraction and recovery agent in this part of the country. If anyone can find him and bring him home, it's Sadie."

"The district attorney says Sierra won't be charged. It was self-defense. She'll need therapy." Cece laughed. "I guess we all will. We Winters are pretty screwed up." She searched Deacon's gaze. "I know Marcus has a lot to answer for and he'll likely spend the rest of his life locked away somewhere, but he was a victim, too, and I'm sorry no one recognized it in time to save him."

Deacon touched her cheek. "At least he can't hurt anyone else or himself. He'll be on a different path now."

"I'm tired." Another raw confession. "Will you take me home?"

"I will."

Cece wrapped her arm around his and leaned against his shoulder. When they were outside and headed across the parking lot to his truck, she pulled him to a stop and stared up into his brown eyes. "I can't leave Winchester until we find Levi and I know Sierra will be okay. But I want to know you better, Deacon Ross."

"I'll be right here with you, Cece Winters. I can't think of anything I would rather do than get better acquainted."

She went up on her tiptoes, put her arms around his

neck and kissed him on the lips. She had spent too long waiting for her life to begin again. She had no intention of wasting another minute.

* * * * *

COMING SOON!

We really hope you enjoyed reading this book. If you're looking for more romance, be sure to head to the shops when new books are available on

Thursday 8th August

To see which titles are coming soon, please visit

millsandboon.co.uk/nextmonth

MILLS & BOON

MILLS & BOON

HEROES

At Your Service

Experience all the excitement of a
gripping thriller, with an intense romance
at its heart. Resourceful, true-to-life
women and strong, fearless men face
danger and desire - a killer combination!

Eight Heroes stories published every month, find them all at:

millsandboon.co.uk/Heroes

JOIN THE
MILLS & BOON
BOOKCLUB

* **FREE** delivery direct to your door

* **EXCLUSIVE** offers every month

* **EXCITING** rewards programme

50% OFF
YOUR FIRST
PARCEL

Join today at
Millsandboon.co.uk/Bookclub

LET'S TALK

Romance

For exclusive extracts, competitions
and special offers, find us online:

f facebook.com/millsandboon

🐦 @MillsandBoon

📷 @MillsandBoonUK

Get in touch on 01413 063232

For all the latest titles coming soon, visit

millsandboon.co.uk/nextmonth

Want even more
ROMANCE?

Join our bookclub today!

'Mills & Boon books, the perfect way to escape for an hour or so.'

Miss W. Dyer

'Excellent service, promptly delivered and very good subscription choices.'

Miss A. Pearson

'You get fantastic special offers and the chance to get books before they hit the shops'

Mrs V. Hall

Visit millsandbook.co.uk/Bookclub

and save on brand new books.

MILLS & BOON

MILLS & BOON

THE HEART OF ROMANCE

A ROMANCE FOR EVERY KIND OF READER

MODERN

Prepare to be swept off your feet by sophisticated, sexy and seductive heroes, in some of the world's most glamourous and romantic locations, where power and passion collide.
8 stories per month.

HISTORICAL

Escape with historical heroes from time gone by. Whether your passion is for wicked Regency Rakes, muscled Vikings or rugged Highlanders, awaken the romance of the past.
6 stories per month.

MEDICAL

Set your pulse racing with dedicated, delectable doctors in the high-pressure world of medicine, where emotions run high and passion, comfort and love are the best medicine.
6 stories per month.

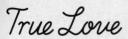

Celebrate true love with tender stories of heartfelt romance, from the rush of falling in love to the joy a new baby can bring, and a focus on the emotional heart of a relationship.
8 stories per month.

Indulge in secrets and scandal, intense drama and plenty of sizzling hot action with powerful and passionate heroes who have it all: wealth, status, good looks…everything but the right woman.
6 stories per month.

HEROES

Experience all the excitement of a gripping thriller, with an intense romance at its heart. Resourceful, true-to-life women and strong, fearless men face danger and desire - a killer combination!
8 stories per month.

DARE

Sensual love stories featuring smart, sassy heroines you'd want as a best friend, and compelling intense heroes who are worthy of them.
4 stories per month.

To see which titles are coming soon, please visit

millsandboon.co.uk/nextmonth

JOIN US ON SOCIAL MEDIA!

Stay up to date with our latest releases, author news and gossip, special offers and discounts, and all the behind-the-scenes action from Mills & Boon...

 millsandboon

 millsandboonuk

 millsandboon

It might just be true love...

GET YOUR ROMANCE FIX!

MILLS & BOON
— *blog* —

Get the latest romance news, exclusive author interviews, story extracts and much more!

blog.millsandboon.co.uk